THE TWO

KEVIN VELA

Charleston, SC
www.PalmettoPublishing.com

The Two
Copyright © 2021 by Kevin Vela

Paperback ISBN: 978-1-68515-341-0.

CHAPTER 1

THE CALAMITY

Matt opened his eyes and rolled over, checking the time on his cell phone. A little after six. He could doze for a bit more. He checked the news feed, and saw there weren't any morning updates. Feeling as if that was a bit odd, he just let his phone slip from his hand and closed his eyes.

Suddenly, his phone buzzed. Annoyed, he picked it up and checked the message. It was his sister, Valerie, texting him that something was VERY WRONG. He noticed about 20 minutes had passed since he dozed off, and figured it was time to get moving. He read the text in more detail.

Something is VERY WRONG! the text read.

"How dramatic," Matt sighed. He waited for more context, as he lay in bed. Sure enough, another text arrived.

My morning podcast is not broadcasting!! the text read.

Matt scoffed and rolled out of bed. Standing up and stretching, he was thinking about breakfast as his pet Beagle, Buddy, excitedly jumped out of the bed. He was assuredly not thinking about breakfast before attending to his dog. Matt followed the anxious dog to the back door and opened it, letting him out for a pee. Walking into his kitchen, he opened the fridge and grabbed the apple juice, pouring himself a glass.

Moving to the laundry room, he picked up the cup and scooped Buddy's dog food out of the container and poured it into his dish. Buddy was barking at the back door, knowing that breakfast was next on his to-do list. Matt grinned and walked back to open the door, letting the dog back in. Buddy scurried towards his food tray while Matt rummaged through his cabinet. Finding some oatmeal, he pulled it out and began preparing it.

Matt and Val were very close as siblings, Matt being four years older. They shared many common interests, but social media was *not* one of them. Val was glued to it, whereas Matt didn't like morning radio, or podcasts, or anything that involved a lot of words—regardless of the topic. He preferred television, if anything. And considering it was a Monday, there would be plenty of Monday Morning Quarterback guys on the air. His phone beeped again, and he saw it was Val, again.

Matt! I'm serious! There is a legit problem here! Are you up yet?? the text screamed.

Matt typed out his reply: *Good morning. Yes, I am awake. I don't care about your podcasts, you know that.*

This might have been a bit meaner than it could have been, but Matt had his morning routine, and Val knew that. She should know better than to bother him about something as trivial as a podcast that's not airing. He turned on the TV… it was just white noise.

"Is the cable out? Come on, it's 2021, that shouldn't ever happen," Matt looked at Buddy, who had joined him by now.

His oatmeal beeped from the microwave, and he took it out. Turning the TV off, he sat down and began to eat. Checking his phone again, there hadn't been any news updates *at all*. Not on the sports sites, the news sites, nothing. He went through his list of favorites, including his daily web-comic, but there was *nothing*. Everything was from the day before—the news stories were all dated for twelve or so hours ago.

Matt checked his WiFi, it was still up and running. The phone was working, he was online. Something definitely felt off. The news didn't just turn itself off. It must have been an internet problem. He stood up from his oatmeal and texted his sister.

Is your internet working? he asked.

It didn't take long for her to respond, *Yes! But there are no updates, nothing! It's as if time stopped!*

Val might be being a little dramatic, but she had a point. Matt walked back into his room and turned on his PlayStation. When the internet was acting goofy, the gaming console was always a good barometer. If the internet was up, the console would connect to it. It booted up, and he started a Call of Duty game. He hadn't been playing recently, but it was an online game. And there was always someone on the planet that was online.

He just went into the standard Team Deathmatch lobby and started a search. He figured it would only take a few seconds, it was always the most popular game mode. Time ticked by and he wasn't put into a game. Thinking that was a bit odd, Matt waited a bit longer. Nothing changed, it just kept searching for a game. Checking his friends list, he saw no one was online. Also unusual, given how he had tons of people on the list, people he didn't even play with anymore.

His phone beeped again, *Have you tried calling the parents? I can't get them to answer!* Val offered.

No, but this seems pretty weird, I can't find a COD match, and there is always a COD match. None of my friends are online either, on PSN or Discord, Matt replied.

Noticing the time, Matt knew he had to get ready for work. Still, something seemed off as he turned the PlayStation off and headed into the bathroom. Brushing his teeth quickly, he combed his hair and walked into the living room again. Buddy was holding his leash in his mouth, knowing it was time for their quick morning walk. He dropped it as Matt approached and hooked the leash onto his collar. Heading for the front door, the duo stepped outside.

The hot air hit them. It was 7am, but the temperature was already over 80. Turning around, Matt locked his door and set off on his walk with Buddy. Looking around, he didn't see anyone else walking their dogs, which also was unusual. In the short two-block walk to the mailbox, they usually saw six or seven people. Everything else seemed normal—the birds were out, the automated sprinkler systems were spraying, Buddy loved to drink out of them.

Still, they saw no people as they got to the mailbox. Matt looked towards the road leading out of the neighborhood, and stood there for a moment. No cars were passing by. He stood there for a good five minutes, not a single car passed by. Buddy was looking at him, this pause wasn't part of their morning routine.

"Come on Buddy, let's head to the edge of the neighborhood for a moment," Matt whispered.

Buddy had zero objections to continuing their walk, as he pointed his nose to the ground and they headed on. Matt would usually let Buddy's nose dictate their pace, but not this morning, as he pulled him along every time he started to veer off. They got to the edge, where the main road was. Matt stood there and looked.

Not a single car. He saw one parked at the streetlight down the way, but there was no one in it. Just...stopped at the light, not moving. It was Monday morning in Austin, Texas. This was a busy street. People should have been on their way to work, kids on their way to school. Yet, there was nothing.

His phone beeped again. Checking it, it was Val. *Matt. I'm getting a little scared. There are literally no people. Is it okay if I come to your place?*

Matt nodded, texting her back. *Yeah, I am going to walk down to the gas station, check on something. But head on over. If you see anyone, let me know, okay?*

He pulled Buddy along as he strode towards the parked car. The road was still completely empty, as Buddy led the way with his nose. Coming to the crosswalk, Matt instinctively looked both ways before crossing the street. He approached the car, noting it was switched off. Looking inside, the car was empty, but in gear. There were no keys, as Matt noticed it was keyless ignition. Backing away, he walked back towards the gas station on the corner. The lights were on, and the door was unlocked. The OPEN sign was illuminated. Walking in, there was no one there. Buddy was sniffing around, but Matt pulled him around the counter to the cash register, he wanted to check something.

His phone beeped again. *Matt! There are empty cars all over the road, none of them are moving! What is going on??*

Val, I don't know. There aren't any people anywhere. Just get to my place, okay? Matt typed back.

Matt checked the register, it was on. He didn't know how to use it, but he tried pushing some buttons. An error message popped up, "Dates do not match."

That confirmed his suspicions, the register was still open, but it was dated for yesterday. The gas station had never closed. He had worked retail in his college days, and knew the registers had to be closed and reopened for each business day. Pulling Buddy along, Matt grabbed a Gatorade and walked out.

As they headed home, Matt texted some of his friends. *Just checking in, seeing if everything is okay.* He also sent one to his boss, asking him if the office was open. No one responded, as he and Buddy walked home. Matt was getting a little more anxious now, as he still saw no one on the road.

Arriving at their house, he unlocked the door and decided to wait for Val. She only lived about 15 or so minutes away, so she should be arriving soon. Sitting on the front step, he let Buddy wander around on the leash while he sipped his stolen Gatorade. A few minutes later, Val pulled up in her Nissan. Getting out quickly, she ran up to him.

"Matt!" Val exclaimed, as she gave him a hug. "What is going on? It's like all of the people have vanished…"

"Yeah, I think that's a literal explanation of what is going on, honestly. Did you see anyone moving on the highway?" Matt asked in a low voice.

"No, and it's Monday morning on I-35. And none of the cars had people in them. It was as if they got snapped.." Val trailed off.

"I think Thanos intended on snapping half the universe, not all but two people. Also, he isn't a real person," Matt grinned.

"Then you explain to me how all the people are missing, yet their vehicles are still on the road!" Val exclaimed.

"I can't, okay? I can't," Matt sighed. "Let's uh,.let's come up with a plan on what we should do, I guess."

"I think we should channel the Good Place and decide between panicking and freaking," Val exclaimed.

"Yes, I think you are already doing that," Matt grinned. "Listen, I am worried, okay? I am. But I don't think it helps if we start freaking out. We still have electricity and running water, so…that's a start. When was the last time you talked to anyone?"

"Last night," Val sighed. "I was talking to Simone, before she stopped responding, I figured she passed out."

"What time was that?" Matt asked.

Val checked her phone, "Last message from her was at 10:37. What about you?"

"I went to bed around 10, let me check the discord chat, there are usually always people talking on there in some thread," Matt offered.

He scrolled through the chat logs, people were talking about various things, one guy was upset about the result of a football game, all of the chats seemed to come to an abrupt end at exactly 10:45.

"It looks like the snap happened at 10:45 last night. All of the chats just stop," Matt whispered.

"What do we do?" Val whispered.

"There have got to be others out there, it doesn't make sense for it to just be the two of us. I mean, two totally random people? I mean, yes, we are siblings, but we are nobodies Val. Why us?" Matt offered.

"I don't know…but I'm glad you are still here," Val whispered.

"I'm glad you are still here too. Did you have any luck getting through to Mom and Dad?" Matt asked.

Val shook her head no. "I want to go check on them," she offered.

"That's a long way, Harlingen. Five hours," Matt sighed.

"Matt?" Val whispered.

"Yeah?" Matt offered. He could tell Val was getting more and more scared.

"Do you think there are zombies out there?" Val whispered.

"Well, I haven't seen any. And…I haven't seen any evidence of any. If everyone turned into a zombie, why were the car doors all closed? But…I think we should minimize the amount of noise we make…for now," Matt sighed. "A zombie apocalypse is something we can't cross off the list just yet. But…I would prefer a Thanos snap to that, if I am being honest."

"Thanos' motivations were to make life better for everyone. Random genocide. How is snapping all but two people better?" Val whispered.

"I don't know Val. I have to believe there are more people out there, starting with our parents. But…it could get a little hairy if we are facing a return to nativism. I have played plenty of those video games, and the common theme is always: people suck. So…let's stock up on some supplies, and head south to Harlingen. Check on the folks. Okay?" Matt offered.

"Okay, whose car should we take?" Val whispered.

"How much gas do you have? Gasoline might become an issue.." Matt trailed off.

"Why don't we head to the dealership then? You know we could get a new car," Val offered.

Val worked at one of the local car dealerships, she knew the ins and outs of that place. And they could get one of those electric cars, eliminating the need to refuel on the way.

"I like that idea. Steal an electric car," Matt grinned.

"Yep. Should we head to the grocery store first? Pick up supplies?" Val smiled.

"Yeah, let's do that. Let me pack a bag, and get Buddy ready. Could you find his crate?" Matt asked.

"Yeah, no problem," Val replied.

Matt walked into his room and grabbed a duffel bag. He was becoming really worried about this current situation, although he wasn't one of those doomsdayers, he certainly wasn't up for a zombie apocalypse. He was also worried about Val, she was way more social than him, and the concept of there not being any people left for her to spend time with was a scary thought. He was sure it was much worse for her.

Packing some clothes, he walked into his bathroom and got his toothbrush and other toiletries. Throwing the bag over his shoulder, he rejoined Val and Buddy. She was grabbing his food, having already packed his small crate into her car. Matt grabbed Buddy himself and they loaded up in her car.

"So, where to first?" Val whispered.

"I think we should go to the Wally World across the street. It has a lot of stuff we can use. It probably has stuff we haven't even thought of.

Then, we can head for the dealership. Do they have that new electric truck there?" Matt asked.

"Yes, it's a display model, no one is allowed to test drive it. Not until the Spring. But…I know where the keys are," Val grinned.

"How far can it go on one charge?" Matt asked.

"Between 200 and 230 miles. It even has a frunk, so we can store a lot in there," Val suggested.

"A frunk?" Matt asked.

"It's a trunk, in the front," Val laughed.

"Oh, okay. Let's get going then. And Val? Try to stay positive, alright? Look, we have each other, focus on that," Matt pressed.

"Thanks Matt. That is a really good thing to focus on," Val smiled.

Val backed up the Nissan and headed for the local store. Despite not subscribing to that "end of the world" conspiracy nonsense, Matt had a few ideas that could help them. And he could only hope that they weren't the last two humans on the planet.

CHAPTER 2

LOOTING

The trio walked into Wally World, automatic doors sliding open. The store was open 24 hours, so the lights were on, everything was working properly.

"There was no one to turn the power off, so that's good. All of the food is still fresh. Why don't we each grab a cart, and grab whatever you think will help us?" Matt offered.

"I would rather stick together, if you don't mind," Val whispered.

"Okay, that works too. You want to take Buddy? I'll grab a cart," Matt handed the leash to her.

She nodded and took it, while Matt grabbed a cart and began their quest. He knew they both had to keep their minds on the task at hand—the idea of them being alone was more than frightening. But—he would take that over the concept of zombies.

"Will you talk about something?" Val asked.

"Sure. You want to talk about survival? Or…?" Matt trailed off. He didn't know what else there was to talk about.

"Yes, talk about survival on a small scale, please," Val said quietly

"Okay, the plan is to steal a bunch of food from this store, then drive to the dealership, and steal their prized electric truck. After that, I want to drive down the road a little bit to the Cabela's, they have more supplies we could use. Then, we can drive for 200 miles, find a nice place to rest and charge the truck," Matt offered.

They were walking down the first vegetable aisle, Val picked up some carrots and bagged them, while Matt picked up some Hawaiian rolls.

"Hawaiian rolls, really?" Val sighed at him.

"If you don't want any, I will eat them all," Matt shrugged.

"I didn't say that, but maybe focus on food that we can preserve?" Val chided him.

"Listen, this is just for the road trip. We aren't filling our cart with cans of beans just yet. At some point, we are going to need to come up with a plan on where we actually plan on living. And what we are doing," Matt sighed.

"I'm not ready to think about that yet. Let's find some more food for the road," Val waved him off.

They walked further down the aisles, Buddy following his nose, while Val picked up some food. Matt picked up his good luck charm, a pineapple-flavored Mexican soda, and put it in the cart.

"You are so silly, every trip you get one of those. Just one, not two or three," Val rolled her eyes.

"I love them, okay? I know they are bad for you, that's why I only get one," Matt grinned.

Val picked one out herself, the cherry flavor. "They are very bad for you, but I like them too."

They filled their cart with groceries, a case of water, some Gatorade, then they came to the frozen section.

"Why don't we go get an ice chest or two? I know electricity is a luxury, all of this food is going to expire at some point soon. We might as well take some of the meat. And ice cream. Chocolate ice cream, specifically," Val grinned.

"I agree. I will go find some ice chests, and some ice. Or do you want to keep staying together?" Matt offered.

"We are okay here, take Buddy and I will take the cart," Val replied.

"Okay, I will come find you in this section in a few minutes. Let's go Buddy," Matt took the leash and they set off. It gave him some time to really think about the future.

No people. But the animals stayed. Hundreds of dogs out there, thousands of dogs, officially on their own. A lot of them wouldn't make it out of their own homes, but some would. Where would they go? Most likely form packs, go feral. What was the plan? Drive south, find their parents' house empty, then what? It was September, still hot. It would be even hotter in Harlingen. When the electricity eventually powered down, they would suffer in the heat.

And they would lose things like the oven, the fridge, Netflix, the Cubs. The Cubs were already gone, Matt sighed. They needed to figure out a method to live, then figure out whether or not they should remain in Texas, or move north. They also needed to figure out if there were any other survivors out there. Just remember the theme of all those video games: *People suck.*

Matt collected a random cart left in the middle of the store, and continued on towards sporting goods. He wasn't sure of the exact location of the ice chests, but that department would have other things they could use. Buddy continued to follow his nose, not a care in the world about their problems.

Arriving in sporting goods, Matt picked out some flashlights, a baseball bat, and then a pair of medium-sized ice chests. Throwing them all in the cart, he headed into the next section, Electronics, picking up some air pods, some charging stations, and a new Mp3 player. He then moved to the pharmaceutical section, looking for all kinds of first aid. He looted everything, bottles of Tylenol, Aleve, Advil, Robotussin, Pepto, all the medicine. He then took all kinds of band-aids, antiseptic, bandage tape.

Moving on, he led Buddy down the pet aisle, picking up a lot of bones for him, treats, a few more collars, a few more leashes, and a rope to play with. Finishing up, he headed back towards the frozen food section and a waiting Val.

Spotting her picking out her ice cream, she offered him a smile. "What's with the baseball bat?"

"Well, we walked right into this store because it never closes. But we probably won't be able to do that with every store. How do you plan on getting into the dealership?" Matt asked.

"Yeah, that's a valid point. We are going to have to break some glass," Val sighed. "I picked out some meat and ice cream. And some cookie dough. What else do you think we should get?"

"I mean, might as well get some milk and OJ, those are going to expire in a week or so. And we will never have milk and cookies again," Matt sighed.

"That really brings me down. Don't talk about that. In fact, let's ban the word 'never'," Val sighed.

"Go get some chocolate milk, and then regular. I'll grab some Sunny D, then we can move on to the next destination," Matt suggested.

"Okay," Val agreed.

"Hey, how about a hug?" Matt offered.

"Good plan," Val relented, hugging him. She took Buddy and went to find the groceries, while Matt pushed his cart towards the exit slowly. He picked up a few more things, chips, granola bars, Skittles. A couple of bags of Skittles.

Walking into the self-checkout area, Matt was looking for batteries. He knew there was an endcap with them, he just needed to find it. Spotting it, he grabbed all of the packs, making sure to get each type. He didn't even know what kind the flashlights used, which is why he was taking them all. Val was coming up to join him with Buddy, asking what the plan was.

"Bag the groceries, I'll get some ice bags from the freezer," Matt said as he walked away.

Val nodded and headed for the self-checkout machine, while Matt went to the freezer and pulled out two bags of ice. Carrying them back to her, he couldn't help but laugh. She was scanning each grocery item and bagging them.

"Hey Val?" Matt teased.

"Hmm?" Val looked up.

"You planning on paying for those?" Matt laughed.

"Oh! Okay, you got me," Val laughed. "No, I do not." She just bagged the groceries, as Matt dumped the ice into the chests. He put the meat, milk, cookie dough, and ice cream into them, as she was finishing up.

"Did you get enough Skittles?" Val laughed.

"I know you prefer chocolate, I grabbed some of that too," Matt grinned.

"I see that, yes," Val shook her head. "Okay, that's everything. Are we forgetting anything?"

"Yeah, my entire cart of supplies. Come on, help me bag these as well," Matt grinned.

"Right, you got a lot of stuff," Val observed.

They bagged all the supplies he had found, finally ready to go. Buddy led them out, following his nose up to the car that Val had double parked in front of the door. Right in the fire lane, just asking for a ticket. Opening the trunk, they put the supplies in first, then the groceries. They put the ice chests in the back seat, then loaded Buddy up, who always loved riding in the car.

"I need to head back to my apartment for a few things, then the dealership, okay?" Val offered.

"Yeah, let's go," Matt replied, hopping into the passenger seat.

Val started the car and put it in motion, driving around some stopped vehicles and heading towards her apartment. Things got very tedious on the highway, as the cars were just stopped, blocking the road. She had to zigzag around them before finally coming to her exit. There was a pile-up at the bottom of the off-ramp, as she stopped the Nissan.

"I was able to get around the pile-up when I took your exit, but this one, we need to push the cars out of the way," Val sighed.

"Yeah, pop the trunk," Matt sighed. He realized he should have put the baseball bat in the back seat, but it didn't matter. Val popped the trunk and Matt dug the bat out. She stayed in the car as he walked towards the pile-up. There were six cars, including a big truck that was really blocking the road. Walking down the line, he arrived at the first car in front and tried the door. It was locked, of course. Looking inside the window, he could see it was still in gear, and the keys were in the ignition.

He readied the bat and took a big swing, smashing the driver side window. Making sure to get all of the glass out of the way, he reached in and unlocked the door, then pulled it open. Turning the wheel to the right, he pushed the car into the grass, out of the way. Picking up the bat he had set down, he walked to the second car and repeated the whole process.

Val got out of the Nissan to help him, as he smashed the truck window, and then moved on to the fourth car while she pushed the truck out of the way. When the truck started moving, the cars behind started rolling down the hill as well.

"Look out! The other cars are coming! It's no big deal, just be mindful," Matt shouted at her.

Val pushed the truck off the road, and the fourth car rolled past her a bit, followed by the fifth and sixth. They piled up again at the bottom, but there was enough room for the Nissan to squeeze around them.

"Okay, let's go!" Val shouted, as they headed back to their ride. Piling in, she squeezed the Nissan through and resumed their journey.

"I know you like this car, but I don't think we are going to have it much longer," Matt said.

"I know. It's okay, it's just a car. It's not practical to be driving a 2.5 liter during a Calamity," Val nodded.

"Is that what we are calling it?" Matt grinned.

"Yes. For now, it's a Calamity. If it turns into a Zombie Apocalypse, we will adjust accordingly," Val replied.

Val continued to drive around the stopped cars in the street, and finally pulled into her apartment complex. Coming to a stop in front of her place, she opened the door to get out.

"I won't be long. Promise," Val turned to her brother.

"Why don't you take Buddy?" Matt suggested.

"You know I try to keep my apartment clean, Matt," Val sighed.

"Yeah, I also know we probably aren't coming back here, Val. So, get everything you need, everything you care about, and say goodbye to this place. And take Buddy. He is the face of comfort dogs," Matt whispered.

"I...I accept that," Val whispered back, as she opened the back door and led Buddy out. Matt waited in the car and continued to think about their upcoming challenges.

He wanted to stop at Cabela's, the place was a walking survival outfitter. It had everything they needed to survive in the event they lost electricity. It also had a wealth of firearms and ammunition. As far as he knew, Val had never shot a gun, but she had time to learn. He knew his old man had a bunch of guns at his place, but they were old, antiquated. Only a few really designed for defense.

Matt let his mind drift over to the Calamity itself. What had happened to all the people? He had slept through it, so he had no idea. But it really was as if Thanos happened. But why were he and Val still there? It didn't make sense. Two random siblings, and no one else? Matt refused to believe that. There *had* to be more humans out there. But did Matt really want to find them? It was possible he was letting the movie and video game scenarios dominate his philosophy.

He checked his phone, none of his friends had responded, and there was still no one on Discord. Nothing on Instagram or Snapchat either. No updates at all. So, if there was someone out there, they probably didn't have a phone, or hadn't thought to post their existence to Instagram yet. Val came out with a bunch of stuff; the Nissan was getting a little too full.

"I think we need to steal another car, Matt," Val offered.

"Agreed. We will have more room once we get the truck. But for now, we can just find a random car," Matt nodded.

"We could go back to your place to get your car," Val suggested.

"It's too much of a hassle. There is one over there that looks like it was searching for a parking spot. We can take that one," Matt pointed.

"Okay, I will make one more trip, and put the stuff in the front seat. Take Buddy and go get that one," Val nodded.

Matt got out of the Nissan, baseball bat in hand, and took the leash from her, heading over to the parked car. Buddy led him on, following his nose. This time Matt smashed the back window, unlocking the door and climbing into the front seat from the back. The keys were still in the ignition, as he had to press the brake to put the car back in Park. Getting it started, he pulled it forward into a parking spot close to Val's.

She came out again, pillows and a laptop in hand. Dumping them all in the front seat, she walked over to where he was waiting.

"Let's head to the dealership next. There is a jewelry store next to it, we can get some new watches as well. I know you never wear one because you would always look at it, but I think we need some," Val offered.

"Yeah, that's fine. Let's get going," Matt replied. "I will follow you."

Val nodded and headed back towards her Nissan. She pulled out of the parking spot and led them towards the dealership, Matt following behind in his newly acquired SUV. Again, zig zagging around parked cars, they weaved through traffic and arrived at the dealership without incident. Hopping out, they linked up and Val asked what they should do first.

"Let's get the truck, and move the supplies. I'm sure when we smash that jewelry store, the alarms will be blaring. I don't want to listen to that nonsense. And I don't want to bring the zombies," Matt grinned.

"Fair enough. I still think it was a snap, but let's not take any chances," Val shook her head with a smile.

They approached the front door, peering inside. Unsurprisingly, they saw no one. Matt looked around for the electric truck, not seeing it. Val motioned for him to smash the door first and he obliged.

"This is the employee entrance—you can't see the showroom from here. Come on," Val said, as she unlocked the dead bolt and opened the door.

"Right," Matt nodded, as he led Buddy inside. Val led them into the main room, and there sitting in the middle was the silver electric truck.

"Here we are, the new electric pickup truck. It isn't hitting the market until next Spring, correction, it's not hitting the market, because there *is* no market. But this one is fully functional. I'll get the keys and charging stations, you start transferring the supplies into it. I can't wait to get it out of here," Val laughed.

"How do you plan on getting it out of here?" Matt asked, curiously.

"Right out the front window," Val smiled. "I liked working here, but I won't miss it."

"Okay then," Matt shrugged, as he walked back to the vehicles outside. He tied Buddy's leash to a pole, not wanting to drag him back and forth. He would need both hands anyway. He started with the ice chests, taking each one to the truck. Val opened the frunk, and he placed them inside. Continuing on, he loaded the supplies next, then the groceries, with Val coming to help him about halfway through.

"Okay, we got everything. Let's start it up, the battery should be fully charged," Val smiled. Matt watched as she hopped into the driver's seat and started the engine. She saw her look of disappointment, as she turned it off and hopped out.

"Bad news, the battery is at 60%. We have to charge it up. No big deal though, with the charging station here, it will only take about 15 minutes," Val reported.

"Oh, is that all? Wow," Matt reflected.

"Only because we have a charging station here. When we get to wherever our new house is, we will have to use the regular outlets. That will take a lot longer. Let's head to the jewelry store while it charges?" Val suggested.

"Okay, let's go," Matt smiled, as he walked to retrieve Buddy, who did not appreciate being tied to the pole outside. His nose had a much larger range than that. "Are we driving, or walking?"

"Might as well drive, it's not like we need to save the gasoline," Val shrugged.

They piled into the Nissan and she drove them across the street and through the jewelry store entrance. Matt was surprised as she went all the way through the door, causing the alarm to start blaring.

"We are here!" Val announced.

"Okay, okay," Matt smiled. They got out and looked through the watches, they all looked expensive. Matt set to smashing the glass with the bat, as Val picked out a ring and some earrings as well.

"I love sapphires, I wish they were my birthstone," Val laughed.

"They are the best color for sure," Matt grinned as he picked out a new watch. Val got one too and they got back into the Nissan where Buddy waited.

She backed it out and drove back to the dealership, asking if they needed anything else.

"Do you guys have some siphon hoses here?" Matt asked.

"I already got some, along with a gas can. I also got portable battery chargers for the truck, as well as the main charger," Val replied.

"Good, at some point, we are going to need gasoline. But we can worry about that when we get to Harlingen, and plan our next move. I know you don't want to talk about that yet, though," Matt sighed.

"I—listen Matt. Do you want to go to Harlingen?" Val whispered.

"I'm not against it. I think we both need to find out whether or not our parents got snapped. I think *not* knowing would eat away at us over time. The question is, do we want to stay there? What is our plan for tomorrow, exactly?" Matt sighed.

"I think we should address that from inside our parent's house, over ice cream," Val answered.

"I agree. Okay, if we are ready, let's go," Matt offered.

Val nodded and they climbed into the truck, starting it up. The battery was at 100%, as Val smiled and drove it straight out the front window and onto the road.

"I've always wanted to do that," Val beamed.

"Really?" Matt asked, surprised.

"Oh yeah, ever since that GTA game. It was fun," Val laughed.

"Well okay then. We can take turns driving, if you want. I know you like driving more than I do, but weaving through traffic is going to be annoying. I'm sure once we get out of town it will be better, if the snap happened at 10:45 last night, the road won't be too busy," Matt offered.

"We will find the best way," Val nodded, as she got onto the highway and headed south.

"Head for Buda, I want to stop at the Cabela's there, finish off our supply run," Matt said, looking out the window.

CHAPTER 3

CABELA'S

Val drove a different, borrowed, truck through the entrance at Cabela's, while Matt and Buddy watched from the electric truck just outside the giant store. The lights inside were off, but there were plenty of windows to illuminate the building.

Val hopped out of the truck, laughing. "Okay, what are we here for?"

"More supplies. Find some camping gear, tents, lanterns, matches, everything. I will check out the guns," Matt offered, as he led Buddy inside, baseball bat in hand again.

"Roger that," Val grinned, as she looked around. It was a huge store, two stories high. An outdoorsman's dream.

Matt knew the guns were in the back on the downstairs level, as he headed that way. Buddy was sniffing the clothing as they walked on, finally arriving at the gun collection; they were running about 100 feet down the back wall. They were also locked inside a glass box, most likely plexiglass. It might take a few swings.

Matt sighed and tied Buddy to a nearby clothing stand, then went down the line, looking for what guns he wanted to take. Finally coming to the home defense section, he took a swing against the glass. It cracked, but didn't break, as he swung again. It took a few more swings but the glass finally shattered and he was able to clear it out of the way.

Grabbing a combat shotgun, he picked it up out of there. Opening the slide, it seemed to be in good working order, as he set it on the counter. He took out another one, setting it down as well. There was a lever action, and then a pump next to them, but he didn't want those. Despite the fact the Terminator made lever action shotguns look easy to use, Matt knew better.

Moving down the line, he saw some smaller rifles, a carbine that he wanted, and a Marlin lever action. Matt didn't have a lot of gun knowledge, really just what his father and grandfather had passed on to him, but he knew he wanted guns that were easy to use—for both himself and Val. He took some swings and smashed the glass again, lifting the carbine out, then the Marlin, setting them both down on the counter. He wanted one more deer rifle, then he would move to the handguns.

Inspecting the deer rifles, there were a lot he didn't recognize. He just wanted a simple, scoped .308 caliber. He saw what looked like another Marlin, this one was probably a .30-06 variant. He liked that rifle, but without a scope, it probably wouldn't serve him too well. Still, he decided to take it; he needed to smash the glass anyway, as he raised his bat one more time.

Taking the Marlin out, he set it on the counter, and looked back at the deer rifles. Spotting a .308 Winchester variant, he pulled that one out. It was heavy, and Matt didn't care for it, so he set it on the ground. Finally, he spotted a Ruger .308 bolt action, with a camo stock. It looked like a nice, simple weapon, so Matt lifted it out. It was much lighter, probably less than ten pounds. He noticed it had "Go Wild" engraved on the stock, as he set it on the counter.

Handguns were next. This was Matt's least experienced field. He had much more time with shotguns and rifles than he did with pistols. Looking at them, he spotted the standard .38 Special for Val. He knew that one would be easy. Smashing the glass, he set it on the counter.

Looking some more, the choices for him were much more complex. He would have to practice a good amount with whatever he chose, as he sorted through the guns. Finally spotting a recognizable name, the Colt 1911. The Marines' weapon. Taking it out, he set it on the counter, then looked through the guns for another one. Finding it, he set that one on the counter as well. He just wanted one more revolver, then he could start looking for ammo. Settling on a .45 caliber Governor to match the Colts, he set it on the counter last.

"Matt? Where are you?" Val shouted.

"Back here!" Matt shouted back. "You good?"

"Yes, I loaded the camping supplies. How are you doing over here?" Val asked.

"I'm good, I got all the guns I wanted. I know you don't like them, but if it's zombies, we will need them. And, we can hunt deer with them.".

"I realize that. But if it's zombies, we have been making a lot of noise, and haven't seen any. Also, the cars wouldn't be abandoned like they were. Still, you are right. How can I help?" Val offered.

"We need ammo. Probably will need a flashlight to see the boxes, I spotted some over there," Matt pointed. "Batteries next to them. Can you get two?"

"On it," Val nodded.

Matt walked around the counter and began inspecting the ammo. There was enough light for him to see the 12-gauge shotgun shells, as he pulled out a bunch of boxes and set them on the counter. Val came back with the flashlights, handing him one.

"Thanks. Okay, you are looking for a box that says .45 caliber, start with that," Matt pointed. "I think this aisle is all shotgun, so move to the next one and tell me what you see."

"Okay, 9 mm, is that millimeter?" Val asked.

"Yeah, you don't need that. Look for .45 and .38. I'll go to the next aisle," Matt replied.

"Here we go, .45. How many boxes?" Val asked.

"All of them," Matt shrugged.

He found the .308 ammo, and started collecting boxes as well. Setting them on the counter next to Val, they realized they needed a cart, or a bag, or something. Then, he spotted portable ammo crates down the aisle.

"Grab some of those crates, we'll use those. I'll keep collecting ammo, we need a few more types," Matt pointed.

Val went for the crates, while Matt continued to search through the ammo, he needed some .30-06 for the Marlin, and some .30 caliber for the carbine. He found the boxes and loaded them onto the counter, looking at the guns. He noticed he still needed ammo for the first Marlin, the .30-30 variant. Heading back, he found those boxes as Val walked back with some crates.

Loading them up, Matt started carrying the crates out to the truck. It took multiple trips, but he got them all in the back. Turning around, he headed back for the guns, which Val didn't want any part of.

"Okay, so, first rule of guns, never point them at people. So, since I'm the only other person, never point them at me," Matt grinned. "The carbine has a shoulder strap, so just throw it over your shoulder. I am going to find some more of those, plus some holsters for the pistols. This place has everything, it's just a matter of looking."

"Should I put the guns in the trunk?" Val asked.

"Yeah, for now. I need to make sure they are good to go—as in—they actually fire. I don't know if these guys put some kind of safety mechanism on them, but first let me get everything we need out of here," Matt sighed.

"After this, why don't we eat? There is a restaurant upstairs, it's decently lit. We need a break," Val offered.

"I'm in on that," Matt nodded.

Val started making her runs, carrying one gun at a time. Matt located some holsters, including a smaller one for the .38. He also found some more shoulder straps. He decided to make one more trip down the gun showcase, just in case he missed something they could use. Coming to the end, he saw an assault rifle with a nice scope on it. He used the flashlight to read the label.

It was a SCAR-17 with a night force scope, Matt could only assume that meant it was a night vision scope. It was advertised as using 7.62 NATO rounds, which were the standard military variant. He figured he would test it out, raising his bat and shattering the glass. Picking up the rifle, it was surprisingly light. He looked through the scope, and sure enough, it was night vision. Setting the gun on the counter, he walked around to find the boxes of ammo.

He piled them into another crate, along with extra empty magazines, and took it outside. Val was on her way back to the counter, and she suggested he start testing out the guns. Nodding, he combined the 7.62 rounds with the other crates and picked up the carbine. Opening the slide, it looked clean and ready to go. Fishing out a round, he inserted it into the barrel and closed the slide. Taking aim, he flicked the safety off and fired into the air.

The gun fired, no recoil whatsoever, which is what Matt expected. It was an extremely efficient weapon for beginners and novices, which is what they both were. Turning the safety back on, he set the carbine down and picked up one of the shotguns. Loading one shell, he fired it off as well. Again, no problem, as there was no recoil.

Val brought out the deer rifle, handing it to Matt. He was actually very curious about this weapon, as he opened the box of .308 and loaded a round. Raising the gun, he looked through the scope, across the highway at a tree in the field. Squeezing the trigger, the gun bucked as he heard the bullet hit the tree. Impressed with not just himself, but the gun, he ejected the spent round and secured the weapon.

An hour later, the truck was packed full and ready to go. All of the guns had worked, and now it was time for lunch. Matt and Val led Buddy up the stairs and into the restaurant, carrying the picnic basket Val had found. Sitting down, Val broke out the snacks.

"Okay, one bone for Buddy," Val smiled, handing the Beagle his lunch. He was all too excited for it. "As for us, I picked up some lunchables."

"Wow, lunchables? Talk about taking us back to high school," Matt grinned. "Do they come with the Capri Sun?"

"They do not, but I brought those Mexican sodas, along with a bottle opener," Val beamed.

"Is that all you brought for us?" Matt asked.

"If you want more you can go back to the truck and get something," Val teased.

"Listen, you said you would handle lunch. So, I will not say a word until we finish our food," Matt grinned.

"That's better," Val smiled as she handed him his lunchable. It had been ten years since high school, and while the lunchable was a fun reminder, they devoured them pretty fast. Matt drank his Mexican soda, which tasted as delicious as always, and waited for Val.

"Darn it," Val muttered.

"Hmm?" Matt grinned.

"Two things….no three. First, I hate you. Second, this Mexican soda tastes amazing, but it's so bad for you. And third…okay. I'm still very hungry," Val whined.

"Why don't you just go get some bags of fish and chips from over there on the counter," Matt pointed. "We can save the rest of the food for when we really have to rest and charge the truck battery."

"Okay, that makes sense," Val sighed as she stood up and retrieved four bags of chips. Buddy didn't have a care in the world as he was chewing on his bone. Matt continued to worry about Val however.

"How are you holding up?" Mat asked her gently.

"I'm not that great, honestly. I thought the concept of all people vanishing was a fairytale reserved for movies and video games. Even if there had been a pathogen or something, there would be bodies. They literally got snapped by the Infinity Stones, which are not a real thing," Val sighed.

"On top of all that, which really sucks, there isn't anything we can do about it. We aren't Avengers, we aren't going to fly across the cosmos and save the universe. We have no way of knowing if there is anyone else out there," Matt sighed.

"We can monitor the internet as long as it is online. I checked it again, still no updates of any kind," Val whispered.

"It feels like we are completely alone," Matt sighed, munching on his chips.

"I'm really glad it's two of us though," Val observed.

"Same. I'm glad you are here with me. Being truly alone would suck," Matt admitted.

"We need to make a rule that says you can't play that hiding trick on me," Val offered.

"But you can play it on me? That doesn't seem fair," Matt grinned.

"Okay, no playing it on each other. *No* pretending to be missing, and no splitting up outside the same building," Val rolled her eyes.

"That's fair. You about done? We should get going," Matt pressed.

"Yeah, do you mind driving? I will get Buddy," Val sighed.

"Sure, no problem," Matt replied.

Knowing Buddy wasn't going to come on his own, Val picked him up, bone and all, and carried him downstairs. Matt followed behind, carrying the picnic basket. He had thought about throwing their trash away, but why bother?

"How much of a bill do you think we racked up here?" Val grinned.

"Oh, five grand, easy. Probably much closer to ten. A couple of those guns were over a thousand. And the ammo? Yeah, probably no less than ten thousand," Matt laughed. "These Texans, they love their guns."

"I hope we only have to use them against things like deer," Val sighed.

"I hope that too, Val. I mean that," Matt whispered.

They climbed into the truck, Buddy shifted around in the back and resumed eating his bone. Val hopped up into the passenger seat and broke out her Mp3 player, as Matt got the truck started. Pulling out, he got onto the highway and began weaving around the parked cars. They were more infrequent as they got out of town, and he was grateful for that. He knew there was a nice rest area around Robstown, and figured they would stop there.

CHAPTER 4

ARRIVING

Matt, Val, and Buddy were lounging in a rest area about 150 miles south of Austin, charging the truck. The charging station had taken them by surprise, they didn't expect to find one. But as Matt remembered, it was a nice rest area. It seemed as if it had been upgraded over the years. They had to break open the vending machines to get some quarters out—the charging station only took quarters for some reason. So, not quite perfect, but it had allowed Matt to shoot the gun again, as he had blown the lock off.

"How long does the charge typically take?" Matt asked.

"Oh, that's a station, so it should take no more than 30 minutes," Val replied, as she ate her sandwich.

Buddy was still on the same bone; Matt had finished up his sandwich and was drinking one of the sodas he had liberated from the vending machine. Val had grabbed a water bottle for herself.

"Probably another 100 miles or so, zig zagging through the traffic. At least there are far less cars on the road. There probably won't be any between Kingsville and Harlingen, so we should make good time," Matt reflected.

"Trying to keep it as short term as possible, what are we going to do once we get to our parents' house?" Val sighed.

"Decide whether or not we want to live there. If we do, take steps to ensure we are as safe and well cared for as possible. If we don't, then we need to decide where we go next," Matt replied.

"What do you think about living there?" Val asked.

"I'm for it. Harlingen is a smaller town, and we are familiar with it. We know where everything is, and the parents' house is across the street from a grocery store, a home goods store, a golf course, tennis courts. We could live there easily," Matt offered.

"Alright. I mean, where would we go, if we didn't want to live there?" Val asked.

"North. I know that's obvious, Harlingen is about as far south as you can get. But if we were to live somewhere else, I would want to move north, to Chicago, or Denver, or somewhere where we could easily survive without electricity. I'm really worried about the electricity just going out someday, and never coming back," Matt sighed.

"Ignoring that long term comment, what work is there to do short term once we settle in Harlingen?" Val asked.

"Oh, a lot. First up, I think we should raid the local Wally World for literally every single perishable item. Then store them in all of our neighbor's houses, use their refrigerators and deep freezes. Honestly, that will take a while. So, no need to go any further," Matt explained.

"Okay, do you think we should steal another electric truck then?" Val grinned.

"Do you think they will have one down there?" Matt asked.

"Absolutely, every dealership in the country was sent one model for its showroom," Val beamed.

"Oh, in that case, yes, we should steal them all. There is one dealership in Harlingen, one in McAllen for sure. Probably one in Brownsville," Matt reflected.

"The battery should be charged, you ready? I will drive the rest of the way," Val offered.

"Okay, sure. I'll get the Beagle," Matt grinned. "Grab some more waters from the vending machine?"

"You got it," Val laughed.

This time, Matt did throw their trash away, and collected Buddy, carrying him to the truck. Val came back with some waters, and she got them moving again. Looking out the window, they had seen plenty of animals. Cows, horses, birds, it seemed to be just the humans that were missing. Matt knew the cows would just migrate, at some point breaking down their fences in search of food and water. Same with the horses. Life would go on—with or without the people.

Val weaved around the occasional stopped car, but for the most part, it was a clear road. She stayed in the left lane, as most of them were in the right, and kept heading south. Matt was worried that finding an empty house would really bring her down, but he didn't know what to do about it.

"We should make another rule," Val offered. "No picking up strays."

"Strays?" Matt asked.

"Stray dogs. I know you love dogs, but we don't know anything about the ones that are going to be roaming. Do you have a plan for that?" Val asked.

"Yeah, but you won't like it," Matt sighed. "For now, we will follow your rule."

"Right then," Val nodded. "Also, no cats. I know that won't be hard for you, since you don't like them."

"At all," Matt grinned. "Buddy would not get along with one anyway."

"Have you thought of anything else we need to do?" Val asked.

"Yeah, but let's not talk about it yet. I am still worried about dealing with the fact our parents got snapped," Matt sighed. "Or zombified, or whatever."

"I think we should live in Harlingen, in our parents' house. That house has our entire family in it, all our pictures, everything. I know it's going to be empty, and I'm okay with it—as okay as I can be. I realize this is more a you thing, this whole apocalypse thing, but that's just how I feel," Val pressed.

"This is barely a *me* thing. I've never been a fan of zombie shows, we don't even watch them. Sure, I have played some video games, and I've heard the basics of how to survive. But honestly, I am just as bummed about this as you. We have to stay positive though, maybe the Avengers are out there trying to save us. I don't know. But Mom and Dad would want us to go on, together," Matt sighed.

"I agree. So, we *will* go on. Come up with the plans, and we will do them. What do you think we should do first?" Val asked.

"Unpack everything, and take stock of the house. Then, take stock of the neighbors' houses. They live in a cul-de-sac, so I figure we should take over each of those houses. I think there are five total, including the parents. It's an older, retired community, so they were probably all home. Which means their cars are there, their houses are stocked with food, so on and so forth. We will try to break in without smashing the glass, if they are like our parents, they probably had a house key under a flowerpot or something," Matt offered.

"Do you think we should get the boat out of the driveway?" Val asked.

"Yeah, no reason to waste driveway space on a boat. Honestly, I think we should steal a lot of different cars. I also think we need to work on obtaining, and storing, gasoline. Every car we are passing has gas in it, so maybe get some trucks with big gas tanks to store it in, for when we lose electricity," Matt reflected.

"What is gas going to do for us when we lose power?" Val asked.

"We are going to obtain some generators, a lot of them, to power our house. They run on gasoline," Matt whispered.

"Oh, that's a good idea. Like I said, I will leave the planning to you. Of course, we will do everything together, but that fact didn't even dawn on me," Val relented.

"Can we talk about something more positive? How about we declare the Cubs 2021 World Series Champions?" Matt grinned.

"Matt, they were 20 games out," Val laughed.

"They went on a miracle run, qualified for the wild card, ran the table, then swept the Astros in the World Series," Matt reflected.

"Was it even possible for them to make the Wild Card?" Val laughed.

"How far back were they from the second spot? Ten, eleven games? Yes, it was possible, it happened. Rule #3. Say it," Matt declared.

"The Cubs swept the Astros, cheaters until the end, to win the 2021 World Series," Val beamed.

"Our shortstop won the MVP," Matt laughed.

They shared a laugh as they drove on, passing through the enormous King Ranch, Val listened to some music, while Matt continued to think about things to do. It seemed to be a never-ending list, but they would manage. Finally, they could see the skyline of Harlingen in the distance, as their trip was nearing its end.

"So, get everything unpacked, figure out what we need, cook dinner?" Val asked.

"Yeah, it's almost 5pm, so we still have time to go out, but we don't have to. Everything can wait until tomorrow. Although I think it would be a good idea to check on the other houses as well. Reduce their electricity usage. Um, I know a couple of neighbors have pets, what do you think we should do about them?" Matt whispered.

"What do you think?" Val sighed.

"I'm not happy about it, but we have to maintain those houses. We aren't just going to throw supplies in them and move on. We have to ensure they don't become infested with rats and mice, especially since we will be storing food there. I don't want the pets. I know it's cruel, but they aren't *our* pets, and they have probably already messed up those houses. Maybe just open the front door and let them run away," Matt sighed.

"Let's move on. I'll focus on unpacking—you focus on the houses. We are going to need more clothes, that should be fun," Val smiled.

"I was never much of a shopper, but yes, we are definitely going to need more clothing. We will have to figure out the best way to wash it all," Matt sighed.

"You didn't like shopping because we went into every store," Val grinned.

"And most of the time didn't buy anything. Only go into a store if you have the intention of buying something. It really became a miserable experience as time went on," Matt grumbled.

"Well, we will only go to a couple of stores, or, I will go shopping for clothing while you work on another project in that area," Val offered.

"I accept that," Matt grinned.

They were coming into the city, and Val had to weave around more cars. Still, there weren't many on the road. Harlingen was mostly a retired community, so by 10pm, everyone was winding down. They certainly weren't on the highway, as parked cars remained sporadic. Val took their exit, and there weren't any cars on the offramp.

"Lucky break, we don't have to push cars out of the way," Val whispered.

"Everyone that lives in this area is in bed by 9pm, and even if they are awake, they aren't driving," Matt reflected.

Val pulled into the neighborhood, driving by the country club, the tennis courts, and the golf course. Coming into the cul-de-sac, their parents' car was in the garage, and the boat was in the corner, as they expected. Val parked in the driveway and hopped out. Matt grabbed Buddy, and headed towards the front door. Taking his keys out, he unlocked it and walked inside. Val followed behind him, quietly.

"Mom? Dad? Are you here?" Matt called out. He knew there would be no answer, but he had to try. They walked into their parent's bedroom, and the bed was unmade. The breathing machines were both lying there, left behind after the bodies vanished.

"They got snapped," Val cried.

Matt offered her a hug, as they cried. Buddy could sense their distress, as he rubbed up against Matt's leg, whining.

"Stay with Buddy, okay? I will fix the bed," Matt whispered.

Val broke the hug and nodded, as she led Buddy into the living room to sit on the couch. Matt got the breathing machines off the bed and into their storage boxes, shoving them underneath. He made the bed and walked out to join Val.

"I think we should sleep in the guest room, it has a King bed, and if they get unsnapped while we are sleeping, they will reappear on top of us if we are in their bed," Matt whispered.

"And we know that's how it works. I hope the Avengers are out there, trying to save us," Val managed. "Despite the fact they aren't real."

"I always said Han Solo is a real person, so, I guess we have to believe the Avengers are too," Matt sighed. "I am going to go check the other houses. Take your time, stay with Buddy, and when you are ready, unpack the groceries and get them into the fridge, okay?"

"Okay. I know the neighbors have a pair of Poms, what are you going to do about them?" Val asked.

"I don't want to even think about it. I am doing their house last," Matt sighed.

Matt walked out the front door, really dreading this particular task. Heading over to their other immediate neighbor's house, he tried opening the door. It was locked of course, so he searched high and low for a hidden key. Under flower pots, on top of the porch light, underneath the welcome mat, there was nothing. A dog started to bark at him, which just added to his problems. It sounded like a terrier, but Matt wasn't sure, he had never spoken to this particular neighbor.

Heading around the side of the house, Matt tried their back door, locked as well. This would be the point of entry, as he headed back to the truck to get the baseball bat. He felt bad about this, but they needed the houses for storage, cold storage even. Trying to convince himself of that fact, he headed for the back door and broke the glass tile next to the deadbolt. Reaching inside, the dog was snarling at him by this point, as he finally saw what breed it was.

"A damn Scottish Terrier, are you serious?" Matt exclaimed. This dog would never welcome him into its house. Matt knew the breed, despite Disney trying to portray it as a loving, friendly dog, it was anything *but*. Giving up, he walked to the next house.

"I can't do this yet," Matt whispered to himself.

Arriving at the next house, he once again searched for a spare key. This time, he found one, as another dog started barking. Another terrier, from the sounds of it. Unlocking the door, Matt peeked inside. And once again, the dog was snarling at him. A Standard Schnauzer. The only difference between this breed and the Scotty was one was black, and the other was grey. Same personality. Closing the door, Matt felt as if the fates were lining up against him.

Moving on to the last house, he prayed it was empty. Alas, it was not, as he heard the baying before he even got to the door. However, this encouraged him. Finally, a likable breed. It was a Hound, Matt didn't know what kind, but the baying told him it was likely a Basset Hound. Sure enough, he peeked inside the window and there was an older, fatter Basset. Matt knew they were friendly, he just needed to offer him a treat and they would be pals.

Walking back to the truck, Val had come out to unload the groceries, and he asked for a dog treat.

"Sure, what have you found?" Val asked.

"A Scotty, a Schnauzer, and a Basset Hound. I haven't heard the Poms barking in this last house next to us, but just give me the treat. I am going to make friends with the Hound," Matt sighed, setting the bat down in the tailgate.

"Matt? You can bring the Hound home, okay? To cancel out the bad karma," Val offered.

"Yeah, thanks Val," Matt nodded, as he took the bone and walked back to the Hound's house. Searching, he found a key underneath the welcome mat, and unlocked the door. The Hound came forward to greet him, as Matt held the bone out. The dog didn't even hesitate as he took it and started to chew.

"What's your name bud?" Matt asked, looking at his collar. The name Fred was on the tag. "Why does everyone name Basset Hounds Fred? It was one movie, sheesh," Matt shook his head.

Standing up, Matt walked into the house, looking for a leash. He found them hanging on a coat rack, taking one and putting it on Fred. Fred was not interested in going anywhere however, as he chewed the bone. Relenting, Matt let go of the leash and searched the house. Unplugging the electronics in the living room, he moved on and did the same in the bedroom. He turned the air conditioner off, and checked the guest room.

He turned off the ceiling fans and headed for the front door, his work complete. He needed to get Fred back to the main house, and then deal with the other dogs. Picking up the leash, Fred came as they crossed the cul-de-sac to meet Val.

"This is Fred, he isn't a stray, he is a Basset Hound with an unimaginative name. And we are keeping him," Matt declared.

"Hey Fred," Val smiled, as she leaned down to pet him. "We will put him in the back yard for right now. I haven't heard from the Poms, maybe they were on vacation again. That woman always traveled."

"I hope so," Matt whispered, as he took Fred around the house and opened the back gate. Letting him inside the yard, Matt closed the gate and walked over to the other neighbor's house. Checking for a spare key, he didn't think he would find one, and he didn't. But there was no barking, which was a welcome relief. Walking back to the truck, he picked up the baseball bat and headed around back. Breaking the glass tile, he reached inside and unlocked the deadbolt, opening the door.

Heading inside, he shouted a hello, just to see if the dogs were there. Nothing responded, so he set about unplugging all the electronics again, and turning the A/C and ceiling fans off. Unlocking the front door and walking out, he waved the all clear to Val.

"I'm finishing up the groceries, next is the camping gear, where should I put it?" Val asked.

"In this house here. Just anywhere. It's empty. I'll take care of the other two dogs now," Matt sighed.

"Do you think if you open the doors they will just run away?" Val whispered.

"No, they aren't that kind of dog, they would just attack us. Those are their houses—they aren't going to leave them. Can you get the shovel out of the garage, and set it out here, for after?" Matt sighed.

CHAPTER 5

COPING

Val handed Matt a pint of chocolate ice cream with a spoon. She sat down next to him with her own pint, and they dug in. Buddy and Fred were hitting it off, chewing on their bones. Fred was an older dog, he could get along with anyone. Matt knew he wouldn't be a problem.

"Today was pretty terrible, so let's just eat this ice cream and go to bed," Val offered.

"I support that," Matt sighed. "Even though I could eat more than this."

"Tomorrow morning, I will cook us a big breakfast while you organize this house. Dad's guns are locked up in the attic, you should see which ones you can use. I spotted the carbine in the closet, and his big gun is in his nightstand," Val offered.

"Okay. But his guns should be in the armory, not the attic. Tomorrow we steal another electric truck, and get more groceries. While you unload them, I will keep working on the houses down the street. I know that that is more physical work for you...but..." Matt trailed off.

"I'm not trading places with you. I'm sorry, I know what you are doing is hard for you, but that's not something I can do. And Matt? I'm sorry, but you really can't bring any more dogs home. Two is enough," Val sighed.

"No promises. Hounds are social with each other, I mean, these two are already getting along fine. Hopefully I find some that will just run away," Matt sighed, as he ate his ice cream.

"Let's save tomorrow for tomorrow, and just focus on the ice cream. Do you think there is anything pressing we need to do before bed?" Val asked.

"No. Let's finish up here, take a shower, then head to bed," Matt replied. "I guess Vic probably got snapped too."

"Getting to downtown Houston to check on her would be a nightmare. If she is still here, she will have the same thoughts we did, come check on the parents. We will be here," Val whispered.

"Did you at least text her?" Matt asked.

"I did, right away. She never responded. If she woke up to an empty world, and got a text message, she would have responded. I will try again, but I am pretty sure she got snapped. And like you said, downtown Houston would be a nightmare. The Astros had a home game last night. We aren't going," Val sighed.

Matt nodded and they finished off their pints, as the two hounds kept eating their bones. He wasn't up for his evening walk with Buddy, as they stood up and rinsed the dishes off. But he did think about their sleeping arrangement.

"I forgot Buddy's bed at my place. And I don't even know if Fred has a bed, I can go back over there and check," Matt suggested.

"I can go. Buddy can sleep with us tonight," Val offered.

"Okay, thanks," Matt relented. "I'll jump into the shower."

An hour later, they were settling into bed, Buddy in between them. It was a king bed, so there was plenty of room. Tomorrow was going to be a busy day again. And with any luck, Matt wouldn't have to deal with any more dogs.

"Good night Matt. I love you," Val whispered.

"I love you too Val," Matt whispered back, closing his eyes.

Buddy woke them up the next morning, ready to go out. Matt got up and walked to the back door, letting both dogs outside. He went into the kitchen to pour himself some apple juice, and look for the dog food. He found both, and drank while pouring some food into the two dishes. He figured Val must have brought back Fred's dish last night as well.

He let the dogs back in, and directed them to their bowls. It was a new house for Fred, but he was settling in quickly. Buddy had been there lots of times, so he knew where things were. Val slowly walked into the room, offering a good morning.

"Good morning. You will have to show me how to make your coffee, so I can know for future days?" Matt asked.

"It's a Keurig Matt. Put the K-cup in and press go," Val muttered.

"I don't know which flavors are yours though?" Matt countered.

"I will set everything up today," Val motioned. "I promise to cook breakfast, after my coffee. What are you going to start with?"

"I'm going to take the bat, and walk the dogs. I'll check out a couple of houses, then come back and go through Dad's closet," Matt offered.

"Enjoy your walk," Val said, starting the Keurig.

Matt put the leashes on each dog, and led them outside, baseball bat in hand. It was around 7:30ish, so it was still a cool morning. They walked out of the cul-de-sac and to the first house on the street. Matt looked around for a spare key, finding it under the doormat. Unlocking the door, the trio walked inside. The hounds followed their noses, but there was nothing to find. The house was empty, as Matt closed the door and let go of their leashes.

Powering everything down, he collected the dogs again and continued on to one more house. Inside, a Chihuahua was barking at them relentlessly. Letting out a sigh, Matt turned them around and headed home. Walking inside, he could smell breakfast cooking, as Val had promised.

"I'm going to put the dogs out back," Matt offered.

"What did you find out there?" Val asked.

"One empty house, powered down, and one Chihuahua. I'm going back to open the door and hope it runs away," Matt sighed.

"I know you hate this. Just open the door and come back, okay?" Val pressed.

"Yeah, I'll be right back," Matt whispered, as he threw Buddy and Fred into the back yard and walked back outside, picking up the shotgun as he went. He headed back to the occupied house, and searched for a key. Finding one underneath the flower pot, he unlocked the door. The Chihuahua was barking entirely too much, but Matt had learned his lesson. Leaving the door open, he headed back towards their house, with the yappy dog following from a distance. As Matt walked further away, the dog stopped following, and wandered off.

Matt was grateful, as he re-entered their house and set the shotgun down in the corner. The breakfast continued to smell really good, and he offered his assistance in the kitchen.

"I'm good. About ten more minutes 'til we eat; go check out the closet, Dad had more clothes than he could wear, I think we should load them up in the truck and dump them somewhere," Val suggested.

"Yeah, I agree with that," Matt nodded.

He walked into his parent's room, heading for the closets. There were a lot of clothes hanging, he didn't think it was fully necessary to get rid of them, and it certainly wasn't a priority. He spotted the carbine leaning against the wall, and checked it. The safety was on, as he ejected the clip. Fully loaded, it was ready to go. He set it back down and walked over to the nightstand on his Dad's side, opening it. The .357 Magnum was there, too big for practical use. He left it there and closed the drawer.

All of the other guns were locked in a gun armoire, safe and secure. The key was in the nightstand, and he fished it out. Unlocking the cabinet, he took stock of the weapons. There were ten of them, two deer rifles, four hunting shotguns, a smaller .410, a Marlin, and a classic M1 Garand. He didn't recognize the last gun, as he picked it up. It was a rifle, really old, from the looks of it. Opening the bolt, he looked at the stamp. .303 Enfield, from World War I.

Shrugging, he put the Enfield back and closed the cabinet. All of the guns had locks on them, but he would worry about that later. He would probably only unlock the Garand, the Marlin, and the .410. But really, the Garand was too much of a hassle, despite its power.

"Matt! Breakfast is ready, what do you want to drink?" Val called.

"Just some OJ is fine, thanks," Matt responded.

"No problem, come sit down," Val offered.

"On my way. I'll leave the dogs outside. Buddy is a horribly effective beggar, I can't imagine how good Fred is at it," Matt laughed.

"There is bacon, so I am sure he would be a nightmare. Still, he seems very friendly. You are right Matt—hounds are nice to be around. But honestly, two really is the max for this house," Val stated.

"I know. The good thing is, hounds run. So, I can just open the door and they will go. Speaking of that, we will have to keep a close eye on them when they are in the back. I know Dad put some chicken wire out there to prevent Buddy from digging, but honestly, I should just lock them on the back porch while we eat," Matt reflected.

"Yeah, that's a good plan. Because they will dig holes," Val pointed out.

Matt walked back to let them in, but kept them on the back porch, closing the door on them both. Then he finally came to sit down. Val had cooked bacon, sausage, and eggs. It honestly looked delicious.

"Thanks for cooking, I appreciate it," Matt offered.

"You are welcome. I am content to do the household chores for now, because you are literally walking out with a shotgun and a shovel, going door to door," Val deadpanned.

"Let's please talk about anything else," Matt sighed.

"So, what do you want to do today? Dealership, then Wally World?" Val asked.

"Yes. I figure start on the meat aisle, and work our way down. Take everything. Preserve it in the houses. Every house so far has a deep freeze, so as long as there is electricity, the meat will endure," Matt replied.

"And then the ice cream?" Val grinned.

"Yes. I mean, this is a huge neighborhood. We can use every single freezer. That is all we are going to leave in operation, I even unplugged the washers and dryers. Everything else is being powered down," Matt pressed.

"It makes sense. We should also look into turning the lights off in the stores as well, if they are even on," Val suggested.

"Right, take as much pressure off the electrical grid as possible, to preserve it as long as we can. And hope a storm doesn't come in and blow it out, because I have no idea how to fix it," Matt sighed.

"We can google it, while we still have the internet. I plan on writing a lot of stuff down, it will take weeks, even months I'm sure," Val offered.

"I agree. Get as much information off the internet as possible. We also need to remember to keep some vehicles operating. We have the parents' car, but I think we should get some new ones from the dealership. Start them, drive them, keep them operating. The gasoline collection can come last, it's not going anywhere. But we should at least get the trucks around— just park them in the Wally World lot. I mean, if it really is just the two of us Val, we have plenty of resources to survive…forever. Even without electricity," Matt whispered.

"Are we just—I guess…we are just accepting the fact the people are gone," Val sighed.

"I would love for them to get snapped back today, sis. But we can't count on it. We have to go on living. I'm not saying it has to be all work. We can go have fun tonight. Play tennis, play golf. Really, we should play golf, before the course dies off," Matt grinned.

"I *do* think that would be fun. But for now, let's continue on. How was your food?" Val smiled.

"It was really good, especially the crispy bacon," Matt grinned.

"I'm glad you liked it. Just rinse your dishes off and set them in the sink. Do you want to take the dogs?" Val asked.

"Just Buddy. Fred isn't getting in that truck, and I'm not carrying him," Matt laughed.

"Fair enough. Get him and let's go," Val laughed.

Matt put his dishes in the sink and went to collect Buddy, Fred wanted to come too but Matt held him back, closing the door on him. He led Buddy out and loaded him into the truck, closing the door on him as well. Going back inside, he gave Fred a bone to make up for being left behind. Grabbing the baseball bat, he made for the truck, where Val was waiting.

"I don't think we will need that, Wally World's don't close," Val smiled.

"I know, but the dealership," Matt shrugged as he climbed in. "Did you notice any pressing needs for the house?"

"Yeah, more K-cups, more apple juice for you. More ice cream," Val nodded. "A lot more ice cream."

"We will get the ice cream, I promise. We will even keep most of it in our house. We can put the meat and everything else in other houses. For now, make for the dealership, we need that second truck," Matt shook his head with a smile.

Val put them in motion, driving out of the neighborhood and onto the highway. The dealership was about six miles down the road, and she weaved around the stopped cars. Spotting the sign, she took the exit and once again there was no pile-up. Driving to the side entrance, she parked the truck and they hopped out, leaving Buddy, much to his chagrin as he barked at them.

Matt shattered the glass with the bat, and they walked in. Finding the truck once again in the middle of the showroom, Val climbed in and checked the battery. It was at 95%, high enough.

"Let me find the chargers and everything, you can drive it out the window this time," Val beamed.

"Can't argue with that," Matt grinned, as he climbed into the driver seat. Val brought the chargers, then went to collect more. "Do you need help?"

"No, I got it. I know what I am looking for!" Val laughed.

"Okay," Matt relented, as she came back with one last load.

"All set, I'll follow you to Wally World," Val grinned.

"Okay," Matt smiled, as he drove the truck out the showroom window, shattering the glass and pulling out onto the street. Heading towards Wally World, Matt took in the sights. There was a golf course right next to their neighborhood, to go along with the country club course inside their neighborhood, so variety wouldn't be an issue right away. There were also tennis courts at the country club, as well as a swimming pool. They would take advantage of those amenities while they still could.

His mind drifted to the island, South Padre, to the east. The salt water would destroy a lot of boats in the coming months, but maybe they could go on a brief boating adventure while they still had theirs running properly. There was also the beach, but getting on the island would likely be difficult, Matt knew there would be a big pile-up on the bridge across. That didn't seem important at the moment though, as he refocused on what they needed to do in the short term.

Matt weaved around a stopped car and took the offramp, figuring they should move that car at some point. Pulling into the parking lot, he double parked in front of the entrance to Wally World. Val came up behind him, and they hopped out together. Val let Buddy down, and they walked inside.

Once again, the lights were on. "I think we should get everything out of the meat and freezer sections, then turn the lights off. We should probably go out tonight as well, drive around, see if any bright lights are on. I am guessing those dealerships will be well lit, those need to be turned off. One way or another," Matt offered.

"Let's grab the carts and get to it then. It's going to take a long time," Val sighed.

"I have good news for you though," Matt offered.

"What's that?" Val asked.

"You can eat the ice cream here, if you want," Matt grinned.

"That is a valid point, yes," Val smiled.

CHAPTER 6

SHOPPING TRIP

ONE WEEK LATER

Sitting at the breakfast table, the pair had just woken up and needed to go over a plan. They had emptied out the nearby grocery store, and had taken a day to recover from that ordeal. It had been much harder than they had anticipated, seeing as how they needed to create space in neighboring homes, which means throwing unwanted items away.

"What are we going to do next?" Val grinned.

"We got everything we possibly could get out of the Wally World, food wise, turned the lights off, I think we should move on to our next store. Which...honestly, should be that big grocery store further up the highway," Matt sighed.

"More food?" Val whined.

"Listen, I know it sucks, but we are on a time restriction with the food. It has expiration dates, and we need to get it frozen," Matt pressed. "We are using about 20 houses right now, that leaves literally hundreds."

"I know. I know you are right, the food should be the priority, but I want to do something else," Val sighed.

"What would you rather do, instead of food?" Matt asked.

"Go clothes shopping!" Val beamed.

"I know you want to do that, especially after we turned all those lights off on the second night. Just think about how much electricity we are saving. But the clothes aren't going anywhere. The milk is. Think about this, once we drink all of the milk we collect, there is literally no more milk," Matt countered.

"Once again, I know you are right. So, the grocery store. Are you at least satisfied with our fleet of vehicles?" Val smiled.

"Yeah, we have to make sure to drive the ones we actually want to work, but the pickup trucks will hold plenty of gasoline, once we get to that step. Honestly, we will never run out of gas, there are so many cars out there. After groceries we should move on to generators and other home goods," Matt reflected.

"Lifting those things will suck," Val whispered.

"Yeah, maybe we can commandeer a forklift. I don't know. We will figure it out," Matt shrugged.

"Have you thought about our veggie problem?" Val asked.

"Yeah, we should just plant. Use the Pom's yard as a garden, it gets good light, as well as good shade. We can grow carrots, tomatoes, squash, I mean, we can grow almost everything. Except pumpkins and watermelon. We can eat the veggies we do have, but they won't last much longer. I guess we have been eating them," Matt offered.

"I agree, we should grow them," Val nodded.

"Let's walk the dogs, then head to the grocery store. It took a week to empty the Wally World, and we just focused on groceries. It will probably take the same amount of time for this one. I know it sucks, but once we get the food sorted out, we can move on to other things at a slower pace," Matt pressed.

"I know you are right about the food expiring. Going into other people's homes…it doesn't sit well with me. And I know you are avoiding certain houses, and I will take care of those. It was smart to set mouse and roach traps in all of them, but I refuse to check those. That's all you," Val waved.

"Yeah, that's not a big deal. I don't care about dead mice. Just chuck them outside, let the birds get them," Matt shrugged. "We should go swimming tonight, you know, do something fun. Mixing in the golf was smart."

"I support that. What do you think the best way in is?" Val grinned.

"Honestly...probably through the club. Unlock the gates from the inside. If they are padlocked... shotgun," Matt shrugged.

"Let's get going. The groceries need to be preserved, after all," Val stood up and fetched the dog leashes.

———

"Tomorrow, we go shopping!" Val proclaimed, as she tossed the tennis ball to Matt in the pool. Five days had passed, and they had emptied out another grocery store.

"Big day," Matt grinned, catching the ball and throwing it back.

"I know you don't like my way of shopping, what would you like to do?" Val beamed.

"It's a mini-outlet, right? I think we can split up, I'll go to the Nordstrom's, probably just focus on that. You can go literally everywhere else," Matt laughed, continuing the toss.

"I will accept that. As for other things to do, I will leave you to your devices. What else are you thinking we should do in the near term?" Val asked.

"Honestly...I know this sounds silly, but I regret not going back to my place to pick up some more of my stuff. I don't have any of my Cubs gear, not even my hats, and it's bugging me. I am willing to drive back alone, if you don't want to go," Matt sighed.

"Nonsense. I had a feeling that would come up again, it's not like you can buy Cubs' memorabilia here. We can head back, it's only 300 or so miles. Drive up, loot, drive back. Just like the first time. We will take Buddy and Fred, in one of the smaller electric cars. Maybe tomorrow?" Val offered, as she threw the ball.

"Yeah, that sounds good. After that, I think we could have some fun at the island," Matt replied.

"South Padre? What do you want to do there?" Val asked, surprised.

"It would be nice to take the boat out, maybe one last time. We could even try to steal someone else's bigger, nicer boat," Matt grinned.

"Go fishing?" Val smiled.

"Maybe. We probably wouldn't catch a lot using artificial lures, but we could. Otherwise, just enjoy ourselves. Maybe even head to the beach," Matt pondered.

"Do you think it will be hard to get over the causeway?" Val asked.

"Yeah, that would be the only challenge, crossing the bridge. There is probably a pileup on both sides of the arch. I'm a bit worried about getting stranded in the boat as well. What if we fish, then the engine doesn't start again? We would have to row back, that would suck. Maybe just go boating, or fish close to the shore," Matt sighed, catching the ball.

"We should start the boat up when we get home, make sure it's in working order. There are also plenty of neighbor's boats we could try out as well. Honestly, I look forward to the beach. I know you love to get in the water, but I could just lie there under the umbrella," Val reflected.

"The salt water is going to destroy so much of that stuff. But we can bring it back, to preserve it. The boogie boards, the umbrellas, it would be fine in one of the houses," Matt pointed out.

"Very true, yes," Val smiled, throwing the ball over Matt's head. He jumped to catch it, but it landed behind him. He waded to retrieve it and tossed it back.

"Honestly, being able to just drive to the beach, straight shot, not having to worry about finding an open spot, that sounds really awesome. If we have to move cars out of our way, we will," Matt grinned.

"I completely agree. We always went to the same spot when we were kids…what was the hotel called? Do you remember?" Val asked, as she tossed the ball again.

"I think it was the Sunrise II. Honestly, now that the food is done, I think we can really relax, take our time. Do some fun things. Without people, the wildlife will flourish. There are so many wildlife refuges we could check out. Ah… should probably avoid the zoos though. I guess there is only the one in Brownsville. I really don't want to think about what's happening to the animals there," Matt sighed.

"I agree, we can start having a little more fun. I'm liking the golf, it's way better than Top Golf. Not having to pay to play makes the game a lot more accessible," Val smiled.

"Agreed. Golf kind of disappeared when Dad got out of the military, it's way too expensive of a hobby. Which is what likely led to the creation of Top Golf. I mean, people our age had no interest in paying fifty bucks per person to play 18 holes. Or more. I mean, 50 bucks was for a cheap course. It's just unrealistic. And now, we are the best golfers on the planet. Take that, wealthy elite," Matt laughed.

"Let's get out, the shopping mall awaits," Val shook her head.

"Alright," Matt relented, heading for the stairs behind her. They got out of the pool and dried off in the shade, before putting their sandals on and walking out the gate that they had merely unlocked from the inside. Getting into their silver electric car, Val drove them home.

Walking into the house, Matt let Buddy and Fred out into the back yard, while Val changed clothes. They had been keeping an eye on the dogs when they let them out, Buddy was prone to digging. She finally came to trade places with him, as he went to change as well. He got his new clothes on and came back into the living room, giving Buddy some love.

"Which cars do you want to take?" Val asked.

"The gas-powered trucks. I will do my shopping, and while you do yours, I will rob some gasoline from the cars around the mall. There is no rush, so take your time. Power down whatever electricity you find," Matt replied.

"Okay. Are we taking the dogs?" Val asked.

"Nah, too much of a hassle. I have a feeling Fred never went anywhere with his people. Let's just leave them both here with bones," Matt grinned.

"Sounds like a plan," Val smiled, fetching some bones and tossing them to the dogs.

"I've got the siphon pumps that we got from Wally World, as well as a large gas can, so it should be easy enough. But I think I will take my time shopping as well," Matt reflected.

"As you said, there is no rush. This is all we are doing today. Tomorrow we head back to Austin, get your stuff, maybe make a few other stops, then the island," Val beamed.

They walked outside, climbing into the gas-powered trucks that they had parked in the Pom's driveway. They drove the vehicles around the block daily, to make sure their batteries stayed charged. Val led them towards the outlet, as Matt followed behind. They had also taken to nudging the stopped cars on the highway off the road, to make everything easier. The outlet mall was about ten exits away, but the road was completely clear.

Taking the offramp, they turned into the mini outlet mall, and Val went to park in front of her store, while Matt parked in front of his. Hopping out, he took out his flashlight and walked inside. The lights were off, and they would remain that way. They had spent a lot of time driving around town at night, powering down lights The dealerships in particular felt extra good to turn off, Matt figured they were saving a lot of electricity. The downside was there was no A/C, so it was pretty warm inside.

Undeterred, Matt found himself some nice clothes. Trying on some pants, and later shorts, they fit well. He knew he needed more shorts, so he took them all in his size. It amounted to sixteen pairs. Bagging them up, he walked out to his truck and tossed them in, before heading back for more. He also completely raided the socks and underwear, taking all of the packs of six. He wanted some shoes, but this wasn't the store for them. He had seen a couple of shoe stores on his way in, so he would head there next.

He figured he could find some better, more climate-friendly tops in the stores on South Padre, as he finished up in that particular store. Exiting, he walked over to the nearby shoe store and once again began by taking all of the socks and insoles. He was honestly happy to be shopping alone, not that he ever minded Val's company, but this was one area where they had nothing in common. Matt just wanted to pick out the things he liked, try them on, and leave. Suggestions were not welcome.

Trying on several pairs of shoes, he again took them all. They varied in type: from hiking boots, to walking shoes, to tennis shoes, to house slippers. He took *everything*. Finally finishing, over an hour had passed.

He walked outside, looking down to see if he could spot Val. Her truck had moved, so he figured everything was good. Time to move on to the second phase of his trip.

Taking the gas can and the siphon hoses out of his truck, he walked to a nearby car. He took notice how this was the only car close to him, he would have to drive to the ones on the outskirts of the parking lot. One of the consequences of the snap happening late at night—no one had been here. Maybe security guards, janitors.

As he got to the car, he realized he had forgotten his baseball bat in the trunk, and went to get it. Smashing the car window, he opened the door and pulled the gas handle, popping the door open. Setting up the siphon pump, he slowly squeezed the gasoline out of the tank. It was working well, not even spilling, as he filled up the gas can and stopped. Walking it back to the truck, he opened the gas tank and poured the gasoline into it. It was a two gallon can, so it was going to take multiple trips.

Walking back on his third trip, he spotted Val coming out and giving him a wave. She wasn't heading his way though, as she entered the next store, flashlight in hand. Matt didn't mind, as he continued his task. They had drained the gas-powered trucks to less than a quarter of a tank, to give them plenty of room to harvest gas from other cars. He had to make two more trips, but he finally drained the car's tank.

Looking around, he spotted another car at the far end of the lot. He wasn't about to walk that distance, so he got in the truck and drove it over to the abandoned car. Smashing the window again, he opened the gas tank and resumed. He finished that one, it had over ten gallons in it, and the truck was full. Getting into the truck, he drove over to Val's location and honked the horn. She came out, asking if everything was okay.

"Everything is good. This gas tank is full, let's switch vehicles. How is your shopping going?" Matt asked.

"Good, I followed your advice, took all the socks and underwear I could find. Now I am working on shoes. I should be done within the hour," Val replied.

"Okay, that works. I am going to take your truck to that small pack of vehicles out there on the frontage road, fill up the gas tank. Then we should be good to head home, take it easy," Matt smiled, as they traded sets of keys.

"Hey Matt? Where are we going to put all these clothes?" Val asked.

"We can bag up the parents' clothing, and put it all in the attic. Or a nearby house. We aren't throwing it away, just moving it, okay?" Matt answered.

"Okay, I support that," Val nodded.

Matt nodded and got into the truck, driving it out onto the frontage road and parking behind a set of stopped cars. Smashing the windows in one trip, he began siphoning the gasoline again. Looking around, he saw some birds flying above, but other than that, no signs of life. He knew the people were gone, but he still held out hope.

An hour later, Val led them back towards home, both gas tanks on full—two less problems to worry about. Matt knew they still needed to harvest and store gasoline, but there was no rush. Not yet, at least. After their island trip, he wanted to work on the generator salvage. They had been avoiding it, but it was finally time.

Parking the trucks in the long driveway in between their house and the Scotty's house, they unpacked their clothing and moved inside. Matt let Buddy and Fred outside, as Val started unpacking their parent's dresser and closet. Matt fetched some trash bags and got the attic ladder down, as she filled the first bag. Carrying it up the ladder, he looked around the attic. There wasn't much up there for them, as he deposited the first bag.

"Honestly, we need to actually get rid of some of Dad's clothes. I'm not putting this all into bags, it would take hours," Val lamented.

"Let's just move them to the Scotty's house then, we aren't using it for anything other than meat storage," Matt offered.

"Okay. I can do this. You want to cook dinner for us? You said you were going to grill something," Val asked.

"Yeah, sure. I can get started on that. You sure you got this?" Matt asked.

"Yeah, it's fine. I know you don't like going into the Scotty's house. I will move Dad's clothes, okay?" Val pressed.

"Thanks Val, I appreciate that," Matt sighed.

As Val started on her task, Matt walked into the kitchen. He opened the fridge and took out a New York strip he had been defrosting, and carried it outside to the grill. The dogs followed him, salivating at the sight of the steak. He fired up the gas grill, not wanting to use the charcoal just yet. It was stored in a different house anyway. Putting the steak on, he sat down in the patio chair and enjoyed the backyard.

They had set up their parents' birdfeeders, having a seemingly endless supply of seed. Harlingen had a lot of exotic birds that weren't native to the rest of the country, but right now it was just a blue jay perched on the birdfeeder. Rising occasionally to flip the steak, he knew he had to go back inside and make the side dishes. He was thinking about simmering some carrots and broccoli when Val came out to join him.

"Hey, I need a break. Dad has way too much clothing, and it's heavy," Val sighed.

"I can help you after dinner, it's no big deal," Matt offered.

"I've got it, I cleared a lot of space out, but we still need to throw some bags in the attic. I checked that guest room dresser, there is plenty of room for your clothes in there. Closet too. This is just a small project," Val grinned.

"A welcome change, I guess. Our projects seem to be massive in scale, emptying out and storing two grocery stores. We haven't even been to the home goods store yet," Matt sighed.

"We haven't even really done an inventory of all of the houses, we just walked in and powered everything down, then threw the food in the fridges. What are you looking for in the home goods store that we don't already have?" Val asked.

"The generators are the biggest thing. You are right about the tools, I'm sure every house has a tool box with the standard fare. But you never know what we might need—might as well take as much as we can. I'm not saying 'empty the paint aisle' or anything like that, just the essentials," Matt laughed.

"Yeah, I don't think painting houses is in our future. At all," Val smiled.

"The steak is almost done, what would you like for sides?" Matt asked.

"We still have those vegetables. I think we need to eat them," Val replied.

"Yeah, I was thinking about simmering some broccoli and carrots. Anything else?" Matt asked.

"No, just keep working on the perishables while we still have them," Val shrugged.

"We are going to build that garden, okay? The seeds are in the home goods store, which we hit next week. After Austin, and the island," Matt pressed.

"I know Matt. Go on, go make the sides, I will take care of the steak, it should be almost done," Val smiled.

Matt opened the back door and headed for the kitchen. The dogs remained with Val, hoping for a piece of the steak. Letting out a sigh, dinner always felt a little down for them, it's when they really missed their friends and family. But they had plenty of ice cream for dessert. So, there was that. Opening the fridge, he took out what was left of the broccoli and carrots, and threw them on a pan. Adding some olive oil, he turned the oven on and let them cook.

HIs parents had an electric oven, and when the electricity went, it would go too. But they had contingencies, Fred's house had a gas oven, and he had spotted some others down the road as well. Matt was hoping his generator plan would work however, when the time came. An idea popped into his head, and he would make sure to share it with Val over dinner.

Walking back to the door, he popped his head out and asked what she wanted to drink. She gave the standard answer: green tea. He, of course, would be having a delicious pineapple-flavored Mexican soda, his one for the week. He got them on the table and went to collect the veggies, as Val walked in with the steak, followed closely by the dogs. Despite the fact they wouldn't be getting any, it didn't stop them from putting on their best begging performances.

Sitting down, Val asked him what he wanted to talk about. "I actually had an idea for power. I'm not sure why I didn't think of it sooner," Matt grinned, as he cut the steak in half and served Val hers.

"Oh yeah? Whatcha got?" Val smiled.

"Solar power. I mean, at least one of these homes in the neighborhood has to be running on solar. It's the latest thing for the wealthy elite. Yeah, it only costs like 30K, but still, that could solve our electricity worries— permanently," Matt offered.

"Oh yeah, you are right!" Val exclaimed. "We should look for one. Do you even think we need to get the generators out of those stores if we have solar power? It's infinite."

"Yeah, I think it would be a nice fallback option, but I don't think we need to work as hard on it. The internet is still up, right? I think we should google solar power upkeep and all that. It can't be easy, I'm sure the panels need to be cleaned regularly. Which we haven't been doing, obviously. We also need to find a solar-powered house. This area has to have some, it's not like it's ever *not* sunny down here," Matt reflected.

"How much do you know about the upkeep?" Val asked.

"Next to nothing. We had to google how to hook the generator up to the house, solar power is another dimension to me," Matt sighed.

"I think it's a good plan, but it might be a little too much to take on. I have read you need to replace the parts every couple of years. We don't know how to do that, or where to even *find* the parts. This steak is delicious, by the way. I'm just saying, I think your original plan to conserve electricity is really smart. We have powered down a lot of the commercial area. But the residential area still needs work. I know why we got away from it, but going house to house and turning off the air-conditioners is a worthy cause Matt," Val pressed.

Matt slowly ate his steak, not wanting to think about the houses. "I know you are right, and solar is probably a lot more work than it seems to be. I guess we can keep going house to house for now. It's been what, over two weeks? Most of the pets have probably died, or destroyed the insides of the house trying to survive. After our island getaway, we can go back to that. Of course, who knows how much power the island is using. But the salt water will take care of that at some point."

They quietly ate their meal. Val sensed his distress about the homes and tried to get them back on track. "So, are we heading to Austin in the morning? Pick up our stuff? I know we got out of there in a hurry because we were worried about our parents, but we left valuables behind. Did you think of any other places you wanted to go while we were there?"

"Yeah, I want to raid the Wally World for all of their pineapple-flavored Mexican sodas," Matt grinned, as he drank his.

"Okay. That's fair," Val rolled her eyes. "You closed those doors behind us, right? So any animals couldn't get in?"

"Yeah, but I would still expect to find some. Rats can get into anything," Matt sighed.

"Well, you are taking the shotgun, in that case," Val glared. "I hate rats."

"I think rats are universally hated," Matt laughed. "I have taken care of the traps in the houses nearby, they are working. How was your dinner? Ready for ice cream?"

"I am always ready for ice cream. And the dinner was great, thanks for cooking," Val beamed.

Matt got up and scooped some mint ice cream into a bowl, and they shared it. They had decided to rotate flavors, to preserve them for longer. Matt had always liked mint chocolate chip.

"Which car do you want to take tomorrow?" Val asked.

"I think one of the electric trucks. We will probably bring back more than we expect. Same route, stop at the Robstown rest area, recharge, head to Austin, loot, recharge at the dealership, head back. We can take Buddy," Matt suggested.

"Want to take a bunch of gas cans, so we can loot gasoline?" Val offered.

"That's a good idea, yeah. The cars are a lot closer together in Austin, it will be easier. The Wally World alone had about a dozen cars in the lot," Matt replied.

"Okay, rinse off the dishes, throw them in the dishwasher, and we can take the dogs for a 'w' before bed," Val grinned.

"Solid plan," Matt smiled.

They rose and took care of the dishes first, then fetched the leashes. The dogs were excited, forgetting about the food immediately as they headed for the door. Matt picked the combat shotgun up and slung it around his shoulder, following Val out.

"I wish you wouldn't carry that around," Val lamented.

"You never know what dangerous animal might come and try to say hi," Matt offered. "I let a lot of dogs run away, and with no people, other predators are free to push into the city. It will only take one encounter to convince you."

"Let's just go," Val shook her head.

Exiting, they led the dogs out into the neighborhood. Matt was thinking about their trip tomorrow, hoping that everything would go smoothly. Buddy just followed his nose, not caring about anything other than being with his people.

CHAPTER 7

GOING BACK

Matt was loading up the truck with his Cubs gear, as Val walked Buddy around the front yard of his old house. It had been an uneventful drive north, but they were able to confirm that the cattle herds were still perfectly fine. He had no doubt that when the time came, they would just break through the fences.

"Just need the katana set and I will be good to go," Matt offered.

"Yeah, take your time Matt. Grab everything you want," Val encouraged him.

Walking back inside, he had taken all of the pictures of his friends and family, as well as a couple of picture frames his grandparents had gifted him years ago. Picking up the Japanese katana set, stand included, he took it out to the truck. Walking in one last time, he did a final check to see if he was forgetting anything. Remembering his car charger, he headed out to his old car and retrieved it.

"Okay, I'm done here," Matt announced.

Val led Buddy back to the truck, and they said goodbye to his house for good. Driving out, they headed to a different grocery store, wanting to pick up the medical supplies there. They had already raided the gas station next to the house, but they knew you could never have *too* much medicine.

Double parking at the entrance, the lights were still on, as Val led Buddy inside. Matt got a cart, and they headed for the medicine aisle first. Dumping everything inside, they walked back to the food, collecting the pasta. It had a lifespan of years, and they already had a lot in the neighbor's houses. Unfortunately, the cases of water were on the very last aisle, and it would take a lot of trips.

"Who designed this store?" Val lamented. "I'll take this cart back to the truck—you can start on the water."

"Copy that," Matt grinned.

Matt grabbed another cart and walked it to the back of the store, loading up cases of water. Pushing it to the front, he joined Val, who was finishing up bagging the groceries. They walked out to the truck, putting the groceries in the trunk, while the water went into the back tailgate next to the empty gas cans.

"We still have room for more water, you want to grab it?" Val asked.

"Yeah, along with some other luxuries, namely those Mexican sodas," Matt grinned.

"Despite them being *bad* for you," Val chided him.

"Listen, we get plenty of exercise every day, I think I can drink pure sugar once a week," Matt laughed.

"I can't contest the exercise. Come on," Val rolled her eyes, heading back in.

They made one more run, then piled into the truck and began their second mission, harvesting gasoline. There was a pileup of cars back at the offramp, so Val turned them the wrong way, heading back up the road. Stopping by the cars, they had brought two siphon pumps, so they could work twice as fast. Matt smashed the car windows with the bat, and opened the gas tanks.

"Have you thought of anything else we should do here?" Val asked.

"No, not really. Head to the dealership after this, charge the truck. The car batteries are all dead by now, none of these cars are going anywhere. This city is dead. Like every other city out there. Let's just finish this and get back to our home base," Matt sighed.

"Hey Matt?" Val called out to him. "You okay?"

"I'm alright Val. I still just feel bad about having to kill those dogs. I mean, if the people come back, how am I going to explain that to them?" Matt sighed, as he began pumping the gas.

"Matt? There are millions of dead pets out there. There was no way to save them all. Without their people, pets die. Sure, some of the dogs and cats might have been able to survive, and are roaming around out there. But the vast majority of them curled up in their human's homes and passed on. That's not your fault. Okay?" Val pressed.

"I guess when our own pets pass on, that will be it for dogs," Matt whispered.

"Not necessarily," Val beamed.

"What do you mean?" Matt asked, curious.

"I have been saving this news for this specific conversation. I know those incidents bother you, so you will be happy to know that I have been secretly taking care of a female Beagle down the block. She is around Buddy's age, it was honestly just pure luck that I found her, since I was skipping houses that were barking at me. But I recognize a Beagle bark," Val laughed.

"Oh wow. That's quite a secret," Matt grinned. "You can move her closer, if you want. I get that we need to keep them separate until it's puppy time."

"I would like to move her closer, yes. Maybe into Fred's house," Val reflected.

"That actually cheers me up a lot. Dogs might be endangered, but the Beagles will live. Of course, I don't really want to think about puppies," Matt smiled.

"I hope we can get to a point where we can think about puppies," Val beamed.

"We will Val. We just need to hit that home goods store, and we will pretty much be done looting," Matt offered.

"I agree, but we still need to finish the homes. It's a big lift, but we have to go door to door, power them down. Air-conditioners are a huge drain on the power grid. If we can turn them all off, we can extend the lifespan by a lot," Val observed, as she put her gas can in the tailgate and took out another.

"Yeah, it should be easier now. It's October, it's been about three weeks since the snap, The Calamity. The pets are, as you said, probably gone," Matt whispered, as he also switched gas cans.

"I need you to smash this window," Val pointed.

"Oh, right. You know, you could do it too," Matt grinned.

"True. But you need the stress relief," Val laughed.

"I guess," Matt sighed, as he smashed the car window. Val opened the door and popped the gas tank open, resuming her task. They had four cans left to fill, it wouldn't be much longer now.

"We should plan our island getaway. Are we taking the dogs?" Val asked.

"Oh yeah. Buddy will love the beach. Bring both of them, for sure. Go home today, start the boat again, we know it's running, but you can't be too careful. Drive it to the island, probably just stay at our own trailer, yeah?" Matt offered.

"Come on Matt, we have dreamed of those sea cottages for years. Why would we stay in our crampy trailer, with two dogs?" Val whined.

"Okay, stay at a sea cottage then. Put the boat in the water, take it for a spin, then make for the island. Clear the bridge, which could be a huge pain. Honestly, I think we should stop the planning at clearing the bridge. South Padre was always crowded, even at night. I'm sure that bridge is packed with cars," Matt sighed.

"I agree; clear the bridge, go from there," Val nodded.

"Let's focus on the fun aspect as much as we can. A lot of that fishing gear should be brought back with us, to preserve it. It will literally rot away on those salt flats, but fishing remains a good source of food going forward. Still, let's hit the beach, drive the boat around, have fun," Matt offered.

"Absolutely, we don't need to preserve much to go to the beach. An umbrella, some towels, some boogie boards, that's it. You want to take an ice chest?" Val smiled.

"Yeah, absolutely," Matt nodded, finishing up his gas can. He got the last one out of the truck as Val put hers in the tailgate.

"The fish should be plentiful, right? I mean, no one has fished there for a month. Even with artificial bait, we should be able to catch a lot," Val offered.

"Yeah, you would think so. We'll do the standard: wake up early, drink a coffee, go. Make sure to bring your Keurig, especially since we don't know if the sea cottage will have one," Matt grinned.

"Don't worry, I will pack accordingly," Val laughed.

"Right, this one is full, let's get going," Matt finished.

He put the gas can in the tailgate, and they climbed into the truck. Val put them in motion, and they headed south towards home. She put her Mp3 player on, and they listened to music. About an hour later, Val came to a stop. Matt had been dozing, and he asked what was going on.

"Look, there is a deer underneath that tree. Do you want to shoot it? Don't act like you don't love venison," Val whispered with a smile.

Matt looked and saw the deer, laying in the shade. It was unusual for them to be out in the middle of the day, but he was fine with it. And he couldn't deny his affinity for venison. The Go Wild was in the backseat, Matt had packed it in a gun case, along with some ammo. Nodding, he slowly got out of the truck, leaving the door open. Quietly unpacking the rifle, he loaded it and looked out at the deer. It was a pair of doe, lying down, not even looking their way at the moment.

Matt adjusted the rifle, clicking the safety off. Val remained quiet, holding Buddy, understanding the basics of hunting. Sighting in, Matt pulled the trigger, the kick caused him to briefly lose the deer in his scope, but Val was there to report the news.

"You got it! Nice shot!" Val exclaimed.

Matt saw the other doe fleeing, while the dead one laid underneath the tree. He secured the rifle, ejecting the round and then the clip. Leaving the bolt open to make sure it was empty, he rested it in the backseat.

"I'll go get it—can you clean out the back as best you can? Put everything in the frunk or back seat. There shouldn't be that much blood, but still," Matt shrugged.

"Can you do something with the rifle?" Val asked.

"Oh, right," Matt sighed. "You need to learn to accept that we need it, it just killed our dinner for the next few days."

"That doesn't mean I want to *touch* it," Val countered.

"Fine," Matt sighed. He put the rifle back in the gun case, and set it on the ground in between the seats. Giving Val a thumbs up, he turned and headed for the fallen deer. Walking over, he enjoyed the view of the open prairie. Arriving at the deer, Matt had shot it directly in the head, which was his intention. Preserve as much meat as possible. Picking it up, it was fairly light, probably less than 100 pounds. Heading back to the truck, Val had cleaned out the back as instructed, and Matt dumped the doe in the tailgate.

Climbing into the front seat, Val resumed their journey. "Okay, so, I will leave the deer entirely to you. Entirely. I will take care of the supplies while you... harvest it," she offered.

"I accept that. Don't let the dogs outside. I will probably just do it in the neighbor's yard. I need Dad's field knife and some plates I guess. I will use the neighbor's plates. I can't wait to eat it, honestly," Matt grinned.

"I am also looking forward to eating it, but nothing that comes before that specific step," Val pressed.

"I know, I got it. I will take care of it. I will be in the Pom's backyard. Make some good sides for us tonight, okay? This will be a great dinner," Matt laughed.

"How about macaroni with the last of our carrots?" Val beamed.

"Wow, you sure went through those carrots fast," Matt teased.

"We are going to grow more, so it's okay," Val laughed.

"I accept your offer, macaroni, carrots, and red wine," Matt offered.

"Absolutely. It's not like we don't have plenty of alcohol for the rest of our lives," Val nodded.

Val continued down the empty road, before finally coming to the rest area. Matt had just stretched his legs, so he let Val walk Buddy around while the battery charged. Looking around, it looked like some critters had dug in the trash, but other than that, it was abandoned. Val brought back some snacks from the vending machine, which they hadn't destroyed, so it was still critter-proof.

"Thanks," Matt whispered, taking the bag of chips.

"You are welcome. Should we head home now? The battery has enough juice to get us there," Val smiled.

"Yeah, thinking about that deer is making me hungry. These chips will be gone in no time," Matt laughed.

"Oh you," Val rolled her eyes as she unplugged the charger and got them going again. "Can you think of anything else you need to harvest that deer?"

"Just an apron that we don't care about. I'll wear some of Dad's hiking boots, and take a gas-powered truck to dispose of the carcass. As in, throw it on the side of the road, in the grass of course, so you can't see it," Matt teased.

"There will be a time when I am accustomed to this, but today is not that day," Val shook her head with a smile.

"I'll be honest, I have never done this before. I just hope I get the meat out of there correctly. I've got a YouTube video to watch though. It will work," Matt grinned.

"Moving on! Um, are we there yet?" Val asked.

"You are the one driving. You can go faster, you know. There is no speed limit, and we pushed the cars out of the left lane," Matt laughed.

Val shook her head and accelerated, wanting to get home and get dinner on the table. Matt wasn't looking forward to field-dressing the deer, but he had to learn at some point. Fileting fish would be much easier, if they caught any.

CHAPTER 8

THE LIGHT

Matt stepped out of the shower in the Pom's house, having been covered in blood after harvesting the deer. It had been a lot bloodier than he expected, but he got the meat cleaned and ready to grill. His bloody apron went into the trash can, as he put some shorts on and walked into the backyard to start the grill. Deciding to use the Pom's charcoal grill, he dumped some in the pit and poured lighter fluid on it. Lighting it up, it reminded him of his childhood when they only used charcoal.

Inspecting the meat, which he had put in vegetable bags, Matt guessed he got about 30 pounds. It was a satisfying result for his first deer. It would feed the two of them for over a week. Heading back inside, he finished getting dressed and cleaned the field knife. Knowing the grisly task ahead of him, he went into the garage to get the tarp, and threw it into the back of the other electric truck.

Walking around to the backyard, he dragged what was left of the deer carcass and heaved it into the tailgate. Some scavenger was about to luck into a fine meal. But that could be after dinner, while Val walked the dogs. It was almost time to go check on Val herself, as Matt went to collect the bags of venison. He threw them all in the Pom's freezer, except for the meat that he would grill tonight.

They were heading to the island tomorrow, and didn't really have a set time on when they would be back. Hit the beach tomorrow, go fishing the next morning, see where they were at. They would have to take food and drink as he wasn't expecting to find a lot there. Maybe that was unrealistic, the nonperishables should still be fine in the grocery stores. Matt was a little curious about how much South Padre had grown, as in, *expanded* down the island. But he would not be going on that drive to find out.

Feeling that the grill had had enough time to warm up, he threw the venison on and sat down in the chair. Val walked outside into their back yard to ask him how it was going.

"I figured you have had enough time to get that carcass out of my sight and off the planet, do you need anything?" Val offered.

"Maybe a Mexican soda? I mean, this would normally be the time to drink beer, but we got no beer," Matt laughed.

"Fair enough," Val smiled. "How much time do we have?"

"About 30 minutes to cook all the meat. After dinner, you can walk the dogs while I eject the carcass from the planet," Matt grinned.

"I'll be right back with your drink then," Val rolled her eyes.

Matt stood up and walked to the fence line, to make it easier on her. She came back with his drink, handing it to him. He thanked her and went back to the grill, flipping the meat. Sitting down, he sipped his soda and enjoyed the birds. Waiting for the meat to finish, he flipped it a few more times. Finally, it was done as he plated it and closed the grill.

Walking back to their house, he entered through the front door and set the plate of meat on the table. Val already had the red wine poured, as she brought the macaroni and last of the carrots.

"It smells delicious, wow," Val observed. "This is a literal example of you putting food on the table, I guess."

"Yeah, pretty much. I didn't do it for that accolade though. You spotted the deer, so it was a team effort. I would have kept dozing," Matt shrugged.

"Still, you shot it. What's the gamer term? *Domed it*," Val laughed.

"You make that sound really cheesy, okay? Let's just eat," Matt shook his head with a smile.

They dug in, both observing how amazing the venison tasted. They once again, did not share any with the dogs, despite their effective begging faces.

"So, when you go to walk Buddy, that's when you stop to check in on the secret Beagle? What's her name anyway?" Matt asked.

"Gracie, according to her house," Val nodded. "And yes, I leave Buddy outside and go feed her and let her out back. I stored some dog food there, so it's easy."

"You can move her to Fred's house so you don't have to go as far," Matt offered.

"I will do that today before I walk Buddy. While you take care of the deportation," Val grinned.

"Sounds good. So tomorrow, head to the island. We will take a gas-powered car, so we don't have to deal with the charging. Honestly, just get everything we need for the beach there, out of one of the shops," Matt shrugged.

"I think moving the cars out of the way will be the biggest obstacle. There could be a lot of them. But we will make it work. Bring the baseball bat, we are going to need it. Also, I think we should take the SUV, since it has a hitch, and we are towing the boat. Did you forget about that?" Val teased.

"I did actually. Yes, we will take one of the SUVs. I don't really care if the turn signals aren't synced up, remember how the parents always struggled with that? It doesn't matter now," Matt admitted. "So, take the boat, move into a sea cottage, probably the one closest to the channel, set up shop, then tackle the bridge."

"Righto. How was the venison?" Val smiled.

"If we have to live off deer, it will be an easy thing to accept. It was so good," Matt admitted. "It barely needed any seasoning."

"I agree. Okay, let's move on to our tasks, then drive the cars around, we haven't done that today. Then we can relax before bed. Big day tomorrow," Val beamed.

"Agreed. Let's hook the boat up tonight, so we can leave right away in the morning," Matt offered.

They rose from the table, rinsing their plates off and putting them in the dishwasher. Val hooked up the dog leashes, and Matt got the keys to the truck and went outside first. He knew Val did not want to look at the carcass, which was fine. It had gotten pretty gross there for a while. Starting the truck, he drove out of the neighborhood and parked on the side of the road. Hopping out, he tossed the deer into the grass, and headed home.

Spotting Val walking towards the other end of the neighborhood, he parked the truck and picked up the dogs. Walking them the other way, he headed for the tennis courts so Val would have plenty of space. The courts were still in good shape, he wondered if they should move the nets inside to preserve them. He also wondered if they had new nets inside the pro shop. Not having his bat with him, he figured he would check some other time.

Turning to slowly head back, he didn't see Val, so he waited a bit longer, unsure if she was already back or still on the way. He was happy to hear her story of finding another dog, and understood why she saved that news for a rainy day. Still not seeing her, he decided to head back, get the dogs into the backyard just in case.

Walking into the house, Val was there already. "Oh, did you get Gracie?" Matt asked.

"Yep, she is in Fred's house, I brought her bed, her blanket, other stuff. I was worried about not taking her with us, but Fred's house has a doggy door, and chicken wire along the fence to prevent digging. Hopefully she behaves herself, if not, I will be sad, but she wasn't our dog," Val shrugged.

"Well, okay then. I'm going to go hose down that tarp, then hook the boat up to the SUV. Can you back it into the driveway?" Matt asked.

"Sure thing," Val smiled, grabbing the keys and heading out. He followed her and got the water hose, cleaning the blood off the tarp. Val backed the SUV up, as Matt waved her back. Signaling stop, he moved the bricks out from in front of the boat trailer tires, then pulled it forward. She came to help him, as they lifted it up and got it on the hitch. Screwing it down, the boat was nice and secure. The wiring was a mess, but as Matt had pointed out, it didn't matter.

"Okay, we are all set for tomorrow. Let's pack some bags then head to bed," Matt smiled.

"Roger that," Val grinned.

Waking up the next morning, Matt and Val got the SUV loaded up with some food and clothing, plus the dogs. Val got them going—she took it slowly, as she had never towed anything before.

"Anything you think we can't get around, just stop and we will move it. No sense in risking the boat," Matt offered.

"Roger that. The road should be relatively empty on the way though, I'm excited," Val beamed.

"Me too. We haven't been there at all this year. It should be fun," Matt smiled.

It only took them about an hour to get there, as the road had been relatively empty. The town of Port Isabel, however, was very crowded. It was the gateway to the island, with a ceremonial lighthouse, and of course, the bridge over the bay. There were a lot of stopped cars blocking the road, and it became impossible for Val to get around them. Matt got out with his bat and started moving them.

They had known this was going to be the most tedious part, as Val got out of the SUV with her own baseball bat and started helping as well. There were a lot of cars on the road, and they weren't even to the bridge intersection yet. Figuring they needed to get them completely out of the way, Matt drove them into the adjacent parking lots. Val copied him, and after an hour, they finally reached the bridge.

It was the nightmare they had been expecting. About 50 cars were piled up across all four lanes. Val asked Matt how they should approach it.

"Let's make this right and head toward the sea cottages. And hope the swing bridge is closed, I don't even know what we would do if it got left open. But I doubt it did, boats don't travel at night like that. There is a boat launch right after the bridge, do you think you can make it to the sea cottages on your own?" Matt asked.

"Yeah, no more hassling with the gate guard, just drive on by," Val beamed. "You said you wanted the one closest to the channel?"

"Yeah...um.." Matt trailed off, looking towards the island. "You see that?"

Val looked in the direction he was pointing. "Is that a new thing? It seems like a huge waste of electricity," she whispered.

It was a green light, pointing straight up in the air. It didn't make sense that it was visible in broad daylight. Nonetheless, they could see it plain as day, and it was coming from the island.

"You can probably see that from space….wow. We need to get over there and power that down. But first, yes, the sea cottage closest to the channel. As mysterious as that light is, it is still on the island, which we have to use the bridge to cross," Matt whispered.

"What if we launch the boat and take it across? Steal a car, head towards that light? I have a feeling that isn't an ordinary thing," Val offered.

"You know what? Yeah, let's do that. The road is clear, head towards the swing bridge. We will take the dogs as well," Matt decided.

Val nodded and they piled back into the SUV. She slowly made her way to the bridge, there were a lot less cars on this particular road. There was a swing bridge that led to a community of trailers, docks, and sea cottages. Matt and Val had spent a lot of time there as kids, and their parents still had a trailer. But they weren't going to make it *that* far just yet.

"Okay, do you know how to do this?" Matt asked.

"Um no. What do I have to do?" Val whispered.

"Turn left here, and back the SUV down this ramp here. I'll get out and spot you. Stop when I say, okay?" Matt offered.

"Got it," Val nodded.

Matt got out and helped Val back the boat down the ramp. She kept it straight, as he signaled her to keep going, as the tires crept into the water. Finally, he told her to stop.

"Okay, put it in park and come on out!" Matt shouted.

Val complied and hopped out. "Now what?" she asked.

"Untie the cables, and I will get in the boat. You have to push the boat off the trailer and into the water. I will start it up, while you park the SUV... over there somewhere," Matt pointed. "Then, bring the dogs back and get in the boat. That's it."

Matt climbed into the boat, and they both untied the cables, Val pushed it off the trailer, and it backed up into the water. Lowering the engine, Matt started it up while Val got back in the SUV and parked it nearby. She got the dogs out and led them back to the water's edge, as Matt crept forward.

Val approached nervously. "This doesn't seem like a good way to get in a boat," she offered.

"I'm not going to contest that—you want to walk over there to that dock?" Matt pointed.

She nodded and led the dogs over, while Matt backed the boat up and steered it towards the dock. Turning right, he drifted towards the pier, and threw the landing cushions out. They bumped against the dock as he grabbed a column. Fortunately, the tide was in, so it wasn't a big step down. Val handed him Buddy, then had to coax Fred into jumping down. It was a struggle but the hound finally complied.

Val was next, but Matt stopped her. "Wait, go get the shotgun and the Go Wild out of the trunk," Matt pointed.

"Why did you bring those?" Val lamented.

"In case we get in trouble, now go on," Matt pointed.

Val relented and brought back the guns, one at a time, handing each one to Matt. Finally, Matt offered his hand and helped Val down into the boat.

"Okay, that's over. You know how to drive this thing, right?" Val smiled.

"Oh, of course. It's easier to go under the swing bridge," Matt grinned.

"Let's go then," Val grinned, as she sat down next to him. The dogs didn't seem too happy, but they would get over it, as Matt pushed off and steered the boat underneath the bridge. They weren't going underneath the bridge itself, but rather, the road that led up to it.

"Okay, ready? I'm going to open it up. Dad and Grandpa always wanted to keep it on 3 RPM for some reason, but that won't be happening today," Matt laughed.

"Go for it!" Val beamed.

Matt opened up the throttle, and the boat raced along, pushing up and over 4 RPM. Matt thought it was funny how the sky did not fall as a result! But there was a weird green light shining in the sky, so, there was that. He pointed to their left, some dorsal fins were breaking the water. Porpoises, still alive and well.

Val laughed at the sight of them, as they chased the boat along. Matt made sure to keep the green buoys on the right, as they zoomed towards the island. Val shouted something at him, but he couldn't hear her. Slowing the boat down, he asked her what was up.

"I was just asking what the floating things are?" Val shouted.

"Oh, the buoys? They are there to mark the channel, and prevent drunk idiots from running aground. Okay, look, we are approaching land, and you see the line of them going that way? This has always been a weird channel; it starts down there and goes all the way down. I am wondering where the best place to dock would be. The light is coming from further down, but I don't want to approach it straight on. I want to come at it from a distance, so let's go ahead and dock right here at this big restaurant," Matt pointed.

"Do I need to do anything?" Val asked.

"Deploy the landing cushions on the starboard side there," Matt pointed.

Val didn't need to ask what was starboard, as she walked to the right side and flipped the cushions over. Matt approached the dock, probably going too fast, he had never actually been allowed to dock the boat before.

"Slow down!" Val exclaimed.

Matt tried to slow the boat down a little bit, and Val grabbed a pylon. Matt quickly grabbed another one and pulled the boat in.

"Let me get out first and tie the boat to the dock," Matt pressed, as he climbed out. She handed him the rope and he tied it to the docking bracket. He moved down and tied the other one and the boat was secure. That just left the problem of Fred. The old, fat Basset Hound.

"What do we do about Fred?" Val asked.

"Leave him there, honestly. Hand me the guns, then Buddy," Matt sighed.

Val handed him the shotgun, then the Go Wild, then the Beagle. He helped Val out, and she took the leash. He handed her the shotgun as well. She gave him a look of disapproval.

"Sling it around your shoulder, and let's go. No pouting, I have a bad feeling about this. Don't act like *you* don't," Matt pressed.

Val slung the shotgun around her shoulder, and Matt checked the Go Wild, making sure it was loaded. It was good to go, and he slung it over his shoulder. The light was north of them, but he steered them directly across the street, due east. It looked like it was emanating from the beach, and he wanted to look at it from a distance at first.

Fred was baying his disapproval, but this wasn't the best thought out plan. They left him behind, crossing the street and into the hotel parking lot. South Padre Island was one big road down, and one big road up. There wasn't anything in the middle, so it was pretty easy to get across it in no time. They approached the pier leading to the beach, and finally got a full view of the light.

Matt took the Go Wild off his shoulder and looked through the scope, resting his elbow on the edge of the pier. He was very surprised at what he saw. Val asked him for an update.

"It's a man, sitting by a fire, with the green light shining *down* on him. It's not coming from the *ground*, it's coming from the *air*," Matt whispered.

CHAPTER 9
THE PROTECTOR

"What? You mean it's an actual person? Let me see," Val pressed, as she awkwardly looked through the scope. "Oh…"

She handed him the rifle back, as he looked through the scope again. The man was just sitting by the fire, seemingly unaware of their presence. He looked familiar, but Matt's feeling was that recognizing him was impossible.

"What do you think we should do?" Val whispered.

"I mean…I guess we should approach him and say hello. I guess. What do you think? We can head back, forget this happened," Matt offered.

"No, I think we should go say hello," Val relented. "You are right, this is very strange."

"Okay, let's walk up the street then approach him from there," Matt said carefully.

Val nodded and they set off again, walking up the street. This was very bizarre, but Matt decided it was worth the risk. If it went bad, he could just shoot the guy. He switched weapons with Val, who didn't question it.

Approaching the light, they turned towards the beach again and walked down another pier. The man hadn't moved, still sitting by the fire. He looked insanely familiar, but Matt just couldn't place him.

"Took you kids long enough. Did you decide I wouldn't bite you right away?" the man growled in a low voice.

"Something like that. You look familiar to me, but we haven't met. What's your name, where are you from?" Matt asked.

"I...I can't remember my name. I can't even remember how I got here. I just know what I am," the man growled.

"Okay, you don't remember anything, you said? That's a bit odd. But you know *what* you are? What are you?" Matt asked, confused.

"I am the Protector," the man growled.

"Of what?" Val asked.

"The Chosen Ones," the man growled.

"Oh, well lucky them. I guess that has nothing to do with us, since we are nobodies. We can offer you some food and drink, then you can be on your way," Matt shrugged.

"You realize he is implying us, right?" Val sighed.

"The girl is right, you are the Chosen Ones," the man growled.

"I feel like this conversation is being ripped out of a comic book, or a bad kids' movie from the 80s. Let's just get out of here Val," Matt scoffed.

"Come on, look at him. He is a real person at the very least. What is it you are supposed to protect us from? And just how *exactly* are you going to protect us?" Val waved at him.

The man raised his hand and five claws extended out of his fingers, at least six inches long, metal. Matt and Val started freaking out.

"Okay, what is that!" Val exclaimed, looking at Matt. "I was literally making a joke—did you detect the sarcasm? My words were literally dripping with sarcasm! Then he gets up and extends claws out of his hands! This makes no sense! None Matt! I am freaking right now, yep, skipping panicking, happy to freak."

"I don't know! I literally have no idea. They don't make sense, it's impossible, humans can't do that!" Matt exclaimed.

"They don't make sense!" Val shouted.

"They don't make sense!" Matt threw his hands in the air.

"Let's get out of here! I'm done! Let's go Buddy!" Val exclaimed, leading Buddy away. Matt followed her, leaving the comic book character there.

"Is this a dream? I am ready to wake up now!" Matt exclaimed.

"Yep, total nightmare! We are walking away from a human being with claws. Can he track us? What should we do? Let's just get back in the boat, he can't get to us in the water. Okay," Val waved her hands in the air.

"I agree, get in the boat!" Matt walked faster.

Val hurried after him, as they crossed the street and made their way to the boat. Reaching it, they dropped Buddy in, Val jumped in after him as Matt untied the lines in a hurry. He started the engine as Val pushed off, and pointed him towards the open water. Matt steered that way and gunned the engine, ignoring the "No Wake" signs.

Coming to a stop in the middle of the bay, Matt stood up and threw the anchor off the side. Picking up the Go Wild, he looked through the scope back towards the island. Sure enough, standing on the dock they had just left, the man was standing there.

"Okay! This is bad. This is very bad," Matt exclaimed. "He is standing right there."

"What in the world is going on Matt?" Val shouted.

"I have *no* idea. First, all the people vanish, then a man with claws coming out of his hands appears! Is he some kind of comic book character? Why can't I remember comics all of a sudden? *I'm sitting down.* I'm done," Matt shouted, sitting down in the seat. "Sitting down. Sitting. Down."

"Okay. Okay. He said he was the Protector of the Chosen Ones, and that we are the Chosen Ones. Ignoring the ridiculous claim that we are the Chosen Ones, he said he was here to protect us, right? Protect us from what? Do you think he has a good track record when it comes to protecting people?" Val asked.

"There are other comic book characters I would rather have protecting us—let me just say that," Matt scoffed. "I just can't remember them."

"Who is he? And does he have a track record of killing innocent civilians with his claws?" Val demanded.

"I don't know, I can't remember!" Matt waved his hand.

"Is he an Avenger?" Val asked.

"Val! *Stop* asking me about him! I can't remember!" Matt exclaimed.

"Well, what are we supposed to do? Okay, let's at least try to figure out what side he lands on. In the world of comics, there are good guys, and bad guys. And he is on the good guy side, right? No, don't answer that, I know you can't remember," Val waved her hand.

"I think if he was on the bad guy side, he would have killed us already. But can we focus on the fact that comic book characters are not *real?* Okay? Can we focus on that for a second?" Matt demanded.

"The light is gone Matt. Clearly, he was sent here. Look, all of the people vanished. We accepted it. We accepted we could not do anything about it. Now, we need to accept this. That man is here. If we don't go get him, he is going to come to us. He will find us, I don't know how I know that, but I do. He will come to us," Val pressed.

Matt sighed and looked through the scope again, the man was still standing there. "He said to us he couldn't remember his name. We need to name him. Any ideas?"

"Sam," Val offered.

"Okay, sure. Sam. Let's go get him," Matt sighed. He stood up, and pulled the anchor up. He hadn't turned off the engine, so he turned the boat and headed back to the dock. This was not how he had wanted this trip to go.

Approaching the dock, Val tossed the newly named man the line, and he took it, before hopping into the boat. Pushing off, Matt turned the boat again and headed slowly back towards their original starting point.

"So, we are going to call you Sam, is that okay?" Val asked.

"Yeah, fine," Sam replied.

"Did you have anything you wanted to do, Sam?" Val asked.

"Protect you," Sam replied.

"Okay, let's skip over that entire conversation for now. In fact, let's just ride in silence, until we get to a place where we can brief you," Val sighed. "Matt? Go faster, please."

Matt opened up the throttle and headed for the swing bridge. It didn't make sense, but Val was right. Even if they left him on the island, he would be knocking on their door in Harlingen tomorrow. Or sooner. And he didn't even want to think about this Chosen One nonsense.

Passing underneath the bridge, they came to a stop in front of the boat launch. Sensing their intent, Sam hopped out of the boat and into the water, pulling them to shore. Matt raised the engine out of the water, as Val jumped out and went to get the SUV. Backing it up, Sam waved her forward and pushed the boat onto the trailer. Matt jumped out and helped pull the boat forward, and they secured the cables around it. Val pulled it out, and Matt and Sam got the dogs out, then the guns. Sam handed the shotgun to Matt, who took it cautiously.

They walked to the SUV, and Sam hopped into the back trunk, given how he was all wet. He lifted Fred up with him, as Matt helped Buddy in. He got in the passenger seat and Val pointed them west, driving home.

"I don't like this," Matt whispered.

"I don't either," Val whispered back. "Does whispering do anything?"

"No, he can probably hear us," Matt sighed.

"Do you think he has other abilities?" Val whispered.

"Yes," Matt relented. "Though I can't remember them."

"This doesn't make any sense," Val pressed.

"None whatsoever. We can go home, eat some ice cream, and try to figure out his purpose," Matt sighed. "A lot of ice cream."

"A lot of ice cream," Val nodded in agreement.

Arriving home with no incidents, Val parked the SUV in front of the Chihuahua's house outside the cul-de-sac. Neither of them wanted to deal with the boat at the moment. And really, it was fine leaving it like that. They all piled out of the vehicle, Matt taking the Go Wild and Sam taking the shotgun. Val shot him a look but Matt just shrugged. The man had metal claws, what did he need a shotgun for?

"We base our operations out of this house. You can sleep in any of these houses in the cul-de-sac. Honestly, *that* one would be best, we are keeping a female Beagle separate in that house, and you could take care of her," Matt pointed at Fred's house.

"Fine," Sam shrugged.

"You don't talk a lot," Val observed.

"Nope," Sam shrugged again.

"Where is that ice cream?" Val sighed.

"Let's just get inside, I'm sure he has one big question on his mind, and we will do our best to answer it," Matt waved them on.

Ten minutes later, they were sitting at the table, Matt and Val had a pint of chocolate ice cream, and Sam had taken a glass of bourbon, which they had plenty of.

"So, about the people," Matt sighed. "We went to bed the previous night, and woke up the next day. Every single person was gone, vanished. The immediate, and prevailing theory was they got snapped by the Infinity Stones, which we know aren't real. We haven't come up with another explanation, we honestly haven't tried to. We just accepted things, and have moved on as best we can."

"I've held an Infinity Stone, so they are very real," Sam offered.

"Which Infinity Stone?" Val asked.

"Val—" Matt tried.

"The Soul Stone," Sam replied.

"Oh…that sucks. That's the bad one, I'm sorry," Val whispered.

"Moving on," Matt sighed. "We have set up our home here as best we can. It's just been the two of us, so it's been hard work. And we aren't done yet. We were taking a break when we found you on the island. How did you get there, exactly?"

"Don't know," Sam shrugged, sipping his bourbon.

"Great. Now what?" Matt sighed, looking at Val.

"What's going on with the memory loss?" Val asked.

"I don't know. I literally cannot remember your existence at all, Sam. You seem so familiar, but I can't place you. And not just that, something else about you just seems off. We think you are a comic book character, but you could be a movie character, we have no idea. You could just be…I don't know. What can you remember about yourself?" Matt asked.

"Not a lot. I have longer term memories, where I have been, what I have done. But names and identities escape me as well. But whatever. What have you done to preserve your life here?" Sam asked.

"Well, we raided the local grocery stores for all the perishables, and froze them in the neighboring freezers. Almost a hundred houses' worth. We are also storing the nonperishable food in those houses, lots of pasta, canned foods, stuff like that," Val started. "We also powered down as much electricity as we could, but we aren't done with that yet. We have a fleet of cars out there, some electric, that we are maintaining. Gasoline will never be a problem, there are so many cars out there with gas in them, you saw them on the way here. Matt wants to raid the local home goods store for generators, grills, stuff like that. We have also touched on solar power, but that looks like a big hassle."

"Not bad for a couple of kids. Moving to a smaller town, preserving electricity, food, you've got guns to hunt, a boat to fish, I've seen worse," Sam reflected.

"Why don't we touch on that? What exactly do you want to do? Please don't say take us anywhere, we are established here, we aren't leaving," Matt sighed.

"I am supposed to be the Protector, but you kids don't seem to need much protection," Sam reflected. "I should get to New York."

"About that," Val cut in. "You can't remember your name, or how you got to that island, but you have other, long-term memories you said? Do you remember where you got these 'Protector' and 'Chosen Ones' titles from?"

"It was a voice that came through the fire, that I did not start. It said I was the Protector of the Chosen Ones, and they would be arriving soon and I should wait for them," Sam shrugged.

"A voice that came through a fire, sure, that makes sense," Val sighed, eating more ice cream.

"So, nothing told you that *we* specifically were the Chosen Ones?" Matt asked.

"No, not specifically. Do you think if I go back, someone else will come find me?" Sam asked.

"No, I don't. So, you want to go to New York? We will give you a running car and a siphon pump, and you can drive there. Come back and pick us up in a jet or something, whatever you guys use to get around," Matt scoffed.

"Alright. I'll take that Beagle with me, in the other house," Sam replied.

"Fine. When do you want to leave?" Val asked.

"Right now. What else am I gonna do?" Sam shrugged.

"Okay, go get the dog, the keys to the red Volvo are right there," Matt pointed. "I would offer you safe travels, but it feels like you don't need them. So, good luck I guess."

"Thanks for the drink, and the intel. I'll come back and get you in about a week," Sam shrugged, standing up.

"Can I see those claws again before you go?" Val asked.

Sam extended the claws out of both hands, before retracting them, as the siblings dug into their ice cream. He took the keys off the wall and headed outside, taking the bottle of bourbon. Closing the door behind him, they let him go.

"Was that all a dream just now? Are we dreaming? That man had claws coming out of his hands," Val exclaimed.

"Please don't talk to me about stress while I am stress eating," Matt pressed, eating his ice cream.

Val continued to eat hers, until they both had finished. They sat there in silence, not wanting to be the first to speak. Finally, Val broke.

"We sure could have used his help with those generators before you let him take off like that," Val pointed out.

"I wasn't going to tell him not to do something," Matt shrugged.

"That's fair. What are we going to do if he comes back in a jet to pick us up?" Val asked.

"Make sure the street is clear so he can land," Matt shrugged.

Val broke into a laugh, "Okay, that's funny, I admit. What should we do now?"

"I have no idea. Our island adventure got cut short, and I'm not up for moving all those cars off the bridge. There were probably hundreds of them," Matt sighed. "It's not even 2 pm."

"Why don't we go to the driving range? I think it will do us some good," Val offered.

"Okay, sure," Matt relented, standing up.

———

Matt and Val were approaching the 18th hole, having decided to spend the rest of the day playing golf. They were at the course across the street this time, and the lack of water was starting to show. At this point, neither one of them cared too much.

"This is the last hole, we have both had a few nightmares, so let's make this a good one. 400 yard, par 4, you're up first," Val offered with a smile.

Matt grinned and took out his driver, launching his ball down the middle of the fairway. Giving way for Val and her Pink Lady, she also launched her ball down the middle. Picking up their bags, they headed out.

"We should find a tougher course, now that we have straightened our swings out, these retirement communities aren't offering much challenge," Val beamed.

"Did you see the one we drove past in Port Isabel? We could try that one. I want to get back on track, somehow. That uh...encounter, has really thrown us off, I feel like," Matt sighed.

"We accepted the snap, The Calamity, we just need to accept this. Trying to figure anything out is *impossible.* Just go with it, I say. We can't undo it, after all," Val offered.

"Do you really think he is going to drive to New York and fly a jet back here?" Matt whispered.

"I do not. I'm not even sure he knew where we were, exactly," Val shrugged. "We didn't tell him."

"There are water towers everywhere, he isn't an idiot. He has probably been to all corners of the planet. I'm talking as if I have accepted it, I don't know how I feel about that. Here is your ball," Matt pointed.

Val took out her 5 iron and smacked her ball into the bunker on the left side of the green. Offering a sigh, they continued on to Matt's ball. He took out his 7 iron and knocked it onto the green.

"That 7 iron is a beast," Val laughed.

"It never fails," Matt grinned, as they walked towards the green.

"Let's once again focus on the short term. What would you like to do tomorrow?" Val asked.

"Sleep in," Matt smiled.

"We can do that. What about after? Come on, come up with a plan. We can go to the home goods store," Val offered.

"Alright. Let's take two trucks, and go get the generators. Along with other things," Matt nodded.

"We will pack snacks. It will likely be hard work. Alright, let me play out of the sand again," Val sighed.

"Your iron shots still veer left a little bit, you need to straighten them out, else you will keep landing in the left side bunkers," Matt smiled.

Val played her ball out of the sand, hitting it onto the green, about fifteen away from the cup. Matt went for the flag while she cleaned the bunker, then he headed for his ball. He gave it a good effort, leaving his putt about six inches short. Tapping in, he collected the flag while Val lined up her own putt. She made it look effortless, as the Pink Lady found the middle of the hole.

"Hey, nice job," Matt laughed. "Putting is definitely one of your strengths."

"I take it a little more seriously than you do—you don't even try to read the green," Val laughed, collecting her ball.

"Come on, let's go have dinner. That was fun, I'm glad we could get our mind off that comic book character with claws for a bit. Venison awaits," Matt smiled.

CHAPTER 10

THE RETURN

ONE WEEK LATER

"Okay, it's been a week, do you think Mr. Sam is coming back in his jet today?" Val laughed, as they ate breakfast.

"I don't know if we are holding him to exactly seven days, but no, I do not," Matt grinned. "I think he will come back here, yes, but not in a jet. And not before next week. It probably took him a while to drive across the entire country. And then do whatever it is he wanted to do in New York. I imagine he is still there, exploring, looking for his people? I don't know."

"If it wasn't for the metal claws, I would have thought he was a loon. But those were *real*. We got a good look at them, they came out of his hands. It wasn't a prop," Val shook her head.

"He was a lot more agreeable to that request than I would expect," Matt reflected. "I hate not being able to remember."

"I think he knew that we were telling the truth about everything that had happened, as you said, he had eyes. He saw everything on the island and in this city. But not being able to remember is just bizarre. It has to be connected to whatever is going on here. If he really does come back here in a jet, we are going to need a lot more ice cream," Val finished.

"Two different worlds, fusing together? I don't know. Anyway, we were going to head back to the island today. Lie on the beach. We got those generators out of the store, and a lot of other supplies, we need a break. Do you still want to go?" Matt asked.

"Yes, I do. And if there is another green light...we will do the same thing. But I think we should focus on clearing the bridge. We aren't taking the boat this time, just go, clear the bridge, lie on the beach. We forgot the suntan lotion last time, but I packed it today," Val beamed.

"We should bring back some fishing gear, so let's take a truck this time. The one with the reinforced grill, so we can push cars out of the way. Let's take Buddy and Fred again, we don't have to worry about getting Fred out of the boat," Matt grinned.

They stood up to take care of the dishes, and the doorbell rang, causing Val to drop her plate on the ground, as the dogs started barking relentlessly.

"Oh my God! That scared me," Val took a breath.

"No kidding, I was surprised too," Matt admitted. He looked out and saw it was Sam, but didn't see a big jet anywhere. "Okay, it's Sam. I'm going to open the door, you good?"

"Yes," Val relented, as she picked up the pieces of the shattered plate.

Opening the door, Matt offered a greeting. "Hey Sam, you scared everyone. I don't see a jet, everything good?"

"Define good," Sam offered.

"Um, is it okay if I don't? Come in, we will get you a drink," Matt opened the door.

Sam walked in and sat down, apologizing to Val for scaring her. Matt handed him a bottle of bourbon and a glass. "We have other booze, I don't know what you prefer," Matt sighed.

"Anything is fine," Sam shrugged, pouring himself a glass.

Matt and Val sat down at the table, and waited for him to get started. He just drank, so Matt prodded him along, saying "I know you are a man of few words, but if you could share some news with us, we would appreciate it."

"There isn't much to share. All of the people look to have vanished... your Infinity Stone theory checks out. What was weird was I didn't find my home, or The Avengers Tower. It's as if I crossed into a different dimension where my people don't *exist*. Where *I* don't exist," Sam shrugged.

"You are taking that news pretty well. How did you get up and back so fast?" Val asked.

"I'm used to these kinds of situations. And I drove," Sam shrugged, as he poured himself another glass.

"What would you like to do next?" Matt asked.

"Like I said, I'm used to this. I will help you kids survive, until something comes along," Sam said carefully.

"Well...we appreciate that. As I said, you can live in the house across the street. Do whatever you want, honestly," Matt offered.

"I'm not a—what's the word you kids use? *Suburbanite.* I spotted a ranch on the east side of town, when we were driving back from the island. I will make my base there. Finish powering down the city, turning the A/C's off, stuff like that. Your plan to conserve electricity is a good one. What have you done about preserving water?" Sam asked.

"Well, we have dozens of cases stored," Val offered.

"I see. Nothing then. Okay, I will fill some ice chests with water, store them here with you. Your water usage should be kept to a minimum, don't run the dishwasher, use your hands. Washing machine...I suppose that is okay. But conserve clothing. I know you have weapons and ammo, have you secured what was in this city?" Sam asked.

"No, it's not zombies, we don't think we will need more than what we have, which is a lot. It's in the house next door. I try not to go in those two houses that much," Matt sighed.

"Matt thinks he earned some really bad karma on our first day down here, I have tried to convince him he is wrong, maybe you could help?" Val asked.

"What happened?" Sam asked.

"He had to kill a pair of unfriendly dogs," Val whispered.

"You showed them mercy," Sam responded. "This isn't my thing either, but those dogs would have starved to the point that they would become a danger to you. Killing them was merciful."

"Yeah, I can tell this isn't your thing. Thanks for trying though," Matt sighed.

"What other work do you have to do?" Sam asked.

"We raided the home goods store while you were gone. Got all the generators out of there, some other things. We probably should finish raiding it and move on to another one. The generators were really heavy for just us, though. We could use your help with it," Val pressed.

"Anything else?" Sam asked.

"Nothing that I can think of. We have been trying to mix in recreation with work. I know you are used to this sort of thing, but we are decidedly not. We still need to do things that make us smile," Matt sighed.

"Why don't you try that island trip again then? I can do the work required here. Take care of the dogs. I'm not a freeloader, I said I would help you, and I will," Sam growled.

"Yeah, I know you aren't a freeloader. You just drove all the way to New York and back here. You didn't have to come back, but you did. In record time, seemingly," Matt offered.

"Even if that fire hadn't told me to protect you, I would have come back anyway. In situations like this, it's best to stay together. I could do this alone, but it's not fair to expect you kids to do that," Sam shrugged.

"Well, we have been on our own for a month now," Val countered.

"That's true, and you have done well for yourselves," Sam relented.

"I think we will take your advice and head to the island. If you need anything, we have food in all the houses, guns in the house right here," Matt pointed. "Camping gear in the house over here, and generators in the third house."

"Got it. You don't have to worry about me, I won't steal from you," Sam nodded.

"I wouldn't accuse you of thinking about it. Do you have any other abilities that we should know about?" Matt asked.

Sam extended his claws and cut his opposite hand. It drew blood, and the siblings watched as the cut healed itself and disappeared.

"It doesn't make sense," Val whispered.

"It doesn't make sense," Matt shook his head.

"Have a safe trip. Come back whenever, I will be around. Take the same weapons you took the first time," Sam pointed at the shotgun as he stood up to leave.

"Hey, one last thing. We are both sorry about your friends and family. We lost ours too. We know you are used to it…but it still sucks," Val whispered.

"Thanks Val. You are right, it does suck. You two seem to be good people, I won't let anything happen to you," Sam nodded, as he exited the house.

Val let out a sigh. "Sam *says* things and you just have to believe him. I feel a lot better with him out there taking care of security and the electrical grid."

"The healing thing is just nuts. It's as if he can't be killed. Remember when I said I would rather have someone else protecting us? I might have gotten that wrong," Matt sighed.

"Were you serious about going to the island? You don't want to keep an eye on him?" Val asked.

"Yeah, I was serious. I want to lie on that beach, and salvage some fishing equipment. Let's take the boat, we can drive it across the bay like last time. I'm in no mood to deal with those cars," Matt sighed.

Sam knocked on the door, and Val moved to open it. "Is everything okay Sam?" she asked.

"There is another light," Sam replied.

"Oh…great," Matt sighed.

He stood up as the group moved outside. It was to the east again, looking much further away. Maybe even coming from the exact same location as last time.

"Okay, I guess we are all going to the island," Matt sighed.

"Yep," Sam nodded.

"Let's get some gear and get moving. Sam? Can you re-hitch the boat to the SUV? We aren't moving the cars," Matt sighed again. "Did you want a gun?"

"Not really my thing," Sam shrugged.

"Okay," Matt relented. "I knew that, but I was still going to offer one."

Matt walked back inside and picked up the Go Wild and the shotgun, carrying them outside. Val packed up some drinks and they headed for the SUV behind Sam, who was already hitching the boat up.

Climbing in, Sam got in the back and Val drove them towards the island. "Can we just go back to when it was the two of us? This is getting pretty crazy. No offense Sam. Any ideas on who it could be?" Val grinned.

"After Mr. Sam here, I don't even want to speculate. Hopefully it's not an asshole," Matt sighed.

They drove in silence, an hour later arriving in Port Isabel once again. The green light looked to be coming from the same location, as Val crossed the swingbridge and backed the trailer down the boat ramp. Sam and Matt got out and spotted her, then Matt climbed into the boat as Sam pushed it into the water. Val parked the SUV while Sam collected the guns, and they boarded the boat.

"It's good that you kids know your way around a boat," Sam offered.

"We spent a lot of our childhood here. Matt in particular always loved boating," Val beamed.

Matt drove them underneath the bridge, then opened the throttle up, once again crossing over 4 RPMs. The porpoises came again, to Val's delight as she pointed at them. Matt smiled and they crossed the bay, coming to the same dock they were at last time. Pulling up, Sam and Val grabbed the pylons and tied the rope off. They all climbed out, guns in hand, and walked across the street to the first pier.

They could see the silhouette of a person sitting next to a fire, as Matt looked through the scope to figure out what they were dealing with.

CHAPTER 11

THE SPECIALIST

"Who is it, Matt? Do you recognize them?" Val asked.

"No, just another random dude. I mean, if we judge by looks, he definitely looks like a bad guy," Matt sighed.

Val looked through the scope and let out a sigh. "He does look pretty scary, I guess let's just go say hi."

"Yeah. Sam? Just don't kill him unless he threatens the two of us, okay?" Matt sighed.

"No promises, let's go meet him. Just walk down the beach this time, instead of circling around," Sam growled.

"Alright," Matt relented.

"How do you think he is going to handle the news?" Val whispered.

"I'm sure it will be a negative reaction," Matt whispered back.

"Try to be nice, okay? That's really all I can offer," Val shrugged

"Of course, why wouldn't I be nice to the scary looking man?" Matt grinned.

"Not ideal for our situation," Val lamented.

"At all," Matt agreed.

They approached the fire where the man sat, and offered greetings. He was wearing all black, with sunglasses and black hair.

"Brave to approach me so openly," the man smiled.

"We don't want any trouble," Matt started.

"Well, you don't look like bounty hunters. But this guy," the man pointed. "He could be a merc for hire. I recognize a killer when I see one."

"Yeah, so do I," Sam observed.

"Are we going to have a problem here?" the man grinned.

"Not with the two of us. What is your name?" Matt asked.

"Hmm. I don't remember my name all of a sudden, I don't even remember how I got here. I just know my title, apparently," the man reflected.

"Right, and what's that?" Matt sighed.

"The Specialist. I take it you guys are the Chosen Ones?" The Specialist smiled.

"I don't know," Matt sighed.

"What planet is this, anyway?" The Specialist asked.

"Um, Earth? What, are you from a different planet?" Matt sighed.

"Never heard of it. Some backwater planet?" the Specialist asked.

"I will take that as a yes. If you want to call it that, sure. You aren't going to like the answers to your next questions," Matt sighed.

"How do I get off this backwater planet?" The Specialist grinned.

"You don't. You can't. And it has nothing to do with the three of us," Matt held his hands up. "Quite simply, the people that used to inhabit this planet never reached the technology of space travel. As far as they were concerned, we were the only living beings in the universe. Extraterrestrials existed only in comic books and movies."

"So...what are you saying? You don't know who I am?" the Specialist asked.

"No idea, man. If you're some famous intergalactic criminal, you have found an ideal situation to lie low. But if you are some thrill-seeking rocket-man, well, this could suck for you," Matt put his hands up.

The Specialist studied them, and then looked at Sam, who hadn't taken his eyes off him. "Who are you supposed to be?"

"Sam," he replied.

"Okay Sam, I'm really not inclined to believe anything these kids are saying. So maybe I can get some answers out of you," the Specialist started.

"Doubt it," Sam shrugged.

"I have ways to get them out of you, I think it's inevitable that we clash so, why don't we get this party started?" the Specialist grinned, as he stood up, taking a knife out.

"Just don't involve us," Matt sighed, taking some steps back.

"You don't seem too concerned about your friend's wellbeing," the Specialist offered. "Normally I would be laughing at that, but something about this whole situation doesn't feel right."

"I'm not going to say anything that you could take as an insult. I will simply say, leave us out of it," Matt sighed.

"Alright then," The Specialist looked back at Sam. "You ready to do this?"

"Whenever," Sam shrugged.

The Specialist moved with lightning speed towards Sam, raising his knife to Sam's throat. Sam didn't even flinch. Whether or not it was designed to be an intimidation move, Matt didn't know, but it didn't matter at all to Sam. Val retreated behind Matt, and the Specialist spun and cut Sam's throat.

"I guess he thought I was bluffing. Now, it's time for some real answers," the Specialist looked their way, turning his back to Sam.

"He didn't think you were bluffing—he just didn't care. I know you think you killed him, but look," Matt pointed.

The Specialist turned to look back at Sam, who hadn't moved, his wound had already healed, as he stood there. The Specialist raised his knife again, cutting across Sam's torso. He cut deep, and watched. The wound healed again, as Sam just stood there.

"Satisfied?" Sam asked.

The Specialist turned and looked at Matt. "What's going on here?"

"As I said, I wasn't going to insult you. I knew you would want to try to establish yourself against him, and I knew I couldn't stop you. But you can't kill him with a simple knife. None of it makes sense, I don't like it any more than you do, but here we are. If you want to keep experimenting with your killing techniques against him, go ahead. Watch out for those claws though," Matt sighed.

"What claws?" the Specialist asked.

Sam raised his hand, extending his claws out of each finger. Despite his best efforts, the Specialist couldn't hide his surprise.

"Okay, why don't we start over," the Specialist offered. "You start."

"What's your name?" Matt asked.

"I don't remember," the Specialist replied.

"How did you get here?" Matt asked.

"I don't remember," the Specialist replied.

"How do you know you are the Specialist, here to assist the Chosen Ones?" Matt asked.

"A voice from the fire told me," The Specialist replied.

"Explain that," Matt pressed.

"I can't," the Specialist replied.

"Explain Sam," Matt pointed.

"I can't," the Specialist repeated.

"How much of this makes sense to you?" Matt asked.

"None of it," the Specialist admitted.

"That's where we are. What would you like to do now?" Matt asked.

"I would like to…get off this beach. Go with you three," the Specialist offered.

"You just tried to kill Sam, so I'm not entirely convinced you aren't a threat to us. The best thing I can tell you is, killing us would not benefit you in any way, shape, or form," Matt pressed.

"I agree with that," the Specialist admitted.

"Does that mean you aren't going to try to kill us?" Val demanded.

"You aren't a threat to me, and I'm not a threat to you. I don't…I don't kill people that I don't *need* to," the Specialist tried.

"Is that really true?" Sam asked, staring him down.

"I don't kill people, that I don't need to," the Specialist repeated.

"He can stay with me on the ranch. I don't want him near you kids. You are going to have to work, same as me. Accept it…or die here," Sam growled.

"Let the record show that I did not make that threat," Matt offered.

"I'm used to it. I accept. I will pull my weight. And hope a solution comes," the Specialist affirmed.

"Great, let's get out of here then," Matt waved them on.

Matt and Val headed back for the pier leading off the beach while Sam followed, making the Specialist come last. Sam didn't seem to care about turning his back on the man, but he had more than his eyes to protect them. They had figured out he had enhanced senses. Walking across the street, Matt came to a stop.

"Why are we stopping?" Val asked.

"The Specialist has another question," Matt replied.

The Specialist was looking around, at the cars in particular. "What happened to all the people?" he asked.

"The two of us went to bed one night, then woke up the next morning and literally all of the people had up and vanished. I know that doesn't seem believable, but that's how it is. We have no idea what happened, or how to undo it, or anything. It is just the four of us. Come on, the boat is this way," Matt resumed walking.

The Specialist followed them, continuing to study the area. There was nothing for him to deduce, but Matt wanted to get away from him all the same. Descending into the boat, the Specialist paused.

"This is much older tech than what I am used to," he reflected.

"As I said, this planet has not even come close to the level of tech you are accustomed to. And considering there are only four of us, that's unlikely to change. Still, I don't think you will have a problem living here, provided you can convince Sam not to kill you. He is the Protector, after all," Matt shrugged.

Matt got the boat going, opening up the throttle and heading back towards their original departure point. Jetting across the bay was never dull for the siblings, as they looked for porpoises. Not seeing any this time around, they passed underneath the swing bridge, and slowly turned towards the boat ramp.

Sam disembarked first, as Val tried to follow him, only to be stopped. "Why don't you kids head back to the beach? Lie in the sun, swim, move into that sea cottage you have been trying to move into. I will take this guy here back to the ranch, just outside of town. Start getting it going."

"Um, okay," Val relented.

"Hey Sam?" Matt offered.

"Yeah?" Sam asked.

"Until we know what is actually going on, and what your titles mean, don't kill him, alright? We might need each and every one of you. At this point, I'm sure we can expect more weirdos to join us," Matt sighed.

"See? The kid isn't so bad. That's about the only way he could convince me to spare your life," Sam told the Specialist.

"I'm used to being the most dangerous guy around. But I actually do think he was going to off me as soon as you kids were clear," the Specialist grinned.

"Yeah, I am pretty sure that was going to happen," Matt sighed. "Also, come up with a name for yourself. There is a grocery store on the road out of town, feel free to raid it. We will catch up with you…later. I'm not sure when. It's up to Sam, I guess."

"I'll be around the houses soon enough. Have to pick up the Beagle. Let's get out of here," Sam motioned to the Specialist.

The two men walked away from them, as Val pushed the boat off. Matt backed it up, then turned towards the sea cottages.

"This keeps getting weirder and weirder," Val whispered.

"No kidding. Let's take his advice, move into the sea cottage, head to the beach, rest and reflect," Matt sighed.

CHAPTER 12

THE BEACH

"I don't think it was a snap," Matt reflected.

They were standing in the water, resting their arms on the brand-new boogie boards they had liberated from a nearby surf shop. Standing behind where the waves crested, they were bouncing with them as they rolled by.

"We have been avoiding this topic entirely, but I guess we need to start trying to come up with an explanation. Why don't you think it was a snap?" Val asked.

"Couple of reasons. Thanos wanted to delete half the universe, at random. He never would have left two random siblings on Earth. Also, there is a massive plot hole in that theory. I'm not sure if you noticed, but every single car out there has been turned off. They didn't run until they were empty, they were turned off. That's too specific for Thanos. Someone literally turned off every single car... it's something else," Matt offered.

"Accepting the fact that we are crossing over into some kind of multiverse, which...I guess I have to accept that...who or what do you think it was?" Val asked.

"Two possibilities come to mind. One less likely than the other. First, it's those omnipotent jerks from Star Trek," Matt shook his head.

"Those pompous beings that snap their fingers and anything can happen? Technically, that is a snap," Val laughed.

"Smart ass. But yes, those guys. But I don't think it's likely," Matt grinned.

"Why not? Didn't he say the trial never ends? This could be another one of his trials," Val beamed.

Suddenly, a huge wave was cresting on top of them—they looked up in shock as it came down on them, sending them under; they lost their boards as they came up from it. Looking back, the wave had carried their boards to the first sandbar and beyond.

"Well then. Maybe they don't like being called 'pompous," Matt laughed, as they made their way to the sandbar. Chasing down their boards, they walked back out to their spot.

"That's funny, I admit. But why don't you think it's them?" Val asked.

"Where is the Captain? Wherever there is an omnipotent jerk, there is a Captain. I don't see one," Matt laughed.

"That's very true. They seemed to hold Captains in extremely high regard," Val reflected. "What is your second theory?"

"It's the Bad Side demons messing with us," Matt smiled.

"I didn't think they could interfere in human affairs?" Val countered.

"The Puppetmaster can. And maybe they have agreed on some kind of bogus experiment. Delete the human race, leave two people, then gradually increase the population to show that humanity sucks," Matt offered.

"Hmm. But how did they land on the two of us? As you have said, we are complete nobodies," Val pressed.

"Maybe it really was completely random. Two siblings, that was their only criteria. Naturally, two siblings wouldn't hurt each other, but as the population count increased, the Bad Side points would start accumulating," Matt shrugged.

"How in the world are they deciding who they send us?" Val threw her arms in the air.

"That's a great question. Maybe they are literally going down a list of fictional characters from different genres, fusing them together into one person. Comics were first, then…I don't know, movies were next? Then it's going to be something like video games, then television, then anime, I don't know. I am grasping at straws, I realize that," Matt shrugged.

"Still, this theory is more plausible. So, over here we have the Good Side choosing their comic book guardian to come help us. They choose a paragon of justice, Bucky Barnes," Val offered.

"Uh—" Matt tried to cut in.

"BUCKY BARNES!" Val shouted.

"Okay," Matt relented.

"And then the Bad Side demons pick their character, an irredeemable villain, Thanos. And then the Puppetmaster lands somewhere in between those two. A medium choice. Sam. A hero, but also an anti-hero," Val finished.

"I can see that, he is definitely in the middle somewhere. Not a paragon of justice—but not a villain. Like I said, I think he is multiple characters fused into one. But I can't remember their names, which is weird. The question is, is this a preset list, or are they adapting as they go? I can guarantee the Bad Side demons were not happy when Sam came here and told us he would take care of us. Which is what led us to the Specialist," Matt grinned.

"How in the world did the Puppetmaster land on him? Can you make a case that he is medium?" Val asked.

"No, he cut Sam's throat after talking to us for less than five minutes, he seems to be straight to the Bad Side. I have no idea how they landed on him. Maybe they broke up the medium into levels, and he is as far down as they can go while still staying in medium. But seriously, no. He is Bad Side, all the way," Matt sighed.

"And the memory loss? Explain that," Val challenged.

"I have no idea. I mean, maybe they don't want to get accused of violating copyright laws...that don't exist in their world. I don't know, but both of them seem like hybrid characters. You know?" Matt shrugged.

"Let's move on for now. And say your theory is correct, and they are pulling from fictional media. Video games could be next, or television. Who do you think they could send?" Val asked.

"I mean, who knows what franchise they will settle on? It could be Mario on one side, Bowser on the other, and Luigi in the middle. I think they will send someone more practical. Maybe an RPG series? A Final

Fantasy hero, a villain, and then they land on a side character. I mean, I can think of a couple that would fit in perfectly with those two loners," Matt grinned.

"If they are fusing them together, I mean, that is right up Nintendo's alley. Half of their characters are just the result of a fusion. But okay, moving on. Television?" Val asked.

"What if they sent the Floridian from the Good Place, wow," Matt laughed.

"Oh my God, he would be the Bad Side choice, they would have to land on someone in between the indecisive buffoon and the Floridian. So, the skyscraper or the Arizona trash bag, fused together. What do you get when you fuse those two together? A medium sized trash dispenser!" Val laughed.

"What about the Busty Alexa?" Matt grinned.

"Oh! Yes, absolutely. With or without her powers, that would be fun. But she could ruin the whole thing for them. I think it really would be a medium size trash dispenser," Val reflected.

"Anyone that comes from that show would likely confirm out theory. But I can just hope for a fused skyscraper and Busty Alexa," Matt grinned.

"Oh you. Anime?" Val shook her head.

"I would love to have a DBZ character. They can all fly," Matt smiled.

"The Prince of Saiyans?" Val beamed.

"Oh God, the late Prince. Not the early Prince. I bet the Bad Side would be pining for the early Prince. And again, that show literally had fusion. It was a silly win button," Matt grinned.

"What if it was a Bebop character?" Val laughed.

"None of them really land in the middle. They are all Bad Side," Matt shook his head. "And a fused together Bebop character would be weird."

"What about that overrated show? The one with the 60 billion double dollar man?" Val smiled.

"Oh, they would send the priest, fused with the lead, for sure," Matt laughed.

"I haven't really seen anything that hasn't aired on Cartoon Network. This is a fun thought experiment...but I think the Specialist is really derailing it. How in the world did they land on him?" Val sighed.

"Maybe they are targeting that particular subset of characters. Loners, outcasts, killers. Or maybe the Puppetmaster sat on the remote by accident! That one is truly out there. I don't know. I think we should wait for the next person, to see if my theory holds any weight. I think if they really wanted to send a bunch of medium people, they should pull characters from that one channel with the YA shows. That entire network screams mediocre. Each show has one good character, at best. The rest, medium. But, if they send the skyscraper, it's basically over. That is essentially a confirmation that they are messing with us," Matt grinned.

"I totally agree with what you said about that network. They have no idea how to land the plane. As for us, I mean, what are we supposed to do? Let's say it is the Puppetmaster, what is the end point? How long does it go on? The rest of our lives? That would be so cruel, I haven't wanted to think about how the people are maybe never coming back," Val sighed.

"It's a good question. Where exactly is this going?" Matt mused.

"And the words that come through the fire?" Val asked.

"Honestly, I think if it is the Puppetmaster, they are literally just ad-libbing it—kinda like how I am ad-libbing this explanation. How do we get the new characters down there? Have a giant green light shine down on them, with a voice that comes through a fire. Oh, and tell them the siblings are the Chosen Ones. That will make their head spin. That is totally something the demon would say," Matt laughed.

"Yes, I can see that," Val rolled her eyes.

"They are flubbing that aspect of the story; we aren't even thinking about it. I hope you can hear us, demons. You all suck!" Matt shouted.

"I hope you choke on your dinner, Puppetmaster!" Val shouted.

"Still, if they are making up the list of new people as they go, and they are watching us, it could suck. Watch them send us two animals fused together," Matt laughed.

"That would be so horrible, oh my God! Imagine trying to communicate with him," Val beamed. "In all seriousness, what should we do?"

"Just, survive. And keep them from killing each other. I really think Sam was going to walk that guy away from us and kill him, for sure. Like I said, I bet the Bad Side demons were fuming when Sam got here, he is literally built for this. He took one look at that guy and decided to kill him. The whole conversation was a waste of time. He wasn't going to see the sunrise tomorrow. I think—I hope I convinced Sam to spare him... for now. But one slip up, that's it. As talented as that Specialist seems to be, he can't beat Sam," Matt sighed.

"Why don't we head back, loot some fishing gear, then go home? Even though...if it really is an experiment, we should probably stop accruing Bad Side points," Val sighed.

"Looting the fishing gear can be the last thing we steal," Matt offered. "It's not like we can go back and undo the stuff we did in Austin, Miss *Drive My Car Through the Front Door*," Matt teased.

"I will accept my Bad Side points for that, there is no appealing," Val laughed.

"I know it's a wild, out-there conspiracy theory...but can you just imagine getting our time in front of the Puppetmaster, I am betting there would be a lot of anger there," Matt whispered.

"Oh, definitely. They are breaking all the rules. We will probably not figure it out for sure anytime soon. And if it's those omnipotent assholes from Star Trek...that just throws everything out the window. They don't have to follow any rules," Val sighed.

"Let's just ride the waves in, get everything packed up, and head back to the boat. I'll drive us to the sea cottage, we can rest a bit, take showers, then start our journey home," Matt offered.

They waded inland, and then caught a wave back to the beach. They had both always loved the beach, especially the boogie boards. Walking to their umbrella, they dried off and put their water shoes on. They had essentially taken everything from the local beach store, noting their prices were outrageous. If anyone was accruing Bad Side points there, it was the shop owners, not the looters.

"I don't like the way the sand feels in my shoes," Val lamented.

"Go rinse them off in the water," Matt shrugged. "That's what I did."

Val walked back to the water and rinsed out her shoes, putting them back on. Looking out into the Gulf, she pointed to the ships out there.

"What do you think is going on with those ships?" Val asked.

"Nothing, they are anchored. They will be there forever," Matt called back to her.

"How is the fishing out there?" Val asked.

"It's deep-sea fishing. So, wonderful. You have never liked the waves though," Matt pointed out. "We could get a really nice boat, to mitigate the effects."

"Do you think it would start up for us?" Val asked.

"Yeah, we could go find one while we are here. It has been a month plus, as long as we find the keys, it should start up. If not, we can ask Sam and the Specialist to take a look at it," Matt suggested.

"That seems like a good project for them once they get their ranch up and running," Val nodded, walking back and picking up the basket of stuff. "I will take the supplies—you take the guns."

"Okay," Matt nodded, slinging the Go Wild around his shoulder and picking up the shotgun.

They headed back towards the pier, crossing the street and walking to the boat without incident. Val set the basket down on the dock and hopped into the boat, while Matt handed her the guns first, then the basket. Jumping in himself, he started the boat while Val untied the lines and they pushed off.

"Can I drive?" Val smiled.

"Sure, just go left here, out the channel, then head south, staying in between the buoys," Matt guided.

"So, I have noticed you completely ignore those 'No Wake' signs, and just open it up right away. I think that I will do that as well," Val beamed, as she accelerated out of the channel and towards South Bay.

It was windy today, and Matt tried to get Val to slow down a bit, because the water was rough, but she learned the hard way as the bow kicked up in the air and she slowed the boat down abruptly.

"Oh! That was scary. Okay, I need a minute," Val put her hands up. "You drive."

"Sure," Matt grinned, as they switched places. "It's windy today, the water is bad for boating. We have to go a bit slower to avoid hitting a cap like that. No big deal."

Matt got them going again, staying on 3 RPMs, occasionally turning into some waves to ease the impact. Passing by South Bay, they came upon the sea cottages. They had set up on the first one at the very end, so they could fish off the pier into the channel if they needed to. Approaching the dock, Matt glided the boat in as Val deployed the cushions and caught the railing. Tying the boat off, they disembarked and headed inside.

"You can get in the shower first; I will get some snacks going. We can head home in a couple of hours. I think we can leave the boat in the water, we come here once a week," Matt offered.

"I agree. The cottage down the street had a nice Gulf boat, you want to go check on that while I shower?" Val grinned.

"Sure, hopefully the keys are in the cottage," Matt smiled.

CHAPTER 13

THE SURVIVALIST

ONE WEEK LATER

Val teed off on their final hole of their day, the 6th. The Pink Lady landed on the green, it was a Par 3. They were playing on the course in Port Isabel, which was in poor condition. Without regular upkeep, the grass was dying off, and the greens were choppy. Not having a care at all, Matt teed off next, also knocking it on the green.

"Are you sure we should be doing this while the guys clear the bridge to get to the green light?" Val asked.

"Sam doesn't want us too close to the Specialist, even though it's been a week and we have had a couple of conversations. So, it's golf," Matt shrugged.

"We have to walk back this way, just take the putters and leave the bags?" Val offered.

"Yep," Matt nodded, as they set off, putters in hand.

"So, any final guesses on who the person at the fire will be?" Val beamed.

"I think we need to settle on a genre. I think it will be a videogame character. What about you?" Matt laughed.

"Also, a video game character. I'm hoping for a female, I could use the help keeping those guys in line," Val laughed.

"Okay, final guesses?" Matt prompted.

"The lead from the Fantasy series. With the anatomically nonsensical chest," Val smiled. "You know, your favorite."

"That's not a bad guess, honestly. She could really help us," Matt reflected. "It's hard to see how she would be a medium though. She would have to be fused with someone else. Still, I hope you are right."

"Did you have a guess, or are you throwing in with me?" Val laughed.

"I'm going to guess the lead from the android RPG, the futuristic one where there are no more humans. She could really help us as well. She at least doesn't need sustenance," Matt grinned.

"I hope you are wrong. Can you imagine trying to make conversation with her? It would be easier to talk to the Specialist," Val beamed.

They arrived at the green, Val got the flag since Matt was away. This particular green was in poor condition, their balls hadn't rolled at all. But again, they didn't mind. Matt lined up his putt, knowing he had to hit the ball with force to get it there, and once again, it lipped out.

"That always happens!" Matt exclaimed. "I always rim out!"

"It's crazy how often it happens, yes. Still, that was a nice putt, good par," Val shook her head, smiling.

Matt tapped in and collected his ball, then went to pick up the flag while Val lined up her own putt. Again, putting it with force, she went a foot too long. Tapping in herself, they high fived, replaced the flag and headed back for their bags.

"Think the guys are done?" Val asked.

"Yeah, they are at least on the other side," Matt sighed. "We can help them finish up if we need to. Or just weave around the cars."

"Yep," Val nodded.

Collecting their bags, they walked across the course to their parked car, and piled everything in. Val got them going, as they headed for the main road, and then the causeway leading over the bay. Following the route Sam had carved out, they drove up the hill and down the slope, seeing that the guys had cleared the arch completely, and were working on the road. Coming to a stop behind them, the siblings got out.

"Hey guys! How's it going? Need some water?" Val offered.

"Thanks," the Specialist smiled. He took the water from Val and drank. "Have you guys finally decided I wasn't a threat?"

"Matt told me you would be insulted if we did that, so no," Val beamed.

"He makes a valid case," the Specialist said sipping the water.

"Have you come up with a name for yourself?" Matt asked.

"Well Sam here suggested 'Bob', I vetoed it. I'm going with 'Jack'," the Specialist shrugged.

"That the name of one of your victims?" Matt grinned.

"Maybe," Jack grinned.

"Okay," Matt shrugged. "Val wants to see your eyes—it seems like you are hiding them on purpose."

"I'll just take my sunglasses off then, how about that?" Jack shrugged, as he removed his sunglasses, revealing his eyes that seemingly glowed red.

"Those are um, intimidating. You really are a scary guy," Val whispered.

"We have a working theory about what is going on here, and your presence is throwing a wrench in it. But you are accustomed to being on your own, so you aren't necessarily bad for this kind of situation. Just follow Sam's rules," Matt shrugged.

Jack put his sunglasses back on and nodded, as they turned to resume work on clearing the road. It took the four of them another 30 minutes, but finally they could drive across, as they piled into the SUV. Val got them going, and they drove straight to the pier next to the green light. There was no point in being cautious anymore. Still, Matt took the shotgun, just in case.

Walking down the pier, they spotted a person staring into the fire. It was a woman, which cheered Val up immensely. Again, she just looked like a normal human being.

"I don't think that's the girl I guessed. It's someone else. The Fantasy character had way longer hair, and she didn't wear clothing like that. Any ideas?" Val offered.

"She just looks normal to me, let's introduce ourselves," Matt shrugged.

Approaching the woman, they could see she had long brown hair, tied in a ponytail, red shirt, brown pants and boots. She looked up and asked them if they were the Chosen Ones.

"We don't really know. What did the fire tell you your title was?" Matt asked.

"The Survivalist," she replied, her English accent catching their attention.

"Okay, so you are English. That's cool. Let's get out of here," Matt waved her towards the street.

"No threat," Sam reported, following Matt.

"At all," Jack added, following as well. "Nice tits though."

"Please ignore them, they are just over this whole affair. My name is Val, I know you don't remember your name, but it's nice to meet you," Val beamed, extending her hand.

The woman shook it, asking what was going on, as they followed the group.

"It's a long story, and we will tell it to you on our way home. For now, let's catch up to them," Val smiled.

The group walked back to their SUV, with Jack getting in the very back. Noting they either needed to bring a pickup from now on, or just take less people, the rest of the group piled in. Val drove them around the still traffic and waited for the obvious question.

"Where are all the people?" the Survivalist asked.

"The humans on this planet all vanished about six weeks ago. It was just us two siblings, then you guys started dropping in. Obviously, something is amiss, and we have a working theory, but there is no way to know for sure," Val replied.

"I'm all for mysteries, but that all sounds impossible," the Survivalist scoffed.

"Then explain where all the people are," Matt shrugged.

"I...can't," the Survivalist relented.

"We know you can't remember your name, so just come up with one on your own. We are going to take these two guys back to the ranch, and then head to the houses with you, get some food. How are things at the ranch Sam?" Val asked.

"Fine," Sam shrugged.

"No complaints," Jack smiled.

"You two look like absolute killers," the Survivalist whispered, looking at them.

"Good survival instincts," Jack grinned.

Sam said nothing as they drove on. Crossing the bridge, their new member looked out at all the empty cars, trying to make sense of it.

"It's just humans that have vanished, there are plenty of seagulls, and I even see dolphins in the bay," the Survivalist whispered.

"Yes, it's just humans. And they are porpoises, not dolphins," Matt whispered back.

Val took them out of town and towards Harlingen, pulling over where Sam directed her to. There was a ranch on the side of the road, a couple of horses were in the paddock, it looked nice. Sam and Jack got out and walked towards it, not even offering a goodbye as Val got them going again.

"Okay, I'm serious, those two looked like killers—who were they?' the Survivalist demanded.

"One of them is a Superhero, having lived a long time and saved the Earth countless times, according to him. But yes, he has killed thousands of people in his day. His title is the Protector, he won't hurt us. The other guy, yeah. He is a killer from outer space. As in, not from Earth," Matt grinned.

"Don't forget Sam isn't human either," Val laughed.

"Right, not human," Matt added.

"That doesn't make sense," the Survivalist retorted.

"Neither does your presence. How did you get here?" Matt asked.

"I…I don't remember. Val was right, I don't even remember my name. What is your name?" The Survivalist asked.

"Matt. We are just two ordinary siblings that woke up to an empty planet one day about six weeks ago. We could use your help with the day to day. We have a good setup in our neighborhood. You can have your own house, a bed, a shower, whatever you don't have, you can loot. I have an assortment of weapons to fend off stray dogs and predators, I will give you one," Matt replied.

"How much do you know about me?" the Survivalist asked.

"Nothing? Do you remember anything about yourself?" Matt offered.

"Oh, come on. You two look like you are knowledgeable people, you must recognize me. I did a world-famous magazine shoot last month. It was all over the news and social media. You don't have to be polite, go on and get the unwarranted flattery out of your system. Then we can actually start solving this mystery," the Survivalist scoffed.

"Aggressive!" Val beamed.

"I'm sorry for not recognizing you. I guess I'm not as tapped into the social media scene as I thought. In the meantime, take some time to let it sink in. You aren't solving this mystery. There are currently five humans on the planet right now. Sam took a week, he drove to New York City, it was completely abandoned. I'm not suggesting you go to that extreme, but we aren't going to pressure you. Just come up with a name for yourself for now. We will show you your house and leave you to your own devices," Matt shrugged.

"Jack took what? Ten minutes?" Val laughed.

"Yeah well, he had to accept things quickly, because Sam was going to run those claws right through him," Matt grinned.

The Survivalist sighed and looked out the window. They drove on in silence, coming into Harlingen and taking their exit.

"Harlingen? Where is that? Where are we?" the Survivalist asked.

"Harlingen, Texas. The southern tip, Mexico is about 50 or so miles to the south. This is where our parents lived, we drove down to check on them and set up our base here. We are using all of these houses to store food and supplies. We check on them almost daily, to make sure mice and other critters aren't getting in. We can show you more once we get inside our house. As I said, take as long as you need to settle in. We will provide you with all the information we have," Matt sighed.

"Alright. I'm sorry for my comment earlier. This is just a lot," the Survivalist sighed.

"Oh—it's okay. Come on, let's get inside," Matt managed as Val parked the SUV in the adjacent driveway and they hopped out.

"This way, we are using all these cars, but this house is ours," Val pointed, leading them on.

"How long have you been on your own, six weeks?" the Survivalist asked.

"I would say so now. We mix in work with pleasure, to help us stay focused. It's mostly golf and the swimming pool, but we have gone boating as well," Matt replied.

"I'll help. Even though I don't think you are being honest with me, I am actually very good in situations like this," the Survivalist admitted.

"We will appreciate whatever help you can offer," Val smiled.

Walking into the house, Buddy and Fred came to greet them, barely even barking at the Survivalist, as they were more focused on food and attention. Val fed them both while Matt led their new member into the living room.

"Let's sit down here, and we can go over our local situation. Sam raided City Hall for a map of the city, and as you can see, we have been working on powering everything down to conserve electricity. All of the residential areas have been completely turned off, and Sam and Jack are working on the southwestern commercial area right now.

We raided the local grocery stores, basically emptying them, storing all of the food in this neighborhood. Freezing the perishables, we have accumulated a lot. Even if we run out, the hunting down here is amazing, and we can fish as well. Food should never be an issue. We also have plenty of water, sodas, juices, honestly it should last us for years. Water shouldn't be an issue either.

When and if the electricity goes out, we have stored generators in this cul-de-sac, along with gasoline in all the trucks you saw out there. Every single car you saw out there has gas in it, so again, gasoline will never be an issue. We can honestly live like this...forever if we need to," Matt finished.

"You have definitely done well in just six weeks. Have you taken any precautions against hurricanes? We are in the middle of the season, and just one could ruin your entire way of life," the Survivalist offered.

"We haven't. Hurricanes are extremely rare here, and we haven't even thought about that. But with no way to predict or track them now, we should probably look into that," Matt relented.

"This looked like a wealthy retirement community, so I'm sure the flood control is top notch. But we should find the houses that are at a higher elevation, and prepare them to be an evacuation point. Do Sam and Jack have an evacuation point?" the Survivalist asked.

"Sam can't be killed, so no, he does not. Jack hasn't even thought about it, I'm sure. But we can talk to them about it," Matt whispered.

"Arrogance is the enemy here, okay? Anyone can be killed, no matter how tough they appear to be," the Survivalist pressed.

"You are right that arrogance is the enemy," Val cut in. "But Sam heals on his own, Jack cut his throat in their first encounter, and Sam just stood there like it was nothing. The cut was gone by the time Jack turned back around. We can show you next time, along with his metal claws."

"That—that's not possible, okay? Whatever you saw, it was a trick, an illusion, it wasn't real," the Survivalist tried.

"If you don't mind, can we move on? I agree with you, set up an evacuation point. Please, continue. What other ideas do you have?" Matt asked.

"Please, if you could?" Val whispered to her new friend.

"Okay, I'm sorry. How are you communicating with each other?" the Survivalist relented

"Like this. Val and I don't split up. Sam comes by from time to time. Whenever the green light appears, we get in our vehicle and go pick them up, then head to the beach. We still have our two phones, and they are still working. But other than that, we don't have direct lines of communication," Matt shrugged.

"Well, we could find phones, I guess. Or short-wave radios. Install one here and at the ranch. If a storm is blowing in, they could warn us. We could head to the evacuation point," the Survivalist offered.

"Yeah, I like that idea. Where could we find a radio, I wonder?" Matt whispered.

"Don't most truckers still use them? We can probably take some out of the big trucks on the highway," Val offered.

"Great idea. We should be able to find plenty, one for each of our vehicles, one for the ranch, one for here. We can do that tomorrow," Matt grinned.

"We should also board up the windows of all the houses you are using, do you have lumber here?" the Survivalist asked.

"Oh, the hardware stores have plenty of precut lumber, they are still full of supplies. As much as we took, it's pretty much impossible to empty out an entire hardware store. We can do that tomorrow as well," Matt offered.

"That's all I have for now. I will think of more as time goes on. Will you show me to my house?" the Survivalist asked.

"Sure, it's this way. You can raid the local stores for clothing. We have only been taking clothes that fit us, so the stores are still full. Come on," Val smiled.

Val led her out and headed towards the Scotty's home, knowing Matt still wanted nothing to do with that place. Matt himself stood up and went to his parents' room, Fred and Buddy close behind. They had come in and parked at the siblings' feet during the conversation. Matt knew they needed more attention, but he was going to get their new member a weapon. Taking out the Marlin 30-06 and the extra combat shotgun, he figured she would be good with either of those.

He laid them on the bed and dug out some ammo, setting a box of each down next to the guns. Laying a hunting vest on the bed as well, he walked back out and sat down, petting the dogs while waiting for Val to come back. Half an hour passed and she finally came back to sit next to him, asking for an update.

"Oh, there is no update, I got a couple of guns out for her, for when she is ready. How is she holding up?" Matt asked.

"She is good, she apologized again for her aggressiveness, and asked me to forward that to you as well. She is very polite, a welcome development. She also said we can just call her Jen, it's nice and simple. She wanted to rest a bit, then she would rejoin us. Why don't we cook dinner for three?" Val smiled.

"Okay, sure. What meat have you taken out?" Matt asked.

"Brisket. What do you think the best way to cook it is?" Val beamed.

"Oh, slow cooker for sure. It's what? 3 pm? We can cook it for about three hours, eat at six. Then go over the plan for tomorrow. Both of her ideas were really good," Matt admitted.

"I completely agree, we hadn't even thought about hurricane season, I'm sure there are a few that have already pounded the country. There is no way for us to know though," Val shrugged. "Come on, let's head to the kitchen."

CHAPTER 14

THE THEORY

The next day, the entire group was raiding the hardware store. Matt, Val, and Jen had spent the morning looting CB radios from the big trucks on the highway, and had gone out to the ranch to drop one off. Sam and Jack had been there, so they came back to help with the looting. Matt didn't really know their morning routine, he had learned they were playing hide and seek at night, to keep their skills fresh. Sam was winning on a constant basis. Jack had the eyesight, he could apparently see in the dark, but Sam's enhanced senses were far superior.

Jen had finally come around to accepting the way things were when she got a better look at the two of them. Specifically, the claws and the eyes. So now they were preparing for a hurricane that may or may not hit them in the months, or years to come. The store was dark, but that suited Sam and Jack just fine, as they hauled lumber out to the two electric trucks.

"Do you think we should go pick up that third electric truck, now that there are three of us in the neighborhood?" Val asked, as they pushed a flatbed out the door.

"There is a dealership in McAllen, and another in Brownsville. We should probably head to Brownsville, since Sam wants to move on to shutting down that electricity next. He found another ranch they can base out of while working on that," Matt replied, handing the second flatbed off to Jack.

"After shutting down the island, don't forget that," Jack grinned, as the siblings headed back inside.

"Right. How is that going?" Matt asked.

"Probably a quarter of a way up the island now," Jack shrugged, as he and Matt lifted the lumber into the tailgate while Val took the flatbeds back inside. "How often does it storm here?"

"Well, thunderstorms are way more common than actual hurricanes. I think it's been 20 years or more since a hurricane hit this area. But thunderstorms—maybe once a month. It doesn't rain a lot here; the drought is real. Fortunately, we have greatly reduced the water consumption, so it won't be an issue for a really long time, if ever," Matt shrugged.

"Have you put in a good word for me with Jen?" Jack smiled.

"I think that comment about her chest and your eyes convinced her you weren't a person she wanted to be around for any reason," Matt grinned.

"You really think me being here is an accident?" Jack asked.

"It's a little weird. We haven't had time to talk about it since Jen got here yesterday, but we seem to have one criminal, one guy that qualifies as medium, and now a person firmly on the good side. But…I lean towards accident, yes," Matt sighed.

"Some kind of force is out there, pulling the strings. None of it makes sense, but what's the endgame? What are we supposed to be doing?" Jack asked.

"I honestly think we are all supposed to survive together, whether it's to prove something, or figure out the mystery, I'm not sure. But I really think all of us need to be alive for the endgame. And more than one of us are worried about you screwing that up, either by killing someone, or getting yourself killed," Matt smiled laconically.

"I can't kill Sam, so you don't have to worry about me killing anyone. The nightly game is frustrating me though, he finds me *every* time. You could help me out a little, telling me a secret or two," Jack teased.

"Fishing for intel huh?" Matt grinned. "As you said, you can't kill him. The best you can hope for is disabling him. If you are just wondering how to win a round of hide and seek, how about this. He has enhanced senses.

He can smell you at all times, he can hear you breathing. How much time are you guys giving each other to hide?"

"He gives me an hour. I felt like I had completely immersed myself into the terrain last night, and he walked up behind me like it was nothing. It made me think he had planted a tracking chip on me," Jack lamented.

"As I said, he is elite. I suggest using the water to mask your scent. Innovate. Probably should take more than an hour," Matt grinned.

"I'll keep those things in mind, thanks," Jack grinned, as they finished loading the lumber. Both trucks were full, so they headed inside to collect the others.

"Hey guys! Come on, the trucks are full!" Matt shouted at them.

"On our way!" Val shouted back.

They rounded the corner and headed out together, gathering at the trucks. Val asked what the plan was.

"You three can take the boards back to the houses, Jack and I will head back to the ranch," Sam shrugged.

"You aren't going to help us?" Jen demanded.

"You want to work with him?" Sam motioned to Jack.

"No," Jen admitted.

"See you later then," Sam turned and they headed off.

Jen waited for what she believed to be them walking out of earshot, before speaking. "I really don't trust them," she pressed.

"Sam heard you, and he knew that anyway. We can only work with what we have. New people seem to drop in every week, maybe we will get another person that you want to be around," Matt offered.

"What can we do about it, Jen?" Val asked. "We trust Sam, and we are leery of Jack. You need to get to that point as well. Anyway, before we board up the houses, why don't we go eat lunch? There is still plenty of brisket."

"Good plan. Jen? You good?" Matt asked.

"As good as I can be. I'm still having a hard time with that healing thing. There is always a logical explanation. Maybe we can talk more about your theory at lunch," Jen sighed.

"Yeah, sure," Matt shrugged. "Let's head home."

Val and Jen got into the first truck while Matt drove the second one, and they drove back to the neighborhood. Parking in the cul-de-sac, they left the lumber for later and headed inside. Fred had taken an immediate liking to Jen, as he approached her, asking for attention. She petted him and sat down at the table, while Val and Matt heated up the leftovers.

"You both said you think it's a *Puppetmaster* surrounded by *demons* arbitrarily deciding who joins you, and they made up some stupid story about telling each of us our role through the fire, and it's not working. And you don't know how long it's going to last, or who is coming, or what we have to do. How do you think we can we find out more?" Jen sighed.

"We can't. We can only go to the light, pick the people up and continue on. It really sucks, we miss our parents and our friends. Not really our jobs, especially since we don't have bills anymore. But…if it really is a sick experiment, we are ready for it to end. And Val has a lot to say to the Puppetmaster about how depraved they are," Matt grinned.

"It's completely unacceptable. But honestly, we don't even know if our theory is correct. We could be completely and utterly wrong. I do believe we should go forward with it though. Trying to earn good points by doing good things is not a bad way to live. Even if we are wrong about the Puppetmaster, and someone else is testing us, it's a sure way to score well," Val pressed.

"After we eat…I need some time. I feel like I helped you guys with a few things, a few important things, now I need some solitude. Is it okay if I take some supplies? I will probably just stay in the city, but I need this," Jen whispered.

"That is completely okay Jen. Take the Marlin, a truck with a radio, go wherever you want. Do anything. Like I said, Sam drove all the way to New York City. You haven't taken any time at all. You can even take Fred—he really likes you. Just try not to go out at night. I don't know the range of those two guys, or where they go, or anything. I just know they are playing hide and seek, and they both excel in the darkness. You don't want to get tangled up with them," Matt grinned.

"Right. Thank you," Jen said as Val served her plate. They sat down and ate, not really having much else to say. Finishing up, Matt helped

Jen pack up some supplies in a backpack, handing her the Marlin and a hunting vest with plenty of ammo that she wouldn't need.

"If you get in trouble, just use the radio. Maybe fire a shot in the air from time to time. I will let Sam know you are out and about, but to stay away. If you get in actual trouble, fire three consecutive shots in the air. The stores should all have a little bit of food, but if you run out, just come back here, we will feed you. If we aren't here, head to the ranch," Matt offered.

"Thanks again. I've been too aggressive with you, I know. I'll make it up to you when I get back," Jen sighed.

Matt nodded, and Jen put Fred's leash on and led him out. He was happy to go with her, as Buddy looked on, expecting Matt to move. He just shook his head and closed the door behind them.

"Well! Just the two of us! Want to get started on boarding up the windows?" Val beamed.

"Sure, let's take Buddy, tie him to a tree out there. And we can talk about anything other than the Puppetmaster, okay?" Matt grinned.

"That's fair. She was being pretty difficult, even *I* admit. I hope this time away helps her. Even if she doesn't believe us, what can she do about it? Help us, or strike out on her own. She isn't that kind of person, right?" Val asked.

"No, she will come back and help us. She just needs a few days. Her ideas were solid though. We have an evac house now, and we are working on getting it stocked up. I don't think it will be necessary, but you never know," Matt shrugged.

"How should we tackle this next project? Which houses do you think we should board up?" Val asked.

"Well, I don't think we should board up the houses that people might be moving into. So, why don't we start at that corner house, and move on down the street. I got the drill and hundreds of screws, along with a wood saw, so we will just go slow and steady. There is no rush, and we can take plenty of breaks. You hold up the boards and I will drill them into the walls," Matt replied.

"You are going to drill into the bricks?" Val asked, curiously.

"We are drilling them on the inside of the houses. Obviously, we can't drill into bricks," Matt grinned.

"Oh! Right. I admit, I have never done this before," Val realized.

"It's okay, neither have I," Matt shrugged. "Let's just do what we can with the lumber we have, then continue it when we are all together again. Tomorrow we can head to Brownsville to get the third electric truck. Sam said there was also a golf course on the south side of town, so maybe we can try that out as well."

"That's something to look forward to," Val beamed.

CHAPTER 15

BONDING

The next morning, Matt and Val were finishing up their breakfast, about to set off on their morning chores, when they heard a truck pull into the Scotty's driveway. Fred was baying out the truck window, as Val went to the door. Opening it, she waved at Jen.

"Hey! Is everything okay? You are back earlier than we expected!" Val shouted.

Jen helped Fred out and walked over, giving Val a big hug, which surprised her.

"Oh...this is nice," Val whispered, as she hugged back. Breaking apart, Jen approached Matt and offered him a hug as well. Even Matt had to admit it felt really nice.

"Hey guys, I just wanted to come back for good. I explored a lot yesterday, then I finished at the ranch, where I really talked to Sam...and a little bit to Jack. And...I need to apologize again for being so aggressive with you two, especially you Matt. You two have taken on a lot, the entire human race vanished, but you are still here, carrying on. That takes more strength than you realize, and if I am going to be here, I need to be supportive. I brought back some venison that Sam shared, so we can eat it later. Is there anything else I can do?" Jen offered.

"Oh, those are very nice things to say, Jen. We appreciate it, Matt especially. Today we plan on going to play about nine holes, then on to

Brownsville to pick up a third electric truck for you to drive. But we can skip the golf, if you want, and go straight to Brownsville." Val said smiling.

"Skip the golf? Why would we do that? No, I'll join you," Jen smiled. "We can talk about lots of things."

"Oh, you play golf? Okay then," Val stammered.

"I'm English, of course I can play golf. Come on, let's go," Jen shook her head with a smile.

"I don't know what being English has to do with it, but okay," Val managed.

"Don't forget, we have to drive the cars first," Matt pointed out.

"Drive the cars? Oh, you mean to keep them running? That's really smart, which ones do you drive?" Jen asked.

"All of the ones here in the cul-de-sac. We just drive them each one time around the entire neighborhood, it's a big circle. Will you help us?" Val smiled.

"Of course, where are the keys?" Jen asked.

"We leave them in the ignition, we don't really have a theft problem here, for obvious reasons," Matt shrugged.

"Makes sense, come on let's go," Jen smiled.

They took Buddy and Fred with them, and headed for their respective vehicles. They had 12 scattered about the cul-de-sac, not including the two electric trucks.

"Hey, we check the houses as well, make sure everything is okay. I set mouse traps, if you could help me with those Jen? Val wants nothing to do with them," Matt sighed.

"Oh, sure. I'm not afraid of dead mice, all the doors are unlocked?" Jen asked.

"Yes, I just check each room, that's enough. If you could take that house next to yours, I would appreciate it," Matt pointed.

"No problem," Jen smiled, as she headed that way.

Matt watched her go, as Val came up and grabbed him. "Quit looking at her ass," she whispered with a smile.

"I wasn't— I was just.. I'm glad we have someone here to help us," Matt relented.

"I am too. And I'm just teasing you, that's the first woman you have seen in over a month. And she is pretty hot. Here is some free advice: While it's been over a month for you, it's only been a few days for her. She isn't going to be thinking about it any time soon. So, behave yourself," Val beamed.

"Thanks for the tip. How are you?" Matt shook his head.

"I'm good. I am glad she came around so quickly. I'm curious about what else she did yesterday," Val grinned.

"We can ask her on the course. Something tells me she is going to be really good," Matt shrugged. "But first let's hit the houses, then the cars. You take the Pom's, I will take Fred's."

———

Hours later, they were standing on the tee box as Jen launched her ball into the air down the right slide, with a slight fade it came back and landed in the middle of the fairway. Matt and Val knew they were in trouble, and it was just the first hole.

"Wow, nice shot," Matt grinned.

"Thanks. These are really good clubs," Jen smiled.

They had liberated the pro shop again, noting how much nicer it was than the one in their own country club. Each one of them had taken new clubs, new balls and tees, and new bags. Val teed up her Pink Lady and launched her own shot down the left side of the fairway, landing about 30 yards shy of Jen's.

"Yeah, these are nice. Too bad most of the course is dead or dying, so we won't get good rolls. But oh well," Val shrugged with a smile.

Matt was last, as he launched his standard drive down the right side, passing Val's and stopping near Jen's ball. They set out, in no particular hurry.

"So, I went to the library yesterday, I had to turn the power on for a bit, it was really hard to find what I was looking for in the dark. But I turned it off when I was done," Jen assured them.

"That's fine, did you find what you were looking for?" Matt asked.

"I did not. I found something completely different, and it...confirms your story about this being a different world than mine. A few months back I did a magazine spread, it was very popular. I needed some money for an expedition in Siberia, and that is usually a guaranteed way to get it. I tried to find a copy in the library, and while I did find that magazine from the correct month, it wasn't me.

Not giving up, I searched for magazine covers my more famous brother had done. Found the right magazines, no brother on the cover. Then I searched for books that my father had written. The library didn't have them. I thought that was believable, this is a small town, they might not have them. I searched for old magazine covers that my brother and I did— nothing. I searched for cover stories of the artifacts I have found—zip. Nothing I have done, nothing my family has done exists in this world. That's when I went to see Sam. But, not before making a stop at the electric company. You guys are so silly. Val? Here is you, that was a nice tee shot, you still have some distance though," Jen stopped them.

Val got her 3-iron out and swung away. Coming up about 50 yards short of the green, they resumed their walk.

"You guys went house to house turning the power off? Why didn't you just go to the electric company and turn the breakers off?" Jen laughed.

"Oh...we didn't think about that....whoops," Matt relented.

"Dumbass!" Val exclaimed, laughing.

"Hey! You didn't think of it either!" Matt shot back.

"I took care of it, all of Harlingen is powered down except for our neighborhood. Here I am. You beat me by a few yards Matt," Jen grinned.

Jen took her 3-iron out as well, and knocked her ball onto the left side of the green. Taking some steps forward, Matt hit his 4-iron onto the front of the green. Continuing on, Matt was embarrassed about the electricity, and he failed to hide it.

"Don't worry about it!" Jen laughed. "It was a great idea to conserve electricity, I can't overstate that. Your methods were a little off, but that's okay. Do you even know where the electric company is located?"

"No idea, but neither did you, and you found it," Matt sighed.

"Hey! I'm just teasing you. You are right, Val didn't think of it either! But we can go town to town now, and shut down the electricity that way. Sam's idea to find a map in City Hall was smart, copy that trick and shut down the whole region," Jen beamed.

"Yeah, that's a great idea. We can start on that tomorrow. Driving around is a little tedious because we haven't cleared the roads, but the Calamity happened late at night, so not many people were out," Matt whispered, as they got to the green, which was pretty much yellow at this point.

"So, you have a brother?" Val asked.

"Yes, a much more famous older brother. He got a five-year head start on his career, because I went to university. He suffered an injury a few years back though, and has largely retired from the field work," Jen offered.

Val was away, she still needed to chip on, and she lobbed her ball to about five feet away. Jen got the flag since she was closer than Matt, who had a long birdie putt coming up. He knocked it to about two feet away, and tapped in for par. Jen was a bit closer, but it was still too far as she also had to settle for par. Val made her par putt look effortless as she knocked it straight in.

"Nice putt Val," Jen beamed, replacing the flag and moving on. Walking up to the next tee box, they saw it was a par 5 of over 500 yards, with a stream crossing the fairway. It was definitely in play from the tee box, as Jen studied the hole.

"Okay, we have to drive over that stream, but avoid those bunkers on the left. This is a mean tee shot, I would say hit a slice straight at those bunkers," Jen offered, as she readied her driver. Swinging away, she also generated great contact as she carried the stream, but her slice took her into the uncut rough. "Too much," she lamented.

"I don't think either of us can even play a slice, fortunately my shots favor the right. Val veers a little left, but I am honestly not sure if she can get it to those bunkers," Matt offered.

"We are about to find out," Val smiled, as she teed up and launched her ball down the middle of the fairway, slightly left, but not enough to catch a bunker. Matt was last, as he sent his ball down the right side, landing cleanly.

They set out down the fairway, heading to the right to look for Jen's ball. The grass was about eight inches high; they would need to avoid the rough at all costs to avoid potential nightmares.

"Our memories have been...altered, or really just erased, when it comes to these new people. You have your memories though, which seems new. But at the same time, Sam doesn't really share a lot. So, it might not be," Matt sighed. "This is all so tedious."

"I have another idea that could help us," Jen offered.

"All of your ideas are welcome," Matt replied.

"There is a small, local airport near here, I could get a plane up and running, take it up occasionally to keep an eye out for storms," Jen smiled.

"Oh—you can fly a plane?" Val stammered.

"Yes, it's just a matter of getting one started, sitting on that flight line hasn't done them any good. Planes are just like cars, they need to be used," Jen pressed.

"Okay, well, if you need any help, let us know. Val doesn't like heights, and I'm not a fan of them either. So, you will probably be on your own for that one," Matt grinned.

"That's fine, we will test out the radios, make sure they work, then I will try to find a plane that I can get running again," Jen whispered, as they looked for her ball. Val found it, deep inside the rough. Jen took her 7-iron out and punched it onto the fairway, but she still had so far to go. "I'm going to try this fairway wood. Um? How strict are we enforcing the rules here?"

"You can adjust your lie if you need to. All we are really enforcing at this point is you have to play your ball," Matt shrugged.

"I can't get to the green, but I want to try out this wood," Jen admitted. She adjusted her lie a little bit, then hit the fairway wood. It veered way right, and she was back in the rough. "This would be one of Val's famous nightmare holes, I suppose."

"It's happened to us all. Any hazards that are on the left, I usually find. Anything on the right, Matt finds. You were too aggressive with that slice. Maybe you were just trying to show off?" Val beamed.

"I was not!" Jen pouted.

"Come on, I have to go back and hit mine," Val laughed. "I am not going to try the fairway wood—I can't make the green so no sense in joining Jen over there in the jungle."

Val walked back and hit her 3-iron straight ahead. She still had over a hundred yards to go, as they moved up to Matt's ball.

"I am going to try the fairway wood as well," Matt grinned.

"Your funeral," Val teased.

Matt swung away, generating good contact and good distance, the shot veered into the rough on the right side though. Not as far as Jen's, which he made sure to point out.

"Let's go. And remember Jen, you have to play it. So, I have no idea how you are going to get it out of there, but I'm sure you will find a way," Val laughed.

They headed down the fairway again, coming to Val's ball first. She was about 175 yards away, but the green was surrounded by bunkers. She decided to play it safe and hit her 5-iron. It was straight on, but landed about 30 yards short. Continuing on, they found Matt's ball first. It was about four feet into the rough, and he decided to play more aggressively, and hit his 5-iron out of there. Val shook her head and watched as he hit it about ten yards short of her own ball.

"Oh, nice save. Come on Jen, let's search for yours," Val beamed.

They found it, about 20 yards into the rough. Two bunkers stood between her and the green, and she decided to try to punch it out towards where Matt and Val were. It didn't go well, as the ball stayed low and landed about five yards short of the fairway. She could play a similar shot to Matt, as she punched it out again, leaving her about a hundred yards short.

"This rough reminds me of home. England always punished you for going wide," Jen reflected.

"You are back in the fairway, you can knock it on the green from there," Matt offered.

"Nothing short of holing out will save this," Jen grinned. "I would still be one over."

Jen took out her pitching wedge and knocked her ball onto the green, about 20 feet away.

Matt and Val took turns chipping on, leaving them each with short par putts. They got the flag and Jen knocked her putt close, tapping in. "Finally. Three over, let's hope someone else has the next nightmare."

"Or no one else," Val chided her.

'Right, sorry," Jen relented, picking up the flag and standing in silence. Matt finally sunk a putt, and Val followed him, both saving par.

"Okay, nice pars guys. Safe to say I will be teeing off last on the next hole," Jen smiled, as they walked on.

"One more hole, then back to work?" Matt offered.

"Let's see how it goes. I think Jen is eager to get back into the match, and she will likely need more than one hole to do it," Val laughed.

They came to the next tee box, seeing it was a 180-yard par 3, with a green surrounded by water. None of them seemed too happy about it.

"We can always skip this hole?" Val suggested.

"No no—we have never done that. It's a straight shot, and the ball isn't going to roll. So as long as you don't go over, you are safe," Matt encouraged her.

"The pond opens up a lot to the right, so as long as you hit your standard left Val, you should be okay," Jen offered.

Val took her 3-iron out and boomed it—even Jen was surprised at the contact. The ball didn't even hit the green as it sailed over and into the water.

"Wow, you guys are great at teeing off. Top Golf fans?" Jen asked.

"Yes, we went there a lot. I guess you didn't have that problem," Val smiled.

"Oh, I went to Top Golf a lot. I assume you mean I had money problems, you are right, but in reality, I usually don't have much free time," Jen reflected.

"I'm sorry. I didn't mean to imply that," Val tried, as she teed up again.

"It's okay. Golf is expensive. This course was probably 100 pounds… er…dollars a person," Jen offered.

Val swung again, generating good contact and landed on the green, safe.

"Nice shot," Matt grinned, as Val and Jen high fived. He teed up his own ball and swung away, knocking it onto the green as well, though not as close as Val. But he would be putting for birdie, while her first ball was swimming.

Jen high fived him as well, and teed up her own 3-iron. She hit it right, but it faded to the left a lot. Matt and Val looked on as the ball landed on the center of the green, about four feet from the pin.

"Wow, great shot," Val whispered.

They high fived again and set off, putters in hand. "Did you test out Sam's healing ability while you were out there?" Matt asked, smiling.

"Yes. I shot him in the shoulder. The round didn't even penetrate his collarbone, just ricocheted off. The wound healed in seconds. It was basically the final nail in the coffin for me. I'm in a different world. I hope I can find my way back to mine," Jen said wistfully.

"I hope so too," Matt whispered, as they approached the green.

"I'm putting for bogey, right? Stupid water," Val growled.

"Yeah, you really rocked that drive. I thought it would land safely on the green, but it went straight over on the fly," Matt smiled.

Jen went to get the flag; she was closest to the hole. Val lined up her putt, but left it short. Matt also left his short, the ball just didn't roll well. He tapped in for par. Jen was last, as she sank her birdie with no drama.

"Okay! I think Matt was the most consistent, so, we will remember that come dinnertime," Val beamed.

"Let's get going to Brownsville. We can find City Hall, turn off the power to the whole grid, then pick up that electric truck," Jen laughed. "Tomorrow I will explore the airport. This was a lot of fun, we definitely have to keep doing stuff like this, as long as the courses are still semi playable."

"When we lose golf, we have tennis, which I look forward to just as much. We also won't have to go as far," Matt smiled.

"Oh? I love tennis, that should be fun too," Jen nodded.

"You play tennis as well?" Val asked.

"When I was young, I had to take all kinds of lessons. Golf, tennis, swimming, equestrian, I barely had time for friends. I admit...this kind of social activity is new for me. I am used to being on my own, maybe one or two more people," Jan reflected.

"Well, I hope you are having fun, we have to make the best of this nightmare," Matt smiled.

"You are right, we are making the best of it. And I *am* having fun," Jen said cheerfully.

CHAPTER 16

THE LEGEND

Matt, Val, and Jen were sitting at the breakfast table, finishing up and preparing for their morning routine. Jen had been successful in getting a plane up and running, and she had been taking off and landing on the golf course in the country club, which they weren't playing at anymore. She had flown around, mapping out how the terrain looked. Sam had asked her to locate any nearby deer farms, and she had found a few to the northwest.

"So, are we expecting another addition to the team today?" Jen asked.

"Yeah, it's been every seven days. The light is usually visible from here, so we can pick up Sam and Jack on our way there. We will take the electric truck, put the two guys in the tailgate. This week we need to take the two boats out, for sure. Keep them in working order, fishing is a legitimate source of food, and those waters should be loaded," Matt offered.

"Agreed. Although I am happy to say my plane idea has been a smashing success," Jen smiled. "Are you two sure you don't want to come up with me for a spin?"

"You are landing it on a golf course, yes we are sure," Val replied.

"I'm about done here, I'll get the dishes in the dishwasher, you guys want to take care of the cars and houses?" Matt offered.

"Absolutely," Val beamed.

Matt collected the dishes and started rinsing them off, while the girls took Buddy and Fred out with them. Matt looked out the window to the east and spotted the green light coming down. He wondered who they would get today. He was hoping for another neighborhood resident.

An hour later, they were driving towards the island, stopping to pick up Sam and Jack, who hopped into the tailgate.

"Hey guys! How's it going?" Val shouted out the window.

"No problems to report," Sam shrugged.

"How is your nightly game going?" Matt shouted.

"He still finds me every time, but I think it's taking him longer now at least," Jack lamented.

Val drove them on, entering the port and passing by the lighthouse. Sam and Jack had pushed the cars off the road entirely, so she just drove on over the causeway. Coming to a stop outside the hotel, they got out and approached the pier. They weren't even carrying guns anymore, they had Sam.

"Any ideas on who it could be?" Val whispered.

"I'm hoping for Han Solo or Obi-Wan, myself," Matt grinned.

"Not your favorite character?" Val teased.

"Um, he would kill us all. It's kind of his thing," Matt shook his head with a smile.

They walked onto the beach, and saw a blonde woman sitting by the fire. Again, she looked like a completely ordinary girl.

"She looks a little more familiar, but I can't place her," Val whispered to her companions.

"I agree, she looks familiar. Maybe they took my advice and fused some television characters? I've given up trying to remember things at this point. Hopefully she is cool about all this," Matt shrugged.

"Who are you guys?" the girl asked.

"We are the only humans on the planet. I'm Matt. This is my sister Val, and this is Jen. The two guys are Sam and Jack. What did the fire tell you?" Matt asked.

"That I am the Legend sent to assist the Chosen Ones," the girl replied.

"Wow, arrogance!" Val beamed.

"I don't like her. She smells of death," Sam growled.

"She has definitely taken lives," Jack grinned. "Can she come to the ranch with us?"

"I think that would be best for now. I really can't remember much about her, only that she seems familiar. But I don't think she is a threat to Sam, and honestly, I think Jack would lay her out as well. Come up with a new name for yourself, okay? We aren't calling you the Legend. I know you can't remember anything; we will slowly bring you up to speed. I think we should film a video to make this easier," Matt lamented.

"I am totally on board with that. Come on, let's go," Val smiled and waved them towards the truck.

"Wait!" the Legend called out. "Did you say we are the only humans left?"

"Yes, I know that's hard to believe, but the sight of the island, and later the city, will convince you. After that, convince Sam you aren't a threat and you can come live in our neighborhood, if you want. You might want to stay at the ranch," Matt shrugged.

"Okay, I'm coming," the Legend relented.

"Why don't we go back to the ranch and film the video? I have my phone, it will help us explain everything to our new arrivals," Val beamed.

"I can tell how this gets old for you, the same questions, over and over again," Jen sighed.

"If we knew what the endgame was, it would be a lot easier to accept," Matt whispered. "Let's head back to the ranch. She isn't a threat; Sam just needs to hear her story."

They piled into the truck, Sam and Jack once again getting into the tailgate, with the Legend following them. Matt told Sam to show her the claws and he did. She didn't even flinch.

"How strong is that metal?" the Legend asked.

"It's apparently unbreakable using conventional means. I've tested it out, can't even scratch it," Jack grinned.

"I bet that comes in handy," the Legend smiled.

Sam just shrugged and retracted his claws, as Val steered them towards the causeway. Driving over the bay, they spotted quite a few porpoises, the lack of human activity was giving them more freedom and confidence. Exiting the port, Val drove them to the ranch. Everyone hopped out, as the Legend looked around.

"This is nice, I like those horses," the Legend smiled.

"Yeah, this is where Sam and Jack base their operations out of. You can spend the night here, then hopefully Sam will allow you to come join us in the neighborhood, if that's what you want. Let's film the video, Matt," Val smiled.

"Alright. I think you should start it, make the introductions, stuff like that," Matt grinned.

"I agree Val, you are the perfect welcoming mat," Jen teased.

"Gee thanks," Val rolled her eyes. Val got her cell phone out and started recording a selfie video.

"Hey newbie! Welcome to Earth," Val started with a smile. "Long story short, all of the humans have up and vanished in the night. And when I say all of them, I mean every single human being on the planet was seemingly blinked out of existence, save my brother Matt and I. Say hi Matt."

Val turned the phone towards him, and he gave a wave. She continued on.

"We were alone for three weeks, when all of a sudden, a green pillar of light appeared from the sky, leading to a man sitting by the fire. Just like you were! And just like you, he had no memory, but we kinda recognized him as a comic book character. Sounds crazy, right? Well, say hello to Sam and his claws," Val beamed.

She turned the phone towards Sam, who extended his claws for the camera to see. Jack cut his arm, and Val zoomed in on the healing.

"Next up came Jack," Val smiled. "He is from outer space. Introduce yourself Jack."

"Jack," Jack smiled, removing his sunglasses and looking into the camera.

"Next up came the super awesome Jen, a survivalist. She is from a wealthy family of adventurers in England, we just can't remember much more than that. Say hi Jen," Val smiled.

Jen waved to the camera, as Val continued on.

"Most recently this familiar blonde appeared. Again, we only have vague memories. She hasn't chosen a name yet, but she will. How is this happening, you ask? Officially, we don't know. But we can confirm that both Sam and Jen have gone out and explored the area, Sam going as far as New York, and they didn't see another soul. It's just us, a group of loners, plus two siblings. We are surviving as best we can, having looted and pillaged plenty of supplies. Well, that's it. Your welcome video has concluded!" Val laughed, ending the video.

"Well done," Jen smiled. "Okay, what's the plan now?"

"I think the three of us should go boating, we haven't done that in over a week. Meanwhile, the Legend here can stay with Sam and Jack, tell them her story, convince them she isn't a threat. Once again, she seems to be normal. Not sure how she qualifies as medium just yet, but I digress. I'll be honest Jen, I don't know how you qualify as medium, but maybe you were sent here to counter Jack. Because he doesn't qualify as medium either. Do you Jack?" Matt grinned.

"Not even remotely," Jack smiled.

"On that note, let us be off. We will come check in after we take the boats for a spin. See you guys later," Jen waved.

They loaded up in the truck, leaving the newcomer with the two guys. Turning around, Val drove them back to Port Isabel, turning towards the swing bridge. Finally arriving at their sea cottage, they all hopped out.

"Oh, this is nice. As nice as it could be right next to those salt flats," Jen observed.

"We have stored a bunch of fishing gear inside the cottage, and back home in Harlingen. But today, let's just take the boats for a spin. We have two, our parents' bay fishing boat, and a larger Gulf boat that we borrowed from one of the neighbors. Which one did you want to take out, Jen?" Matt asked.

"Oh, it doesn't matter. I'll take the smaller boat, and just follow you guys?" Jen offered.

"Okay. The wind was a bit stronger than I would like, but the big boat shouldn't be affected by it. I'll open the throttle up, just follow behind in our wake. Oh, and we ignore the 'No Wake' signs. It's a personal vendetta," Matt grinned.

"Well...okay. I guess sinking the other boats is no big deal, right?" Jen managed.

"I don't think some waves will cause them to sink," Matt laughed.

"Fair enough," Jen smiled.

They walked into the cottage and got the keys to both boats, which were docked next to each other. Jen headed for their smaller boat, while Matt and Val descended into the Gulf boat, which was called the *Invictus II.* Starting the engines, they untied the lines and pushed off. Matt turned the big boat around and headed out towards South Bay. Opening the throttle up, Val looked behind them and saw Jen following, offering a wave.

"This never gets old! Let's see what this big boat can do!" Val beamed.

Matt accelerated and they raced across the bay, porpoises coming up next to them to ride the waves they were generating. Matt wound the boat around the open water, taking big turns. Finally, they came to a stop in the middle, as Jen pulled up beside them.

"Hey! This is a nice boat, I can tell you guys take care of it. What kind of fish can you catch here?" Jen shouted.

"Speckled trout and sand trout for the most part. Redfish are uncommon, or *were* uncommon. There used to be strict enforcements on sizing. Out in the Gulf they have Kingfish, a lot of chicken dolphin, red snapper, grouper, sailfish. Our only problem is bait, we only have artificial lures, so we probably couldn't catch as much as we could with shrimp. But we don't need to catch too many to feed us all," Matt reflected.

"Want to head back?" Jen offered.

"Yeah, follow us. How is the water for you?" Matt asked.

"Oh, following in your wake smooths it out. You are right though, the wind is picking up. Let's go back," Jen replied.

They pointed their boats back towards South Bay, and Matt led them on. Arriving at the docks, Matt let Jen go ahead of them and dock on their pier, while he docked on the one behind it. Tying the lines off, they all climbed out.

"You guys made a good choice, moving down here," Jen offered. "You have hunting and fishing, we will never run out of food. I think.we should talk about your working theory on what is really happening here back at the house. Are we bringing the new girl?"

"As long as Sam allows it," Val smiled.

"Right then, do we need to do anything with the boats?" Jen asked.

"Just get the engine out of the water, I will take the keys inside," Matt replied.

Jen hopped back in the boat and raised the engine, while Matt walked the keys back into the warm sea cottage. They piled into the truck and Val drove them back towards the ranch. Coming to a stop, the ranchers walked out and the Legend climbed into the back seat.

"She is clear. Any big plans we should know about?" Sam asked.

"Nothing Sam. Do you guys need anything here?" Matt asked.

"Nothing. Stay safe," Sam replied, heading back inside with Jack.

Val put them in motion and headed towards Harlingen. She asked the Legend if she had settled on a name.

"Carly is fine. Thanks for trusting me," Carly offered.

"No problem. You just needed to convince Sam, I never thought you were a threat, even though I can't really remember your background," Matt shrugged.

"How much do you know about me?" Carly asked.

"Very little, honestly. Whoever is pulling the strings here is wiping our memories. It really seems like you either dated a billionaire, or you are a billionaire. Or both," Matt reflected.

"How do you know that?" Carly asked.

"Television show? We are pretty sure you are a television character, but honestly, you might be from comic books. Jen here—she may be a video game character. Sam is like you, maybe movies, maybe comics. Jack is from movies—or video games. I know it's a lot to take in, and it doesn't seem believable at all, but it's the truth. Our memories are being wiped each new arrival, so we really don't know what's going on," Val sighed.

"I didn't believe them either, but I went to the library, looked myself up, couldn't confirm my existence at all. And…there are no people anywhere. None of it makes sense, but here we are. Try to stay positive, it can crush your soul if you let it," Jen pressed.

"I have plenty of experience with my soul being crushed, believe me. I won't be a problem. Sam's claws seemed normal to me, so I feel like I am probably ahead in that regard," Carly shrugged.

"Yeah, pretty much. Do you have any special abilities? I can't remember," Val asked.

"No, just a regular human with some skills. No super powers," Carly smiled.

"When we get home, we will cook dinner, and go over our working theory. It will seem out of this world to you. But we believe in it. And it stops at a certain point," Val whispered.

"I'm willing to believe anything at this point," Jen offered. "The healing ability did it for me."

"Like I said, I have died, been buried, been resurrected, so I'm up for just about whatever," Carly shrugged.

Val turned into their neighborhood and into the cul-de-sac. Hopping out, she pointed at Jen's house. "That is where Jen is staying, if she will have you, you can stay with her. If not, you can stay in the house right there," she offered.

"Anywhere is fine," Carly nodded.

"She can stay with me, I don't mind," Jen smiled.

"Let's get inside and cook dinner, then we can record our theory on another video. Because I don't want to do this over and over," Matt grinned.

"Sounds like a plan!" Val beamed.

CHAPTER 17

THE CALM

They were sitting at the dinner table, having cooked some steaks for everyone, along with some frozen veggies. Sipping some wine, Val started the video.

"Hello again, newcomer. We are sitting here over dinner, about to share our theory about what in the world is happening on our planet. As we said in the welcome video, all of the humans have disappeared. It started out with just my brother and I, and as of this recording, four people have been beamed down to join us. From fictional universes. Or alternate universes. Or—somewhere. Matt? Take over!" Val laughed.

"Right, so I believe a television show has taken over our world. How that is possible, I don't know. But the people vanished—they didn't die—they vanished. And left everything behind intact. So, I think it's an omnipotent Puppetmaster, testing humanity. For what reason, I don't know. What the endgame is, I really don't know. And what the test parameters are, I have no idea.

I think the Puppetmaster has two advocates, one from the Good Side, and one from the Bad Side. They each are choosing people to come and join us, and the Puppetmaster is either choosing someone in between that range of characters, or fusing them together, I'm not quite sure. But they end up with a medium person, so to speak," Matt offered.

"What about Jack?" Val asked.

"I think he was an accident, he really doesn't count as medium, even with his anti-hero shenanigans. I think the Puppetmaster made up for it by sending us Jen, who also doesn't seem medium. Jack is on the bad side, and Jen is the good side. Our most recent addition, Carly, fits the mold of a medium person. It's also possible that they are fusing people together without knowing what the result will be, then just going with it. That's honestly all I have," Matt finished.

"What about the voice in the fire?" Jen asked.

"Oh, right. I think that's a bogus stunt that they ad libbed in there. They needed to give us some direction, and they winged it. We aren't even paying attention to it right now. Unless it says something different," Matt shrugged.

"This concludes our theory. We don't know why it's happening, how it's happening, or what the endgame is. We are relatively sure that all of the people have to survive, or the test fails. But again, our theory might be wrong, and it could be something completely different," Val admitted. *"Bye!"*

Val ended the video and they resumed eating. Figuring Carly had some questions, they waited for her to ask them. However, she remained silent.

"These are cute dogs. I am guessing they are the only ones alive?" Carly smiled at Buddy and Fred.

"There is a female Beagle at the ranch, did you meet her?" Matt asked.

"Oh, no. I didn't go inside," Carly admitted.

"Well, yes. These are the only pets that survived," Matt sighed.

"I'm sorry again you two. Especially you Matt. I realize this is the fourth time you have done this—you must be tired of it. I compare myself to Carly here, who doesn't even have a question, and I'm embarrassed. I was too hard on you both," Jen sighed.

"Stop apologizing already, please," Matt managed.

"You are making him very uncomfortable," Val beamed. "You were too aggressive with us, but you have apologized and we have moved on. How is the food?"

"Oh, it's delicious. Thank you for cooking. Again, this sure beats being marooned on an island, every day," Carly smiled.

"You are very welcome, Carly. I am glad you are handling this so well," Val laughed.

"The time I spent traveling, I ran into this very scenario a few times. This is without question the best situation I have encountered though. I mean I *was* marooned on an island once. You have food, shelter, luxuries. I'm not going to drag you down," Carly assured them.

"So, you have your memories? You just can't remember your name. It seems like Jen has her memories as well. I wonder if that means anything. Because Val and I can't remember you," Matt reflected.

"It's only vague patches. We can identify your genre, that's about it. But it's as if all of our knowledge regarding each one of you has been deleted from our brains," Val offered.

"It is very strange. But we can't do much about it. Do we have any plans for tomorrow?" Jen asked.

"You can take your plane up, the rest of us will take care of the morning chores. After that, I've got nothing," Matt shrugged. "Carly? Do you play golf?"

"Never," Carly smiled. "But don't let me stop you."

"Do you play any sports?" Val asked.

"No," Carly admitted. "I was never into them."

"We could go swimming," Matt suggested.

"Yeah, we could. Let's just play it by ear," Val beamed.

"Okay, I will get the dishes, since Matt got them last time. Then I will retire to my house. Carly? I'm in the room on the right as you enter. The one on the left is open. We can loot some clothes for you tomorrow," Jen offered.

"Thanks, I appreciate that," Carly nodded. "Do you need any help?"

"No, I got it," Jen assured her.

"Okay, I am going to turn in early then. There are a few things on my mind. Good night guys," Carly stood up and exited the house.

Matt and Val helped Jen carry the dishes into the kitchen, and she rinsed them off and started loading the dishwasher. Val pulled Matt into the living room and they sat on the couch. She clearly had something on her mind, but she was going to wait for Jen to leave.

"Okay, good night guys. I will take the plane up in the morning, report anything I find," Jen offered. "How about some hugs?"

"Sure," Matt replied, standing to hug her. Val was next, and Jen headed out.

"Suggesting we go swimming, really? Trying to get them into bikinis? Val teased.

"Come on, that was not my intention and you know it. I was just trying to think of something we could all do. It's a huge pool, and Carly doesn't play sports," Matt rolled his eyes.

"I know, I just like teasing you. You barely looked at Carly, you are all about Jen, huh? You have never liked blondes," Val laughed.

"And I don't like the name she picked out. It literally just screams blonde. I know she is a badass, but I can't contest your analysis," Matt grinned.

"You have to keep taking it slow with Jen, just like I told you," Val advised.

"I'm not doing anything in regards to Jen, jeez. She is a wealthy, highly acclaimed treasure hunter. A global icon. I'm nobody," Matt scoffed. "My lack of familiarity with her turned her off completely."

"You are one of three men left on the planet. The other one is Sam, and Jack has a snowball's chance in you know where. At some point, Jen will want some attention. That being said, I think Carly was willing to sleep with either of us tonight. She has no boundaries," Val laughed.

"Really?" Matt asked.

"Yes really. She figured out right away you weren't interested, but she was eyeing me. Maybe I should invite her over. How could I do that without making it weird with Jen though? I guess I will wait until tomorrow," Val reflected.

"Okay then, I am over this conversation. Shall we head to bed then?" Matt rolled his eyes.

"I'm glad we are getting more personable people. I agree with what you said, Carly is right down the middle. Medium all the way. I wonder who is next? What genre is left? Anime?" Val wondered.

"Getting an anime character would be weird. I think it might loop back around to comics," Matt offered.

"I can see that. The videos were a great idea, I know you are getting tired of the same questions every week. And after the skepticism from Jen, it sure was nice to get someone that didn't care at all. She is a lot closer to Sam in that regard," Val smiled.

"It definitely makes things easier," Matt admitted.

"Alright, let's head to bed. Tomorrow we will introduce Carly to the morning chores, wait for Jen to get back, and go from there," Val smiled.

The pair stood up from the couch and headed to their rooms. Val had moved into their parents' room, figuring they could each be sharing a bed with someone else at some point. Matt led Buddy into his room, where the Beagle curled up in his own bed. Changing clothes, he flopped down himself and fell asleep.

———

The next morning, Matt and Val were showing Carly around the neighborhood while Jen had taken the plane up to check the weather. Carly had adjusted quickly, more than content to be a part of the team.

"How did you sleep last night Val?" Carly grinned.

"Oh, I slept alright. I take my Benadryl and pass out," Val smiled.

"Well, if you want someone to snuggle with, I'm available," Carly beamed.

"Wow, you called that one," Matt shook his head.

"I would like that Carly, thank you," Val laughed.

"I can snuggle with you too Matt, unless you are holding out for Jen," Carly teased.

"As I said, Jen is a wealthy, renowned treasure hunter, and I'm a nobody. She isn't interested, no matter how much you guys insist otherwise," Matt rolled his eyes.

"You know there are currently six humans here, right? Wealth and status went out the window when the rest of humanity went. I dated a billionaire, but he never cared about the money. Jen doesn't either," Carly encouraged him.

"I would advise continuing to take it slow. I will tell you when the time is right," Val teased.

"It does kind of help to have a sister on your side," Carly laughed.

"Hey guys, are you receiving me?" Sam called on the radio.

Matt walked over to the truck and picked up the transmitter.

"Yeah, go ahead Sam," Matt replied.

"Jen just radioed that a huge storm is heading our way, possibly a tropical storm, and it should get a little stronger yet. She recommended beginning evac procedures. And she asked one of you to pick her up at the airport," Sam finished.

"Copy that Sam! We will begin preparing now. What are you and Jack going to do?" Matt asked.

"We will head to the neighborhood as well. Possibly ride out the storm in the cul-de-sac while you guys take shelter in the safe house. Don't worry about coming to pick us up, we will just walk," Sam signed off.

"Okay guys, did you hear that? A storm is coming in. It will likely be just rain, but we should prepare anyway—it is good practice I guess. We have already blocked the back doors to these houses in the cul-de-sac with sandbags, and we have boards for the windows. Carly? Can you help me with that? And Val? Start the evacuation procedures Jen and I set up. Get the dogs there first. We have the safe house stocked with food and water, a generator in case the power goes out. Get our valuables there as well, in case the worst should happen. You know, the family photos, heirlooms, stuff that wouldn't survive water. But I'm sure we will be fine," Matt assured them.

"Do you really think the boards are necessary for a rainstorm?" Val asked.

"Eh, probably not. We can skip that step. But the danger of flooding is real. Let's get everything off the ground that we can, starting in our house. Rugs, chairs, nightstands, stack it up on the tables and beds. Carly? Can you help me while Val gets the dogs to the safe house?" Matt asked.

"Absolutely. Val? Are you okay?" Carly asked.

"I'm good. I'll take the dogs to the safe house then come back and help you guys. Oh, Matt? You need to head to the airport to pick up Jen, remember?" Val pressed.

"Oh, right. Yeah, I will do that now then," Matt relented.

"I will start preparing the houses for flooding. It would have to be a lot of water to get up this driveway, but you never know," Carly observed. "Get back here safe and sound Matt. And be nice to Jen."

"I'm always nice to Jen," Matt stammered.

"Just go Matt, before you start blushing," Val teased.

Matt sighed and headed for a gas-powered truck, he wasn't sure about how well electric vehicles handled rain, but that was probably silly of him. He knew the automakers weren't that dumb. Climbing in, he started it up and headed off. The sun was still out, so he figured he had time. Driving to the airport, he looked for Jen. Not seeing her, he drove through the gate, literally, and onto the tarmac.

Honking his horn, he looked around the flight line, not seeing her anywhere. It was possible she wasn't back yet. It had taken him around half an hour to get there, which should have been enough time for her to land. He picked up the radio and called her.

"Jen? Are you there? What's your status?" Matt asked.

"Hey! I'm over here in hangar four, can you come get me, or do you need me to come to you?" Jen replied.

"Oh, where is hangar four? I'm on the tarmac, I can head for the flight line," Matt offered.

"It's down at the very end of the flight line, to the left. Can you drive down?" Jen asked.

"On my way," Matt replied.

He steered the truck down the flight line, spotting the hangars. Jen was standing outside of the last one, waving. He honked in acknowledgement and pulled up to her. Hopping in, she greeted him.

"Hey, thanks for coming to get me. It's a big storm, circling, trying to become a hurricane. It looks like it will max out at a Category 1. By the time it hits us, it will be a tropical depression, probably dumping lots and lots of rain. I figure we have about two hours, max. Let's head back," Jen pressed.

"Okay, thank you for warning us. It's uh, really amazing to have you here," Matt managed.

"They are having fun with you about me, aren't they?" Jen sighed.

"What—what makes you say that?" Matt asked.

"It's not fair to either of us. You are a lot more nervous around me, and I know it's because they are teasing you. I'll stop them," Jen growled.

"You are very perceptive," Matt observed.

"And you are smarter than you give yourself credit for. We are all in this together, and I want us to be on the same page. I have had all kinds of suitors, most of them were completely unwanted. I don't look at you that way, Matt. So please don't be nervous around me, it's going to make me feel bad," Jen sighed.

"I don't know what to say, okay? I'm not good at this. Let's just get back to the neighborhood and continue to prepare. Val is taking the dogs to the safe house, and Carly was getting the houses ready to fight flooding. There was a flood here…a long time ago. It got into that house, but we weren't there for it. But I know it's possible," Matt whispered.

"Where are Sam and Jack?" Jen asked.

"They are walking back from the ranch," Matt replied.

"We can split up. Have Val and Carly stay in the safe house with the dogs, Sam and Jack in my house, and you and I in your house. If we need to evac, we can," Jen offered.

"Oh…are you sure?." Matt tried.

"Yes Matt. I'm sure. I know they are having fun with you about it, but I don't have any issues being around you. You are good company. And I trust you," Jen pressed.

"Okay then. That's a good plan," Matt relented. "There were a couple of cars in the street, we should get them into garages. We boarded up the windows of the safehouse, but not the ones in the cul-de-sac. We have sandbags to fight the flooding, is there anything else we should do?"

"There are generators in each house, right? I can't think of anything else," Jen whispered, looking at the sky. They spotted clouds on the horizon, maybe another hour until they would hit them. Pulling into the neighborhood, Sam and Jack were walking towards the cul-de-sac, and Matt stopped to pick them up. He drove on and pulled into a garage that one of them had left open.

"What's the plan?" Jack asked.

"You and Sam are going to stay in that house," Matt pointed. "Get everything off the ground, fight the water if it comes. Val and Carly will be in the safehouse with the dogs, and Jen and I will be in our house. Let's check in with the girls, see where they are at."

Carly came out from Fred's house to greet them. "Hey guys, I got all of these houses prepped. Everything off the ground, sandbags are laid on the front porch in front of the doors. Where do you want me?"

"With Val and the dogs in the safe house. She won't want to be alone," Matt pressed.

"No problem, I'll head there now. It's that big house next to the golf course, right?" Carly asked.

"Right, turn left at the corner, it's on that hill. The windows are boarded from the inside. Put the sandbags at the front door when you get in. You have your radio if you need help," Jen finished.

"Good luck guys, see you later," Carly nodded and jogged away.

"Let's get inside, use your radio if your house has water coming in and you need help," Matt told Jack.

"Roger that. This rain could be a good thing, as long as it doesn't overstay its welcome," Jack grinned, heading off.

CHAPTER 18

THE STORM

Matt and Jen walked into the main house, Carly had indeed stacked all of the chairs on the table, and everything looked as prepared as it could be. They just needed to move the sandbags in front of the last door and they would be ready. It took them a few minutes, and Matt asked if she wanted to join him on the couch.

"Do you have playing cards?" Jen asked, as they sat down.

"Oh, yeah. And dominoes. Maybe a few board games as well. We should check in with Val on the radio, make sure they have everything they need first," Matt offered.

"Good idea," Jen whispered, as she went to the radio, which was resting on the bar.

"*Hey Val? Do you read me?*" Jen transmitted.

"*Hey Jen, I read you. Are you guys all set up there?*" Val asked.

"*Yes, how about you?*" Jen replied.

"*Yes, Carly just got here. We are all good, we see the storm clouds moving in. Going to set the sandbags up on the front porch. Is Matt behaving himself?*" Val asked.

"*Yes Val. You are making us both uncomfortable with your game, if you could ease off a bit, we would appreciate it,*" Jen sighed.

"*Okay, I'm sorry. I need to help Carly—do you have anything else for us?*" Val asked.

"Just make sure the generator is off the ground, you guys put it on top of a table in the garage, right?" Jen pressed.

"Right, it's safe. I will talk to you guys soon," Val signed off.

"I knew she would shoot her shot in there," Matt grinned.

"It's getting a bit tedious, maybe we should just shag and get it over with?" Jen rolled her eyes.

"That's a pretty lame pick-up line," Matt laughed. "What kind of card games do you play? We have some cribbage boards."

"Oh, I would like that. I'll clear the table off, it's not going to flood straight away," Jen smiled.

"I'll get the cards and board," Matt grinned, heading for his parents' room. Opening the closet, he dug around up top and pulled down a container of their playing cards, complete with cribbage boards and dominoes. Heading back to the table, Jen had gotten them some drinks and was sitting down.

"Have you ever ridden out a hurricane before?" Jen asked.

"No, but we have come close a few times. Austin is centrally located, so there isn't as big a danger. But it's not impossible, we have just been lucky. What about you?" Matt asked as he started shuffling the cards.

"I was shipwrecked on an island by a storm once. It was hellish, I was glad when that particular adventure was over," Jen reflected.

"That happened to Carly as well, as she pointed out, this is a much better situation," Matt grinned.

"Oh, no doubt. This house beats a cave any day," Jen laughed, as she took her cards.

"How big was the storm heading our way, really?" Matt whispered.

"It was above average Matt. It wasn't a standard thunderstorm. I don't know where it came from or where it's been, but I saw the eye. It's going to be a lot of rain. We will do our best," Jen whispered back.

"Do you think we should board up the windows? I mean the back porch is essentially all windows," Matt sighed.

"Do you have boards big enough?" Jen asked. "This house has a lot of windows."

"We cut some, yes," Matt relented.

"In that case, I don't think it would hurt to board the back porch," Jen nodded, setting her cards down.

Matt set his cards down as well, and they stood up and headed for the back porch. They had stored the boards there, along with the drills and screws. Jen picked up the first board and held it upright against the wall, while Matt screwed in the bottom first, then the top. He needed a stepstool, so he fetched it out of the kitchen.

The rain was starting to fall as they continued on, boarding up the entire back porch. Heading back to the table, the radio squawked again.

"Hey guys, it's Val. It's starting to rain here, pretty heavily. Just making sure the radio is still working?" Val transmitted.

"All good here, are you receiving?" Sam replied.

"Yes, I hear you Sam. Matt? Jen?" Val asked.

"Hey Val, we are all good here. How are the dogs?" Matt asked.

"Buddy is nervous, as always. Fred doesn't seem to care, he is too old for this I think," Val laughed.

"Okay, thanks for checking in. See you soon," Matt signed off.

"Let's get back to our card game. The rain is really coming down now, but we have time," Matt smiled.

"Worried about your sister?" Jen asked.

"Only a little bit, she has Carly, Buddy, and ice cream. She should be okay," Matt grinned, as he sat down again.

They started playing their game as the rain came down outside. It was heavy, and the wind really started to blow. But it didn't seem out of the ordinary, as they got pretty deep into their game.

"10 points," Jen offered, as she counted her hand and moved.

"14 points," Matt nodded, as he moved. It was close, as Matt picked up his crib, when the radio squawked again.

"Hey Matt, water is starting to come up the driveway to this house," Sam transmitted.

Standing up, the pair looked out the front window. Water was indeed coming up the driveways, as the storm wasn't letting up. It wouldn't be long until it reached the house. The wind was howling now, Matt hoped Val was okay. The rain wouldn't bother her as much as the wind.

"Yeah, this is going to be a problem. We have walled off the doors as best as we can, but do you have any other suggestions on how to keep the water out?' Matt whispered.

"Just mops, fans, and buckets," Jen offered. "We are going to be okay Matt."

"Yeah, I hope so," Matt relented.

"Come sit down on the couch," Jen pressed. She led him over to the couch and they sat down. She surprised him by taking his hand. "It's okay to be scared, there is no one here to tease you about it."

"I uh...thanks Jen. You are really nice to be around," Matt managed.

"I have been through this a lot. Do you have lanterns or flashlights in case we lose power?" Jen asked.

"Both, in my room," Matt pointed. "We should get them out now."

"I'll get them," Jen assured him, standing up and going to collect them. She brought back two lanterns and two flashlights, and sat back down.

"Let's check the driveway again," Matt tried, but he was interrupted by the power going out. "Great. This is what I was so afraid of, losing power and never getting it back."

"It's okay Matt. You planned for this, we have a generator in the garage, I'll go hook it up and turn it on," Jen pressed.

"Hey Matt. We just lost power here, going to turn on the generator you set up. Val? How are you doing?" Sam transmitted.

"We still have power here, the water isn't even on our driveway yet. We are good. I'm scared, but I have Carly, Buddy, booze, and ice cream," Val replied.

"See? They are okay, Matt. I will be right back," Jen assured him, picking up a flashlight. She walked out into the garage, leaving Matt to his worries. He was really worried about fixing the electricity grid, and repelling the floodwaters. The lights came back on, and Jen walked back in.

"Matt! The water is coming onto the front porch, but the power is back on," Jen shouted to him.

"Okay, yes I can see that," Matt replied. "Thanks for handling that."

Matt stood up and walked over to her, looking out at the front porch. It was filled with water, and it wouldn't be long until the level reached the doorway. He hoped the sandbags would work—he had never seen them in action before. Jen surprised him by offering him a hug.

"It's okay Matt. It's okay to be nervous. We will handle it, just relax," Jen whispered.

"Thanks Jen, I might have already said this, but it's really nice to have you here," Matt whispered back.

"I'm glad to be here with you guys," Jen assured him. "The garage though, it's going to get hit. There isn't anything on the ground, but the wood cabinets are going to be ruined. Water was already seeping in—we didn't have enough sandbags."

"It's okay. As long as the generator is off the ground, we will be alright," Matt shrugged.

They looked outside again, the wind was still howling, and the downpour continued. It would likely be hours until the storm passed. But the sandbags appeared to be holding, as no water was leaking through the front door. Walking back to check the back porch, everything was okay there too.

"Come on, let's resume our game. We don't have anything pressing yet," Jen offered.

"Okay," Matt relented.

They sat back down at the table, and Jen shuffled the cards. Dealing their hands, Matt started to pick his cards up when they were interrupted by a thunderous crash. They lost electricity again, and the wind was howling louder than ever. Matt's heart was pounding as he tried to figure out what was happening. He could barely breathe. Jen had also been scared; she recovered a bit faster.

"Oh my God, what was that?" Matt gasped.

"I think—I think a tree came down. Are you okay? Just focus on breathing for now," Jen managed.

They collected themselves and walked into Val's room. It opened up into a back patio, which was essentially gone. The roof had caved in, and their prized avocado tree was falling through. Water was coming into the room from the rain.

"It's a lost cause Matt! We have to abandon the house, I'm sorry!" Jen shouted as the wind was howling. "We need help! I'll radio Sam!"

Jen made her way in the dark towards the radio, picking up the transmitter.

"Sam? Can you read me?" Jen transmitted.

"Go ahead Jen," Sam replied.

"Go to channel 2," Jen pressed.

She changed the channel—she didn't want Val to hear this yet. *"Are you there?"* she asked.

"Yes, what's your status?" Sam asked.

"A tree just came down on the back porch, the roof is caved in, and water is coming in. We have to abandon this place, can you come help us?" Jen asked.

"On my way," Sam signed off.

Jen walked over to light the lantern, and they both waited for Sam. He waded through the water and up over the sandbags as they opened the door for him.

"How bad is it?" Sam asked.

"It's bad, it knocked the power out, probably for good. Water is coming in, I…I don't think we can save the house," Matt sighed.

"I will do what I can. There is a radio in the Pom's house, sandbags, everything you need to survive. Did Val get all the family heirlooms out of here?" Sam asked.

"Yes, all that's left is the furniture, but it's not essential. We will evacuate to the Pom's house, hopefully the water hasn't come in. Will probably need to start the generator though," Matt relented.

"Take some fresh socks and shoes, if you don't already have some there. Put your raincoats on and get going. I will go get Jack to help me," Sam growled, turning back towards the Scotty's house.

Matt nodded and the pair collected some supplies, including their cribbage board and dominoes, the lantern and flashlights, and finally, clothing. Putting their raincoats on, they waded out into the water. It was past their ankles, as they made their way towards the Pom's house. Walking in, Matt nearly fell on the slippery tile, water had seeped in.

"I've got you," Jen pressed, as she grabbed his arm, helping him catch his balance.

"Thanks," Matt managed. "Let's regroup here, check the status of the house. Can you go turn the generator on? I will call Val on the radio."

"Yes, I'll be right back," Jen assured him.

Matt nodded and walked into the living room where the radio was. Water was seeping in—they needed to address that immediately. But first he needed to tell Val he was okay.

"Hey Val, come in. Do you read me?" Matt transmitted.

"Yes Matt. Is everything okay?" Val whispered.

"Jen and I had to evacuate to the Pom's house. We are all okay, but the avocado tree fell on top of the back porch, caving the roof in. Sam and Jack are trying to mitigate the damage now, but I don't know if they are going to be able to save the house. Water was pouring in from the rain. How are you guys?" Matt sighed.

"I am about to start drinking. We still have power here, the dogs are very nervous. I'm glad you are okay Matt," Val managed. *"Here is Carly."*

"Matt? I will take care of your sister, okay? You guys stay safe over there. Hopefully the storm will pass within the hour," Carly pressed.

"Thanks Carly. Make sure she doesn't drink too much," Matt signed off.

The electricity came on as Matt stood up to address the water situation. It was seeping through the front door, as Jen came back in from the garage through the side door.

"The garage is full of water, corner to corner. Where are the mops? We need to get this water out of here," Jen pressed.

"They are in that closet," Matt pointed.

"Hey, are you okay?" Jen came over and hugged him. "I'm sorry about your house. Did you check on your sister?"

"Yeah, they are still okay there. Val is going to start drinking, she is probably really scared. I hope Carly can help her through this as well as you are helping me. Thanks for your support, Jen," Matt managed.

"It went from a scary situation to a really bad situation fairly quickly. I honestly thought we would be okay, then a tree fell on us. That's a lot.

Now if you are ready, let's mop up this water and reinforce the sandbags," Jen pressed, breaking the hug.

"Yeah, okay. This house doesn't have a back porch as extensive as ours, so we can concentrate on the front. Let's start with the sandbags. I think they had fallen off the front step, that's why water is coming in. If we can fix it, we can block the water again," Matt offered.

They walked to the front door and were surprised to find Jack bringing over a pair of sandbags, thrown over his shoulders. He waded up to them and dumped the bags at their feet.

"These aren't doing anything in your old place. Figured you could use them here," Jack offered.

"Yeah, thanks Jack," Matt responded.

"I have two more trips to make, be right back," Jack smiled, wading back.

"He is really strong," Jen whispered.

"Yeah, let's stack these up a little better," Matt grinned. They stacked the sandbags on top of each other, creating a new wall to block the water. Jack brought over two more sandbags, and they told him that was enough. He nodded and headed back. Closing the door, they got the mops out and started clearing the floor tile of water.

As they were finally finishing, the storm was beginning to pass. The wind had died down a lot, it was just steady rain now. The water wasn't receding just yet, but Matt and Jen were finally able to sit down on the barstools and rest. It was only then that they realized how dirty they were.

"Um, would you like to shower? I think we have some of the old owner's clothes here, they should fit you until you can get back to your own house," Matt offered.

"That's kind of you. I will clean up a little bit, thank you," Jen relented, standing up. "Hey Matt? You did great. Your plan was a good one. It's not your fault a tree went down, no amount of planning could have prevented that."

Matt nodded and they parted ways, searching for some clean clothes. Matt and Val had put clothes for them each in every house, so he found some quickly. Hopping into the shower, he rinsed himself off and got out, getting dressed. Walking back into the living room, Jen was still in her room, so he broke out some snacks and water.

She finally came back in, wearing some sweat pants and a matching sweatshirt. "There wasn't much in there for me, but this will do until I can get back, as you said. Hopefully another tree doesn't fall on us," Jen lamented.

"That was terrifying, I admit," Matt sighed.

"Oh, completely. I was scared Matt. I was. There is no shame in it," Jen offered.

"Thanks for saying that, you don't seem to scare easily," Matt managed.

"Still, I can be. And I was," Jen grinned. "The storm is finally passing. I think the danger is over. Should we continue our game?"

"Yes, I would like that," Matt smiled, as she sat down.

CHAPTER 19

THE WRECKAGE

Hours had passed, and the water was finally receding from their driveways. The storm was completely gone, and Sam was out exploring the wreckage. He had checked each house in the cul-de-sac, and came back to issue a report.

"All of the houses, except for Jen's, had water come in. But it's not serious, they will still be habitable. I got the power turned on in them. I am going to get the power on in each house we put a generator in, which should be about 30. Then I will head to check on Val and Carly, who didn't lose power.

As for your house, the back room next to the porch is ruined, it's a complete loss. It looks like it was an add-on, so we can seal it off, save the rest of the house. Water came into Val's room, but we managed to keep most of it out. Wall off that back room, and it will be fine. Do you need anything here?" Sam asked.

"Jen could use some of her stuff from her house, other than that, we are okay," Matt replied.

"What do you need?" Sam asked.

"Just some pairs of jeans, some shirts, new socks and shoes. Thanks Sam," Jen replied.

"You are welcome. I will be back with your stuff soon. Then back to work," Sam shrugged.

Sam waded back towards Jen's house as they closed the door. "Nothing bothers that guy," Jen observed.

"Nope. He has seen everything," Matt shrugged. "Thanks for sticking it out with me, I think we had it worse than everyone."

"We are a team Matt. Come on, let's talk to Val and Carly on the radio," Jen waved.

They walked back inside and Jen called the safehouse. It was Carly that answered.

"Hey guys. Everything is good here, the storm is passing. How are things there?" Carly asked.

"We are good. Sam is making some rounds, he will check on you two soon. How are things over there? How is Val?" Jen asked.

"She is resting in bed, she got pretty scared with the wind, and you having to abandon the house. I stayed with her until the storm passed. Should we try to link up?" Carly asked.

"Sam will come to you, make sure the road is passable. He doesn't seem fazed by anything," Jen replied.

"And Jack?" Carly asked.

"I don't know what he is doing," Jen admitted.

"Are you sure that's okay?" Carly pressed.

"No, I will try to reach Sam," Jen whispered.

Jen stopped transmitting and looked at Matt nervously. "Do we have any weapons here?" she asked.

"No, but I don't think Jack is going to do anything. You guys are way too suspicious of that guy," Matt scoffed.

Suddenly, Jack leapt at them through a window, shattering the glass and slashing Matt's arm. He fell down, yelling in pain. Jen tried to hit him, but he punched her in the face, knocking her out.

"Finally get to rid myself of you two," Jack grinned. "The storm threw Sam's senses off—he doesn't even know where I am."

"Jack! Why are you doing this? What do you hope to accomplish?" Matt demanded.

"Satiating my primal urges, for one. And I am tired of being looked down on," Jack growled.

Matt backed away from him on the ground, as Jack stalked him. "You are an idiot, Jack! I've never looked down on you! You are throwing your life away! What's your endgame, huh? Even if you kill us, Sam will kill you. How does that help you?"

"You are right Matt. This isn't personal, I actually like you. But the fire told me if I kill the Chosen Ones, I can get off this planet. I have been biding my time, looking for an opening. This storm provided it. Sam is away, and like I said, the storm has thrown his senses off, I can make my escape after. I only need an hour or so to get in front of him and stay there. Then it becomes a battle of wills. I don't believe anything you guys have said about him. He might be a good tracker, but I'm the better killer...nnghh.." Jack trailed off. Looking down, blood was coming out of his chest. Sam retracted his claws and let Jack's dying body fall to the ground, not offering any words.

They watched Jack die, and Sam helped Matt to his feet. "You okay kid?" he asked.

"Yeah, he cut my arm, but I'm good. Thanks Sam," Matt managed.

"Just doing my job. I will get rid of the body. You take care of the girl," Sam shrugged.

Matt looked down at Jack, disappointed. "I liked him, I never wronged him in any way," he sighed.

"You liked the idea of him. But you didn't know him. I did. He was plotting against us from the moment he cut my throat. I never took my eyes off him. He was a murderer, and proud of it. And now, he has paid the price. Go on kid, get out of here. Take the girl to one of the rooms, I'll get rid of the body," Sam shrugged.

Matt sighed and picked Jen up, carrying her to the bedroom. Laying her down, she had a bruise on her face, so he went to get a washcloth. Gently applying it to her cheek, she stirred, raising her hand and grabbing his.

"Oh...that hurts. What happened? Are we safe?" Jen whispered.

"Yes, Sam saved us. I'm sorry I put you in danger," Matt sighed.

"It's not your fault Matt," Jen managed. "Is he dead?"

"Yes, Sam killed him. He is gone," Matt nodded.

"Matt? You are bleeding. Your arm," Jen pointed, still wincing in pain.

Matt hadn't even felt the cut, as he looked to see. Blood was streaming down his arm—Jack had cut him deeper than he had thought. He was serious about trying to kill them. "I don't…I don't know how to treat it. Can you help me?" Matt whispered.

"My head is still spinning—I might have a concussion. We need help again. Can you radio Carly?" Jen managed.

"Yeah, I will bring the radio back here," Matt sighed. Standing up, he went to fetch the radio. Bringing it back and sitting on the bed, he picked up the transmitter.

"Carly? Are you there?" Matt asked.

"Yes Matt. Is everything okay?" Carly asked.

"You were right Carly. You were right," Matt sighed. *"We need help, can you collect Val and drive the truck here? We are in the Pom's house."*

"We are on our way Matt," Carly signed off.

Jen extended her hand again, as Matt took it. "We survived Matt. Focus on that," she whispered.

"Only because of Sam," Matt sighed.

"You are a good person, and you see the good in people. I saw Jack and I saw a murderer, a monster in the dark, a huge threat. I never wanted to be around him, no matter what. I'm glad Sam picked up on that," Jen sighed.

"I'm sorry again for putting you in danger," Matt said quietly.

"I don't blame you Matt. Could you help me to the sink? I need to throw up," Jen managed.

Matt picked her up and carried her to the bathroom, as she leaned over it. He tried to give her some privacy but she grabbed his hand. He stayed as she vomited. She gave him a nod as he picked her up and carried her back to the bed. She took his hand again and closed her eyes.

"Is it too soon for laughs?" Jen whispered.

"I would say yes, since I'm still bleeding," Matt grinned.

"Fair enough. Just rest with me here until our help arrives," Jen closed her eyes.

Matt sat there next to her, holding her hand, trying to figure out what went wrong with Jack. He literally gained nothing from trying to kill them.

He couldn't get off the planet, he couldn't escape Sam, he couldn't do anything. Thinking about the conversation on the beach, and what Jack said, he didn't kill people that he didn't need to. Sam called him out right there, from that moment on, he never took his eyes off Jack. He placated his desire to play hide and seek, but he made sure Jack didn't get near the neighborhood. And he found him, every time.

"He was way out of his league," Matt whispered to himself.

"Talking about Jack?" Jen whispered.

"Yeah. He was no match for Sam. He never even heard him come up from behind, I barely saw him. It was just the claws through his back, and it was over," Matt reflected.

"I was no help, he caught me by complete surprise. I'm sorry about that," Jen sighed.

"It's okay. It's my fault, not yours. I let him in," Matt sighed.

"I can tell it's going to be a battle to get you to stop blaming yourself," Jen whispered.

They heard the truck honking outside, as Carly and Val pulled up. The water was still in the street, having not receded. Matt stood up and went to greet them. Val came in first, jumping into Matt's arms.

"Oh my God! Are you alright?? Did Jack do something stupid??" Val exclaimed.

"Yeah. We won't be seeing him anymore. He thought the storm had interfered with Sam's senses. He was wrong," Matt sighed.

"That cut looks deep. Do you need me to stitch it up?" Carly offered.

"I do, yes. Jen has been concussed—she needs an ice pack. And I need stitches. Can you go get the first aid kit out of our house? Matt asked.

"I will be right back. Val? Stay here with your brother and Jen," Carly pressed.

Val nodded and they walked into the bedroom to join Jen while Carly waded back through the water again. Matt sat down, while Val sat next to Jen and took her hand.

"Oh, hey. I think you are stealing Matt's spot," Jen whispered.

"I will relinquish it then," Val shook her head with a smile and gave way. Matt took Jen's hand again and they waited for Carly to come back.

She finally got there, handing an ice pack to Jen, who accepted it. Then she examined Matt's wound.

"You are bleeding everywhere. We should move to the bathroom. I need to clean this, then stitch it up. Want morphine?" Carly whispered.

"Yes please. I'm nowhere near as strong as you or Jen. I couldn't do anything against Jack," Matt sighed.

"Don't say that. Come on, let's go," Carly picked up the kit and led him into the bathroom. Sitting down on the edge of the tub, he let Carly look at his wound.

"I need to clean it first," Carly whispered. She picked up a hand towel and dampened it, then wiped the blood off his arm.

"How is Val?" Matt whispered.

"She is having a rough day. She downed some glasses of alcohol, ate a bunch of ice cream, now she is laying in there, likely crying on Jen's shoulder trying to mask it. I will take care of her for the next few days, while you and Jen take it easy," Carly whispered back.

Carly gave Matt a shot of morphine in the opposite thigh, and gave him a few minutes. Then she applied the antiseptic, causing Matt to hiss in pain. He squeezed her hand, as the pain sharpened for a moment, then finally stopped altogether as the morphine was kicking in. She then proceeded to stitch up his arm. He didn't ask her if she knew what she was doing, knowing that she did. He winced in pain as she slowly stitched him up.

"Jack wasn't your fault. Sam knew he would make a move, he set a trap, he killed him. It's over," Carly assured him.

"How do you know that?" Matt asked.

"He told me. I think he was testing me—he is very efficient at his job. I literally got on my knees and asked him for a chance, I know he is still watching me though. I promise Matt, I'm on your side," Carly pressed, as she continued to stitch him up.

"I know Carly. If you weren't, Sam would have never let you come here. As you said, he knows what he is doing," Matt relented.

"Val feels bad for teasing you about Jen. But we couldn't help but notice the chemistry building in there," Carly grinned.

"She helped me through the storm, and she was mad at you guys for teasing me. She is very perceptive. Still, I feel like I put her in danger," Matt sighed.

"And you are wrong. You aren't responsible for Jen, and you aren't responsible for Jack's choices. Val and I promise to stay out of your way in regards to her from now on," Carly assured him.

"How are things going between you and Val?" Matt grinned.

"You are having a rough day, are you sure you want to know?" Carly beamed.

"No, I'm not sure. Just tell me she is okay," Matt relented.

"She will be okay," Carly nodded. "I will admit though, ever since you mentioned that swimming pool, I cannot get the image of Jen in a bikini out of my head. You are a real rogue for suggesting that."

"Oh, come on. I was just thinking of things for us to do together, since you don't play sports," Matt scoffed.

"I know, but still. I think your days of golf are over for a bit. I'm done with the stitches. I'm going to bandage it up now. How are you feeling?" Carly smiled.

"Oh, I stopped feeling the needle a while ago. That morphine really works," Matt stammered. "Thank you for helping me."

"You're welcome. Come on, let's get you back in bed. You need to take it easy," Carly beamed, finishing up with the bandage.

She helped Matt stand up, the morphine was having an obvious effect. They walked into the bedroom and Val gave way again, letting him lie down next to Jen.

"He got a dose of morphine, and it looks to be knocking him out. Why don't you two rest, while we try to assess what work needs to be done? We should have brought the dogs, I guess we can go get them. Come on Val," Carly waved her out.

Val gave them both a kiss on the forehead and left with Carly, closing the door and turning off the light.

"Well Matt," Jen whispered, taking his hand.

"Yeah?" Matt whispered back.

"I guess you got me in bed. Didn't take as long as you thought, huh?" Jen teased.

"Oh jeez. This is never what I envisioned, I hope you know," Matt rolled his eyes.

"I do know that. Like I said, you are a good person. Those two have had one thing on their mind since we were eating dinner last night. But you have been a breath of fresh air. Let's just rest, as they said," Jen whispered.

"Alright," Matt relented. He was really feeling the effects of the morphine, and couldn't even form words, as he passed out.

CHAPTER 20

RECOVERY

Matt stirred, waking up in the dark. It was night outside, he had no idea what time it was. Jen felt his movement and woke up herself.

"Hey, how are you feeling?" Jen whispered.

"I'm alright. My arm is in pain, but other than that, I'm good. How are you?" Matt asked.

"My cheek hurts, and I still can't focus too well. Will you get me some water?" Jen asked.

"Sure thing," Matt replied, standing up.

He slowly opened the door and walked into the living room. Sam was sitting on the couch, resting, or so Matt thought.

"Hey kid. How ya feeling?" Sam asked.

"I'm good, my arm hurts, but I'll be okay. Jen has a concussion, and she is requesting some water. Do you know what time it is?" Matt whispered.

"It's 2am. The storm is gone, the water is draining. I helped it out a bit on that front. It should be completely gone by the morning," Sam shrugged.

"And Jack?" Matt sighed.

"Laying in the country club for now. I will get rid of the body permanently when the water drains," Sam shrugged again.

"It was what he said on the beach right? He doesn't kill people that he doesn't *need* to. You never believed him," Matt observed.

"Right. You saved his life later, but he was on borrowed time. He vastly overestimated himself, I let him think that using the water masked his scent, but it didn't. I might have let him get a little too close, but it worked out. He was feeling himself as he stalked you, never even saw me coming. I guess that surgical shine job was a poor investment," Sam observed.

"Nice eulogy," Matt grinned.

"I thought so," Sam allowed himself to smile as well.

"I'm heading back to bed, thanks for being the best Sam," Matt shook his head with a smile.

"No problem kid," Sam finished.

Matt walked back into the bedroom with Jen's water, he had remembered to grab a straw, figuring it would be hard for her to sip anything. Handing it to her, she thanked him.

"Oh, thank you for bringing a straw, that is very thoughtful of you," Jen whispered.

"I figured you wouldn't be able to sip it. How is your cheek?" Matt asked.

"It's still throbbing. I need some aspirin. I'm sorry, do you mind? I should have asked for that sooner," Jen lamented.

"No problem, there is some in the bathroom," Matt grinned. He walked into the bathroom and collected some aspirin, opening it and pouring some tablets into Jen's hand. She took two and drank the water.

"Lie back down here with me," Jen set her hand on the bed.

Matt complied, lying down and taking her hand. "We don't have to talk... I know your mouth is sore. Let's just try to sleep again, it's two in the morning," he whispered.

"Are you tired?" Jen asked.

"No, not at all, honestly," Matt admitted.

"I'm not either. So, let's talk about some things, okay?" Jen whispered.

"Sure," Matt relented.

"If you could be anywhere right now, on this empty planet, see anything, where would you be?" Jen asked.

"I think the only answer is right here next to you," Matt grinned.

"Oh God," Jen rolled her eyes and smiled.

"Did I get that one right?" Matt smiled.

"Okay. Let's talk then. Believe it or not, despite all of your unwarranted flattery, as I like to call it, there is something that I am not good at," Jen whispered.

"What's that?" Matt asked.

"This. I'm not good at this right here. I can dedicate myself to helping someone, but I have never dedicated myself to *being* with anyone. I just don't have the time," Jen whispered. "But I like this feeling, it's nice to be next to you right now."

"It's not like I am good at it either. I've been single forever now, because I don't know how to get past the first conversation," Matt whispered back.

"Our first few conversations were rough, and it was my fault. We are past that now. And I have plenty of time on my hands. I think we should stop making excuses and just commit to taking things slowly. Today was not a good first date! But we can try again. Properly. For now, we go slowly. Let me take the lead. I will keep those two off you." Jen offered.

"For a bruised cheek you seem to be saying quite a bit. Are you nervous?" Matt teased.

"A little bit. As I said, it's been nice to be here with you, taking care of each other after we were nearly killed. A lot of my relationships start this way. But…. they also don't make it past the next morning, nine out of ten times. So, we go slow. One day at a time," Jen grinned.

"Okay. We go slow," Matt whispered. "Let's try to sleep again."

"Okay," Jen nodded.

———

The sun was coming up, and Matt stirred again. Sitting up, he looked at Jen, who was sleeping. She felt his movement though and took his hand.

"Good morning," Jen whispered.

"Morning," Matt replied.

"Go see what it looks like out there, while I get a bath going. You can join me if you want," Jen grinned.

"I thought you were taking things slowly?" Matt whispered.

"We are. But we both need a bath, again. Might as well save water," Jen tried.

"I will say nothing," Matt shook his head. "Do you want a drink or anything?"

"Just some juice is fine," Jen whispered.

"Okay, be right back," Matt nodded.

Matt walked into the living room to find Sam, Val, and Carly quietly eating breakfast. Val got up immediately and came to hug him on his right side, since his left arm was out of action.

"How are you feeling?" Val said with concern.

"My arm is sore. Jen is sore as well. What is our status here?" Matt sighed.

"We have a lot of work to do, but Val insisted on waiting for you two to wake up. Do you need anything?" Carly asked.

"Just some juice, two glasses please," Matt sighed.

Val handed him his already prepared glass of apple juice, and went to prepare another. Matt drank his and took the new glass.

"We really can't help you—she is concussed, my arm is out of action. Good luck out there. Sam? Anything I need to know?" Matt asked.

"We got it, kid. Go rest, you have done enough," Sam offered.

"Okay, thanks," Matt relented, as Val shooed him back into the bedroom.

Walking in, he heard the bath going, and decided not to walk in on Jen. Instead, he gave it a few minutes then knocked on the door.

"Jen? Are you...decent?" Matt asked.

"Yes Matt. Come in," Jen replied.

He slowly opened the door, not sure if it was really okay. He peeked in, Jen was standing over the bath, wearing her tank-top and shorts. She looked his way and accepted the glass of juice.

"Get as undressed as you want to, and get in. I will sit on top of you," Jen offered.

"Oh um, sure. Can you...help me get my shirt off?" Matt stammered.

"Of course," Jen nodded, as Matt tried to raise his arm but failed.

"I can't...I can't yet. I'm sorry," Matt gasped in pain.

"It's okay. How much do you value this shirt?" Jen asked.

"Oh um, not at all. I don't even know where it came from," Matt shrugged. "Why do you ask…oh.."

Jen proceeded to tear his shirt right off, surprising him. She asked about his pants and he didn't want them either, but was able to slide them off. Stepping into the bath, the water was hot as he sat down in it. Jen dimmed the lights, then climbed in after him, and slowly sat on his lap, shifting her weight to avoid his left arm.

"Have you…done this before?" Matt whispered.

"Don't ask questions like that," Jen grinned. "Just be still, hold me in your arms."

"Okay," Matt relented, as he wrapped his right arm around her. He closed his eyes and they just lay there in warm bliss.

Val came into the bedroom, calling for them. "Matt, Jen? Um, where are you guys?"

"In here! Don't come in, what is it?" Jen asked, annoyed.

"Oh…um? Is everything okay? What is going on?" Val asked, confused.

"If you insist on being a nosy neighbor, we are taking a bath together. Did you need something?" Jen demanded.

"Oh! I'm sorry, I just brought you breakfast, I will leave it here on the bed. Bye!" Val exclaimed, scurrying away.

Matt and Jen could only laugh, as they returned to their bliss. Half an hour went by, and she finally said something. "I like this. I like the quiet. I think…if we are going to do this…we should do it quietly to start. Neither of us are good at talking, so, why risk it? Will you wash my hair?"

"Oh…you finished that so oddly. But sure, I noticed you brought the cup with you," Matt whispered, picking it up. Filling the cup, he slowly rinsed her hair. She reached forward and grabbed the shampoo, handing it to him. He ran his hands through her hair, having to use a lot more shampoo than he was accustomed to.

"Just like that Matt. Run your hands through my hair," Jen whispered.

He continued, growing more comfortable with it. Finally, he used the cup to rinse it out again. Finishing up, he set the cup down and wrapped his arm around her again.

"Let's get out Matt. I will go first. Don't come out until I say, okay?" Jen whispered.

"Okay," Matt nodded. "What are we going to do about those nosy neighbors?"

"Oh, I will handle them. Don't worry. Like I said, I will take the lead Matt," Jen grinned, as she stood up and got out of the bath. It was impossible for Matt to not look at her amazing legs, but he remained silent as she dried off and exited the bathroom.

Some time passed and she called to him, telling him it was okay to get out. Matt rose and exited the tub, draining it. Pulling his pants on after drying off, he entered the bedroom, where Jen was waiting with the breakfast tray.

"Let's go into the living room and eat," Jen offered.

"Okay. Um? Can you help me with a shirt?" Matt asked.

"After breakfast," Jen grinned.

"Okay," Matt shrugged.

They entered the living room, finding it empty. Sitting down at the table, Val had made them pancakes and eggs. Jen got them some more juice as they dug in.

"How is your head?" Matt asked.

"My cheek is still sore, and I feel like I have a minor concussion. But we will use that excuse to get out of doing chores," Jen replied. "Your arm?"

"It hurts. I don't need it as an excuse, it's a legit injury," Matt grinned.

"Look outside, the water level has completely receded. We can head back to your house after breakfast," Jen offered.

"Sure," Matt shrugged.

"Did you want to do something else?" Jen asked.

"No. I want to see the damage to our house. Whether or not it's salvageable. I know there is a lot of work to do," Matt relented.

"And we won't be doing it. It's going to be up to Sam and the girls. I will be ready before you, but I still need at least a day," Jen pressed.

They finished up their meal and headed over to Matt's house. Jen surprised him again when she took his arm, but he didn't object. They just needed to feel each other out. Entering the house, Buddy and Fred came up to greet them.

"Oh, hey guys!" Val shouted from her room. "In here!"

They walked into her room, and found the three of them cleaning up the back room, or what was left of it. The avocado tree was gone, Matt was kind of confused about that.

"What happened to the tree?" Matt stammered.

"Sam chopped it up and we got it out of here. There is a hole in the wall, as the tree knocked the doors down. But we think it can all be fixed. How was your bath?" Val beamed.

"It was really nice," Matt admitted.

"I bet," Val laughed.

"Can we talk to you two ladies in the living room for a minute? You don't mind, right Sam?" Jen asked.

"Go ahead," Sam shrugged.

The four of them walked into the living room, sitting down. "How are you two doing?" Jen asked.

"We are okay. You?" Val asked.

"I think it's safe to say yesterday was our worst day since what you call The Calamity," Jen whispered.

"Oh, definitely. It absolutely was," Val nodded. "I went through a lot of ice cream and booze."

"Carly? How do you think Val is holding up?" Jen asked.

"I think she is okay, as she says. Yesterday was, as you said, really rough. But we got through it," Carly grinned, taking Val's arm.

"Yes, so did we. And rest assured, it was harder for us," Jen pressed, taking Matt's arm. "First a tree fell on us, then Jack tried to kill us. Carly, you saw it in Jack too. What do you think happened?"

"He saw an opening, he took it. I'm not like him, I never enjoyed killing. I look back at it with a lot of regret. Jack didn't. I'm glad you two survived, how did Sam get back so fast?" Carly asked.

"He never left. He created an illusion of an opening for Jack, and Jack fell for it. He was a talented killer, but as I told him, Sam is on another level. Plus, he has enhanced senses. It wasn't even a fight, Sam walked up behind him and ran his claws right through him," Matt reflected.

"Can we please talk about anything else?" Val sighed.

"Sure. I know you two have been having fun with Matt about me, and I would like for you to stop. It's not fair, or even nice. Neither of us are good at being with another person, and you are making it harder. So, from now on, any teasing will result in chores for both of you. While we slack off," Jen pressed.

"That's fair. I'm sorry for that. I didn't think we would encounter a near-death situation, much less two. And I learned being with someone can really help you through it," Val sighed, looking at Carly.

"I have been through plenty of near-death situations, as I said, I didn't survive some of them. And I can confirm, a partner helps immensely. We are happy for the two of you," Carly smiled.

"Can we please talk about anything else?" Matt sighed.

"I need to change your bandage. Or can you take care of it, Jen?" Carly grinned.

"I could, but I don't think I should try to focus that much. If you could handle it please Carly?" Jen whispered.

"That's fair, you are concussed, after all. Your bruise looks pretty bad," Carly relented.

"Matt has been a true gentleman and not commented on it, but it feels awful," Jen sighed.

Carly stood up and moved next to Matt, unwrapping the bandage. She stopped herself, not wanting to get blood on the furniture. "Should we move to the bathroom? This is a bloody bandage," she offered.

"Oh, right. Sure," Matt relented, standing up. They left Val and Jen, moving into the bathroom. Matt sat on the tub again while Carly fetched the first aid kit. She unwrapped the bandage and examined the wound.

"The stitches are holding, you have been taking it easy, which is good. How are you feeling? I won't betray you, you can talk to me," Carly whispered.

"I'm disappointed in myself for trusting Jack. All of you saw right through him, he said the fire told him if he killed us, he could get off this planet. He has been lying to us since his first second down here. I never suspected it, and I put Jen and Val in danger," Matt sighed.

"How much experience do you have in situations like this?" Carly whispered, as she wrapped a new bandage around his arm.

"Oh, none whatsoever," Matt admitted.

"What did you do for a living before The Calamity?" Carly asked.

"I worked for the government, it was an easy desk job," Matt whispered.

"So, you have no experience, no background in this kind of situation. That's not your fault Matt. Sam apparently is heavily experienced, he was pretty tough on me at the ranch. I felt like he was staring into my soul at one point. But he cleared me. He never cleared Jack. Don't beat yourself up over it. Come on, let's go back," Carly smiled, as she finished up his bandage and helped him stand.

"Thanks Carly, I appreciate it," Matt relented.

"Val said you didn't like the name I chose. Is it that bad?" Carly grinned.

"It's pretty terrible," Matt smiled.

"I can pick a different name, it's no big deal," Carly shrugged.

"It's up to you and Val. How are things going there?" Matt asked.

"We are sleeping together. But you knew that," Carly teased.

"Yeah, I figured you were on an accelerated timetable, especially after Jack," Matt admitted. "Let's check in with Sam. First I want to try to get a tank top on though."

They walked into the bedroom, and Matt found a tank top in the back of the closet. Pulling it on slowly, he winced as he had to lift his arm. Finally, they walked into the back room, where Sam was assessing the damage. Matt asked for an update.

"We need to fix the electricity. Your idea to use generators was smart, and I went house to house making sure the generators were on or the power was working. It looks like two blocks lost power, everything else is up and running. We can fix up the back room after. How is Jen?" Sam asked.

"She has a mild concussion—she probably needs a day. She feels bad about it, but...." Matt tried.

"No reason to. I'll take Carly, we will try to locate the line that is down, go from there. You, Jen, and Val stay here with the dogs. Where is Gracie?" Sam asked.

"Back at the safehouse," Carly replied.

"Okay. How is your arm?" Sam asked.

"It's sore. I can't lift very well. It's going to be a long recovery," Matt sighed.

"You did good kid. You distracted him long enough for me to get behind him. We will take care of the electricity and bury Jack somewhere. A ditch feels right," Sam grinned.

"I can't argue with that. Be safe out there. Please bring Carly back alive," Matt sighed.

"No problem," Sam shrugged. "Let's go girl."

"Are you always this friendly?" Carly deadpanned.

"Ask Jack," Sam growled, as they headed out the hole in the back wall.

"I'll be fine Matt," Carly assured him, as she followed Sam.

CHAPTER 21

GETTING CLOSER

Val was sitting in the loveseat with Buddy, and Jen was laying on top of Matt on the couch. It was a new position for them both, and neither had any complaints. Fred was sitting on the ground beside them, as Jen petted him. The lights were off, to help Jen.

"I'm going to start making lunch," Val whispered. "They should be back soon—it's been over an hour."

"I don't even know what time it is," Matt admitted.

"It's daytime," Jen waved her hand in the air.

"Beauty *and* brains, you are doing well Matt," Val laughed as she stood up with Buddy and moved into the kitchen.

"Try to keep power consumption at a minimum. Maybe just sandwiches today," Matt rolled his eyes. "I guess time has never been a big deal to you on your adventures."

"No, never. I mean, sure I was aware of where the sun was at, and how close nightfall was, but the exact time never really mattered. Knowing the time is a luxury, it's not necessary. Humanity lived a long time without using clocks," Jen whispered.

"I guess I take it for granted," Matt reflected.

"Let's just rest while she makes lunch. This is nice, isn't it?" Jen whispered.

"Yes, it's very nice," Matt admitted.

"If you were wondering, I have not done this before," Jen grinned.

"I was wondering, but I wasn't going to ask this time," Matt smiled.

"Quick learner," Jen teased.

"Never shared body heat with anyone in a freezing cave?" Matt offered.

"Not the same at all. I'm not counting it," Jen grinned.

"Okay," Matt whispered. He didn't want to talk too much, figuring it was best to just stay quiet. His curiosity wasn't strong enough to risk spoiling their comfort.

"You still aren't fully comfortable with this, are you?" Jen whispered.

"Your perception is remarkable," Matt admitted.

"I told you I would take the lead, but we will talk more tonight when we are alone," Jen assured him.

Val came in with some sandwiches and sat down in the chair next to them. "I just made some PB & J, I realize Jen is probably still unable to chew solid foods, but these should be easy enough. Should I radio Sam and Carly?"

"Nah, Sam is fine. And if Carly needs a break, she can come back. Honestly, there is probably much more work to do than they let on, Sam just didn't want to make us feel bad," Matt shrugged, as he accepted a sandwich.

"Carly told me your cut is more serious than you are letting on, so I guess it's contagious," Val grinned.

"Well, my bruised cheek and mild concussion are exactly what they appear to be, so I am breaking the mold, as always," Jen smiled, as she slowly ate her sandwich.

"I think it's going to be a bit before we are back to normal, sadly," Val sighed.

"Just think, we have another person coming in what, five days? It's getting to be a bit too much," Matt offered, as he ate.

"Hopefully they can make the seamless transition, the way Carly did," Jen offered. "Too bad about her name though."

"You don't like it either? I told her Matt didn't," Val grinned.

"She offered to pick a different one, I hope she comes back a new woman," Matt smiled.

"Oh you," Val rolled her eyes. "How are you feeling Jen?"

"I'm okay, thank you for the sandwich. I agree with Matt, Sam and Carly might be gone for a while—we should do something together. Did you want to play dominoes?" Jen offered.

"Sure, but I'm not very good at it. I will warn you: Matt is hyper competitive when it comes to dominoes. He will try to block the board, as often as he can," Val grinned.

"I can't dispute that, I do like winning in dominoes," Matt waved his good hand in the air. "I will leave it to you two to shuffle though, I really only have one arm at the moment."

"Also, I am not trying to get you two off that couch, if you want to continue to lay there, you may," Val pointed out.

"Oh, we will have plenty of time for that tonight. Let's play," Jen grinned, as she rolled off the couch.

Val stood up to fetch the dominoes, laying them out on the dinner table. Matt and Jen had some bad memories there, and they asked if they could play at the kitchen table instead.

"Oh, sure. Is that where you two were when the tree came down?" Val whispered.

"Yeah, it was extremely scary. I'm glad you and the dogs weren't here for it," Matt sighed.

"It even scared me. The water was pouring in, it was a really bad situation," Jen reflected. "But it's okay now. Come on, let's play."

They played for hours, until Sam and Carly finally came home. Walking in, Carly plopped down in the empty chair at the table, while Sam stood next to it.

"Welcome home—are you guys okay?" Val asked.

"Just tired. Sam seems to have endless stamina. We have some things we need to go over. Who is winning your game?" Carly asked.

"Matt, of course. It's uh, 755 for him, 460 for Jen, and 325 for me. He is ruthless, he always has been. I don't care at all, but I think Jen is quite annoyed," Val beamed.

"It's crazy how good he is at this," Jen grumbled.

"Should we prepare dinner? Are you guys done for the day?" Matt asked.

"We are done, yes. The electricity is working again, Sam fixed it while I evacuated the flooded houses. But... he thinks we need to move," Carly whispered.

"I know this is your family home, but it's not a good base anymore. The cul-de-sac withstood the flooding, but this whole side of the neighborhood is fried. All the kitchen appliances are shorted out, we had to move all the frozen food out of the freezers and down the road to the other side. If we stay here, we would have to go farther to take care of those houses. The safehouse is already good to go, and we prepared the two neighboring houses for living as well. I'll repair the back room, the wall, and the roof, but I still think you should relocate," Sam finished.

"That's fine. The safehouse has four bedrooms, right? We can move there tonight. Pack up everything and go. I know Carly is tired, so why don't we eat first, she can take a nap, then we can go," Matt offered.

"Thanks for doing all that work," Val whispered.

"You're welcome. It's been a very rough few days. After we get you moved, you kids can relax. I will handle the rest of the repairs," Sam shrugged.

"How did you drain the water so fast?" Jen asked.

"I opened the manholes," Sam shrugged.

"How?" Jen whispered.

"His claws are unbreakable metal—they can cut through anything. You gonna stay for dinner Sam?" Matt asked.

"Yeah, I will eat with you guys. Then head off to the home supply store, we need bricks and mortar for the back wall," Sam replied.

"Val? Do you mind cooking tonight? I would, but I only have one arm," Matt sighed.

"I will help," Carly smiled.

"Thought of a new name yet?" Matt grinned.

"You can call me whatever you want Matt," Carly teased. "After dinner, I will change your bandages, then we can move."

"Okay," Matt held his hand up.

"Come back to the couch with me," Jen rolled her eyes.

"Sure," Matt smiled, standing up and following her back into the living room. He lay down first, and she slowly crawled onto him, minding his arm. Settling in, they dozed while the girls worked in the kitchen, and Sam spent time with the dogs.

———

An hour later they were eating dinner at the table, Val had made chicken fettuccine, a wonderful dish from their childhood. Even Sam was enjoying it.

"Thanks for cooking," Sam offered.

"Oh, you are welcome, Sam. We are not used to having you here, but we appreciate everything you have done for us," Val beamed.

"It's my job. I'm good at it," Sam shrugged.

"You prove that every day," Matt nodded.

"I'll help you with the dishes, then you guys can get moving to the safehouse. You should drive all the vehicles there. Carly and I pushed the unused ones down the road, so there is plenty of space for the fleet," Sam offered.

"Yes, thank you Sam. Carly? Can you change Matt's bandage? And Jen? Maybe you can start packing the trucks with our stuff?" Val smiled.

"Yes," Jen nodded.

"Come on Matt," Carly grinned.

"Remember what I said Carly?" Jen pressed.

"Yes, I got it," Carly nodded.

"Scary," Matt whispered, as he followed her into the bathroom. Sitting down on the edge of the tub, he asked her what that exchange was all about.

"Val and I wanted to tell you this, and we cleared it with her first. We feel like the sooner you accept it, the happier you will be," Carly teased, as she unwrapped the bandage.

"Not shady at all," Matt sighed.

"We want to tell you that Jen isn't spending time with you, getting closer to you, because you are the only man available. She isn't settling for you Matt. She isn't the kind of woman that settles for anything. Literally, nothing. Even I know that, and I have only known her for a few days. She wants to get closer to you because you are worth it. So, stop thinking she is too good for you, and *especially* stop thinking you aren't good enough for her," Carly chided him.

"Did you uh...rehearse that?" Matt stammered.

"Val and I went over it a few times," Carly grinned, as she wiped the dried blood off his arm. "This scar is going to be with you for the rest of your life. But the stitches are holding, you are doing a good job of taking it easy."

"Maybe you just did a good job of stitching me up," Matt grinned.

"Not bad," Carly beamed. "Did you really want me to change my name?"

"Even Jen took a shot at it today," Matt whispered. "I'm sorry if that offends you."

"It doesn't, it's not my real name. I can't remember my actual name. Why don't we come up with one together?" Carly smiled, as she wrapped a new bandage around his arm.

"Only if you really want to," Matt whispered.

"I told you I don't mind. No one seems to like it, even I am having second thoughts. What about Simone?" Carly offered.

"That was the name of Val's good friend, it might be a bad memory for her," Matt whispered.

"Caitlyn? Or Caty, with a C?" Carly grinned.

"Caty with a C is good," Matt nodded.

"Caty is in then," Caty grinned. "See how easy that was? I have had all kinds of names. You would think I am an ex-stripper. No jokes."

"I would never have said that! A spy would probably be what I would have gone with," Matt laughed.

"I like that better too. A spy," Caty grinned. "Come on, let's get ready to move."

"Thanks for helping me with this, by the way. And thanks for your uh...encouragement, regarding Jen," Matt smiled.

"You're welcome, Matt. You and your sister are good people. I don't have any idea about what's really going on, but I do know that much," Caty assured him.

"Thanks again Caty. I enjoy your company as well," Matt grinned.

Matt and Jen were lying in their new king-size bed in their new home. Matt was very quiet, allowing Jen to control the situation. Buddy was in between them, and Fred was laying on the ground next to Jen's side of the bed.

"Are you okay? You seem nervous," Jen grinned.

"Maybe I am a little more nervous tonight, since I am fully awake and lying in bed with you," Matt admitted.

"We are just going to lie here, okay? I want to talk to you about a couple of things. They will probably make you uncomfortable, but I will get us through it," Jen assured him. "Take my hand."

She extended her hand over the Beagle and Matt took it, caressing it.

"Tell me what you were thinking when Val first suggested we get together," Jen whispered.

"How do you know she did?" Matt asked.

"Just assume I know everything going forward, it will make your life easier. Now tell me," Jen grinned.

"I was thinking you had absolutely no interest in me, and you never would," Matt whispered.

"Why? Because I am rich and famous, and you are just some guy?" Jen offered.

"Yep, pretty much exactly that," Matt nodded.

"I see. Tell me what you were thinking when Jack was trying to kill us," Jen whispered.

"I was...I was thinking of some way, *any* way to save you," Matt reflected.

"Mmhmm. And now tell me what you were thinking in the bath this morning," Jen finished.

"I was just thinking about how insanely beautiful you are," Matt grinned.

"Right. You think I took a bath with you because you are the only man available?" Jen asked.

"No, you could have taken a bath by yourself, easily," Matt admitted.

"That's right. I could have done that, very easily. But I didn't. I took a bath with *you*, and instead of asking you why you think that is, I will just *tell* you, to make your life easier. Because I wanted to. If I didn't want to be right here, I wouldn't be. The life and death situation is over; the adrenaline is gone, and I am still right here. I'm not ready to tell you I love you, or bed you yet, but I am very content to lie in your arms Matt. You are a good person, with a good heart. And that's more than I can say about so many of my ex-suitors," Jen finished.

"Um...okay. You want to...get a little closer?" Matt whispered.

"Yes," Jen replied, as she shoved the Beagle down to the foot of the bed and laid her head on his right shoulder. Buddy was not amused, and came back to lay next to her. "We will take another bath tomorrow. I will continue to wear the pants in this relationship! And yes...it's a relationship."

"Okay," Matt whispered, as they closed their eyes and went to sleep.

CHAPTER 22
THE SUNWALKER

The group was driving over the causeway, heading towards the light. Jen had almost fully recovered, only her bruise remained. Matt however, still had a bad arm, and he rode in the back next to Jen. They were still taking things slowly. Still hadn't kissed, but Matt felt like it needed to happen soon. He was content to let Jen take the lead, but he figured she could even sense that the next step needed to come.

Val and Caty were closer than ever, they kissed regularly. Caty was in the front seat as Val drove them on. Sam was the same as always, focused on work. He had insisted they bring weapons this time, if he deemed the person a threat, they wouldn't leave the beach alive. Matt didn't argue, he had completely misread Jack, so he left it to Sam.

Val parked them in their hotel and they hopped out, Jen with the shotgun. Sam led them on, as they walked down the pier. Matt saw it was an African American man, wearing all white, a trench coat, sunglasses, a staff on his back. Even his hair was dyed white.

"Wow," Matt whispered.

"You recognize him?" Jen asked.

"No, but his outfit is sure snapping. Again, memory loss. I...don't even know what to say," Matt put his hands up.

"I recognize him, we have tangled a few times. He doesn't kill humans—but—he isn't exactly compatible with us," Sam snarled.

Approaching the fire, the man looked up. "Who are you kids? Are you the Chosen Ones?" he growled.

"I guess. What did the fire tell you?" Matt sighed.

"I am the Sunwalker. Real genius, that fire. I recognize you, want to tell me what's going on?" the Sunwalker growled at Sam.

"These four are human, no threat to you. There are no threats to you left," Sam shrugged.

"There are always threats to me," the Sunwalker said in a low voice.

"You want to fill us in on what this guy is?" Jen asked.

"He is a vampire," Sam shrugged.

"Say what?? It's broad daylight!" Val exclaimed.

"I guess that explains why he is called the Sunwalker? Still, are you really a vampire? I don't suppose you eat food?" Matt sighed

"Blood," the Sunwalker growled.

"Terrific. This is definitely a problem, Sam? You say he doesn't hurt humans? What is he going to do when he figures out he is fresh out of food?" Matt demanded.

"Die," Sam shrugged.

"You expect me to believe that?" the Sunwalker growled.

"Val, you want to play the video?" Matt sighed.

"Please don't destroy my phone. May I approach?" Val whispered.

"Go ahead," the Sunwalker said slowly.

Val looked at Sam, who nodded. She held her phone up and played the video. The Sunwalker watched it, showing no emotion. It ended and Val stepped back.

"Who was that guy with the weird eyes? I don't see him here," the Sunwalker growled.

"He was a threat to us," Matt sighed.

"No longer," Sam finished.

"I see. I know you aren't a man to trifle with. So, I will be brief. I am going to take a look around. If I am convinced you are telling the truth, I will join you. If not, then you won't see me again. Clear?" asked the Sunwalker..

"Fair enough. I am still a bit concerned about uh…feeding you," Matt sighed.

"Seems like it's a huge problem," Val cut in.

"I guess he will have to figure it out. See you later, Sunwalker," Matt waved, heading back to the truck. Jen followed him, and the others fell in line.

"Can't think of a single use we have for a vampire," Matt muttered.

"Let's just head home. Sam can keep working on your house, and we can do other things," Caty grinned.

"Sounds like a plan," Jen smiled.

"We could have at least offered to take him somewhere," Val whispered.

"He made his intentions clear. He will come back to us at some point, as Matt said, he has to," Sam shrugged. "He drinks blood."

"We need a gameplan for that," Matt sighed, as he climbed into the truck.

Val got them going, and they drove on in silence. Jen took Matt's hand in the back seat; it was something they liked doing.

"What are you thinking about?" Jen whispered to him.

"What we are gonna do about the Sunwalker? And what you have in mind for when we get home?" Matt whispered back.

"You will like it," Jen grinned.

"I have faith in you," Matt relented.

Val pulled up into the driveway, and they got out. She asked Sam if he needed anything, and he shook his head no and wished them well. Walking inside, she announced lunch would be in a few hours, then both couples retreated to their rooms.

"What did you want to do?" Matt asked.

"Is the suspense killing you?" Jen teased.

"Not really. Your company is enough for me," Matt said cheerfully.

"You are a terrible liar," Jen grinned. "I am going to change into something more appropriate, then we will get in the shower."

"Oh, okay," Matt managed. He was already wearing a bathing suit, in case they had wanted to go swimming. He managed to get his shirt off, though his arm was still bothering him. Jen stepped into the large walk-in closet while Matt looked at his arm in the mirror. He couldn't see the wound through the bandage, but at least it wasn't bleeding anymore.

Jen came out wearing a dark purple bikini, putting her hand up on the wall. Matt could barely look at her, as she laughed. "I'm told this is your favorite color. I like the way it looks on me. What do you think?"

"It's plain to see how you sell so many magazine copies, that's for sure," Matt managed.

"Just the idea of seeing me in a bikini sells. Come on, let's get in the shower. It's okay to look at me, I want to see how brave you are," Jen teased.

Matt managed to look her way—her body was glowing in that bikini. She turned the water on, it was a big shower stall with good pressure, and then she summoned him.

"Come on. I'm having fun teasing you, but I am a little nervous myself," Jen grinned.

"I think you are just saying that to make me feel better," Matt observed.

"Maybe I am," Jen whispered as she took his hand and led him into the shower. She leaned against the wall as he put his hands around her waist, and she wrapped her own arms around his neck. "Let's make the first one a good one."

Matt leaned forward and kissed her, running his hands up her back and unsnapping her bikini top. She moaned into the kiss as it fell to the ground. Finally breaking away, they gasped for air.

"Oh, braver than I expected. Come on, kiss me. But be careful with your hands, I can hurt you very easily," Jen whispered.

They kissed some more, as Matt gently caressed her breasts. She allowed it, but started to run her own hand slowly up his left arm, towards his wound. He lowered his hands and she followed suit, smiling in between the kisses.

He ran his hands down her backside, slowly reaching inside her bottoms and grabbing her ass. She moaned again and squeezed his arm aggressively, causing him to wince. He didn't back down though, continuing to squeeze her ass. She squeezed his arm even harder, laughing.

"Can you withstand me?" Jen grinned.

Matt finally let go and she did as well. His arm was bleeding, but they kept making out. Finally, they were beginning to lose the hot water and decided to get out. Jen picked up her top and put it back on, shaking her head with a smile.

"That was fun. Let me look at your arm," she grinned.

She undid the bandage and inspected it. "The stitches are still holding, barely. You almost made it a lot worse. I'll get a new bandage," Jen smiled.

He didn't object as she stepped out of the bathroom, looking back to see him admiring her. Noting he had found some courage, she came back with a new bandage and wrapped his arm.

"Can I ask a question?" Matt offered.

"It's 'May I. May I ask a question.' Go ahead," Jen grinned.

"Was that a good first kiss?" Matt teased.

"It was. As I said, braver than I expected, straight for the bikini. I didn't think you had it in you. But that's good Matt. It's been a week. Did you want to talk about whatever it is you have been feeling bad about?" Jen offered.

"How did you know about that?" Matt sighed.

"Matt, you are surrounded by three women, it's going to be hard for you to hide your feelings from now on. Our new team member isn't going to be any help on that front, if he even decides to be a member of the team," Jen rolled her eyes.

"We should talk about that particular subject over lunch. But yeah, I did want to tell you something. I...I'm sorry about your career. I know you love it, and I haven't wanted to talk about it. But I don't see how it continues with us here. Out of all of us, you have definitely lost the most. And I can't do anything about it," Matt whispered.

"That's really good of you to say Matt. I knew you wanted to talk about something, but I didn't think it would be this. It's very thoughtful of you. I am sad about the prospects of my career being over. I'm sad about potentially not seeing my home again. I know there is nothing that can be done about it, and that's not your fault Matt. I don't know what is really going on here, but...I'm glad we can face it together," Jen managed, as she wiped a tear away.

She leaned forward and kissed him, to his surprise. Breaking away, she stepped back into the walk-in closet to presumably put some more clothes on. He sat down on the bed, looking for his shirt. His arm was sore again from her squeezing it, but it was worth it in his mind, as he pulled the shirt on. She came back out, having just put on a see-through robe.

"If you are wearing that to lunch I hope you are prepared for stares," Matt grinned.

"Think it will create jealousy and desire?" Jen laughed.

"Definitely," Matt smiled.

"Thank you for saying those things Matt, it was nice of you. Don't feel bad about it, okay? Let's snuggle a bit, I think we have some time. And I will remind you to be careful with your hands," Jen teased.

They lay down and closed their eyes, Matt couldn't resist caressing her ass again as she squeezed his arm and smiled.

"I have to ask you something Matt," Jen whispered.

"Go ahead," Matt grinned as she rubbed her ass.

"If you could get me back to my world, but it meant we would never see each other again—would you do it?" Jen asked.

"Oh, definitely. I want you to be happy, Jen. And I know you will only truly be happy once you are back in your world. So, if I could get you there, I would," Matt assured her.

Jen was quiet, as she let go of his arm and closed her eyes. He also let go of her ass and wrapped his good arm around her.

———

A few hours later, they were sitting at the table eating lunch with Caty and Val, who were indeed staring at Jen.

"Soo…what are we going to do about this new guy?" Val managed.

"I'm more concerned about what we are going to do about this bikini," Caty offered with a smile.

"What bikini?" Jen asked.

"The bikini that you are wearing to the lunch table," Val pointed out.

"Oh, it's very comfortable. And a nice color," Jen smiled.

"Uh huh. Anything to add, Matt?" Val glared.

"The Sunwalker is a problem," Matt smiled, as he ate.

"He drinks human blood? That's a problem," Val pressed. "You don't have to point out the obvious."

"Do you think he eats anything else?" Carly asked.

"My vampire knowledge is pretty limited. I have seen some movies, read *Dracula*…that's about it. Val is the one that went to see "Twilight" a dozen times," Matt offered.

"I was TWELVE," Val snapped.

"So, you matched the number of times you went to see the movie with your age? Kids these days," Jen laughed.

"Moving! On!" Val pointed her finger in the air.

"Do you think he is a threat to us?" Caty asked.

"That's Sam's department. A vampire that doesn't hurt humans seems pretty odd to me. Maybe he is from that anime about a vampire that hunts other vampires. They make the best hunters, after all," Matt shrugged.

"Do you think he is more dangerous than Jack?" Val sighed.

"Well, he is physically superior to Jack, more skilled, so yeah. I would say he is more dangerous than Jack. But is he dangerous to *us*, that's the question," Matt replied, concerned.

"What do you think he is doing right now?" Val asked.

"No idea. It's possible he is heading for us—it's possible Sam went to kill him. But it would make more sense to wait, the longer the Sunwalker goes without food, the weaker he will be," Matt reflected. "Even I know that."

"Terrific. I think it's time for a drink," Val sighed, standing up to get a bottle of booze.

"Do you think he fits into your theory about what's going on here? Is he medium?" Jen asked.

"No idea. I think he is another person that has been fused. There is no way he wears white on a regular basis. But if he really is a vampire hunter, I guess he could fit that medium mold. How he helps us, I have no idea, but that might not be their intention. If they were looking to split the difference, they accomplished that," Matt nodded.

"Say he wants to be our friend—how do we help him? He needs blood, I am just not going to let him suck mine," Jen pressed.

"I think we should go check out a local hospital. Pick up some empty blood packs, fill them with ours, freeze them here. That's my best idea. There are four of us, we can ration them. I think he will be agreeable," Matt offered.

"And if he isn't?" Caty asked.

"Then he dies, one way or another," Matt shrugged.

"Let's clean up, and head to the hospital. Try to make contact with Sam. Take some weapons, just in case," Jen pressed.

"Are you going to uh, go in that?" Caty asked.

"No, I need to put some sandals on, obviously," Jen rolled her eyes.

"That's not what I meant," Caty deadpanned.

"If you don't want to go, just stay here with Val," Jen shrugged. "Matt and I will be okay."

"Okay, let's get going then, all of us. Clearly, Jen's confidence is overpowering us all, but there isn't anything we can do about it," Val smiled. "Someone else needs to drive, I have had a few swigs."

"You know we can't be pulled over, right?" Matt teased.

"It's still not safe to drive while impaired," Val countered.

"Okay, fine. Jen? Caty?" Matt asked.

"I can drive, no big deal," Caty rolled her eyes.

"Her name is Carly, FYI," Val glared.

"We picked out Caty?" Matt stammered.

"I nixed it," Val shrugged. "Come on, let's go."

CHAPTER 23

THE BLOOD SOLUTION

The group was walking into the local hospital, armed with the two shotguns, to salvage some medical supplies. Not entirely sure where to look, they decided to stay together. Jen had put some yoga pants on, but it had hardly done anything to reduce the staring. She had one of the shotguns slung around her shoulder, looking around the ER.

"Okay, I guess we'll just search through the cabinets and stuff, I don't really know where they keep empty blood bags. We should also find some syringes for withdrawing blood," Matt suggested.

"Please don't mention syringes again, or show them to me, or anything," Val pressed.

"She doesn't like needles, come on, let's go," Matt grinned.

They went room to room in the ER, finding plenty of half filled, contaminated blood packets, but no unused ones. Deciding to split up, they moved into the living ward, where regular patients would usually be kept.

"Here are a few empty ones, unused," Jen took some out of a cabinet.

"Okay, we should be able to find plenty in this area then, let's keep going," Matt whispered.

"Why are you whispering?" Jen asked, curiously.

"I don't know, this place is pretty creepy, I don't want to wake up a zombie, or something," Matt shrugged.

"You are so silly. Can I ask you something? You don't have to answer, in fact I know it's too early to ask this, but out of curiosity, if you could get me back to my world, and had the option of coming with me, would you?" Jen asked.

"It is...pretty early for that kind of question. You are talking about moving in together after a week. And it's a lot more complicated than it normally would be. You live in England, right?" Matt asked, as he picked up some empty packets.

"Yes. I know it's too early—I get that. I shouldn't have brought it up," Jen relented.

"It's okay. If my world was restored, would you want to stay with me?" Matt asked.

"I....you are right. Let's revisit this in a few months, okay?" Jen whispered.

"Okay," Matt grinned. "Taking things slowly, remember?"

"Yes. Come on, we have all we can carry. Let's head back to the truck," Jen offered.

They walked out of the living ward, through the ER and outside, where they had double parked. Throwing the packets in the tailgate, they headed back inside to get more.

"How many do you think we need?" Jen asked.

"I have no idea. No reason not to take them all though," Matt shrugged.

"We still need to find some syringes. I am guessing the other team wants no part of those," Jen grinned.

"Pretty much guaranteed. Might as well look for bandages as well, this place has everything," Matt offered.

They continued their search, not sure where Val and Carly were, but Matt had a few guesses. Picking up more empty packets, they were really looking for syringes at this point. Finally finding some, they took as much as they could carry and hauled it back to the truck. Still not seeing Val, Matt shrugged and went back inside for one last trip. Once again, they carried a full load out to the truck, but Val and Carly were still MIA.

"You got your pistol? Fire a shot in the air," Matt said.

Jen took the Colt out and fired a shot. They waited, and the missing pair finally showed up.

"You guys finished?" Val beamed.

"Yeah, you good?" Matt asked.

"Yes, we were just talking. I really wanted nothing to do with this particular mission. Carly didn't mind, right?" Val laughed.

"Not at all, I enjoy all of your company. I'm so used to meeting people then never seeing them again. And while I won't say this is a great situation we are in, you guys have definitely made the best of it, and I am happy to be a part," Carly smiled.

"She is so nice. It doesn't even hurt not remembering her, it's more fun to listen to her talk about herself," Val beamed.

"Come on, let's head home," Jen grinned. "I want to go swimming."

"Oh, I guess the pool is next then," Val laughed.

"I guess so. Think the chlorine will hurt my wound?" Matt asked.

"You should definitely not submerge it, just sit in the shade and relax," Carly smiled. "I need a swimsuit though."

"Oh, we can stop on the way home and get one. We have to go past some stores," Val offered, as she started the truck and they steered towards home. "I'm thinking blue."

"Of course, you are," Carly grinned.

———

Two hours later, Jen was swimming some laps, while Matt, Val, and Carly sat on the step at the edge of the pool. Carly had indeed picked out a blue bikini for Val. They had dragged an umbrella over to the edge to give them some shade, and brought some drinks from home.

"So, Matt. That woman is gorgeous. You know that right? How are you keeping it together?" Val teased.

"It's uh, it hasn't been too bad. She actually doesn't enjoy talking like the two of you. It seems like she is good at literally everything, but she is just as nervous about a relationship as I am. I want to ask her out on a date, but where would we go?" Matt sighed.

"You don't have to go anywhere, we can cook dinner for you two, play some music, and leave you to it. She doesn't expect you to take her to some glamorous club or anything," Val offered.

"I agree, just wear really nice clothes, and treat it like a date. You said she was a professional adventurer? She has probably never even worn heels. Talk about your lives, what you hope for, what your relationship goals are. And just compliment her appearance one time, when you first see her," Carly offered.

"You uh, you been on dates like that, Carly?" Matt asked.

"No, it's just wishful thinking. I never really went on dates. It was straight to sex. He was a wild child, then he was a hero. He never cared about dates. Then the assassin came, and uh, yeah. No need to talk about that," Carly grinned.

"Why don't you come on a date with me then? Have you ever worn heels? I will dance with you," Val smiled.

"Oh…I would like that, yes. I guess I have to find something to wear. Maybe Jen and I can go shopping together," Carly managed.

Jen came over to them, asking how they were.

"We are good, how was your swim?" Matt asked.

"Lonely," Jen shrugged.

"Hey, I literally cannot swim with you, on account of not being able to lift my arm. Blame these two lazy bums," Matt grinned.

"I am," Jen laughed.

"Oh stop. I have drunk too much to go swimming like that," Val scoffed.

"Carly? Those scars on your back? Where are they from?" Jen asked.

"I've had a rough life, Jen. Savagely tortured a few times. I would rather not relive it," Carly whispered.

"Oh, in that case, I won't bring it up again. I'm sorry," Jen offered.

"It's okay. Do you have scars from your adventures?" Carly asked.

"Only a few, I trust that Matt has not betrayed their locations?" Jen teased.

"He has not. He does have a question however," Val beamed.

"Oh? What is it Matt?" Jen asked.

"Would you like to go on a date with me tomorrow night, Jen?" Matt asked.

"Oh," Jen looked away. "Of course. I would enjoy that. I have nothing to wear for such an occasion."

"I don't either. You and I can go shopping tomorrow," Carly offered.

"Of course. Dark purple or dark green, right Matt?" Jen grinned.

"Anything you want, Jen. I don't set those kinds of expectations," Matt waved.

"I see. Well, I will keep that in mind," Jen smiled.

"And blue for me, right Val?" Carly asked.

"Absolutely. Blue," Val beamed.

"Unless someone wants to stay, should we retire then? Tomorrow is a big day all of a sudden," Jen smiled.

"Sure," Matt grinned, as they stood up and exited the pool. Matt handed Jen her towel, and then her mesh robe, while the others dried off. The safehouse was much closer to the pool than their old house, so they had just walked over. Heading home, Jen took Matt's hand and they walked in silence. The two couples were polar opposites, Val loved to talk to Carly, but Matt and Jen were content to just hold hands and enjoy each other's company.

Walking into the house, they were surprised to find Sam there, with the Sunwalker. "Oh, hey," Matt stammered.

"What were you kids doing?" Sam asked.

"Well, we went to the hospital to pick up some supplies, then we went to the swimming pool," Jen offered. "Is that a problem?"

"I told you, they have accepted their situation here, and they aren't trying to do anything about it," Sam told the Sunwalker.

"What can we do?" Matt shrugged.

"Well by all appearances, it doesn't look like you can do anything. So why bother? It makes sense," the Sunwalker growled.

"I told him you have a video—will you share it with him Val?" Sam asked.

"Yes. Again, please don't break my phone. You seem to be the kind of man that lashes out," Val whispered, as she dug her phone out.

"I don't hurt humans, only vampires and their minions," the Sunwalker growled.

"Well, we are not minions, I can assure you," Matt offered.

"I know that," the Sunwalker replied.

Val set the phone down and played the video for him. The Sunwalker watched with curiosity, but wasn't moved by Matt's theories.

"That all sounds like a load of bull to me," the Sunwalker finally said. "I'm not the result of some fusion, I have a lifetime of memories. Plus, I know this guy, the one you call Sam."

"It's a theory, it could be wrong, I have no idea," Matt shrugged. "Your exact identities are a mystery to us all. But the people are gone, there is no denying that. They didn't die, they vanished. Why don't we move on to what exactly you want to do—I know you don't want to stay here with us, but I also know you *need* us to survive. So...talk."

"You are right on both accounts. I need you to help me live. This is as close as I will ever come to asking for help," the Sunwalker said quietly.

"Yeah, I'm not trying to pick a fight with you. How much blood do you need, and how often do you need it?" Matt asked.

"Once a day should be enough to keep me going. But I need a full blood packet. And...I could use it soon, your wound is affecting my senses. I need blood,' the Sunwalker growled.

"You can take it from my left arm, it's dead anyway," Matt offered.

"What happened to you?" the Sunwalker growled.

"The threat got close to him," Sam intervened.

The Sunwalker turned, "I take it you won't be taking that risk with me."

"No, I will not. Try to go around me and you are dead," Sam growled.

"I've learned about you in our previous engagements. I know there is nothing I have that can defeat you. But as I said, I don't hunt humans, and my track record proves that," the Sunwalker growled.

"It does. And it's the only reason you walked off that beach. But go feral, threaten these kids, and I will put you down," Sam said with menace, extending his claws for added emphasis. "Come to me for your daily blood dose, I will be in the house at the entrance to the neighborhood.

You can't mask your scent, so don't try. The last guy thought the storm threw my senses off."

"Nothing throws your senses off. I told you, I won't try anything. Also, this is why I think the kid's theory needs some work. We have memories of each other. But, that doesn't help us survive. I will stop by once a day to get my daily dose, then leave you all to your devices while I try to figure out a plan for me," the Sunwalker growled.

"Fair enough. Um, Carly or Jen? Do you want to draw my blood? Jen? Why don't you do it, so Carly can take Val into the other room?" Matt asked.

Val was already standing up and leaving, as Carly followed her. Jen picked up a syringe and told Matt to make a fist. He complied, and Jen found a good vein to extract some blood from. She emptied into the packet, and asked the Sunwalker if that was enough.

"Honestly, no. I need one more syringe worth. Again, this is not my thing, at all. But I will show some gratitude," the Sunwalker replied.

Jen waited, and then had to prompt him. "You can do that now."

"Thank you," the Sunwalker growled.

Jen took some blood from Matt's other arm, and handed the packet to the Sunwalker.

"Do you have a straw?" the Sunwalker asked.

Jen stood up and went into the kitchen, finding a straw and bringing it back. Expecting another thank you, the Sunwalker offered it. Satisfied, Jen sat down again.

"We are going to need some help with this. You just took a lot of blood from me, we will need to rotate. But I want to make sure we aren't wasting our time helping someone that is plotting to kill us. Sam? You got any ideas?" Matt pressed.

"Kill him," Sam shrugged.

"I agree. That's the best way to eliminate the threat," the Sunwalker growled. "I'm a burden to your survival. I hunt vampires. There are no vampires. I need human blood to survive. There are four humans, plus Sam. I give myself eight days, that's two doses from each of you, then you are all tapped out. What happens then?"

"Six days from now, we get another person. That could add to our blood donations. Provided they are human...and that's not a guarantee. A week after that, another member. So on and so on. The more people we add, the less of a burden you are," Matt offered.

"As you said, assuming we get more humans," Sam offered. "Matt, you said after Jack arrived, we might need all of us at some point. That option is officially off the table now. We killed Jack. Killing one more won't make a difference if we really did need everyone."

"Jen? What do you think?" Matt asked.

"I know you want to do the right thing, Matt—so do I. No one is wrong here. He is a burden, he doesn't help us, but his burden will lighten as time goes on. Theoretically," Jen sighed.

"You are uh, a vampire, right? Can't you go into a deep sleep, until we have more blood supply?" Matt asked.

"Hibernation," the Sunwalker growled. "Not a bad idea. I've never done it before, but it's possible. Just one problem. I actually do need a coffin."

"I don't pretend to understand vampire lore. But uh, we can find you a coffin. This city is a retirement community, there are plenty of funeral homes around. Will any coffin do?" Matt asked.

"Yes," the Sunwalker growled.

"Sam? Why don't you just take him to a funeral home, set him up? If we need him, we can wake him. If not, well, you could theoretically sleep for years, right?" Matt offered.

"Right. Thanks for the blood, you ain't bad kid," the Sunwalker growled, as he and Sam stood and left.

"I think you handled that well," Jen grinned.

"It helped that he was honest about his uselessness. Do you want to head to bed now?" Matt offered.

"Yes. Tomorrow is a big day, I'm looking forward to it. I admit I am a little nervous—formal dates aren't something I do a lot," Jen smiled.

"Same. Come on, let's head to bed then. Buddy and Fred are already there, I'm sure," Matt grinned.

"Just know that if you try to grope my breasts again you are on the couch," Jen teased.

"I can accept that, especially since you specifically avoided mentioning your booty," Matt laughed.

"I did specifically avoid that, yes," Jen grinned.

CHAPTER 24

PREPARATIONS

The group had finished their morning drives, and Jen and Carly were heading off to shop, while Matt and Val were staying home to take care of the dogs. It had been a while since they were alone together, and Val was eager to catch up.

"How is your arm?" Val asked, as she walked into the kitchen.

"It hurts every day. I can still barely raise it. Carly said I would have the scar for the rest of my life," Matt lamented.

"I'm glad Sam was there to save you guys. I'm also glad I wasn't there to suffer any of that," Val sighed.

"Same. What should we do for dinner tonight?" Matt asked.

"I'm thinking I will slow cook this brisket all day, then make you some brown rice. The storm washed away our garden, so we are once again out of vegetables until we get the new one planted. Still, it could have been way worse," Val reflected.

"Well, a tree fell on our house, the garden washed away, that whole side of the neighborhood flooded, I got slashed in the arm, Jen got concussed, I'm not sure how much worse it could have been," Matt grinned.

"Oh you. The tree falling must have been terrifying. I miss that avocado tree. But there is another one about four houses down. It should produce fruit next year," Val smiled.

"How are things going with Carly?" Matt asked.

"Oh, great. She has been through a lot. She is used to one-night stands, but she is happy to do relationships too. She just wants to belong somewhere, and she feels like she is welcome here. And she is a great kisser," Val beamed. "How are things going with Jen?"

"Really good, I think. We are much quieter than you two, and are taking things slowly. At first, I thought she was way *too much* woman for me, but she is just as nervous about a relationship as I am. I don't think she has ever been in one—she has never had the time. She is sad about her career, and I feel bad that there is nothing I can do about it," Matt sighed.

"Yeah, that is a shame about her career. She was a globetrotter, now we are all unlikely to ever leave this area. Still, I'm very happy for you two, you both deserve to be happy in this impossible situation. And like I said, she is beautiful," Val offered.

"Thanks. I guess she is a fictional character, but…she is real to me," Matt whispered.

"Of course. We still don't truly know what is happening, but what was up with the vampire hunter?" Val asked, bewildered.

"I think they are getting lazy, phoning it in. We aren't dedicating any brain cells to their talking fire, and they have likely given up on it entirely. I mean, the Sunwalker? He said it, real genius thinking there. Does he qualify as medium? Sure. But how are we supposed to keep him alive? He straight up said we could probably safely supply him for eight days. It wouldn't be surprising if Sam killed him, honestly," Matt sighed.

"I would hope he wouldn't do that, but I'm not donating any blood, so if killing him makes it easier, just don't tell me about it. I'll delete him from my brain," Val waved.

She put the brisket into the slow cooker and turned it on, as they walked into the living room and sat down with Buddy and Fred. "Do we even know where Gracie is now?"

"No idea," Matt admitted. "I guess ask Sam the next time you see him."

"Do you have clothes for tonight? You don't want to underdress," Val grinned.

"I do. I got some nice clothes from Nordstroms, just in case. I had plenty of time. Maybe we can find some music to play? I haven't even looked to see if these people have anything," Matt offered.

"You are right, our parents' jukebox is back in our house, but we can take the dogs and go get it. Dad had approximately 1.2 million songs on it, what did you want to listen to?" Val grinned.

"I have no idea. What are you and Carly planning on doing?" Matt asked.

"We are going to hang out next door. Tonight is all about *you and Jen*. We will do a double date soon, but tonight it's all *you two*," Val beamed.

"Okay. Let's get the dogs and walk back to our house. I'll take the Marlin, just in case. We haven't seen any wild dogs or anything, but that doesn't mean there aren't any," Matt shrugged.

"I think Sam's presence has kept them away, or put them in the ground," Val grinned.

"I would tend to agree," Matt smiled, as they put the leashes on Buddy and Fred and headed out. It was another beautiful day, and Matt realized he had lost track of time completely.

"Do you know what today is?" Matt asked.

"It's November 4th. We skipped Halloween, oh well. Carly put a hot costume on and gave me a lapdance, so that counts," Val laughed.

"I don't think Jen even cares about that holiday, we missed it completely," Matt grinned.

"Still, Thanksgiving is coming up. We have all the food for it, frozen or stored. Should we do a feast?" Val beamed.

"I think so. We even have turkeys, of all sizes. No idea what house they are in, but Sam and Carly should know," Matt laughed.

"This area took a lot of damage, branches are everywhere, I think the water is still in some of these houses. We should do something about that," Val whispered.

"We can ask Sam. There isn't much I can do with one arm," Matt sighed, as they arrived at their old cul-de-sac.

These houses looked much better—the sandbags had saved them from more damage. But their garage doors were decaying from the water.

Entering their house, Matt walked to check on the back room. He was surprised to see Sam had walled it off with bricks. Not bothering to paint them, the house was at least livable now.

"I got the jukebox, let's go. I can't believe I forgot it—do you see anything else we should take?" Val asked.

"No, not really. We got all the pictures, jewelry. What about Mom's china?" Matt asked.

"I think we should definitely get that, but not now. I need help with it, and you only have one arm for Buddy. Come on, let's head back. Can you take Fred?" Val asked.

"Of course," Matt took the leash from her and led the dogs out. Neither of them were difficult to walk on the leash, they didn't pull at all. Fred was happy to walk anywhere with them, and Buddy just followed his nose.

"I don't even think the two of them care about the lack of people. Fred seems to have gotten over the loss of his previous owners pretty quick," Val reflected, as they headed home.

"He is pretty old, as long as he has people, he is gonna be happy. And Buddy and I have been on our own forever. He knew you, of course, and the parents, but no one else," Matt shrugged.

"They both like Jen and Carly, so that's really working out. Let's get back and pick out your outfit. I think we have plenty of time, those two will likely be out a while," Val grinned.

"What makes you say that?" Matt asked.

"Jen probably had some other things she wanted to check on. And Carly wanted to do her own shopping. I told her the shopping was only okay here, but we could go north later if she really wanted to," Val shrugged.

"What is she shopping for?" Matt asked.

"Just some things she liked to have around. She spotted your katanas, but I told her it was too soon to ask for them," Val grinned.

"I doubt she finds anything like those in Harlingen. Maybe a pawn shop," Matt reflected. "But I doubt they are combat ready."

They walked in the front door, Val set the jukebox down on the table and started scrolling through the music. Matt left her to it as he unhooked the dogs and got them some water. Sitting down on the couch, they were out of things to do until the evening.

———

Hours later, Val was reading a cookbook while Matt was petting Buddy, as Jen and Carly walked in.

"Hey guys, Val? Could you come help us with our stuff? Matt? Stay over there, I want to surprise you, and you only have one good arm anyway," Jen called out.

"This one arm thing is getting a bit old," Matt lamented.

"You probably have a few weeks before you have full motion again. It was a bad cut," Carly commented as she took some shopping bags into the bedroom.

"Thanks for the help, Val. And thanks for cooking, it already smells delicious. What time do you think it will be ready?" Jen asked.

"Oh, there is no set time. But it should be nice and tender by five or six. Let me know what time you want to eat and I will make the rice. We are completely out of fresh veggies, I have frozen ones, but those feel cheap," Val sighed.

"I don't mind, I spent exactly no money on anything today, so there is no such thing as cheap," Jen grinned.

"Fair enough," Val laughed.

"What time is it now?" Jen asked.

"3:30," Matt replied.

"Okay, I am going to start doing my hair and getting ready. I haven't done this in a long time, I used to hate these kinds of functions. But—I feel completely different today," Jen beamed.

"How often did you have to go to functions?" Val asked.

"They were mostly fundraisers, a few times a year. It was always so tedious, so many people. But money doesn't grow on trees," Jen reflected. "I guess this is my first, formal date with a man. There were plenty of one on one interviews, but...this is new."

"Come on, let's start getting you ready. Carly? Will you keep Matt company?" Val grinned.

"Sure thing," Carly rolled her eyes.

"You don't have to do that, you know. I have Buddy here, you can go do something fun if you want to," Matt offered.

"Like what? Be by myself? No thanks. How are you?" Carly asked.

"I'm good. Like I said, my arm is sore. How often did you do formal events and stuff?" Matt asked.

"All the time, every weekend. Every night. It was fun for a while, I did a lot of stupid things. I thought they were harmless, but they weren't. Obviously, everything changed after the shipwreck. Every function I went to after that was a mission of sorts," Carly reflected.

"Did you have any luck shopping out there? Val said you were eying my daisho set. You miss your weapons?" Matt grinned.

"Not really. I didn't have an attachment to any particular weapon. The local pawn shops had a bunch of trash, all fake. Where did you get your swords?" Carly asked.

"Art dealer from Japan. He was trying to sell me some other crap, said it was historical. I think he was saving the katanas for someone else. I made him a good offer though, then asked him why he was behaving so dishonorably. He relented after that," Matt reflected.

"That's basically the kiss of death right there. You knew exactly how to get to him," Carly grinned.

"Yeah. I wanted the katanas, I got them. If we were in a situation where I thought you needed them, I would let you borrow one. But I don't think we are," Matt shrugged.

"Can we talk about something else?" Carly asked.

"Um sure. What is it?" Matt asked.

"Have you gotten anywhere thinking of what the endgame is for us? How much longer do you think this is going to go on?" Carly asked.

"I honestly have no idea. I would hope a year, but it could be longer. It's a horrible game, someone is playing. Val is going to be so mad if we ever meet the Puppetmaster," Matt grinned.

"Do you need help getting ready as well? Did you move your stuff?" Carly asked.

"Yeah, I moved it into the other room. It's not time yet though. It won't take me hours to get ready," Matt replied. "You can change topics pretty easily."

"I'm used to it," Carly shook her head. "Still, we should move in there. At the very least, it will make Jen think you are putting as much effort into it as her."

"You think she is that easily fooled?" Matt teased.

"No, but I was hoping you would be," Carly rolled her eyes and stood up.

They walked into the third bedroom, which also had its own bathroom, and Carly sat Matt down to check his bandage. It was still hurting him a lot, as she looked at the wound.

"The stitches are starting to loosen, I should reapply them," Carly whispered.

"Do you think they can hold until tomorrow? I would rather not do that tonight," Matt lamented.

"I think so, we can do them in the morning. You really have to take it easy though. I'm...I'm not trying to interfere in your date tonight, Matt..." Carly trailed off.

"I understand what you're saying, thanks Carly. I don't think we are at that point yet...but that could be subject to change tonight. She is taking the lead," Matt waved her off.

"Okay Matt. The good thing is Jen knows it's a serious wound, she won't risk hurting you. Let me bandage it up again," Carly whispered.

"Thank you, Carly, for helping me with this," Matt whispered.

"You're welcome, Matt. I hope you enjoy your evening. Val and I will serve you guys some dinner, then head out to have our own fun. Maybe in a few days we can switch places, then go on a double date! And hope our next addition doesn't feel left out," Carly grinned.

"Yeah, or maybe it will be another weirdo that won't even *want* to live here, or be *allowed* to live here," Matt rolled his eyes.

"Seems like it could go either way, I wonder what criteria they are using," Carly smiled.

"It's been really hard to figure out, we have been reduced to guessing. The Sunwalker knew Sam, Sam has held an Infinity Stone, we think he is a comic book character, so I guess the Sunwalker is too," Matt sighed.

"Let's just hope for someone that doesn't need human blood to sustain themselves," Carly grinned. "Do you need help getting dressed? It will probably be hard for you to put your long sleeve dress shirt on, and then button it."

"Yes, please. If you don't mind," Matt whispered.

"I don't mind. I enjoy your company Matt. It's nice to just be...normal for a change," Carly beamed.

"I enjoy your company as well Carly. You are really fun to be around, but I still don't know that much about your past," Matt grinned.

"It's a bad history. If I could go back and change a few things, I would," Carly offered, as she unbuttoned Matt's dress shirt, and then his arm cuffs. "It should be easy to get in this shirt now, just take it easy with that arm."

Matt nodded and turned around, as Carly lifted the shirt onto him. He ran his left arm through the sleeve slowly, and she came around to help him button it.

"I think when you recover your arm's strength that we should start hitting the gym. I know we have been working a lot, but that's not the same as exercise," Carly offered.

"Yeah, I'm open to that. I'm sure we could find one, turn the power on with a generator. I have bad feet though, believe it or not. So, no treadmills for me," Matt grinned.

He pulled his pants on, and then slowly got his socks and shoes on. He was having a hard time tying them, and Carly helped him.

"Thank you," Matt whispered.

"You're welcome again. Anything else?" Carly grinned.

"Yeah, my jacket," Matt grinned.

"Oh, duh. Here, let me help you," Carly smiled. She picked up the jacket and held it up, as he put his arms through it. Closing it, she admired him.

"You look great Matt. Is there anything else I can help you with?" Carly offered.

"No, thank you for your help, Carly. I can't believe Val just nixed our name change," Matt smiled.

"Yeah, I didn't like Caty that much after a bit. She refused. I think you will get used to Carly," she laughed.

He brushed his hair and they walked out together, Matt lamenting that he had no cologne or anything. Carly asked him where he left his, and he just smiled.

"Back in Austin. It didn't seem pressing when it was just me and Val," Matt grinned.

"That's fair. Jen will understand," Carly laughed. "I'll go check on them. Be right back."

Carly walked into the main bedroom, and came back out a few minutes later, giving him an update.

"Ten more minutes. You should stand up—you don't want to be sitting when she walks out here. She looks amazing, by the way. Um, yeah. She looks amazing. I'll start pouring the wine for you guys," Carly stammered.

"You okay?" Matt grinned.

"She is just really beautiful. You look handsome as well Matt, I should have pointed that out earlier. But you probably won't even see us when she walks in. Actually, I will get the dogs out of here first, then come back and pour the wine," Carly managed, leashing up the two hounds and leading them out.

Val came into the dining room, offering a thumbs up and fetched the wine. She actually served the brisket and rice, then scurried out of the house. Matt was confused, but he just figured neither of them wanted to take any attention away from Jen. Or something like that.

CHAPTER 25

THE DATE

Matt continued to wait, the meat smelled wonderful, but he was much more focused on his date. Finally, Jen came into the living room. Wearing a long, sparkling, purple evening gown, with a ruffled top, and a long slit going up her leg. Her hair was curled, she was wearing it down, not in her ponytail. She had put makeup on, and she looked absolutely amazing.

"Good evening Jen. You look beautiful tonight. May I escort you to your seat?" Matt offered.

"Thank you Matt. You look handsome as well," Jen smiled, as she took his arm. He walked her to her seat, and scooted her chair in.

"I see someone has already poured the wine, stealing your job, but that's okay. We will teach them proper etiquette for next time," Jen smiled.

"I wasn't fast enough to stop them, I'm sorry," Mat lied. He had no idea what she was talking about, Val surely knew more about etiquette than he did. Moving to his seat, he sat down.

"Shall we propose a toast?" Matt offered.

"Of course, what shall we toast?" Jen smiled.

"You assured me you would take the lead," Matt teased.

"That's true. Nice save. To our health and relationship Matt," Jen beamed.

"To our health and relationship," Matt raised his glass and they drank. He let Jen pick up her silverware first, and she took a bite of the brisket.

"Oh, this is nice and tender. The chef did a good job," Jen observed.

Matt took his own bite, and it was delicious. He asked her what they should talk about, and she started with a question.

"You dodged my question the other night, but it was an acceptable way to answer. I will ask you again, because I am curious about you Matt. If you could go anywhere, see anything right now, where would you go?" Jen smiled.

"Oh, Japan. For sure. It's my favorite country that I have never visited. It's always been a dream of mine to visit Japan. I am a huge fan of Japanese history," Matt replied.

"What parts?" Jen asked.

"Definitely the Sengoku period, and the rise of the three unifiers," Matt replied.

"Do you know their names?" Jen asked.

"Oh yeah. Oda Nobunaga, Toyotomi Hideyoshi, and Tokugawa Ieyasu. I'm even a fan of their Generals, specifically Date Masamune and Honda Tadakatsu," Matt offered.

"The One-Eyed Dragon, and the Warrior who surpassed Death. Honda Tadakatsu, I have his sword in my collection," Jen grinned.

"Um…really?" Matt stammered. "How in the world did you get that?"

"I don't have his main sword, but one of them. The Emperor gifted it to me, for recovering one of Japan's long last artifacts," Jen reflected.

"You actually met the Emperor of Japan?" Matt whispered.

"Well, yes. But I didn't look upon him. I knelt and kept my eyes down, and he asked me to raise my hands to receive a gift, and he gave it to me, then left. Honestly, I have probably never been more nervous," Jen smiled.

"That's really amazing," Matt managed.

"I'm glad to see you are a true fan of history, Matt. I would love to go to Japan with you, it's lovely this time of year. Do you have any other destinations you would like to see?" Jen smiled.

"Honestly I don't. I...I can only afford to save up for one dream at a time. We have been to Europe. There are a few places we missed, but they are all missable in comparison to Japan," Matt replied.

"That's fair. Where were you born Matt?" Jen asked.

"The Netherlands. I love that country, it's so beautiful. The tulip fields, the people, it's just a great place," Matt reflected.

"I agree, the Dutch are so nice. What would you like to talk about?" Jen asked.

"What was the Japanese artifact you recovered that earned you an audience with the Emperor?" Matt asked.

"Oh, the hammer of Masamune," Jen replied.

"That uh—that would do it, yes. I am surprised they lost it," Matt whispered.

"They said it was stolen during the Bakumatsu, but I learned that was false. It was actually hidden during that time, to prevent it from being stolen. But the man that knew where it was located didn't make it out of Kyoto alive," Jen offered

"I see. I wonder how they settled on Honda's sword," Matt whispered. "He was known for his spears. He is one of their best warriors, even Nobunaga praised him."

"And that man did not like to praise anyone. I think they felt like I had earned a gift, but not an actual treasure of Japan. They don't part with their history easily. I was grateful, I never do anything for the reward, I just want to restore lost history," Jen smiled. "I noticed you had your own daisho set, it looks very real. But it's not."

"Um, what?" Matt asked.

"Oh? You thought it was real, didn't you?" Jen teased.

"The swords are real," Matt tried.

"Well, they will cut. But does that really count as real? They weren't forged in Japan. They are Korean. I'm sorry if that ruins your mood," Jen grinned.

"It kinda brings me down, yes," Matt sighed.

"I will make it up to you later. I promise. I have spent a lot of time in Japan, I am very well regarded there. And I can spot Korean fakes very easily as a result."

"Is there anywhere that you are less regarded?" Matt grinned.

"More places than you would think. Probably can't go to France anytime soon, or Cairo, or Moscow, or Bangkok or Vienna.." Jen trailed off.

"Okay, I confess, that is more places than I would have guessed," Matt smiled.

"I do have an invitation that I would like to extend to you for tomorrow," Jen teased.

"What's that?" Matt asked.

"Come up in the plane with me, if you would?" Jen beamed.

"Oh...you trapped me. Very well, I accept. I feel like I have to, but I suppose that's well played on your part," Matt eyed her slyly.

"How was your dinner?" Jen asked.

"It was delicious," Matt replied, as he sipped his wine. "Yours?"

"It was very well cooked. What shall we do next?" Jen smiled.

"Would you like to dance?" Matt asked.

"I would. You nailed that question, but I wonder how well you dance?" Jen beamed.

"Not well. I don't even know the proper stance, I just used the old one that kids use," Matt admitted.

"That's acceptable. I will teach you another time, for now, that position allows us to get close, which I completely support," Jen smiled.

Matt stood up, and offered Jen his hand. She accepted it and stood, walking over to the jukebox. She had put some requests in at some point, and Val had tracked down those songs.

"What kind of music do you like, Jen?" Matt asked.

"Well, my favorite band is and always will be Queen. But we will dance to classical," Jen laughed. "Do you have something you would like to dance to?"

"Sinatra. That's basically all I have," Matt grinned.

"Well, you could certainly do worse than just having Frank Sinatra," Jen laughed, and started some music. "Which is your favorite?"

Jen approached him, and wrapped her arms around his neck while he put his around her waist. "Definitely "Fly me to the Moon". But I like this one too," Matt whispered.

She had started with "The Best is Yet to Come", but assured him his song would be coming up soon. "I owe you a kiss for bringing your mood down about your swords," she whispered to him.

She leaned in and kissed him, he kept his hands in place, but savored her taste. "Your lipstick..." he whispered.

"It's cherry-flavored, yes. I hate lipstick, I do. Carly told me to give you a pass for leaving your cologne in Austin, so...I will. Just for tonight though, you have to go get some for our next date," Jen whispered.

"You don't have to wear lipstick for me, Jen. I don't have any expectations like that," Matt whispered.

"Val told me that, yes. She said you don't care what I do, but appreciate it all the same," Jen whispered. "That's an uncommon trait. Most men have expectations, but she said you only have preferences, but won't even mention them unless I ask. And...I won't ask."

"Val was gossiping a lot about me, huh?" Matt grinned.

"Not as much as you think. I think she is truly over the moon that I am blessing you with my affection," Jen whispered.

"I am certainly grateful for every moment of it," Matt whispered.

"That's the right response, bravo Matt," Jen smiled, leaning in to kiss him again. She was a really good kisser, as she held onto it. The next song began, it was Matt's favorite.

"This is it Matt. Do I need to take the lead again?" Jen teased.

"Nah, I got it. Jen? I love you," Matt whispered.

"You got it, bravo again," Jen beamed. "I love you too Matt."

They slowly danced, and the next song began. Matt thought it was Bing Crosby, but he wasn't quite sure. He didn't want to ask for risk of seeming uncultured to the most cultured woman he had ever met, so he just continued to dance while Jen leaned against his chest and hugged him.

"How is your arm?" Jen whispered.

"It's holding up okay. Carly said she needed to reapply the stitches in the morning, but I can make it," Matt assured her.

"That's good. Because I want to take you to bed after this next song," Jen grinned.

The last song was Dean Martin, for sure. Playing his most famous track, they continued to slowly dance.

"I've never taken the time to slow down and love someone Matt. But I am glad I finally did," Jen whispered.

"I am too, Jen," Matt whispered. "It feels like you are making it easy for me tonight."

"That one was an accident," Jen beamed. "Come on, let's go to bed."

She turned and headed for the jukebox, turning it off. Taking his hand, she led him into their bedroom, where she let her dress fall down. Stepping out of her heels, she looked back at him, as he slowly got out of his jacket, then his dress shirt. She helped him with the buttons, and ripped it off. She was wearing purple lingerie, and fell into the bed, smiling.

"Use your hands as much as you want tonight, I promise not to take it out on your arm," Jen smiled.

"Sounds like a plan," Matt smiled as he pounced on her.

An hour later, Matt was sitting in the bathroom, while Jen was stitching his arm. She had put her lingerie back on, but nothing else. It was to make up for accidentally grabbing his arm. He had taken morphine again, and was embarrassed about it.

"Stop feeling bad about the morphine, even I would have taken it with a cut like this," Jen tried.

"How often have you had morphine on your adventures?" Matt grinned.

"Almost never, I admit," Jen stifled a laugh. "Be quiet, I am concentrating."

"You said you would take it easy on my arm," Matt chided her.

"Your strength overwhelmed me," Jen rolled her eyes. "I am sorry though."

"It's okay, it was worth it," Matt grinned.

"Oh you. But it's official now, we are *together*. I love you Matt. And I love being with you," Jen whispered, as she finished stitching up his arm.

"I love you too Jen. And I am grateful to be blessed by your affections," Matt smiled.

"You are hitting on all the easy ones tonight. Come on, let's go to sleep," Jen smiled, as she helped him up. Once again, the morphine was crushing him, as he leaned against her and got into bed. She laid on top of his right side, taking his hand. "Good night, Matt."

"Good night, Jen," Matt whispered.

CHAPTER 26

TAKING FLIGHT

Waking up the next morning, Jen rolled off of the bed and stood up to stretch. Matt looked on in amusement as she looked back at him and smiled. Extending her hand, she pulled him out of bed and asked him how his arm was feeling.

"It's still sore," Matt whispered.

"Still think it was worth it?" Jen teased.

"Oh, absolutely. Would you like to get in the shower?" Matt grinned.

"How can I refuse that?" Jen smiled, and they walked into the bathroom. Turning the shower on, it was easy for them to get undressed as they stepped into the stall. Jen wrapped his arms around him and they shared a kiss.

"What's on your mind?" Jen whispered.

"Just reflecting on how lucky I am," Matt whispered back.

"Hmm, I don't mind that," Jen grinned as they kissed some more.

Getting out, they got dressed, Matt a little more slowly, and walked into the living room. Buddy and Fred were there waiting for them, but Val and Carly didn't appear to be up yet. Matt let the dogs outside while Jen poured him some juice and made herself some coffee.

"Want some breakfast?" Jen offered, as she poured the dogs some of their own food. They were still outside, but she knew their routine.

"Sure. How are the rations looking on that front?" Matt asked.

"Right now, it looks like we have Chex Mix and milk, which Val must have opened yesterday. Let's try to eat some, quietly," Jen grinned.

"Let me get Val's Keurig ready, and let the dogs in, while you prepare the food," Matt whispered. The Keurig needed water, so he filled it and stuck Val's new K-Cup in, so all she needed to do was push Go. Then he let the dogs in, who went in a straight line for their food tray.

"What have we been doing with our trash? I haven't even noticed," Jen asked as they sat down.

"We are using the dumpsters behind the Wally World for now. When they fill up, we will move to the next store. We know the critters that trash brings, so we aren't leaving it in the neighborhood," Matt whispered.

"I guess that's all we can do. We could find the landfill around here," Jen reflected.

"I'm just grateful we have water and electricity, honestly. Val pointed out whatever our carbon footprint is, we can't make up for the loss of 7+ billion people. The Earth is doing better than it has been in centuries," Matt grinned.

"She is right. Let's get ready to go, let them sleep in. If they are even here; they might be next door," Jen offered.

"Well, the dogs are back, so that tells me they came here at some point. But yeah, we can get moving," Matt nodded.

"Nervous?" Jen teased.

"Not as much as you think, I have been in a small plane before when I was a kid. It was fun. It's not like a rollercoaster," Matt grinned.

"That's fair. Come on, I will rinse the dishes out, while you go get dressed. You are slower than me right now," Jen smiled.

Matt stood up and moved back into the bedroom, pulling some pants on slowly then his socks and shoes, which he did even more slowly. He was tired of his arm always hurting, but it beat the alternative. Jen came in and threw some clothes on as well, and they headed out.

Jen drove them to the airport, through the smashed gate and fence line, and headed down the flight line.

"You took the direct route, I see," Jen teased.

"I was in a bit of a hurry," Matt grinned. "And I had no idea where you were."

"That's fair. You should radio Sam, let him know we are going up," Jen offered.

Matt picked up the radio and transmitted.

"Sam? You out there? Come in Sam," Matt called.

Some time passed and finally Sam replied.

"Yeah, go ahead Matt. What is it?" Sam asked.

"We are taking the plane up today, going to survey the damage the storm left, and scout out for more storms," Matt replied.

"Good plan. Let me know if you find anything we need to address. I'll continue to work," Sam signed off.

"That guy doesn't talk," Jen offered.

"It's okay, he is there when we need him. He prefers to be alone," Matt shrugged.

"Here we are, hangar four. We are going to need to fuel the plane, there is a gas truck inside this hangar, that's why I parked here. Let's inspect the plane first," Jen pressed.

They got out of the truck and walked into the hangar, it looked to have weathered the storm just fine. Jen's plane was in the very back, facing the wall.

"Well, that's inconvenient, we are going to have to turn it around," Matt lamented.

"Yeah, I didn't have time when I parked it here. It's easy to push though, even for one person. I know your arm is bad, so don't strain yourself," Jen grinned.

"How embarrassing," Matt sighed.

They pushed the plane out a bit, parking it next to the gas truck. Jen hooked up the pump and started it, then walked around the plane, inspecting it for damage.

"It looks okay. As long as the engine starts, we should be fine," Jen observed.

"That's very reassuring," Matt laughed. "As long as the engine starts."

"If it doesn't start, we don't go," Jen shrugged. "It's not going to just turn off mid-flight, if that is what you were worried about."

"Okay, what's next?" Matt asked.

Jen turned the pump off and disconnected it. "Push the plane onto the flight line, start the engine, take off," she grinned.

"Okay," Matt shook his head. They took their places on the wings and pushed the plane out of the hangar. Turning it around, they resumed pushing it onto the end of the flight line. Jen climbed into the cockpit and started pushing some buttons, while Matt just stood outside his door. It was going to be hard for him to climb in with just one arm.

The engine turned over a few times, then finally started. Matt was surprised at how loud it was, as he managed to climb inside the passenger seat. Jen handed him a headset and he put it on. She had hers on already, along with some sunglasses. She handed him his own pair.

"Can you hear me?" Jen asked through the headset.

"Yeah!" Matt shouted.

"Okay! We will let the engine run for a bit, then take off. First, we will head for the island, then fly around inspecting the damage. Ready?" Jen offered.

"Go for it," Matt grinned.

Jen pushed up on the throttle and the plane started to accelerate. It was a smoother ride than Matt expected, as she pulled back on the handle and the plane lifted off. Climbing to about 1,000 feet, she steered them towards the island as Matt looked around.

"What do you think?" Jen beamed.

"Nice takeoff," Matt grinned. "What a view."

"More unwarranted flattery?" Jen laughed.

"It's never been 'unwarranted," Matt laughed.

Looking out the window, they saw several trees were down, some fences were broken, and cow herds had let themselves out. There was no fixing that, but it wasn't a problem. Coming to Port Isabel, Matt spotted the lighthouse, and the swing bridge, as Jen steered them towards their sea cottage. A sailboat was drifting around in the channel, it had likely shaken loose from its mooring lines. But they spotted their boats, safe and sound.

Flying east, Jen scanned the horizon while Matt looked down at the Gulf. "I really want to go deep sea fishing when my arm is better," he offered.

"Have you done it before?" Jen asked.

"Yeah, on a charter boat," Matt replied.

"What's your best catch?" Jen smiled.

"A 70-pound sailfish," Matt beamed.

"That's not bad," Jen nodded.

"What about you?" Matt asked.

"800-pound tuna," Jen laughed.

"You are such a showoff," Matt rolled his eyes.

"It took five hours to land it, I was dead for days," Jen laughed.

"I don't think the fish get that big in the Gulf," Matt offered.

"They are probably very rare. But there is a fish I would like to catch, it's divine," Jen reflected.

"Wahoo?" Matt grinned.

"You know it," Jen beamed.

"We will make that happen," Matt smiled.

"The skies are completely clear, let's head back," Jen offered.

She turned the plane around, and headed back towards the island. They had flown about 20 miles out, and it took them a few minutes to get back. Looking down at the city, Matt was still surprised to see how it looked. Completely abandoned, the grass was starting to disappear. It was long dead, and was now turning into dirt. She flew over the golf course, and it looked barren.

"I think our days of golf are over, look how much the grass has died. It went from being too tall to not even there," Matt pointed.

"Without water, it can't survive. And we aren't wasting water. Fishing and tennis aren't dependent on that though, so when you recover, we can move to those sports," Jen assured him. "And we still have the driving range."

"That's true, at least there is that," Matt nodded.

Coming back into Harlingen, Jen lined up with the flight line, and set the plane down. It bounced on the runway, and Matt teased her about it. She waved him off and taxied back to the hangar. Turning the engine off, they jumped out and pushed the plane back inside to its original parking spot.

"That was fun, I'm glad you invited me," Matt smiled.

"I'm glad you liked it. Let's head home. We need a new project to work on, got any ideas?" Jen beamed.

"No, I haven't been thinking about it since my injury. How about you?" Matt asked as they climbed into the truck.

"We should ask Val and Carly if they want to have their formal date tonight, and go from there," Jen smiled.

"I agree. Val really did a good job cooking for us, but they both got out of there quickly, I think your dress was overpowering them," Matt teased.

"I'm glad you liked it," Jen smiled. "It was nice to be able to wear something and not have to worry about being critiqued for choosing a certain designer or not having my hair done the right way."

"I thought your hair looked perfect, I don't see how anyone could have critiqued that," Matt offered.

"People can always find a way," Jen assured him.

"It's true, people do suck," Matt lamented.

"I miss some people, but society in general, *nah*," Jen shook her head.

"Your profession took you away from people a lot, so I can see how you don't even notice their absence," Matt offered.

"It's true, as I said, I am used to either being alone, or being in a small group like this one. I'm happy here, with you guys. With you Matt," Jen whispered.

"I'm happy for that. We are making the best of it, and I think Val is finally used to it. Carly has helped a lot, I'm sure," Matt grinned.

Jen pulled into the neighborhood, parking the truck in the driveway. She asked Matt if they should drive the cars, and he nodded.

An hour later, they walked into the house where Buddy and Fred greeted them. Carly was sitting at the table, eating some Chex Mix.

"Hey guys, where were you?" Carly asked.

"We took the plane up, scouted around. Where is Val?" Matt asked.

"Sleeping in. Bigtime," Carly rolled her eyes. "How was your date?"

"It was wonderful," Jen smiled.

"It really was, thanks for all your help, Carly," Matt grinned.

"Did you want to change your stitches now Matt?" Carly offered.

"Nah, Jen changed them last night," Matt waved.

"Oh?" Carly asked.

"I grabbed his arm by accident, they popped right out. He says it was worth it though," Jen laughed.

"I bet," Carly grinned.

"It's already eleven, you must have worn Val out, sheesh," Matt scoffed.

"Shush," Carly smiled. "What else did you want to do today?"

"We were going to ask you if you wanted to have your date with Val tonight, but she appears to be sleeping the day away," Matt grinned.

"I think she wants to do it tomorrow. When she is ready, we are going to go shopping. Did you guys want to come?" Carly asked.

"I am shopped out. And Matt doesn't like shopping. I think we will go to the pool while you guys are out," Jen replied. "Pick up some cologne for Matt though."

"Copy that," Carly finished, picking up her bowl and rinsing it out.

Val came into the kitchen, pushing Go on the Keurig and sitting down. "Good morning," she grumbled.

"Good afternoon. You feeling okay?" Matt teased.

"I'm fine. Carly kept me up last night. How was your date?" Val managed.

"It was wonderful, you did a great job on the brisket. Then we danced, then we made love, then I ripped his stitches out," Jen laughed.

"It really hurt, but I maintain it was worth it," Matt shook his head with a smile.

"I'm happy for you two," Val rolled her eyes, moving back into the kitchen to collect her coffee.

They let Val drink her coffee, knowing she wouldn't want to talk before she finished it. Buddy came up and asked for attention, and she petted him.

"What is on the agenda for today?" Val asked.

"Well, Matt and I took the plane up, flew around, came back, drove the cars, came back again, all before you finished your morning coffee. Now I think you are going to go shopping?" Jen teased.

"What are you going to do next?" Val sighed.

"Go to the pool, apparently," Matt grinned.

"Have fun," Val finished, standing up to get dressed.

"How late did you guys stay up Carly?" Matt whispered.

"Four or five. We were having fun. Sounds like you guys were too," Carly grinned.

"We were long asleep by then, the morphine knocked me out again," Matt admitted.

"There is no shame in it," Carly assured him.

"How often do you take morphine for your injuries?" Matt countered.

"Let me think...never," Carly laughed.

"Uh huh. Let's get dressed and head to the pool Jen. These two are impossible today," Matt sighed.

Jen walked into their room and started to change, while Matt followed her. Carly stopped him as he walked by.

"Hey Matt? We are happy for you two. I know you felt like you didn't deserve a woman like Jen, but if she didn't want to be with you, she wouldn't be. I don't know what's going on here, or how long we are going to be here, but she is making her own choices," Carly assured him.

"Thanks Carly. Despite this horrible name you chose, you continue to be good company," Matt grinned.

"I'm going to get you back for that one of these days Matt," Carly teased.

"This is going to seem random, but have you ever been deep sea fishing?" Matt asked.

"I've been out on yachts, does that count?" Carly asked.

"Probably not, did you even feel the waves?" Matt grinned.

"I have a bad history with boats, you know that," Carly chided him.

"That's true, I had forgotten about that. I'm sorry, I won't mention it again," Matt relented.

"It's okay, I am just teasing you. If you want to go deep sea fishing, I will be there, Matt," Carly assured him. "Enjoy the pool."

CHAPTER 27

SEASHELLS

It had been a few days, but curiously, the green light had not come from the sky. The team had been preparing for it, but when it didn't show, it left them with nothing to do. Carly and Val had gone on their own date, pretty much copying the theme from Matt and Jen's. There wasn't a lot they could do, but they had dressed to the nines anyway.

"So...we were planning on going to the island today to pick up our newest member, but with no light....what do we do?" Val asked.

"Well, we could still go to the island. Take the boats out. Jen and I found the shelling island we used to go to as kids, we could do that?" Matt offered.

"Oh yes. I love that idea. Let's go," Val beamed.

"Shelling?" Carly asked.

"We go and collect sea shells, it's fun," Val smiled. "Do we need anything from here?"

"Just your swimsuits and water shoes. We have buckets in the cottage. Maybe take a few fishing poles, even though I can't cast. Grab the dogs, they might like it," Matt grinned.

They collected Buddy and Fred, throwing them in the truck. Val radioed Sam, telling him they were heading to the island, just in case the light showed up late. He told them he would meet them there at some point. She got them going, and Buddy stuck his head out the window and let his ears fly.

They got to Port Isabel without incident, as Val steered them over the swing bridge and up to their sea cottage.

"Hey Jen? Why don't you take the *Invictus II* out for a spin, it needs a run. Just drive once around the bay and back, okay?" Matt asked.

"Sure Matt. You guys load up the other boat while I am gone," Jen beamed.

Val walked up the steps and fetched the keys, tossing them to Jen. She boarded the big boat and started it up, while Carly untied the lines and pushed her away.

"This is a nice setup you guys have here," Carly smiled.

"We uh, moved into this sea cottage, because it's both bigger, and closer to the channel. The smaller boat is actually ours, but we just commandeered the first big boat we found keys for," Matt grinned.

"We store everything inside, and more back in the neighborhood, the salt water destroys stuff here," Val lamented.

"I can see that, yeah. What do we need?" Carly asked.

"Just one bucket for each of us, the net, a fishing pole, some artificial lures, and an ice chest of drinks, which we have in the truck," Matt pointed.

Carly fetched the ice chest while Val handed him the buckets, and they started loading the bay boat. Matt started the engine, and let it run while they waited for Jen to return. Buddy was sniffing around the boat, and Fred was just staring at it from the dock, not wanting to jump in. They spotted Jen bringing the *Invictus II* back, and Carly helped her dock. Turning the engine off, they tied the lines off and joined Matt and Val. Jen picked up Fred and dropped him onto the bow, and he jumped down onto the deck. Laughing, Jen pushed the boat off and Matt steered them out into the channel.

"How far is it, Matt?" Val asked.

"Not terribly far, it's around the jetties, in Boca Chica. I had forgotten the name of the place, but that's where we are headed. We could have driven a car, but nah. The boats need use, and this way is just more enjoyable. Still, Jen, can you drive? My left arm is still bothering me too much to turn the wheel," Matt sighed.

"Of course, sit down here next to me and give me the heading. Everyone get in your seats—we are moving out. Carly? That means you, sit down," Jen beamed.

Carly had been standing on the bow for some reason, and she came to sit next to Val. Matt just waved Jen towards the island and she opened the throttle up, taking off. The porpoises came, and Carly was amazed, having never gotten that close to them before. Jen steered them around the salt flats and towards the jetties that Matt was pointing to.

"Oh, that opens into the Gulf? But there is a cut right there, I'm assuming that's the way we are going?" Jen asked.

"Right, steer us that way, take it easy, the waters are a little rough," Matt grinned.

Jen slowed down a bit, heading into the cut. Matt pointed out the little island, it was more of a peninsula, and she beached the boat, raising the engine out of the water.

"Val? Throw the anchor, if you would," Matt called out.

"Okay, um? How exactly?" Val asked.

"Pick it up and throw it over the side," Jen laughed.

"Right," Val relented, picking up the anchor and dropping it into the water. The boat turned with the rope, pulling against it until coming to a firm stop.

"Okay, you may safely disembark. Don't forget your buckets. Jen? Can I hand you the ice chest and towels?" Matt offered.

"Um? Where are we supposed to disembark, exactly?" Val stammered.

"You really don't remember this huh? I guess you were pretty little at the time," Matt grinned. "I will show you."

Matt hopped out of the boat and down into the water. Carly followed him, wading ashore. Jen handed Matt the towels, and jumped out herself. Val handed her the ice chest, and hopped down. They waded ashore together, as Matt deployed the towels. They realized they forgot the dogs when both of them started baying at them. Buddy was wanting to jump into the water, he just needed a little more encouragement.

"I guess we forgot the hounds," Matt grinned, wading back. He took Buddy in his right arm and carried him ashore, as Jen went for Fred. She dropped him into the water and he swam ashore on his own. Matt put the lead on Buddy and tied it around the ice chest handle. He was a Beagle, and he would literally run away at the first chance. They didn't have a lead for Fred, so they just hoped he would stick close to Jen.

"It would be a good idea to deploy the suntan lotion first. Then just go pick up the shells you like. We used to look for whole sand dollars, starfish, and hermit crabs. And if someone wants to go fishing, the gear is in the boat," Matt offered.

They took turns applying the lotion on each other, then they broke up. Val paired up with Matt, and Jen and Carly headed off together.

"So, I'm not trying to pull you away from your girlfriend, but there is something I am curious about," Val beamed.

"What is that? I'm not telling you how she is in bed," Matt grinned.

"What is it like being with such a prominent global figure that we can't remember?" Val beamed.

"It's really intimidating, I try not to think about that fact, at all. She is the most amazing person I have ever met. She met the Emperor of Japan, Val. A literal deity. *No one* meets the Emperor of Japan. Honestly, she isn't out of my league, because I am not even *in* a league. It's really hard to not believe she is just settling for plain old Matt," Matt whispered.

"Well, you are wrong. But she is very intimidating, so I can't tell you that you are horribly wrong. I know we have all told you this—if she didn't want you, she wouldn't be with you. I think she is very happy, and if she isn't, then she deserves all the acting awards on the planet. You did it right, you took it slow, you respected her, and you let her take the lead. I wish we knew how long this stupid experiment was lasting, so I could comment more on the long-term outlook of your relationship, but I hope that stupid Puppetmaster is choking on her drink," Val laughed as she picked up a sand dollar.

"How are things with Carly?" Matt grinned.

"Amazing. I love hanging out with her every day, then bedding her every night. Our date was a lot of fun, when are we going to do our double date?" Val beamed.

"Soon, I would say as soon as tomorrow, since we had a no show today. Maybe we are done getting new people," Matt shrugged, picking up a starfish.

"I doubt it. The Sunwalker was weird, what if we get a Nightwalker? Can only join us at night?" Val offered.

"Oh jeez, don't say that. We would have to go wake the Sunwalker up. One vampire is bad enough, we can't sustain two," Matt lamented.

"How is your arm?" Val asked.

"It is still very sore. I still need a few weeks, I think. Jen wants to go catch a wahoo, and so do I. But I have to be at 100% to go deep sea fishing. You don't have to go if you don't want to, but I think it would be really great," Matt offered.

"I will take some motion sickness medicine and suck it up. I'm not passing on any group activities if they don't involve heights," Val smiled, picking up a big starfish.

"Couple more weeks, it will be fun. We have to go way out to catch wahoo, so we will definitely attract some porpoises," Matt grinned.

"So, I've got a question. What is a wahoo?" Val laughed.

"It's a rare fish, like a barracuda, that's the best description I can offer. It's delicious," Matt smiled. "If we catch one, it could feed all of us for days."

They made their way around, joining Jen and Carly, who had full buckets. Walking back to the towels, Matt asked if anyone wanted to fish while the others sunbathed. Jen volunteered, and set out to get the rod and tackle. Matt knew she didn't need help, as he sat down on the towel. Carly shot him a look and laid down in the middle, while Val laid to her left. Buddy sat next to Matt as he petted him.

They watched Jen set up her artificial lures and cast her line out into the channel. Fred was close by, watching. None of them could take their eyes off her, as she shot them a smile. Finally, after several casts, she hooked something.

"Oh, I think she has one!" Val exclaimed. Soon enough the fish started jumping out of the water.

"Oh man, a skip jack, have fun Jen," Matt laughed. "Huge fighting fish."

Jen and the fish were battling it out, as it jumped out of the water repeatedly. She didn't seem to be making much progress, as she tried to reel while it was in the air. Finally, she started making her way back towards land, pulling the fish out of the water and onto the beach. Matt got up and went over, it was about 18 inches long.

"Looks good, want to keep him? We can cook it when we get home," Matt grinned.

"Heck yeah, I didn't fight like that just to let him go," Jen laughed. She brought the fish next to them, getting the hook out and heading back for the water. The fish was literally flapping around on the sand, and Val wasn't thrilled. Buddy was very curious, however.

"Um Matt? A little help?" Val sighed.

Matt grinned and threw the fish in his bucket, where it flapped around even more. Val wasn't amused but that was all he could do until it died. Buddy was watching it intently; he had never seen a fish before. Jen was back at it, and Carly and Matt went back to checking her out. They broke out some drinks, content to lie there until Jen was finished. Finally she hooked another fish.

"Oh, she has another one," Val observed. "No jumping, what could it be?"

"It's not pulling too hard, probably a sand trout," Matt guessed.

The fish actually started to pull harder as Jen got closer to landing it, causing her to back up again. She finally got it on land and Matt saw it was a flounder.

"Don't see too many of those anymore. Looks like it would have to be thrown back if there were people here to enforce the rules. Oh well, come throw it in the bucket Jen!" Matt shouted.

Jen smiled and brought it back, tossing it into the bucket next to the dead skip jack. It flapped around a little bit as she walked back to the water. No one objected as she cast her line out once again. Buddy and Fred continued to watch, seemingly wanting to help.

"Dinner is coming along nicely," Matt grinned.

"And yet all you are thinking about is dessert," Carly teased.

"I doubt it, Matt isn't that kind of guy. Despite the fact she is looking gorgeous out there," Val laughed.

"I'm actually a little concerned about what Val was saying earlier about a nightwalker," Matt sighed.

Before anyone could say anything, Jen hooked another fish. This one was pulling hard, as she backed up, but it pulled more line out.

"It's a big one, probably a stupid hardhead. A catfish. Something no one wants," Matt grinned.

"We will see," Val smiled.

Jen landed the fish, it was a prized speckled trout, a big one. Matt cheered her on as she brought it over. It was as big as the skip jack, as she tossed it in the bucket.

"I believe I have taken care of dinner. Shall we go?" Jen beamed.

"Absolutely, I'll get the bucket of fish and the Beagle, Carly, can you get the ice chest? And Val, the towels and sea shells?" Matt asked.

"Yep!" Val exclaimed.

They packed up their gear and waded back into the boat. Matt turned his back to the bow and hopped up, bottom first, his arm just wouldn't let him pull himself in like the others. He helped Carly with the ice chest, then took her hand and helped her into the boat. Jen handed him Buddy, and then she and Val lifted the fat Basset Hound up. Carly helped with Fred, then helped Val get in the boat. Matt went back and started the engine while Jen stayed in the water.

"What's going on?" Val asked.

"Carly? Can you get the anchor?" Matt asked.

"Yep," Carly nodded, as she pulled the anchor into the boat. Jen was directly in front of the bow, and pushed the boat into the channel. Matt steered it out, as Jen quickly hopped in and slid down off the bow.

"Oh, that worked well," Val beamed.

Jen smiled and came to take the wheel, turning them into the channel.

"This was so much fun guys. Thank you," Jen laughed, as she revved the engine and accelerated towards home. The porpoises came again, as Carly pointed them out. Matt just took in the view as Jen brought them into the final stretch. Docking, Carly and Val grabbed the pylons and tied the boat off. Val headed towards the sea cottage, but Matt stopped her.

"Wait! We aren't just heading home this time. Val, help us unload the boat. Then Jen and I will fillet these fish, or I can do it, and you guys can relax. One of you three needs to wash the boat though," Matt grinned.

"I will help you Matt, and Val can wash the boat while Carly loads the truck," Jen offered.

"Sounds like a plan," Carly grinned.

"How do I wash the boat?" Val asked.

"Get the water hose, hose it down. Look at how sandy it got. Get it all off. This used to be my favorite chore," Matt grinned.

"Didn't you hate all chores?" Val teased.

"Yep. Except this singular one," Matt laughed.

They got the boat unloaded, and Matt walked inside the sea cottage to collect a fillet knife, bringing it back to the dock. Jen laid the fish out and Matt cut into them. It took about one second for them to attract guests.

"Wow, they are literally flocking to you guys!" Carly laughed.

"Yeah yeah," Matt sighed, tossing some pieces of flesh into the flock of seagulls. He got the skip jack done and Jen put the fillets into a ziplock, waiting for him to finish. The flounder was a bit harder—it was just a weird fish. He did his best. Jen offered some help but she didn't know the exact method either. He tossed the rotting carcass into the water and the seagulls flocked to it. Last was the trout, he was a lot more careful with it, it was good meat. Finishing up, Val had finished hosing the boat down and was getting out.

"You are right, that is a fun chore," Val beamed. "But we still have to get the dogs."

"Yep," Matt grinned. "Did we get all the gear inside? Let's pack up, get the Beagle and head home."

CHAPTER 28

THE NIGHTWALKER

The group was eating the fish at the table, dogs in their respective positions, when Sam knocked and entered.

"Hey guys. Is that fish?" Sam asked.

"Yeah, would you like some? We saved you some pieces," Matt offered.

"Yeah, thanks," Sam nodded, taking a plate Val was offering. "This is good. I have news."

"Finish your food and share it," Val smiled.

"Yeah, I will," Sam nodded, eating the rest of the fish. "So, the green light is back. It's shining down, bright as ever."

"Terrific," Matt muttered. "A light at night. What does that tell you? Based on the last person to arrive?"

"It's not good. I think we should even consider waking him. Which means you guys need to donate some blood. Are you up for that?" Sam growled.

"Yeah, I am. Meanwhile, Jen? Can you get the SCAR, it has a night-scope. Carly, grab a shotgun as well," Matt sighed. "The clips to the SCAR are in the drawers beneath it, Jen."

"On it," Jen nodded. She and Carly headed towards the gun cabinet in the guest room, while Matt got the blood packs and the syringe out.

"I will go start the truck," Val offered, heading out.

"Sam? I need you to draw the blood," Matt sighed.

Sam nodded and found a good vein, extracting a syringe and depositing it into the blood packet. He took one more dose from the other arm, declaring them done.

"If it's a vampire, what do you think we should do?" Matt whispered.

"Same thing we always do, kid. Make an offer, decide whether it lives or dies," Sam growled.

"How often have you fought vampires?" Matt asked.

"Enough to know they are a pain in the ass," Sam growled. "But it's nothing I can't handle, and with the Sunwalker, I might just leave it to him. It's his field."

"So basically, the offer will be—hibernate or die?" Matt offered.

"Yep," Sam growled.

"Okay," Matt shrugged.

Jen and Carly came back in, Jen was carrying the SCAR, with the strap wrapped around her shoulder, and three extra clips in her gunbelt. Carly just had the shotgun in her hands.

"You look like you know what you are doing, so let's go," Sam growled.

"Good to go Matt?" Jen grinned.

"Oh yeah, you definitely look like an expert carrying that weapon, but I don't think regular bullets would faze a vampire. Let's go pick up the Sunwalker," Matt sighed.

They piled into the truck, Sam getting in the tailgate, as Val drove them out. She asked Sam where the funeral home was and Sam just pointed west, so she steered that way. He guided her there and they came to a stop.

"Keep the engine running Val," Sam growled, as the rest of them got out. She just nodded as they entered the dark funeral home. Sam opened a coffin, and inside the Sunwalker was sleeping, staff in hand.

Opening his eyes, he looked at them. Matt handed him the blood packet, complete with straw. Taking it, the Sunwalker drank. It had an immediate effect, as he sat up, looking at them for an explanation.

"You kids have a vampire on the loose or something?" the Sunwalker asked.

"We think so. The light didn't come until nighttime. And that's telling us it's some kind of trouble. This is your field, we could use your help, if you are up for it," Matt offered.

"Count me in," the Sunwalker growled, getting out of the coffin. He followed them outside and jumped into the tailgate with Sam.

Val said nothing and steered them towards the island. Driving in silence, the green light was shining down brightly as they arrived an hour later. At Sam's direction, she parked further down from the light, and they got out. Walking down the pier, Jen peered through the night-scope, but it wasn't necessary.

"It's a vampire alright," the Sunwalker growled, as they could see the creature's blue eyes looking their way, even from a distance.

"It's a woman," Jen declared. "Wearing black latex, long hair."

"Seriously?" Matt scoffed. "Probably a character from that mediocre movie series."

"That series was hot garbage," Val declared.

"It would be easy to fuse together a bunch of characters and this was the end result. The lead was the only reason to watch, I'm guessing she was involved," Matt sighed.

"Oh, I'm sure she is a real succubus, lure you in with her prized booty, then suck your blood. Are we doing this or not," the Sunwalker growled, beginning to head towards the fire, staff in hand—it actually extended out into a spear of sorts.

They caught up with him, and to Matt's surprise, he didn't tell them off. Slowly, they approached the fire, she was snarling at the Sunwalker, and he returned the greeting.

"Who are you? Where is this?" the woman asked.

"What did the fire tell you?" Matt sighed.

"That I am the Nightwalker, destined to walk by the Chosen Ones," the Nightwalker growled.

"Real genius, that fire," the Sunwalker muttered.

"What a nightmare," Val whispered, moving behind Sam. "Do you think those idiots are on some kind of vampire binge?"

"Yeah, I actually do. Listen, Nightwalker. I am going to make you an offer, then leave. Hibernate, or fight it out with the Sunwalker until one of you dies," Matt offered.

"Or, fight it out with the Sunwalker anyway, and then go hibernate," the Sunwalker growled.

"Let's go," Matt waved the rest of them on. Sam stayed behind, as they made their way off the beach. Jen was keeping an eye on them, as Sam was slowly deploying his claws. The Nightwalker saw them, but didn't waver, as she drew her own sword and attacked the Sunwalker..

"Run!" Jen shouted.

They ran off the beach, towards the truck, Matt looking back to see the Nightwalker leaping into the air, with the Sunwalker following her. She was still snarling, but he wasn't backing down, as they moved to hand to hand.

Arriving at the truck, Val got it started and sped away. Driving over the bridge, Jen declared they were clear and they relaxed a bit.

"Okay! This is getting out of hand, not one vampire, but two?? What in the world?" Val demanded.

"Am I the only one that noticed the Sunwalker was right? She did have a great ass," Carly laughed.

"Oh you," Val glared. "Matt?"

"I mean, I agree with Carly, she was hot," Matt shrugged.

"I give up. We are going home," Val sighed.

"What about Sam?" Carly asked.

"He will be fine," Val declared.

"Yeah, don't worry about Sam, swords can't hurt him. We will check in with him in the morning, see how it went," Matt sighed.

Val drove them home, getting out of the truck and leading Carly inside. Not even offering a good night, they went into their room and closed the door. Jen just shook her head and went to put the gun away, while Matt poured them some wine. He gave Val a 50/50 chance of coming back for a glass as he set four on the table. She did in fact, come back for two of them and headed back to her room. Matt smiled and waited for Jen.

Coming in, she sat down and sipped some wine. "In all seriousness, what do you think we should do?"

"Nothing? Those two wanted to fight it out, and Sam wasn't moving either. We did the right thing. We will try to pick up the pieces in the morning. Do you want to head to bed as well?" Matt grinned.

"It ended up being a long day, let's just go to sleep," Jen whispered.

"I agree. Tomorrow we can regroup. I think Val wants to have our double date, but you will get a say as well," Matt grinned.

"That sounds lovely. I hope they picked out multiple dresses, wearing the same outfit is unacceptable," Jen teased.

"If you are taking a subtle shot at me, I have plenty of different shirts and jackets. It was all free, so I took a lot," Matt laughed.

"Bravo, Matt. Come to bed," Jen stood up and led him into their own room, with Buddy and Fred following. Jen changed into something more comfortable while Matt unmade the bed. He picked Buddy up and fell into bed. The Beagle moved down to the foot of the bed and lay down, while Fred lay in his own bed on Jen's side. She finally came and snuggled down next to him, taking his hand.

"Good night Matt," Jen whispered.

"Good night Jen, I love you," Matt whispered back.

"I love you too," Jen grinned.

———

Hours later, Matt thought he heard the front door open, and Buddy waking up and growling confirmed it. Figuring it was Sam, he sighed and stood up. Jen woke up as well, but he left her there to check out the situation. Surprised, he went back into the bedroom and told Jen to get dressed and join him. She nodded and slowly got moving.

Walking out together, they found Sam sitting at the table with the Sunwalker, and to their enormous surprise, the Nightwalker.

"Good evening. What is going on?" Matt managed.

"We got it out of our system, we couldn't go any further, now we are here," the Sunwalker growled.

"Too angry to ask for help?" Sam growled.

Relenting, the Sunwalker continued, "I need blood before I go back to hibernate. The succubus does as well."

"I am not a succubus," the Nightwalker hissed.

"What happened on the beach?" Matt sighed, sitting down.

"I killed her several times, cut her head off even, she reappeared by the fire every time," the Sunwalker growled.

"Did she ever kill you?" Matt asked.

"Tch," the Sunwalker scoffed. "Once. I also reappeared at the fire…I can't explain it."

"So, it's hibernation then. You understand why, right Nightwalker?" Matt asked.

"Yes. You can't sustain two of us," the Nightwalker growled.

"Right. I can't even give you blood tonight. Jen? Will you help them?" Matt asked.

"Yes," Jen whispered, rolling her sleeves up while Sam got a fresh syringe and blood packet.

"We can only give you one packet for the two of you. You are going to have to share," Matt offered.

"Fine," the Sunwalker growled.

"Thank you," the Nightwalker added.

"To think the vampire has more manners than the vampire hunter," Sam growled.

"Tch. Whatever man. None of this makes sense," the Sunwalker scoffed.

Sam filled the syringe twice, then offered the packet to the Nightwalker first. She drank half of it, then handed it to the Sunwalker. He took it, glared at her, flipped the straw over, and drank. Finishing, he stood up.

"I'll say it again, you kids ain't bad. It was smart to come and get me, if another problem arises, you know where to find me. Just make sure to bring blood again. Can't imagine you needing the succubus for anything," the Sunwalker growled, walking out of the house.

The Nightwalker glared at him as he left, then turned back to Matt and Jen. "I appreciate the blood. I'll go hibernate now, wake me if you need something," she offered, standing up herself and leaving.

Sam let them go before starting again. "The regeneration thing was weird. I even killed her once, and she reappeared by the fire. Someone out there is definitely pulling the strings. Keep doing what you are doing, I will take care of security," he growled.

"How is Gracie?" Matt asked.

"She is fine," Sam shrugged, standing up. "She is a good dog."

"Have a good night, Sam," Matt relented. Sam walked out and closed the door behind him. Matt looked out the window, the two vampires were long gone.

"Well, that was...something," Jen offered.

"I'll bandage your arm, then we can go back to bed," Matt sighed. "I wish we could get a normal person for once."

He wrapped Jen's arm in bandages and led her back to their room. Buddy and Fred hadn't moved, as they got under the blankets and fell asleep.

CHAPTER 29

THE DOUBLE DATE

Two days later, Carly was examining Matt's arm in the bathroom. Both he and Jen had needed a day to recover from the blood drainage, but tonight they were having their double date. Carly was checking in with Matt, while Val and Jen were already preparing themselves.

"It's looking better. I would say another week, then we can take the stitches out. Maybe sooner. How has it been feeling?" Carly asked.

"It hasn't been bothering me as much, I can lift it a lot more now. I still feel it, but it's nowhere near as bad as it used to be. I appreciate all the attention you have given it," Matt relented.

"It's no big deal, Matt. I like taking care of you, even Jen knows it. She could do this, but she understands a gal's need to be around a guy from time to time. Are you nervous about tonight?" Carly teased.

"No, I've already done this once. I've basically accepted that Jen is everything. I think Val might be in trouble though, she doesn't like being put on the spot," Matt grinned.

"She can be very indecisive. Should I warn her?" Carly smiled.

"No way. I didn't have any warnings, no, she is just going to have to answer the questions," Matt laughed.

"How about just a hint? Make my night easier for me? I'm here taking care of you, after all," Carly chided him.

"That's fair. Okay—Most desired vacation destination," Matt grinned.

"Oh, that's going to be rough. I have asked her that very question, she demanded parameters. What are the parameters for that?" Carly laughed. "Did you struggle with that question?"

"Oh no. I answered right away, it has probably raised Jen's expectations. If I knew my answer that fast, she is going to want at least something. She will probably turn to you next," Matt smiled.

"Hmm, I'll work on something. Thanks for the hint. We are several hours away, you probably don't want to get dressed right now. I can come back and help you, if you need it?" Carly offered.

"Honestly, it's the dress shirt. If you could help me with it when the time comes, I would deeply appreciate it Carly," Matt said smiling.

"Of course. Don't be embarrassed. I will come see you when the time arrives. Until then, just relax. Take care of the dogs, check the meat," Carly smiled. She stood up and exited the bathroom, heading to her own room to get ready. Having four bedrooms was pretty convenient in this case. Matt exited as well, heading for the kitchen.

Val had suggested brisket again, but Matt had shot it down. Jen wasn't allowing the same outfits, there was no way she would allow the same meal. He had settled on individual 12 oz sirloins that he had started by baking in the oven. He would move them to the grill when the time got closer. He wasn't sure what the exact time was, but Jen had assured him she would give him plenty of notice to cook dinner, then get ready.

An hour passed, Matt was outside checking the garden, it was in a sad state of affairs. The only crop that was growing were the carrots. But even they were barely making it. He picked a few and took them inside, washing them. They looked edible, but he wasn't going to eat them, and certainly wasn't going to give them to Jen. Letting out a sigh, he moved to the freezer, picking out the pre-approved bag of baby carrots.

Carly came in, telling him they would be ready in about an hour. He nodded and got the sirloins out of the oven; they had just been warming. Moving outside to the grill, he threw them on as Carly followed him. She was wearing a long blue dress, and stood back so nothing coming off the fire hit her.

"You look really nice Carly," Matt offered.

"I'm not good at this, Val is going to help me when she is finished. I feel like if I walked out like this I would just disappear before Jen," Carly lamented.

"Jen isn't good at it either, she just has more experience. But she doesn't like dressing up," Matt assured her.

"Well, for not liking it she sure knows every single detail of it," Carly laughed.

"Like I said, experience, as well as expectations. She was front page news, if she made a mistake, it would be all over the world in five minutes. I told her to take it easy this time, because of you and Val, I hope she listens," Matt grinned.

"Same. What is your plan here? Grill the steaks, then go get dressed?" Carly asked.

"Yes, that's the plan. You don't have to stay out here with me if you don't want to," Matt replied.

"Don't say that. I have to help you get dressed, remember? Then I am going to go get help from Val. No one can be late, because we don't have a set time. We are multitasking the food, and you have a bad arm," Carly chided him. "How long for the steaks?"

"Not long, they were baking in the oven, so I am essentially heating them up so they will be fresh. I nearly forgot the carrots, they are in the pan, can you go turn the stove on?" Matt asked.

"You got it," Carly smiled.

Carly went inside, Matt didn't even watch her, she looked back to see if he was, and turned the stove on. The carrots started to sizzle as Matt got the sirloins onto a plate and brought them inside. Setting them on the counter, he moved towards his own room as she followed him, while the dogs stayed beneath the steaks they could only dream about.

"I am going to suffer tonight because of you," Carly teased, as she unbuttoned his purple dress shirt. Jen had made him switch colors with her.

"What do you mean?" Matt asked, curiously.

"I bet Val you would look at me while I walked away from you in this dress, and she said not only would you not, but you would barely even see me. You are all about Jen and we all know it," Carly laughed.

"Well, if you knew that, why did you make the bet?" Matt grinned.

"Fun," Carly shrugged.

"Hey," Matt said gently. "I do see you, Carly. I already told you that you look nice, and I meant it. I know you are only half ready right now, I'm sure you will look lovely by the time we are at the table. Did you work on your answers?"

"Yeah, I know what I am going to say, thanks for the hint. And thanks for saying those things. Here, let's get you in the dress shirt. Purple? Really?" Carly teased.

"Jen chose our colors tonight," Matt shrugged. "You and Val aren't doing a theme?"

"She told me blue, so I am in blue," Carly shrugged as well as she lifted the dress shirt onto him. Buttoning the shirt up, then the cuffs, she smiled. "Once again you look very handsome, Matt."

"Thank you, Carly. And thank you for your help. Can you go get the carrots off the stove, while I finish up here? Then you can go get ready," Matt said, smoothing his shirt.

"Of course, see you soon," Carly smiled, as she headed out.

Matt slowly slipped into his new suit jacket, buttoning the two bottom buttons, and applied the cologne Jen had found for him. Heading out himself, Carly had simply turned the stove off, so Matt took the pan of carrots off the burner and served them onto a platter. Making sure he had the wine partially opened, he simply waited for the women to arrive.

Jen actually came first, perhaps she believed if she was first, it would give the other two their own moments in the spotlight. She was wearing a long, dark green dress, with a slit that only came up to her ankles. Her hair was once again curled and down, this time a side ponytail.

"Good evening, Jen, you look lovely tonight," Matt smiled.

"Thank you, Matt. You look handsome as well, I like these colors for us," Jen beamed.

"I do too," Matt smiled.

"I know they are your favorite colors for me to wear, I thought I would share them with you," Jen smiled.

Val and Carly came out together, Val was in a red dress, and Carly was in her blue. Their hair was down as well, and they looked very happy to be there.

"Good evening, Val, Carly. You both look lovely as well," Matt smiled.

"Thank you, Matt. I love how you two are matching," Val beamed.

"Thank you, Matt," Carly whispered.

Val and Matt escorted their dates to their seats, and scooted them in. Matt helped Val sit down as well, then went to get the food. Serving it, he brought back the wine and opened it. Pouring each of them a glass, he sat down.

"Thank you for cooking Matt," Jen smiled.

"Yes, thank you Matt," Val beamed.

"So, Val," Jen started. "I asked Matt this last week, and he answered right away. I enjoyed his answer a lot, so now I will pose the same question to you. If you could vacation anywhere right now, where would you go?"

"Oh…are there parameters for this question? Like, is time traveling allowed?" Val asked.

"There are no parameters, and while I won't say time traveling is impossible, it is not allowed. I am talking about right now, present day. No humans to hinder us. Where would you go?" Jen smiled.

"I think…I would go to Rome, most likely. Or Greece. Ancient history interests me," Val managed.

"Rome is always wonderful. I have tried extra hard not to burn any bridges there," Jen smiled.

"What um, how do you burn bridges, exactly?" Val asked.

"Oh, you know. Blow things up, steal things, shoot people, that kind of stuff. Carly? What about you? Where would you go, if you could go anywhere right now?" Jen smiled.

"I spent a lot of time traveling the world as a Superhero, I never really saw any of it. I think I would also like to go back to Rome, as a tourist, as a lover," Carly offered. "I'm surprised to hear you have shot at people Jen. But then again, you handled that assault rifle easily when we went to pick up the Nightwalker."

"Plenty of bad people have taken their shots at me. Most, if not all of my expeditions have greedy competitors, pirates, thieves, you name it. I would much prefer to not have to shoot people, but I'm not delusional about what ambition does to men," Jen reflected.

"Well, there are no more men out there, so…if we could move on please," Matt whispered.

"Matt is correct, let's move on. How is your arm, Matt? I am anxious to go on our next adventure," Jen smiled.

"Are we sure that's polite dinner conversation?" Val offered. "I think our next adventure involves our beds."

Carly stifled a laugh as Matt could only shake his head. Jen was more composed than all of them, "Actually, I believe it's deep sea fishing. I want a wahoo, and Matt wants his big blue."

"Big blue?" Carly asked.

"Blue Marlin. I have always wanted to catch one. The sailfish was fun, but he was small," Matt smiled. "I think next week, I should be good to go. The stitches are falling out, so we can head to the island, prepare the boat and the gear, pick up our next person, drop them off somewhere, then head out. I am really hoping it is just a normal human being this time around," Matt grinned.

"Do we have the necessary gear for deep sea fishing?" Val asked.

"Yes, it's all in one of the neighboring houses. Four big poles, plenty of line, a gaff, a net, plenty of lures. The one thing we need is live bait, but I have an idea for that. We can trap some perch, use the bigger ones," Matt replied.

"I'm not very functional in the morning, so I will need time. What time do you want to push off?" Val asked.

"No later than 6am, it will probably take a good hour to get far enough out for wahoo," Matt grinned.

"This is literally the only thing on Earth Matt will get up early for. Fishing," Val rolled her eyes.

"He will get up early for me if I ask him to," Jen smiled.

"That's true, yes," Val admitted.

"How was the sirloin?" Matt asked.

"Oh, it was very well cooked, baking it first was a good idea, no way to undercook it, well done Matt," Jen beamed.

"I agree it tastes wonderful. I wish our garden was doing better, I don't know what the problem is," Val lamented.

"Sunlight, most likely," Matt offered.

"Yes, we probably need to adjust the amount of sun the crops are getting," Jen nodded.

"Are we dancing next?" Carly asked.

"Yes, if everyone is finished, let's move to the dance floor," Jen beamed.

The couples stood up, and Jen put some more Sinatra on. Carly was still very nervous as she danced with Val, who was trying to encourage her. Matt held Jen close as Sinatra sang.

"Dance with Carly next Matt, she isn't feeling good," Jen whispered.

"What do you think the problem is?" Matt whispered back.

"She likely feels very out of place in this setting," Jen offered. "Do whatever you have to make her feel like part of our group, Matt."

"Ah...you know what? I think I know what's going on," Matt whispered. "Turn Val away from us, okay?"

"Of course," Jen smiled. "I'm glad you figured it out as well."

The song ended, and the couples swapped places, Jen grabbed Val, while Matt grabbed Carly. Carly was very quiet, as the next Sinatra song started. Jen turned Val away, as promised, so Matt could talk to Carly.

"Are you okay?" Matt whispered.

"Yes, I'm fine Matt," Carly whispered back.

"You are a poor liar," Matt teased, as he pulled her closer. "What's wrong?"

"I just don't feel...comfortable here," Carly relented.

Matt slid her hands down her backside, causing her to gasp. "What can I do to fix that?" he teased again.

"Matt," Carly gasped, as she looked at Jen and Val, who were not looking at them. "Please."

Matt lifted his hands back up and smiled. "I know what's going on Carly. I'll help you with it. Meanwhile, why don't you and I go out tomorrow? We can do whatever you want, wear whatever color you want."

"I—.I would like that Matt," Carly relented, looking Val's way again. Jen still had her turned away. "Maybe we can take the *Invictus II* out? Make sure it's ready for an actual fishing trip?"

"Sure Carly. I would like that," Matt grinned, as she rested her head against his shoulder. The song ended and they switched partners a third time. Matt and Val started to dance together.

"I've never seen you like this Val. It makes me happy to see you so happy, in these dark times," Matt grinned.

"I can safely say we are making the absolute best of a horrible experiment that people should be boiled alive for," Val beamed.

"How is Carly?" Matt whispered.

"She seems kind of down, I don't know why," Val lamented.

"I have a guess. You have helped me with Jen, I guess it's time for me to return the favor. She seems to be working really hard to keep you happy...are you uh, reciprocating?" Matt asked.

"I feel like...maybe I should focus more on that," Val relented.

"Maybe you should, yes. It's a horrible experiment for us all, and Carly needs some attention. She and I are going out tomorrow, you know, take her mind off things. When we come back, you should have something nice ready for her," Matt offered.

"I agree Matt. I will definitely focus on that," Val nodded.

"Let her choose the colors for your next date as well. I think...she might be tiring of blue," Matt whispered.

"But it looks so good on her," Val whined.

"I'm wearing purple for Jen," Matt countered.

"That's fair. Alright," Val relented. "Thanks Matt."

They switched partners again, finishing with their original dates. Matt nodded to Jen that everything was going to be okay. She nodded back and they danced in silence. The songs came to an end, and they finished the evening.

"Thank you for the wonderful evening. We will see you tomorrow, good night," Jen smiled.

"Good night," Carly whispered.

"Good night," Val beamed.

CHAPTER 30

MATT 3 CARLY

"Let me know when you see the fish," Matt offered. "I have to drive the boat until then. Just focus on reeling it in like I showed you."

"How am I going to see the fish while sitting in this chair?" Carly asked, bewildered. She was sitting in the fighting chair, reeling in the first and likely only catch of the day. She and Matt had taken the *Invictus II* out, about a mile or so offshore. Matt had set up some artificial lures, and they had hooked their first catch.

"You will see it, trust me," Matt laughed.

Carly reeled the fish in, pulling back on the rod. About five minutes later, she finally understood what was going on. "Oh, I see it! Right there in the wave!"

"Okay, keep reeling," Matt shouted back. He saw the scales reflecting off the sunlight as the fish swam inside the wave. She still had about 20 more yards of line out.

Carly kept reeling, as Matt kept an eye on the fish. When it got to be about five yards away, he let go of the wheel and walked back to the stern, grabbing the line. He motioned with his fingers to keep reeling, as he pulled the line in as well. Finally seeing the blue tail, he pulled the fish in.

"Benito, exactly what we need," Matt grinned.

"He fought like a demon," Carly admitted. "Still, that was fun. Want to keep going?"

"We can if you want, I'll throw this guy in the storage bin, one second," Matt grinned, as he used pliers to get the hook and lure out of its mouth. Picking the fish up, he tossed it in the front storage bin and came back. The other rod was ready to go, as he dropped the lure in the water and let the line out. Readying the second rod, he repeated the process and walked back to the wheel. Carly followed him, smiling.

"Thank you for today, Matt, this is really nice," Carly beamed. She was wearing a white bikini, and kissed him on the cheek, asking if that was okay.

"You can get as close as you want," Matt grinned.

"Oh you," Carly laughed. "You were right about everything, just so you know. Val promised to make it up to me."

"I know she did. She has been trying to block out the situation, and probably forgot it takes two people to make a relationship. I'm sure everything will be better now," Matt grinned, as he pulled Carly closer to him.

"Watch it, mister. I know you like to use your hands," Carly pushed him back.

One of the lines started singing again, as the rod was being pulled violently. "Saved by the fish," Matt grinned.

He went back to reel in the other line quickly, as Carly sat back in the chair again. Putting the rod through the holder, he encouraged her to reel away as he got back on the wheel.

"I think this one is way smaller, not fighting nearly as much," Carly shouted.

"Nah, not smaller, dumber. He is swimming towards the boat," Matt laughed as he slowed the boat down.

"Oh, you are right, I see him already. It looks yellow!" Carly offered.

"Great news. It's probably a dorado, which means dinner," Matt smiled.

"There is the ten-yard ribbon," Carly reported, as the black ribbon tied to the line passed by.

"Coming," Matt grinned, as he pulled the line in again. Carly kept reeling as Matt looked for the fish. Once again, it came tail-first as he reached in and grabbed it. "Yep, dolphin. Good size, about 15 inches. Could be bigger, but still, this should feed all of us tonight."

"Oh, I recognize that fish," Carly smiled.

"Yeah, it's very recognizable," Matt grinned, as he threw it in the front storage bin. "Want to keep going?"

"Absolutely, provided you don't make any more advancements towards my ass," Carly laughed.

"No promises," Matt smiled as he got the lines out again.

"How about one more, then head home?" Carly smiled.

"Okay, make it count," Matt nodded, as he drove the boat. She stood up again and joined him.

"Can't stay away from me, huh?" Matt teased.

"I enjoy your company a lot, I admit. Your sarcasm makes me laugh," Carly grinned.

"I try my best," Matt smiled.

The line started singing again, the fish were abundant with no one out there catching them. Matt walked back and repeated the process, getting the other line in first then giving Carly the rod.

"Oh, this one is much meaner," Carly growled.

"Yeah, I'll be back on the wheel, help you out a bit," Matt grinned as he accelerated a bit, pulling the fish along. It was technically cheating, but no one was going to call them out on it.

"Matt...it's heavy. I can barely pull it," Carly lamented.

Matt walked back and hooked the rod to the chair, and helped her pull back on it. "You can use both hands now, the rod is tied down, it's not going anywhere. Pull back, then reel down. You are right, whatever is out there, it's mean," Matt offered.

He got back on the wheel while Carly continued the fight. It was much easier with both hands, and she was starting to make progress.

"Whenever you feel it swimming towards you, focus on reeling, don't worry about pulling," Matt pressed. "The more you do this, the easier it will get. You have to learn to let the fish tire itself out. You don't have to constantly reel."

"Right," Carly grunted, as she continued to pull. Twenty minutes went by, Matt had come back to help her pull a few times, but they still couldn't see the fish.

"What do you think it is?" Carly growled.

"It could be a big benito, that fits the profile. They love fighting. You still have a lot of line out, keep pulling," Matt encouraged her.

"Look I see it, it's huge. There's the ten-yard ribbon," Carly pointed, gaining confidence.

Matt came back, gaff in hand, and pulled the line. "Keep reeling, it's not over yet. I need to gaff it, so you have to get most of the line in. I see it now."

"What is it?" Carly growled, as she kept reeling.

"It's a huge yellowfin, you are doing great, keep reeling. Here comes the ten-yard ribbon going out again, you've got this. Don't worry about pulling, reel," Matt encouraged, as he set the gaff down and pulled the line in. The ribbon passed by again, as he continued to pull. The fish was on its side, exhausted, but not giving up. "You got it, keep reeling, another couple of feet."

Matt picked up the gaff again, and readied it, as the fish broke the surface. He hooked it in the gills and pulled it up over the side. It crashed down, flopping around, having lost the battle.

"Oh my God, it's huge," Carly exclaimed.

"This is a great catch, good job Carly," Matt beamed. "I'll get you some water, wait there. Don't worry about the fish."

Matt got a water bottle out of the ice chest, but he could see it wasn't going to be enough. Laughing, he picked up the hose and deployed it. Instead of protesting, Carly opened her arms and let the water hit her.

"That feels amazing," Carly laughed.

Matt handed her the water bottle, and got the pliers to get the hook out of the tuna's mouth. It was buried deep in there, so Matt just shrugged and cut the line. Hooking the fish onto the scale, he weighed it.

"35 pounds, that's great Carly," Matt laughed.

She was beaming as he threw the fish into the storage bin and came back to collect the rods. Securing the rods, he walked her to the front of the boat with him.

"Let's head in. We got dinner, and bait for our next real trip. You are going to love this part. Sit in the chair there," Matt smiled.

"This is really great Matt, thank you," Carly laughed, as she sat down next to him. He turned the boat towards the island and opened the throttle up. The engine roared and they started speeding home. They were about three miles out, and he knew they would have company before long.

"Look!" Matt pointed.

"Oh!" Carly exclaimed, as porpoises were riding the bow waves. A few of them were fully breaking the water, jumping with them. Carly laughed as the porpoises followed them all the way in. Water was coming over the bow as they sped through the waves, undaunted. Cutting across the jetties, they pulled into the bay, losing their escorts.

Matt approached the dock, and Carly deployed the bumpers. Catching the pylon, she held on as Matt stopped the boat and tied the stern line off. Cutting the engine, Carly got out and tied the bow line while Matt went for the fish. He handed her the ice chest, and then the fish, from smallest to biggest. She struggled with the tuna, just setting it on the dock as he climbed out.

"Want a picture?" Matt teased.

"Nah. What is the plan now?" Carly smiled.

"I am going to fillet the dorado and tuna, can you wash the boat down, then unload it completely?" Matt asked.

"Absolutely," Carly beamed. She collected her sarong and put it on, watching to see if he was looking her way. He humored her by looking, then smiled and collected a fillet knife.

The dorado was easier, as seagulls flocked to him. He put the fillets on a plate then threw the carcass into the water. The tuna was tougher meat, but he carved it up as best he could, harvesting a lot of it. Throwing the carcass into the water as well, Carly was finishing up washing the boat.

Matt put the fillets in the ice chest, then loaded it into the truck. Carly helped him put the rods inside the sea cottage, along with their other supplies. Finally ready to head home, she gave him one last big hug then hopped into the passenger seat as he steered them towards Harlingen.

"Did you want to make any stops?" Matt offered.

"No, I'm good Matt. Thank you. Just take us home to our coping family," Carly laughed.

"Jen said they were going to go out and shop today, I think she wanted me to take a full day with you," Matt reflected.

"That is really nice of you both, I can't say that enough. We both smell like fish, maybe we can shower together?" Carly teased.

"I'm down for that, but I use my hands a lot in the shower," Matt laughed.

"I'm the one that made the invitation," Carly beamed.

"Okay then," Matt grinned.

They made it home, and Matt threw the benito in the deep freeze while Carly took the ice chest inside. He let her decide which fish they wanted to start eating first, and put the other fillets in the freezer. The dogs were at their heels, and Matt let them out into the backyard while Carly headed towards her bathroom, making sure to look his way first. He got the dogs back inside quickly, he didn't want to leave them out unattended, and followed Carly.

She already had the water going, and had lost her sarong. She started to tease him but he was already out of his shirt, there was no second guessing.

"I'm surprised, I know you are all about Jen, but still eager to get in the shower with me," Carly grinned.

"Jen knows where I am, come on, let's get in. You sure Val is okay with this?" Matt teased.

"Yes, one of the differences between Val and I is she is okay never seeing another man again, but she knows I enjoy everyone's company. Being marooned on an island makes you appreciate everything," Carly smiled as she stepped into the shower stall.

"Jen realizes that too, you need to be around a guy every now and then. With my arm almost fully healed, we will have to find something else to do together. Because this isn't going to be a regular thing, I'm sure you know that," Matt grinned.

"Which means I have to take advantage of it, right?" Carly smiled as she wrapped her arms around his neck. "Will you kiss me?"

Matt leaned forward and kissed her, letting his hands slide down and grab her ass. She moaned and kissed him some more, before breaking away. He let go of her as she turned around and leaned back against him, letting the water come down on them both.

"You've done a great job of cheering me up today, Matt. I will make it up to you soon, I promise. Let's wash our hair and get out, we still smell like fish," Carly laughed.

"Let me wash your hair, Jen really likes the feeling of my hands in her scalp," Matt grinned.

"You seem to be great with your hands, I notice," Carly beamed, as he picked up the shampoo. Lathering her hair with it, he scrubbed her scalp as she moaned in pleasure. "That does feel good."

He rinsed it out, and gave her a spank, as she smiled and stepped out of the stall. He finished washing his own hair quickly and stepped out as well. Drying off, they walked back into the living room, where the dogs seemed to be demanding attention.

"I'm not going to ask to snuggle with you," Carly whispered.

"Okay, don't ask then," Matt shrugged, as he laid down on the couch and extended his hand towards her. Rolling her eyes, she relented and lay down on top of him.

"That was well played on your part," Carly teased.

"You made it easy," Matt grinned.

They napped for a while, until they heard the other truck drive up. Hopping off of him, Carly looked for her sarong, but realized she had left it in the bathroom. She scurried to get it, Matt didn't really understand why, as he continued to lie there and pet Buddy. Coming back out, she sat down in the rocking chair next to him as Jen and Val walked in, bags in hand.

"What did you guys find?" Matt asked.

"More clothing. I picked out some dresses for you Carly, in the color you requested," Val smiled. "How was the boating?"

"It was great, I caught dinner," Carly beamed.

"Oh? What did you catch?" Jen asked.

"A tuna and a dorado. I put the tuna in the fridge, there is a lot of it," Carly laughed.

"How big Matt?" Jen asked.

"35-pound tuna. Close to shore, I was surprised. But Carly did well," Matt smiled.

"That's great. Let us wind down, then we will grill it for you guys," Val smiled.

Jen walked over and sat down on Carly's lap, which surprised her.

"Oh," Carly whispered. "Thank you, Jen, for sharing Matt with me today. I appreciate it."

"You are welcome. I think things will start to get better going forward. Val appreciates everything you have done for her, but now it's time to start your actual relationship. Now, how did you handle the waves out there?" Jen smiled.

"Oh, I barely noticed. Honestly, the fish were hooking so fast, I didn't have time to notice them," Carly observed.

"It's true, we probably only spent ten total minutes trawling. The fish were really running. We got a benito as well, I brought it home. We can use it as cut bait for your wahoo," Matt grinned.

"How is your arm, Matt?" Jen asked.

"It's good. I didn't really struggle with it. Carly was in the chair, but I stayed busy. I think with three other fishermen, I will be fine. I am a bit worried about Val and the waves, but if we put her in the chair, she will be okay," Matt offered.

"I agree. Let's pick up our next member, then go fishing that next morning. Maybe they will even join us," Jen smiled.

"I hope so. It's been a weird couple of weeks," Matt sighed.

CHAPTER 31

THE ROBOT

Val drove them over the causeway towards the light. It was daytime, and that was already better news. Sam was in the tailgate, while Carly rode in the front, a lot happier. Coming to a stop, they piled out, Jen had the shotgun, just in case. Walking down the pier, they looked towards the fire, looking to see what they were dealing with.

"Are you kidding me?" Matt exclaimed. "They are trolling us."

"What is it?" Val asked, bewildered.

Standing by the fire, it was an oddly shaped robot-like creature, an upside-down triangular box shape, with two wheel, and a rabbit antenna. Matt figured it was a fusion, but he definitely recognized the base model, and asked Jen for the shotgun. Confused, she handed it to him as the robot spotted them.

Coming forward to greet them excitedly, Matt knew that once it started talking, it would never stop.

"Greetings, fellow travelers! My name is Y4K-TRP, but you may call me Yaktrap! I am a cheap knockoff of a far less popular design, I bet those people lost their jobs! You are the first people I have seen since arriving here! And boy, am I glad to see you! Wow, those are some BABES!" Yaktrap exclaimed.

"Yuktrap," Matt sighed.

"Did it just call us babes?" Carly offered.

"It's *Yaktrap*, chum! And yes, you are a babe! Can I hang with you? Can we go steady? Would you like to hear about what I have done up to this point in life?" Yaktrap offered.

"No, to all of those. Let's get out of here," Matt scoffed. "Feel free to stay here, Yuktrap."

"It's *Yaktrap,* again. And no way am I staying here, letting you take all of these babes with you. Who are you, scary looking man? You have a face only a mother could barely love," Yaktrap demanded of Sam.

Sam ignored the robot and followed the group back towards the truck. Yaktrap followed after them, still talking. Piling into the car, Yaktrap boosted himself into the tailgate, continuing to demand answers.

"Listen, I know we just met, but I was serious. You are ugly, dude. You need help. You need good old Yaktrap. With my expertise, I can turn you into a man that the ladies flock to, like me, or that other guy driving the truck. Did you see how he had three women next to him? They didn't even look at you man! And it's all because of your face! Where can we go to fix it? I'm not familiar with this area, so you will have to guide me. Don't worry about locked doors, I am an EXPERT at opening doors! There is no door that can stop Yaktrap! Oh, this is a nice view, we can see a lot from up top this bridge. Hey? Do you know why we have stopped here, at the highest point of this bridge? Buddy! I am talking to you!" Yaktrap declared.

"Sam!" Matt shouted.

Sam quickly grabbed the robot and tossed him off the bridge, much to his shock.

"WAAAAAAAAAAAAAAAAAAAAAAAAAAAAAAAAAAAAAAHHH-HHHHH!!!!!!!" Yaktrap screamed, as he hit the water.

Matt got out and looked over the bridge, making sure the robot sank. Content, he got back in the truck and headed home.

"What in the world?' Val asked, bewildered.

"It's a robot, from a very fun video game series. He is a comedy relief character, very, very annoying. But he is used well, in the context of the videogame. Not in a real-life situation. At all," Matt laughed. "It's weird that I can remember him, maybe he was an accident. Or..he said he was a knockoff. But the similarities are absurd."

"You didn't even ask him about the fire," Jen offered.

"I didn't ask him anything. I don't care what his title was, he is on the bottom of the bay," Matt shrugged.

"Okay. So, in the morning, we wake up early, drive to the boat, shove off?" Jen moved on quickly.

"Yep. We are leaving the house at 5am. This is literally the only thing I would wake up at 5am for. Carly? Make sure Val is in the truck. I don't care how it has to happen, just get her in the truck. Okay?" Matt laughed.

"You got it," Carly beamed. "I don't think she will be with us until our escort comes."

"I agree. But it's okay. She insisted she would not skip any group activities," Matt grinned.

"I have nothing to say at this time," Val declared.

They pulled into the neighborhood and parked the truck in the driveway. To their utter shock, and disdain, Yaktrap was there waiting for them.

"How the heck did he get here?" Val demanded.

"No idea," Matt growled, as he took the shotgun again.

"Listen here chap, I'm sure that was just an accident—" Yaktrap started, but was cut off by Matt blowing him away with the shotgun. The robot flew backwards, dead. His body disintegrated into red cubes that evaporated upwards. They heard a hum from the side of the house and then a voice.

"*RRRRRREEESPAWN!*" the voice sounded.

Once again, Yaktrap came around the corner and approached them. "I'm sure you think that was funny—" he started, and once again he was cut off by the shotgun blast.

"*We are sure that was an accident, but if not…you do you!*" the voice sounded.

Yaktrap came around the corner again, "Listen—" he started, but Matt just shot him again.

"*Keep up the great work!*" the voice sounded.

Yaktrap barreled towards them, seemingly unfazed by the danger he was heading into, as Matt blew him away yet again.

"Living is hard, dying is easy!" the voice sounded.

Yaktrap peeked around the corner. "How much ammo you got left, chum?"

"No idea! Come here and let's find out!" Matt laughed.

Yaktrap sighed and came around the corner, sulking. Matt gave him a moment, as the robot pointed at him. He pulled the trigger again, and the robot flew back, dead.

"I admit, this is fun," Val beamed. "Even though I don't understand what's happening."

"We hope you are having a great time.. if not..we are having a great time!" the voice sounded.

Yaktrap peeked around the corner again. "Will you, uh.. consider a truce?"

"Yeah!" Matt declared.

Yaktrap perked up, for some reason, and came around the corner. Starting to say something, Matt cut him off with another shotgun blast.

"Oh hey, it's you again," the voice sounded.

Yaktrap came around the corner again, still sulking. He stood before Matt, as he pulled the trigger. The gun made a clicking sound, it was empty.

"Oh! Click click! Out of ammo! What a shame!" Yaktrap declared.

"Sam!" Matt waved his hand.

Sam deployed his claws and cut Yaktrap in half, effortlessly. His body disintegrated again.

"If you come back disfigured or deformed, simply die again, we will fix you right up!" the voice sounded.

"As fun as this is, we can't keep this going. We need a solution," Jen pressed.

Yaktrap came around the corner again, right into Sam's waiting claws.

"I have an idea, let's step inside for a second. Sam? Keep killing him," Matt grinned.

"We hope you enjoyed your experience. If not, keep doing it until you do," the voice sounded, as Matt led the girls inside.

"Okay, Jen, Carly? You two wearing your bikinis underneath there?" Matt smiled.

"Of course," Jen smiled, as Carly nodded.

"Strip down to them, please. I have a great idea, just smile and go with it, okay?" Matt grinned.

"What are you scheming, I wonder?" Jen beamed, as she took off her jeans shorts and tank top. Carly did the same and they slipped back into their sandals and followed Matt out.

"Hey Yuktrap! Yuktrap! Where are you?" Matt shouted. He didn't hear the respawn device, and Sam was just standing there.

"He hasn't come around the corner yet," Sam growled.

"Retract your claws for a second, you will know when to deploy them again," Matt grinned.

Sam complied and Yaktrap peeked around the corner, noticing Jen and Carly immediately.

"You want a truce?" Matt offered.

The robot nodded and came around the corner, staring at the two girls.

"So, I have an offer for you Yuktrap," Matt started.

"Yaktrap," the robot tried.

"From now on it's going to be Yuktrap. Do you want to live here with these babes or not?" Matt shrugged.

"Yuktrap," the robot relented.

"We are willing to let you in the house, but you have to pay the rent. We don't take freeloaders, believe it or not, the situation here is pretty bad. So, we need all the help we can get. Are you ready to pay up?" Matt asked.

"Name your price, chum," Yuktrap replied, staring at the two girls still.

"All it will take is your voice box," Matt smiled.

"My voice? You want to take my beautiful voice? How will I seduce these beautiful ladies? How will I fix this ugly dude's face? I can't. I can't do anything without my voice," Yuktrap stammered.

"Sure, you can. These ladies can give you plenty of attention without you making a sound, this one here loves to have fun," Matt teased, as he slid his hand down and squeezed Carly's ass. "If you don't like it, you can stay here with Sam. Forever."

Sam deployed his claws, inspecting them. Carly was faking a smile and hissing at Matt to let go of her ass, which he finally did. Jen just rolled her eyes. Yuktrap looked at Sam, and his claws, then back at Jen and Carly. Then back at Sam. Then back at Jen and Carly.

"You make a compelling argument, chum. Here you go," Yuktrap relented, extending a tray out of his mouth and handing Matt his voicebox.

"Okay, you made the right choice. In you go," Matt grinned, as he led them all back into the house. Sam headed out, but not before Val brought him a lunch bag.

"Thanks Val," Sam nodded, and walked off.

Entering the house, the girls got dressed again as Yuktrap inspected the house. Buddy and Fred came up to him and started sniffing. Carly took the time to glare at Matt.

"Way too handsy, Matt," Carly growled.

"Oh, come on, I had to sell it to Yuktrap. And look, it is already paying off, he is completely quiet," Matt waved her off.

"Questionable methods, remarkable results, where have we seen that before?" Val beamed.

"If you don't want his affections Carly, I can always stop sharing him," Jen laughed.

"I didn't say that! But I have to get something out of it. He can't just grab my ass whenever he wants!" Carly shot back.

"That's fair Matt. You should kiss her to make up for it," Val beamed.

"I'll allow it," Jen shrugged. "The robot is quiet, so we all win."

Carly grabbed Matt and kissed him, biting his lower lip, tasting blood. "Ow, ow!" Matt howled in protest.

"Now we are even," Carly grinned ferociously, wiping the blood off her lips.

Yuktrap was standing behind them, hands outstretched, seemingly wanting his own kiss. Carly kicked him across the room instead.

"Not in your life, Yuktrap," Carly hissed.

"I said you could live here, I never said I would share the affection," Matt laughed at him.

Yuktrap got up and waved his arms aggressively, flipping Matt the bird. No one cared, he was quiet.

"Okay, I guess I should go over your chores, Yuktrap. These are our two dogs, Buddy and Fred. You have to let them out daily, watch them, let them back in. If they dig out and run away, I am holding you responsible. You have to feed them, and play with them. They like to play ball, and tug of war. If they run away, or anything happens to them, I am hanging you, upside down, from the top of the bridge. You won't die, so you won't respawn. You will hang there, forever. Clear?" Matt finished.

Yuktrap looked at the dogs, then Jen and Carly, then Matt. He nodded slowly. Satisfied, Matt turned back towards the kitchen.

"Let's eat, then rest up for tomorrow. I'm looking forward to it. We can leave Yuktrap here to take care of the dogs. Carly? I'm sorry for grabbing your ass like that," Matt offered.

"I'm not sorry at all," Carly grinned, still savoring his blood.

"Okay, that's acceptable," Matt shrugged.

Val rolled her eyes as they gathered in the kitchen to start an early dinner. It was going to be a big day tomorrow, and they needed to be ready for it. Matt was relieved they didn't get another nightmare at the beach. As annoying as Yuktrap was, he wasn't a threat, or a burden. Especially without his voice.

CHAPTER 32

DEEP BLUE SEA

It was 5:45 in the morning, and Jen pushed the gulf boat off from the pier. They had everything loaded, four rods, an ice chest of drinks and light snacks, a storage bin with ice, a storage bin without ice, their radio, standard fishing equipment, and Val in the front seat. She hadn't said a word all morning, as predicted.

Jen and Carly sat in the back seats, wearing purple and white bikinis with sarongs, respectively. Matt steered them towards the jetties and opened up the throttle, again ignoring the No Wake signs. Breaking out into the Gulf, Matt accelerated even more, heading due east. The sun was starting to come up, so he could see the water in front of them. Racing seaward, their escorts showed up quickly.

Val perked up as the porpoises were once again breaking the water and jumping with them, riding the bow waves. She was smiling in no time, wearing her own red bikini and sarong, as they sped on. Jen reached over the side and petted them, as Val went to join her. Matt raced on, until they were about ten miles off the coast. He slowed the boat down and started getting the lures ready.

Jen and the girls put some suntan lotion on, then fishing hats. Jen rubbed some suntan lotion on Matt as well, as he put his own hat on. She then took the benito out and started cutting it up, while Matt dropped the first artificial lure into the water. Jen set up the cut bait line and dropped it into the water as well, as Matt got back on the wheel and started trawling.

"Are we just using two rods?" Val asked.

"For now, yes. Did you take the medicine?" Matt asked.

"Yes. How long do you think it will take to hook our first—" Val started.

She was cut off by the line starting to sing loudly. Jen was beaming as she sat Val down in the fighting chair.

"Not long," Jen offered, as Matt got the other line in. The artificial lure had been hit, and Jen lifted the rod and tied it to the fighting chair. "Have you done this before?"

"I have not, I am extremely nervous," Val admitted.

"Use both hands to pull back on the rod, I'll help you. Then reel the line in as you drop the rod," Jen encouraged her.

Val started reeling, as the fish was swimming towards the boat. She reeled faster, taking advantage of the stupidity. She spotted it in the waves.

"Oh! Is that it? That's amazing, you can see it in the waves!" Val exclaimed.

"I admit I was shocked when I first saw it too," Carly laughed.

"Ten yards, slow down Matt," Jen called out, as he slowed down.

Jen reached in and pulled the fish in, tail-first. "Benito," she reported.

"Great, we need more," Matt grinned.

"Easiest benito ever, he swam right up to the boat," Jen laughed. "Great job Val."

She got the pliers and got the hook out, dumping the fish into the storage bin. Matt came back to deploy the cut bait again, while Jen got the artificial lure going.

"Which one do you think your marlin will hit?" Val asked.

"Neither of these, we will get the third line out soon," Matt grinned, as he headed back to the wheel and got them going.

"What happens if both lines get hit?" Val asked.

"It gets more complicated," Matt shrugged.

"Val," Jen chided her, shaking her head.

"Was that a jinx?" Carly laughed.

Sure enough, the artificial line started singing again, and almost immediately after, the cut bait got hit as well.

"Whoops!" Val beamed.

"Jen, get Val set up on the artificial line again. I will get the cut bait line ready for you," Matt pointed. Jen quickly got Val going again, while Matt picked up the other rod and walked it back towards the bow. Jen crawled onto the bow itself, as Matt handed her the rod. Taking it, she sat down, legs extended, as Matt turned the boat sideways, giving both lines as much distance from each other as they could.

"Carly! Help Val, the boat is locked in like this until one of you lands your fish, and Jen's is way out there!" Matt pressed.

Carly was already helping Val pull the rod back. "It's heavy Matt," Carly offered.

"Jen? How are you?" Matt asked.

"My fish is sprinting away, I'm letting it run," Jen reported.

"Copy that," Matt sighed, as he walked over to help Val and Carly. It was a heavy fish, as they reeled aggressively. The fish ran left, away from Jen's line, turning Val's chair with it.

"Where is it going?" Val stammered.

"It's okay, let it go," Matt encouraged her, as he pulled the rod back with her. She reeled it in, as the fish turned towards the boat. Val reeled aggressively, spotting the fish in the wave. That sight motivated her, as she continued to reel. The fish turned away again, and they pulled the rod back.

The ten-yard ribbon passed, and Matt went to get the gaff. Jen was still fine, reeling her line in slowly. He gave her a thumbs up and she nodded, unconcerned. They spotted Val's fish in the waves—it was another yellowfin. Pulling the line up, Matt gaffed it and got the fish into the boat.

"Good job Val. Rest up," Matt grinned. He got back on the wheel and Jen signaled she was ready. They were going to chase her fish. Gunning the engine, Matt accelerated towards it as Jen reeled the line in. They got close enough and Matt turned the boat, while Jen stood up.

"Carly! Come take Jen's rod for a minute," Matt pressed, as Jen handed her the rod and jumped down into the seating area. Sitting down in the other chair, Jen took the rod back and resumed reeling. She looked like an expert as she brought the line in. The ten-yard ribbon passed, but they still couldn't see the fish as Matt brought the gaff back.

"Kingfish," Matt reported, as he gaffed it and got it in the boat. "Good size."

Matt got the hook out and dropped the king into the storage bin with the dead benito. Coming back to Val, he unhooked her tuna and threw it into the storage bin as well.

"Everybody okay? Carly you are up next, Val needs a break. Jen? You good?" Matt asked.

Jen was already cutting another piece of benito up, as she dropped the line into the water. "You are asking after one catch?" she teased.

"Jen is fine," Matt rolled his eyes as he got the artificial lure back into the water. He decided to deploy the third rod, as he went to collect the dead benito. He ran the hook through its eyes, as it twitched one last time. Jen nodded as he dropped it into the water and let the line out. Securing the line onto the upper railing to keep it from getting tangled, he got back on the wheel.

Val came and sat next to him, grabbing a water out of the ice chest.

"If you get hot, we have the hose. Carly can testify it feels great," Matt grinned.

"Where does the water come from?" Val asked.

"The ocean," Matt shrugged.

"Oh," Val realized.

"Oh my God look!" Carly exclaimed, as the third line started screaming. They looked back in time to see a big marlin descending into the water. It had hit the benito.

"The previous struggle must have attracted it," Jen beamed, as she got the other two lines in. "Come on Matt. This one is all yours."

The marlin jumped again, as Matt got the third rod down and walked it to the fighting chair. The fish was pulling mightily, as it started to run. Jen tied the rod to the chair, smiling. She went to drive the boat while Val and Carly looked out, watching the marlin jump again. It was already over 100 yards out, as Matt let it run.

Finally, he decided it was time to fight back, as he started pulling back on the rod and reeling it in. Jen accelerated and pulled the fish back as well, as Carly helped Matt pull back. It was going to take a while to land this fish.

"Can you eat Marlin?" Val asked.

"Oh, definitely. It's a tasty fish. Much better than swordfish," Jen grinned. "I'm sure this area didn't allow you to keep them, but we will be taking it home, provided Matt wins the battle."

Matt continued to reel, but the marlin was undeterred as it pulled more line out. A full hour later, the 100-yard ribbon passed by. Val couldn't believe it when Jen told her that was just 100-yard. She had thought it was the ten-yard, but that one was a different color. The marlin had gone deep, trying to get away.

"It's coming back up, watch the water to see if it jumps again," Matt grinned, as he reeled aggressively. He could feel the fish surfacing. Sure enough, it jumped again, much closer to them.

"Oh, it's enormous," Val exclaimed. "Where are we going to put it?"

"The left bin has plenty of room, we specifically put ice in there for a marlin," Jen grinned. "Don't worry, you will have a role to play."

They spotted it in the waves, looking on in awe as its scales reflected the sun. Jen pulled Carly back with Val, this was when a marlin was at its most dangerous. It could jump into the boat if they weren't careful. It broke the water again, about 30 feet away, and they got a good look at it. Over six feet long, it probably weighed at least 300 pounds. Matt continued to reel aggressively; he didn't want it to jump again.

The ten-yard ribbon passed, as the marlin was exhausted. It was floating on its side by now, out of energy. Matt called Val forward.

"Okay look, it's spent. We have to get it in the boat, you are going to trade places with me. Just hold the rod, okay? It's tied to the chair, it's not going anywhere," Matt assured her.

Jen was putting gloves on, and handed Carly a pair as well. Matt put his own gloves on, and leaned over the side, grabbing the marlin's sword. Jen grabbed the gaff and hooked the gills, while Carly grabbed the tail.

They pulled it up together, flipping it into the boat. Its dorsal was pointing outwards so it was no threat, as Matt held the sword down.

"Oh my God,." Val whispered.

Matt was actually close to crying—it had always been his dream to catch a marlin. Jen patted him on the back, knowing he was both tired and grateful.

"Are you okay?' Jen whispered.

"Yeah, I'm good. I have just always wanted to do this," Matt admitted.

"Congratulations, Matt," Val beamed. She had known about his marlin fantasy for years. "What do we do now?"

"Let's weigh it, let it die, then get it into the storage bin," Jen pressed, as she tied the weight rope around its tail. It took both Matt and Jen to lift the fish up off the deck. Carly reported the weight, not believing it.

"467 pounds," Carly whispered. "Wow."

"It's probably a male," Matt offered. "Do we want a picture?"

"Yes, we do," Jen beamed. "Val? Will you do the honors?"

She stood next to the marlin, while Matt stood on the other side of it, as Val dug her camera out. Snapping the photos, Jen was beaming.

"That is about the only thing that can take the attention off of Jen," Val laughed.

"Oh stop," Jen rolled her eyes. The marlin was taking its last breaths as they got it down and shoved it into the storage hold. Jen got the live bait line out, and then the artificial lure, while Matt rested by the wheel. Accelerating, he resumed trawling.

"Okay, Carly, you are officially next," Jen laughed.

"No problem, I take it Matt is done?" Carly teased.

"Oh, no teasing. That was over a 90-minute fight, he is exhausted," Jen chided her.

"Yes ma'am," Carly smiled.

The artificial line started singing in no time, and Jen got the other line in, then gave Carly the rod. She reported it wasn't heavy, as she reeled.

Val went to check on Matt. "How are you?" she smiled.

"I'm great. Are you having fun?" Matt asked.

"I am. All the excitement has kept me focused on the here and now, instead of the waves. That was the biggest fish I have ever seen," Val beamed.

"There are much bigger ones out here, trust me. The female marlin can get way bigger. But we only have room for one, a second one would just be recreational. And we need the food, so we won't deploy a marlin line," Matt grinned.

"They seem to be biting really fast, do we even need a third line?" Val asked.

"Not right now, two at once was more than enough. I'm glad Jen is here though, she makes it easier on me," Matt admitted.

"Is there anything she isn't great at?" Val whispered.

"Not that I am aware of," Matt whispered back. "There is the ten-yard ribbon, go see what it is."

Val walked to see as Jen was pulling the line in, gaffing the fish, she reported a dorado. Flipping it into the boat, it was bigger than the last one, as Carly was smiling. Matt nodded as Jen got the fish into the storage bin. He stood up and redeployed fresh cut bait, and Jen came back to get the artificial lure back out.

Resuming their trawling, it wasn't long before the live bait started singing. Jen was taking this one, the wahoo was more likely to hit that line. Matt reeled the other line in as Jen sat down in the chair and reeled. She didn't need any help, as they stood by and watched. The ten-yard ribbon passed by in seemingly no time, as Matt pulled the line closer to him. It was another big kingfish, as he gaffed it and flipped it up.

Redeploying the lines, they kept alternating as the fish kept coming. 10am passed, and they had about 20 fish in the storage bin. Mostly dorado, a few kingfish and a couple more benito.

"Is everyone okay? We can stay out as long as Carly and Val are good and the fish are still active," Matt offered.

"I'm tired, but we can keep going, as long as the fish keep biting at this rate," Val replied. "I know Jen wants her wahoo."

"We don't have to get it on this trip," Jen assured her. "We will do this again—it's been a wonderful success."

"That's true," Val admitted. "How about 30 more minutes?"

"Okay," Matt nodded.

The live bait line started singing, as Jen reeled in the artificial lure. It was Carly's turn, as Matt noticed right away the fish was really pulling.

"This feels like a big one," Matt grinned, as he tied the rod to the chair.

"It could be Jen's wahoo, do you want to take it Jen?" Carly offered.

"Oh no, I'm fine Carly. Go ahead," Jen waved her away with a smile.

Carly started pulling, as Matt got the boat going again. Jen helped her pull back on the rod.

"Matt? Go faster, this is one is super heavy," Jen called out. "It's not a wahoo."

"Okay," Matt replied, accelerating.

The minutes ticked by, as Carly was barely making progress. The fish was diving, and she couldn't stop it. The 100-yard ribbon went out, and she was not amused. Matt had stopped the boat again and walked back to help pull.

"What do we think it is?" Val asked.

"It could be another marlin, or a sailfish. Carly is right, this sucker is heavy," Matt growled, as he pulled back on the rod. "He is going deep. You got this Carly—we are here to help you."

"I appreciate that, Matt," Carly growled, as she tried to reel. The fish wasn't having it, as it continued to dive. The 200-yard ribbon went out, and Carly was getting frustrated.

"Trade places with me, Carly," Jen offered.

"Thanks Jen," Carly relented, as she stood up. Matt was also well-rested, he could help if needed. Val and Carly had caught most of the fish, they weren't up for a war.

Jen pulled the rod, the fish had finally stopped diving, probably because it had gotten to the bottom. Matt asked Val to check the depth gauge, and she reported 240 feet. The fish had dived all the way to the bottom. Jen started reeling, pulling the fish back up.

A full hour had gone by, and only the 200-yard ribbon had passed. Matt was in the chair now, pulling the fish. Val asked again what they thought it was.

"It's gotta be another big marlin," Matt guessed.

Another long hour ticked by, as the 100-yard ribbon slowly passed by. Jen traded places with Matt again, and continued the fight. Val was fading, as Carly hosed her down. She appreciated it, but it was noon, the hottest part of the day, even if it was November. This had not been the gameplan. The line was getting closer now, as Matt asked them to keep an eye out while he got both gloves on and the gaffe.

The ten-yard ribbon passed, and Matt asked Carly to get back in the chair, so he and Jen could land the fish. They still couldn't see it, as they looked down into the water. Carly reeled, as Matt pulled the line up. Finally, he saw the tail.

"Oh," Matt realized.

"Enough 'Oh's,' what is it?" Val demanded.

"It's a black tip. Jen? Get the gun," Matt pointed.

"Right," Jen nodded, as she walked to the wheel.

"A black tip what?" Val demanded.

"It's a shark, Val," Matt grinned, as he gaffed it, pulling its head out of the water. He held it there while Jen brought the M1911 and put a round through its skull.

Flipping the dead creature into the boat, it was a four-foot black tip shark.

"Oh," Val whispered.

Matt was grinning, as Jen was shaking her head, laughing. "What a catch," she smiled.

"I haven't caught one of these since before Val was even born. And it was only about a foot long. But—delicious," Matt beamed.

"Oh, it's a fine meal. No doubt," Jen laughed. "Let's get it in next to the marlin."

"Right," Matt nodded, as the two of them lifted it and carried it forward, throwing it in next to the marlin. Coming back, Matt asked Val to hand them both some water. She obliged them and offered to hose them down. They accepted, and Val enjoyed it, hosing down Carly as well.

"Okay, let's head home. Val? Can you tie the rods off in their holders?" Matt asked.

"Right," Val nodded, picking up Carly's rod and securing it inside the holder. Matt turned the boat west, the skyline had all but faded from view completely. They were probably 25 miles out.

"Carly? Can you refill the gas tank? It's at about half, and it will likely take over an hour to get home," Matt pointed.

"Right. You okay?" Carly asked.

"Yeah, I'm good. I'm just tired, and hot. My arm is sore," Matt admitted.

"Matt? I can drive. I'm still good to go," Jen beamed.

"Of course, Jen," Matt relented. He gave way and she took the wheel, waiting for Carly to finish pouring gas into the tank. Completing her task, she sat down next to Val and they put their feet up on the stern.

"Ready!" Val declared.

Matt sat down next to Jen, as she accelerated. The engine roared and they sped off, heading home. The wind and water felt great, as their escorts showed up in no time. Breaking the water, the porpoises were calling out in mid-air, much to Val and Carly's delight. Riding the bow waves, they had attracted a big pod. Jen drove them on, as the boat cut through the waves. She spotted a buoy on the horizon, and headed towards it. It was the main shipping lane—they could follow it all the way in.

Surprising them all, Jen slowed the boat down. The porpoises left, as Jen crept up to the buoy. Matt knew what she was doing, but he wasn't sure if any of them were up for it.

"You looking for cobia? That would be all you, they can't handle it," Matt grinned.

"You telling me you wouldn't help land a cobia?" Jen teased.

Her confidence was amazing, as he held his hands up. He couldn't refuse her on any topic.

"Um, what are we doing? Home is that way?" Val pointed.

"Jen wants more," Matt shrugged as he stood up and walked to the back of the boat. Looking over the side, he searched. Not seeing anything, he shook his head no.

Jen drove them on to the next buoy, determined. It took two more, but finally Matt held his hand up. Looking back at her, he smiled and nodded. Swimming about 30 feet down was a cobia, circling the anchor line.

"Are you sure you want to do this? We barely have any room," Matt grinned.

Jen ignored him, cutting a piece of flesh off the benito and attaching it to the marlin line. Staring at Matt, she walked back and dropped the line into the water, letting it sink. Val and Carly were bewildered, as Jen just smiled. Matt matched her stare, as the cobia swallowed the meat.

"Up," Jen looked back at Carly, who gave way. The line was going out, as Jen sat down. Matt hooked the rod to the chair, and Jen laughed as she started pulling.

"What is going on? You drive up to a buoy and catch a fish? How is that possible?" Val demanded.

"It's a special fish, they like to hang out around anchor lines of buoys. Cobia. C-o-b-i-a. I have caught one before, remember? The ling?" Matt smiled.

"Oh! That?? I remember how wonderful it tasted," Val beamed.

"It's on the line now," Matt grinned.

"Where are we supposed to put it?" Val laughed.

"You can sit with it on your lap, I guess," Matt shrugged.

Jen was pulling the fish in aggressively, not letting it dive. Matt watched as she pulled him up. Getting the gaff ready, he wanted patiently, as the ten-yard ribbon passed. He drove the gaff into the creature, pulling it into the boat.

It was about three feet long, as Jen put the rod back in its holder and tied it to the boat. Walking back to the wheel, they left the fish there on the deck.

"Um?" Val pointed.

"Hold on!" Jen called out, gunning the engine and accelerating. Matt laughed and sat down, as they sped home.

CHAPTER 33

CLEANING UP

"Sam? Are you receiving me?" Matt transmitted.

"Yeah, go ahead Matt," Sam growled.

"We are about two miles out, coming in with a boatload of fish. We could use your help unloading it all," Matt pressed.

"I am waiting at the sea cottage with Gracie, see you soon," Sam signed off.

Matt set the transmitter down and looked back at Val and Carly. The cobia was dead, it had taken them over an hour to get in, and the fish was still sitting on the deck. Val had gotten over it, and was enjoying the company of the porpoises. Jen raced them on, cutting through the jetties and turning them towards their docks. They spotted Sam standing on the dock, with Gracie tied to a pylon. Jen waved, as Carly tossed him a mooring line. Catching it, Sam tied it off and helped Val and Carly out of the boat.

"The generator is on, the A/C is running. Go cool off," Sam pointed.

"Thank you, Sam," Val managed, heading inside.

"She is exhausted. Carly? You can head in and rest if you want to, we got this," Jen offered.

"No, I will help. There are so many fish," Carly smiled.

They started unloading the fish, handing one to Sam, then one to Carly, as they walked back and hung them from the display board. Finally unloading the entire right storage bin, Sam looked at the fish.

"That's quite a catch," Sam growled.

"Still have three left," Matt grinned, as he and Jen lifted the cobia up to him. They realized they hadn't even gotten the hook out of its mouth, and looked for the wire cutters. Sam simply extended his claws and cut the line.

"Right," Matt relented.

Sam grinned and walked back to hang the cobia. Coming back, he admitted he was curious about what was left. Matt and Jen pulled the black tip out first, lifting it up and weighing it first.

"55 pounds," Jen reported, as they took it down. Lifting it up to Sam and Carly, they carried it back and hung it up. Walking back, Sam asked what was left.

"We are going to need your help getting it out of the boat. We can't lift it up to you," Jen admitted.

"Really?" Sam asked.

"Yep," Matt smiled, enjoying Sam's surprise. Sam shrugged and hopped down into the boat. Matt and Jen grabbed the tail, and pulled the big blue marlin out.

"Wow," Sam whistled.

He helped them lift it up, throwing it onto the dock. It was over 6 feet long, all 400 pounds of it. They all disembarked, exhausted.

"You kids go rest, I will fillet these fish. Do you want to preserve the carcasses?" Sam growled.

"Don't fillet the three benito, we will take those back whole. They are marlin bait, the rest of them, get all the meat off them that you can, then throw the carcasses into the water," Matt waved. "I promise we will come help you, we just need to rest for a bit."

"No problem. This is you guys literally putting food on our table, which is normally my job. You all look exhausted, even you Jen. Rest, recover your strength, I'm not going anywhere," Sam growled.

The three of them headed inside the sea cottage. Fortunately, it had two bathrooms, one on each floor. Val had taken the downstairs one, and Carly headed that way. Jen led Matt upstairs, and turned the water on, filling the tub. Taking off her sarong, she pointed to the tub. Matt got in first, lying down. She flopped down on him, he didn't even complain as he held her and closed his eyes.

"Today was so much fun Matt, thank you," Jen whispered.

"You made it amazing Jen. Every second with you is a treasure," Matt whispered back.

"Such flattery," Jen grinned. "But I will allow it."

"That haul will feed us for months," Matt whispered.

"And we don't have to share any with Yuktrap," Jen teased.

"Still can't believe he is here," Matt rolled his eyes. "Let's rest, then go help Sam. We still have a lot of work to do."

"Agreed," Jen closed her eyes. They lay in the bath for about 15 minutes, before Jen started rinsing them with water. Standing up, she stood in front of him as he admired her long legs. She looked back and smiled, stepping out.

"Do you do that on purpose?" Matt grinned.

"I can't do anything about it, so might as well let you enjoy it. Come on, let's go," Jen beamed, as she pulled him up. Putting on her sarong, they walked outside in their water shoes, having never bothered to take them off.

Sam was working on the fish, still having over half the haul left, not even counting the three monsters. There was another station at the end of the dock, as Jen handed him a water bottle. He thanked her and set it down, as Matt looked into the channel. Some carcasses were floating, as well as some dead seagulls.

"They got a little too close huh?" Matt laughed.

"They never shut up," Sam growled.

"I realize this isn't your thing, but we appreciate the help," Matt grinned, as Jen was setting up the other station.

"It's no problem kid. Those are impressive trophies, they will feed us for months," Sam growled. "You are right, hunting is more my thing, but even a hunt doesn't yield that much food. How are Carly and Val?"

"I think they are asleep. Val was pretty exhausted. The black tip added another two hours to the trip, we had planned on coming in sooner. But once she tastes it, she will forget about those complaints," Matt grinned.

"How far out did you guys go?" Sam growled.

"About 30 miles. I don't think it's necessary to go that far, but Jen wanted a specific fish, which we did *not* catch. I will talk to her about it for next time, I think we can stay closer to home," Matt shrugged. "Do you need anything?"

"Take these fillets inside, and bring me a fresh plate," Sam growled.

"Copy that," Matt grinned, picking up the fillets. Sam hadn't bothered to label them, but it didn't matter too much. He would grill all of them, except for the cobia. He would fry that one, most likely. Walking inside, he emptied the fillets onto a fresh platter and took the empty one back out to Sam. Jen was already working on her own fish, and he would check in on her soon.

Carly came out to check on him, and he offered her a hug, which she accepted. "Today was so much fun Matt," she whispered into his ear.

"I loved it too. I really did. I'm glad you were there Carly. Even Sam is out there singing our praises," Matt grinned.

"How is your arm?" Carly asked.

"It's sore, I am embarrassed to admit. Jen is out there filleting the fish with Sam. I want to go take her place, but she will refuse me, I know," Matt admitted. "How are you and Val?"

"Val is dead to the world, already snoring. I am tired too, but I want to help. Want me to wash the boat?" Carly smiled.

"If you don't mind. I wanted another picture with the marlin, but oh well. Let Val sleep," Matt shrugged.

"Let's go then," Carly grinned, as they headed out. Matt took Sam another platter, and went to check on Jen while Carly broke out the water hose. She started by hosing Jen down, causing her to scream. Shooting a glare her way, Carly laughed and didn't even think about repeating the stunt with Sam.

Matt approached Jen and checked on her. "Well, other than that sudden shower, it's easy Matt. Don't be embarrassed about your arm. You contributed plenty today, if you don't believe me, look at the marlin," she pointed.

"Thanks for being so amazing, Jen," Matt whispered.

"It's a team effort. I won't ask where our fifth member is, I know she is sawing logs," Jen beamed.

"Even Carly is tired, but she wanted to help. She had a great time, I know it," Matt grinned, as they got hit by another blast of water. "If you want to go swimming, that can be arranged!" he shouted.

"Don't overestimate your abilities Matt. I can throw you both in that moat with ease," Carly laughed.

"I can't contest that," Matt relented.

"I can," Jen grinned, as she tossed a carcass into the water. "Probably."

"I have my doubts," Matt grinned. "Only a few left, then the big ones. I think we should let Sam handle those with his claws."

"He already said as much. He will carve them up, I am doing the rest, he has the cobia over there now," Jen pointed out. "Will you take these fillets inside, and bring me another platter, along with some water?"

"Sure," Matt replied, picking up the platter and taking it inside. Emptying it onto a cutting board, he scooped up a water and brought it back to Jen. Heading back inside, he started putting the fillets in ziplocks. It took a while, but he bagged them all up and tossed them in the near empty refrigerator. Walking back outside, he took Sam's platter, which was the entire cobia, and walked inside. Bagging it up, he wrote cobia on each ziplock and threw them in the fridge.

Heading back out, Jen was done with her fillets, and was helping Sam with the shark. Carly was finishing up the boat and climbed out of it, asking if they needed anything else. Jen shook her head no and she went inside to crash with Val. Matt joined the pair, switching out the platters. It took another 30 minutes to harvest the shark…and all that was left was the marlin.

"That's the biggest fish I have ever seen," Sam growled, as they stared at it.

"Cut off the sword and the tail, it will lighten the load a little bit," Jen offered.

Sam extended his claws and sliced them off, but they knew it was a fool's hope. They would have to harvest it there on the ground. It took an hour, but they finally got all of the usable meat bagged and refrigerated. Matt and Jen were tiring, as Sam asked them what else they needed.

"We need some more ice chests, to get all this meat home. Can you go loot some? I know there is no ice to be had," Matt sighed.

"Sure, no problem. Why don't you two go get some sleep? I will have everything back here by the time you wake up. Can I leave Gracie here?" Sam growled.

"Yeah, she will be fine inside," Matt relented. He walked to the Beagle and untied her lead from the pylon, bringing her inside with them as Sam headed out.

"Let's get in bed Matt. Everything else can wait until we wake up," Jen led him to their room.

"I don't even know what everything else actually is, at this point," Matt admitted.

They collapsed into the bed, as she rested her head on his shoulder and took his hand. Falling asleep within minutes, they were completely out of energy.

———

Three hours later, Matt and Jen rose from bed. Putting their water shoes back on, Matt didn't even remember taking them off. She smiled and they exited the room, finding Sam sitting there drinking a beer with Gracie.

"Hey Sam. Anything to report?" Jen asked.

"I went and found ice chests, along with ice trays in neighboring freezers. Made a full batch of ice so far, working on the second now. Also got the boat fully unloaded, all of your gear is over there," Sam pointed. "Carly and Val are still passed out. What do you want to do?"

"How much longer do you think until that ice is made?" Matt asked.

"Should be ready now," Sam growled.

"Okay, let's load the fish into the ice chests, and the chests into the tailgate. Once everything is ready, we can wake those two up and head home. Jen and I will cook dinner, and we can eat together in Harlingen," Matt offered.

"Sounds like a plan," Sam growled.

It took an hour, but they finally got all of the fish loaded. It was ten ice chests' worth, as Sam lifted Gracie into the tailgate and Jen went to wake up the sleeping couple. Carly came out, carrying Val in her arms as she was just too tired. Matt helped them into the back, as they climbed in and Sam sat next to them. Matt got into the driver's seat, while Jen got in the front passenger seat and they headed for Harlingen.

Two hours later, Matt was serving some dorado to the entire group. Val had completely recovered, and they were savoring the aroma. Yuktrap had done his job and taken care of the dogs, and for that, Matt had rewarded him with his life. Nothing else. The robot was pretty ungrateful as he continued to wave his arms around, but no one had any interest in charades.

"Today was truly wonderful, one of our best days," Val beamed. "I'm sorry I passed out for like, five hours there."

"It's okay, the motion sickness medicine knocks you out once you stop moving. We all took pretty long naps," Matt shrugged.

"You kids put in the work today, this fish is excellent," Sam growled, as he ate.

"It's nice to have you here Sam, you rarely eat with us," Val laughed.

"Sam helped a lot, he filleted the fish, then sliced up the big ones with his claws. It would have been really difficult for us to harvest that marlin without him," Matt grinned.

"It was a small contribution compared to actually getting all that food in the boat," Sam shrugged. "I'm sure those two big ones didn't come easy."

"They did not. As much fun as that was, it wiped me out. What adjustments can we make to perhaps lighten the burden?" Val asked.

"The biggest one is I don't think we need to go out that far. I know Jen wants a wahoo, but we didn't get one, is that really a problem? Jen?" Matt prompted.

"Oh, I completely agree, the mahi-mahi is delicious. We don't need a wahoo, I just wanted one. Next time, we will stay closer to home," Jen pressed.

"When is next time?" Carly smiled.

"Honestly, we can do this as often as you guys want. We don't have to keep the fish—we can just go out for recreation. The fish we brought home today will feed us for months," Matt shrugged.

"To answer your question Carly, we can go again tomorrow, if you want," Jen beamed.

"Um, I am definitely not going again tomorrow. But don't let me stop you," Val put her hands up.

"Why don't we go next week, after our new team member gets here? Who knows, they could actually be a contributing member. No Yuktrap, I don't count you," Carly teased.

Yuktrap threw his hands in the air, three successive times. It was easy to guess what he was asking, as they laughed at him.

"What do you think next week will bring? You said Yuktrap was videogames?" Jen asked.

"It's anyone's guess at this point. But it seems like we are scraping the bottom of the barrel," Matt sighed, glaring at Yuktrap, who again threw his hands in the air.

"I mean, if he can quietly take care of the dogs, I think we should throw him a bone every now and then," Val smiled.

"You guys can throw him a bone whenever you want, just don't kill him. And never give him his voice back," Matt grinned.

Yuktrap threw his hands in the air again, as Val just rolled her eyes. "Thank you for cooking Matt. Today was awesome, as I said. I am going to retire, if you want to leave the dishes for tomorrow, I will do them," she offered.

"I am going to head out as well, Gracie is waiting outside. I will see you kids later. Good job today, thanks for the food," Sam growled, as he stood to leave.

It was just Matt, Carly, and Jen now. Matt asked what they wanted to do. "I will follow Val to bed, good night, guys. I was going to offer a trade, but I changed my mind," Carly beamed.

"If you want a kiss good night, just ask," Jen teased.

"How…how did you know?" Carly stammered.

"It was super obvious to even me," Matt laughed. "You don't have to offer a trade—I can kiss you without groping you."

"Maybe I like the way your hands feel," Carly smiled, as she stood to leave.

It was just Jen and Matt now. "What would you like to do tomorrow?" Matt asked her.

"Take the plane up, maybe throw Yuktrap out of it," Jen smiled.

"We can do one of those things," Matt grinned.

"Got any special ideas for tonight?" Jen teased.

"I do, but I will let you take the lead, as always," Matt smiled, as he took his plate into the kitchen.

"Good night Yuktrap, I am going to go sleep with my boyfriend now. But hey, you got the dogs, right?" Jen winked at him.

Yuktrap threw his arms in the air again, flipping Matt the bird. They laughed as they headed for the bedroom, leaving the robot all alone. Matt knew it was his least favorite thing in the world, but he absolutely did not care.

CHAPTER 34

THE FALLEN

Val drove them over the causeway yet again, towards the light. Parking at the hotel, they hopped out. Jen had the shotgun, as Sam led them down the pier.

"Here is hoping for a human being," Matt rolled his eyes.

They approached the fire, and they could see a woman sitting by it. Brown hair, down to her shoulders, she was wearing all black. She looked up and spotted them, as they offered greetings.

"Oh, I recognize her! Ugh! Why can't I remember??" Val exclaimed.

"Who are you guys?" the woman asked.

"What did the fire tell you?" Matt started.

"That was I was the Fallen, sent to aid the chosen ones," the Fallen sighed.

"That's definitely not an accurate description of her, I just can't remember," Val shook her head.

"I have no idea who she is, do you remember anything about her?" Matt asked. "Given her height, I guess we can say the vampire streak is officially over."

"Are you trying to pick a fight?" The Fallen stood up.

"Wow, okay, I admit, she is tiny. How tall are you, really?" Val grinned.

"I'm 5'2, thank you," The Fallen hissed.

"With heels?" Carly added.

"Without heels," The Fallen snapped, stepping forward.

"Do you know anything about yourself, other than you're short?" Matt asked.

"Screw you guys, I am out of here," The Fallen growled.

"Okay, let's go home," Matt shrugged. "Big day tomorrow."

"Wait! Okay, listen. Her stature surprised even *me,* but come on. She can be helpful to us, she is *human,*" Val offered.

"Are you sure?" Sam growled, stepping forward.

The Fallen happily punched Sam, sending him flying backwards. He didn't go down though, coming to a stop.

"Okay, so she is strong. But we have to keep her away from the Sunwalker, if you think our mockery was mean, they will be fighting, right away. And I don't like her chances," Matt pressed

"I agree. That guy just wants to fight. But come on, she has superhuman strength, she can hold her own," Val smiled. "I'm Val, by the way. Will you come home with us? We have food, shelter, a slave robot. We aren't your enemies. We are just regular people. Plus Sam."

"Okay, it beats staying here on this beach. But stop making fun of my height, I can't help it. And I really can kick the crap out of a bunch of humans," The Fallen growled.

"We know you can't remember your name, so you will have to choose one. I'm Matt, this is Jen. And this is Carly. We are the only humans on the planet. Come on, let's go," Matt grinned.

"Um, can you run that by me again? Where are all the people?" The Fallen asked.

"They are gone," Val smiled. "We have videos, but let's head home first. Sam? Will you clear her please?"

"She isn't a threat, let's go," Sam growled.

"Did you just say—" The Fallen started in.

"Are you a threat to us? Are you going to hurt us? Attack us?" Jen cut her off.

"No, I don't attack humans. But I don't appreciate the disrespect," The Fallen scowled.

"We will make it up to you soon. For now, let's go," Jen waved her on.

They headed towards the truck, the Fallen bringing up the rear. Val was in good spirits, confident the animosity would pass quickly. Matt opened the back door and turned towards the Fallen.

"You can either get in the middle, or sit in the tailgate with Sam. We have about 30 miles to travel, it's up to you," Matt offered.

"I'll sit in the middle, I don't mind," The Fallen pouted, climbing into the truck.

Matt sat next to her as Val got them going, tossing Matt her phone. "We have a video here," he began. "To help you acclimate."

Matt started the video, and the Fallen watched. "That doesn't make sense," she deadpanned.

"Yes, the common response," Matt grinned. "Yet, here we are."

"What are you doing about it?" The Fallen asked.

"Nothing," Matt shrugged. "A couple of us took some time to accept the way things are, but there is nothing we can do about it. You can take as long as you want. Go explore the abandoned city, pick out some new clothes, do whatever. We will give you a car and a gun, just in case some critters come say hello."

"I don't need a gun," The Fallen scoffed.

"I don't even think you should go," Val offered. "Come home with us, eat, wake up in the morning, go fishing. You can take my place."

"I'm not going fishing if the planet doesn't have any people on it," The Fallen waved her off. "There are productive things I could do. I'm sure I will think of them any minute now."

They waited in silence, as time passed. A lot of time. They pulled into their neighborhood and got out of the truck. Walking inside, Matt summoned the robot.

"Yuktrap! We brought you home your own girlfriend. Watch out, she is being mean at the moment, but she is all yours," Matt laughed.

"I officially don't like you, and will not be staying," The Fallen growled. "What is that??"

Yuktrap approached, extending his arms towards the Fallen, hugging her. She picked him up and threw him across the street. It was a hilarious sight as he landed with a thud.

"Oh wow, nice throw," Val laughed. "I'll get lunch started. More shark!"

"I want a full briefing on what is happening here," The Fallen demanded.

"I nominate you and Carly, Val, you are a fan of hers," Jen grinned. "Come on Matt, let's go secure the shotgun and snuggle."

"Matt? My phone?" Val prompted.

"Oh right, here," Matt handed her the phone, and Val started the second video for the Fallen. He walked into their bedroom as Jen put the shotgun away.

"I still feel embarrassed about how aggressive I was with you," Jen whispered.

"Don't. The situation never stops getting more absurd. She will come around, I was just completely shocked at how tiny she was," Matt grinned. "Come on, let's lie down, I think she will come visit us soon."

"Okay," Jen smiled, as she lay down on top of him and they shared a kiss. Rolling over, they reflected on what was happening. "Do you think this experiment will ever end?"

"I don't know. Part of me thinks yes, part of me thinks no. But I think we are making the absolute best of it. And I feel blessed to have earned your affections," Matt whispered.

"It's easy to be with you Matt. You are happy just holding me, you don't even ask for things like sex," Jen reflected.

"I am happy just being loved, yes," Matt whispered.

There was a knock on their door, and the Fallen walked in.

"From now on, wait for a response," Jen growled.

"I—I accept that. I'm sorry," The Fallen relented, looking away.

"Well, what do you want?" Jen demanded.

"How long have you guys been at this?" The Fallen asked.

"Over two months now, we have to make sure to remember Thanksgiving is coming up. I think it's this week, actually," Matt replied.

"You are really going deep sea fishing tomorrow morning?" The Fallen sighed.

"That's the plan," Matt nodded.

"I need a day, is that okay? Give me a day, Val offered to take me out shopping, I have nothing to wear. I realize, that if we are the only humans on the planet, we need to get along," The Fallen relented.

"That's fair, you can take a day. We can push the fishing trip back, it doesn't matter. We haven't even finished the shark from last week. It's just leisure. Take your time, go shopping, absorb it. We aren't doing anything to try to address the lack of people, and we aren't going to. We aren't going anywhere else. This is our home. Sam is in charge of security—he has already killed one threat to us. Two more are out there hibernating. I'm honestly glad to have another human with us," Matt offered.

"Do you have any other abilities, other than super-human strength?" Jen asked.

"I'm a capable fighter, I have a blade that I can usually summon, but for some reason I can't, and haven't been able to since I arrived. Also, I'm immune to magic," The Fallen replied.

"Your strength can really help us out there in the Gulf. Enjoy your shopping trip, get a bikini with a sarong so you can match us. Or, if you are more conservative, we understand," Jen shrugged.

"I'm not sure Yuktrap would understand," Matt teased.

"What is that thing about?" The Fallen asked.

"It's a really, really annoying robot, I coerced him into giving up his voice box. If you kill him, he will respawn outside, voice box restored. It's really bad, don't do it. You can kick him around as much as you want, make him do chores, enslave him, I don't care. If you want to give him attention, you can, but don't say I didn't warn you," Matt grinned.

"No thanks. See you guys later," The Fallen sighed, closing the door behind her.

"That went better," Matt offered.

"You should have apologized about mocking her height, but oh well. You can later," Jen observed.

"There is no way she is 5'2 without heels," Matt whispered.

"I agree, but come off it already. As she said, she can't help it," Jen rolled her eyes.

"I forgot to remind her to choose a name, I'm sure Val will though," Matt offered.

"Yes, I'm sure. Let's resume our nap," Jen grinned.

"I'm not complaining about holding you in my arms, but do we need to rest if we aren't going fishing tomorrow?" Matt asked.

"I guess not. We can go try to be more social with our newest member then," Jen replied, sitting up.

They stood and opened the door, rejoining the group. The dogs were meeting their new member, while Yuktrap sulked beside her. Buddy and Fred instantly turned to come greet Matt and Jen, as they sat down on the couch.

"How's it going?" Matt grinned.

"Good. This robot looks incredibly sad," The Fallen observed.

Yuktrap extended his robotic hand to the Fallen, and she reluctantly took it. He looked up at her, hoping for some more affection.

"Don't fall for his tricks, he just wants his voice back so he can annoy you constantly," Matt grinned.

"If you give it to him, you are taking him to live next door," Jen pressed.

"Yeah, he can't live in this house while being able to speak," Matt laughed.

The Fallen looked at the robot, then at them. "I'm not sure who to believe right now, but I don't entirely think you suggesting killing him is on the level. Can you just give him his voice box back?"

"Nope," Matt shrugged.

"Why not? Do I have to take it from you?" The Fallen growled.

"I threw it overboard, it's on the bottom of the bay. I assure you, I will never willingly give his voice back," Matt grinned.

"Okay. You are just a jerk. I'm going to stay next door. Val? I will see you later," The Fallen scoffed.

"Bye," Val beamed.

The Fallen stood up and led Yuktrap out, closing the door behind them.

"You are being a jerk, you know," Val chided him.

"Tch, if she thinks she is going to give Yuktrap his voice back and be proven right, she is delusional. I literally give her 60 seconds after he starts talking to come back here and apologize to me," Matt scoffed.

"You gonna take that wager, Val?" Jen teased.

"No, I am not. On this particular issue, Matt is right. Trying to restore his voice is a mistake," Val relented.

"She picked a name yet?" Jen asked.

"Not yet. We are going shopping tomorrow. I will help her with it. Carly? Are you coming with us?" Val smiled.

"Only if Yuktrap isn't. What are you two going to do Matt?" Carly asked.

"I think we will head to the island. Take the bay boat out, lie on the beach. You are welcome to join us Carly, if you don't go shopping with them," Jen smiled.

"It will depend entirely on where Yuktrap is. I am not hanging out with him," Carly grinned.

"That's fair. Either way, we are splitting up. Try to stay out of trouble, Matt," Val grinned.

"Not sure how I could get *into* trouble, but okay," Matt shrugged. "Carly knows the route to me."

Val just rolled her eyes and stood up. She was going to visit the Fallen, she declared. Buddy and Fred didn't make a move to follow her, so she left on her own. Carly stood up and moved to the couch next to them.

"Did you guys want to do anything?" Carly grinned.

"What did you have in mind? You have that look in your eye," Jen teased.

"We could have some fun in your room. I'll submit to your whims Jen, in exchange for some affection," Carly laughed.

"Really? Not getting enough attention from Val?" Matt teased.

"I'm getting plenty of attention, but maybe I want more," Carly grinned.

"You wear what I say, you do what I say, you take the punishment that I say, and maybe you get some affection in the end," Jen offered.

"Deal," Carly grinned.

Hours later, Carly was passed out on the bed in chains, having secretly revealed them to Jen. She had been relentlessly tickled and spanked, and finally had succumbed to exhaustion. Matt and Jen were making out when she stirred.

"Ohh…." Carly whispered.

"Oh, finally awake? Want some loving?" Jen beamed.

"Yes please," Carly managed.

"Matt or me? Matt will cost you 100 more spanks. I'm free," Jen laughed.

"I—I will take you Jen. I can't handle anymore spanks," Carly whispered.

Jen laughed and shifted underneath her, kissing her while her hands were cuffed behind her back. Matt enjoyed himself by spanking her red ass, while she howled in protest.

"Quiet, kiss me," Jen grinned.

Carly relented and made out with Jen, while Matt rubbed her ass. Finishing, Jen pushed her off the bed. Carly hit the ground, not even caring about being topless.

"That's all Carly. You may go," Jen pointed to the door.

"Please let me stay here with you two," Carly pleaded.

"Hmm, alright. We are going to bed though;we aren't going to wake up and free you. If you want to stay here, you are sleeping in those shackles," Jen grinned.

"Fair enough," Carly relented, climbing back into the bed.

"Where did you find these?" Matt asked.

"Police station," Carly smiled.

"I see. That's not bad," Matt grinned, as he got under the blanket. "Good night, Carly."

Jen got them both under the blanket, and bid her good night as well. They fell asleep quickly, tomorrow would be another interesting day.

CHAPTER 35

GAME NIGHT

The next morning, there was a knock on the door. Jen bid Carly to go answer it, laughing.

"Jen! I'm half naked!" Carly protested.

"So? It's either the Fallen, or Sam. Go answer it," Jen pointed. "Or never come back here."

"Oh...okay," Carly relented, standing up and shuffling her chained feet over to the bedroom door. Struggling to open it, she managed to walk out.

"That was mean," Matt chided her.

"She wants to passionately make out with you. I am making her take the long road," Jen shrugged. "If she didn't want to, she could have quit."

"Why do you think she wants to kiss me so much?" Matt asked.

"It was the bet against Val that she lost," Jen grinned.

"She told you that?" Matt asked.

"Yep," Jen smiled. "I'm allowing it."

"Okay then," Matt shrugged.

Carly came shuffling back in, the Fallen and Yuktrap in tow. She had her back to them, not wanting Yuktrap to see her.

"Yuktrap? Get out," Jen pointed, she wasn't dressed herself. "Carly? Face the wall, legs spread."

Yuktrap sulked and rolled himself away, as the Fallen sighed and closed the door. "What is going on here?" she demanded.

"We just woke up, we aren't dressed, and we don't want to be around Yuktrap. What is it we can do for you?" Jen asked.

"And that?" The Fallen pointed at Carly, who had complied. "She willingly put herself there," Jen shrugged. "What do you want? Have you decided to join our group yet? Or do you need more time?"

"I need more time, I'm going shopping today, with Yuktrap and Val. We are going to kill Yuktrap and restore his voice. Then I am going to come back here and establish some ground rules," The Fallen growled, looking at Carly.

"We aren't obliged to follow any rules you think you can set," Jen shrugged. "If you don't want to be a part of our group, there is the door. I understand you need a day, go take it. But stop trying to bully us. You aren't intimidating, at all. You are actually going to get two days, because we are going to the island today, waking up tomorrow and going fishing. If you want to be there, Val will drive you. No Yuktrap. Is there anything else?"

"I might have been confused about who was actually in charge here—" The Fallen started.

"Well, you shouldn't be anymore. Now, anything else?" Jen grinned.

"Yeah, I have something else," Matt cut in. "If you insist on restoring Yuktrap's voice, you will be going against the wishes of the entire group, Val included. So, 30 seconds later, if you want to come back to us, you are going to have to get down on your knees and beg."

"That is not going to happen," The Fallen snapped.

"Keep it up and I will take your clothes," Jen grinned. "Matt is right, Yuktrap does not deserve to have his voice restored. You are completely wrong on that issue. Defy us, and it's your pride that will suffer."

"I'm leaving," The Fallen scoffed, storming out.

"Go give Carly some attention, then let's get going to the island," Jen laughed.

Matt stood up and walked over to where Carly was standing. She had her back to him, so he gave her a spank and grabbed her chin. She looked at him enticingly.

"Hmm, what is missing here? I think fishnets and a gag," Matt whispered into her ear. She opened her mouth and smiled. He gave her a light kiss.

"Come on Matt. Don't be shy, it's no big deal. Kiss her. Use your hands," Jen laughed as she got dressed.

"Think I was being shy?" Matt whispered into her ear.

She shook her head no, as he smiled and kissed her, while groping her breasts. She squealed as he squeezed them. "Bite me and it's over," he whispered. She nodded and they kissed some more, as he slid his hands down her backside again. Finally breaking away, Matt smiled and started to get dressed. They left her there for a bit, before Jen finally walked over and unchained her.

"You okay Carly?" Jen whispered.

"Oh, I'm fine. This was fun. May I get dressed?" Carly beamed.

"Of course. Bikini, we are heading to the island. Tomorrow we go fishing, with or without the Fallen. Do you think we are being too hard on her?" Jen smiled.

"I mean, we all needed some time to digest it. But siding with Yuktrap is not buying her any sympathy. She is going to regret it," Carly laughed. "I can't wait to get back out there in the Gulf tomorrow."

"Oh? You really liked it, huh?" Matt teased.

"It was a lot of fun, I could do it every week," Carly grinned. "I felt like I was getting better at controlling the fish as time went on."

"No reason not to. What else is there to do?" Matt shrugged.

"Let's do the work first. Take the bay boat out, make sure the *Invictus II* is good to go. We should take another can of gas, or just steal it from a car on the road," Jen pressed.

"I think we should just steal it, there are plenty of cars parked close to the sea cottage. Then wait and see if Val brings the Fallen to us tonight. If not, we shove off at 6am" Matt grinned.

"Agreed. Is everyone ready?" Jen asked.

They nodded, and walked out. Feeding the dogs, they petted them and said goodbye, getting into the second electric truck next door. Val's was gone, they figured they were already out shopping.

Heading to the island, they quietly drove, looking out at the pastures. The grass was mostly dead, but the palm trees were alive and well. Arriving in Port Isabel, Matt drove them over the swing bridge and they got ready to take the bay boat out. Noticing the high wind, Matt stopped them.

"There is a storm coming in. I don't think it's another hurricane, but we should scrap this. Head back," Matt offered.

"Agreed, the winds are too high to take the bay boat out. Let's head back to Harlingen," Jen nodded.

They piled back in the truck and headed home. Matt asked if that meant more playtime with Carly, and she could only smile. He pointed out that wasn't a no, and even Jen had to agree. Pulling into the driveway, they got out and headed back inside. They could see the rain in the distance, and got on the radio.

"Hey Sam, a storm is blowing in. Better get inside for a bit," Matt transmitted. *"Val, if you are receiving this, should head home."*

"Roger that Matt, we saw it too, and are coming back," Val responded.

Matt wasn't worried about Sam; he was sure he could smell the rain before they even saw it. Heading over to the couch where the girls were petting the dogs, he sat down, asking what they should do now.

"Let's wait for the rest of our group, see where they are at," Jen grinned.

They heard the truck drive up, and Val led the Fallen inside. Matt asked about Yuktrap, and Val said he was respawning at this very moment. They had run him over with the truck.

"Okay, 30 seconds," Matt grinned.

Yuktrap came in the door, talking.

"Yes! Yaktrap is back, baby! And it's all thanks to you, my Angel! Shorty—you're my Angel, you're my darling Angel, Nnce Nncce unnce uunce," Yuktrap rapped. "I am alive!" he spun around. "I am never surrendering my voice again. Never! Ahahahahahahahahaha. Angel! Let's get in bed, get out of those clothes, let's go baby! I am your one and only Yaktrap!"

The Fallen fell to her knees in front of them. "I surrender. I'm sorry. You were right Matt. Here, take my clothes," she begged, as she took her shirt off. "Just take his voice away again!"

Val was beaming as Carly just burst out laughing.

"Haha! Jokes on you saps, I am never taking my voice box out again! Never!" Yuktrap declared.

"Pants too, Fallen," Matt grinned.

Without hesitating, she ripped her pants off and held her hands up.

"Okay, his voice box is inside that disc tray on the bottom of his face. Rip it open, then rip the voice box out. Give it to me and you get your clothes back. You can keep the name though, Angel is fine," Matt grinned.

Angel didn't hesitate as she shoved Yuktrap over and ripped open his disc tray. "Noooooooooo...." he started, but Angel took the voice box out and offered it to Matt.

"Okay, a deal is a deal. Put your clothes back on," Matt laughed as he stomped on the voice box with his foot. Yuktrap looked on in sadness, but Angel no longer felt the sympathy for him that she once did.

"Thank you, Matt. I apologize for my behavior. You were right, I was wrong. That robot should never be allowed to speak again!" Angel stood up and put her pants on.

"Let's sit at the table, play cards, get to know each other better," Matt grinned. "Yuktrap? Let the dogs out, before the storm blows in. Then serve us some drinks."

The robot slowly rolled over to the door and opened it, ushering the dogs outside. He was sulking again, but no one paid him any mind as they sat down at the table.

"What should we play?" Val beamed.

"Just poker maybe? We have a chip set, Val, do you know where it is?" Matt asked.

"It's in my room, be right back. Yuktrap! Hurry up with those drinks!" Val yelled at him.

Yuktrap let the dogs in and slowly rolled into the kitchen, getting them some cold waters. He rolled back and put one at each seat of the table, as Val walked back in with the chip set and cards. Matt started shuffling as Val passed stacks of chips out. Yuktrap finished serving the drinks then rolled over to Angel, holding his hand out.

"You made me look like an idiot, standing up for you. I lost my clothes because of you, I am never holding your hand again, get out of my sight Yuktrap," Angel hissed.

Yuktrap lowered his arm and slowly rolled over to Jen, standing next to her in silence as Matt dealt the cards.

"So, Angel, where are you from?" Matt asked.

"Las Vegas. I had to move out into a suburb during high school, it's where a large cult of witches lived, I had to battle it out with them," Angel smiled, taking her cards as they threw their chips in.

"Standard poker, right?" Jen asked.

"Yeah, just five-card draw," Matt smiled. "Sooo…you hunt witches?"

"Yes, I thought you knew that," Angel offered.

"No, I did not. I would not have guessed that. It really does seem like the Puppetmaster is on some kind of supernatural binge. Val? Did you know about her profession?" Matt asked.

"I remembered it involved the supernatural," Val nodded. "I think you are right though, fusion."

Jen pushed some chips in, and Angel and Val folded, while Carly and Matt called.

"Two cards, please," Jen asked. Matt dealt her two cards. Carly asked for one, and he took two himself.

Jen pushed more chips in and Carly called while Matt folded.

"Two pair," Jen smiled.

"Three nines," Carly beamed, taking the chips. Matt handed her the cards and she started shuffling.

"I get it, okay, I do. There were four of you, plus Sam. You can't do anything about it, so you just survive, mixing in recreation with work. You don't have magic here, and you aren't going anywhere. I'm in," Angel declared.

They ante'd up as Yuktrap began to move around, looking at their hands. Matt threw him a bone and showed him his cards as he pushed chips in.

"Cheat and you are outside in the rain," Matt grinned at the robot. Yuktrap nodded and moved around. Angel shooed him away, still mad. But the rest of them shared their hands.

"Straight, nine high," Matt smiled.

Jen sighed and threw her cards away as Matt took the pot.

"Val said you had houses and houses of supplies. Is there anything else you need?" Angel asked.

"Nope. We are set," Matt shrugged, as he dealt the cards. Yuktrap moved around again, as Angel continued to shun him.

"Val pointed out you have a vampire problem," Angel offered.

"It's not a problem, per se. They are hibernating," Val corrected her.

"They are vampires, they *are* a problem," Angel countered, pushing chips in. Val and Jen folded, leaving just Matt and Carly.

"All of the humans on the planet are in this house. Human extinction means vampire extinction. They both know that, and they are willingly hibernating to preserve themselves. One of them is a vampire hunter, so now we have a vampire hunter and a witch hunter. He isn't very friendly, and we are going to keep you two separated. I'm sorry for mocking your stature, but rest assured, it was tame compared to how he would behave," Matt sighed.

"Lame apology," Val observed.

Angel pushed a lot of chips in, as they both called her. "Want to try again?" she growled.

"I am sorry for mocking your stature. It surprised me. Not because you are short, but because you are supposed to be a witch hunter," Matt offered.

"Not much better," Jen teased. "You had no idea she was a witch hunter until five minutes ago."

"Flush, Jack high," Matt sighed.

"Flush, King high," Carly laughed.

"Four sevens," Angel growled, taking the pot.

"Nice hand," Matt grinned, tossing her the cards. Yuktrap clapped his hands, but Angel was glaring at Matt.

"I'm sorry for mocking your stature, it was wrong," Matt tried.

"I accept your apology," Angel growled, as she shuffled the cards and dealt them. "Tell me about this supposed vampire hunter."

"He is called the Sunwalker. Sunlight doesn't hurt him. But he needs human blood to survive," Matt offered, as he pushed some chips in.

"I have never heard of a vampire immune to sunlight," Angel observed.

"Now you have," Val smiled, as she called.

Jen and Angel folded, and it was down to Carly, Matt and Val. Matt pushed more chips in and Carly folded. Val called and they revealed their hands.

"Flush," Matt smiled.

"Full house," Val beamed, as she took the pot. Angel handed her the cards and she shuffled them as Yuktrap mocked Matt.

"It's raining Yuktrap, be careful. Wouldn't want a lightning bolt to hit your antenna," Matt grinned.

"Why not?" Angel growled.

"He would die and get his voice back," Val laughed, as she dealt the cards.

"Good reason," Angel conceded.

"Now that our plans have been rained out, what is on the agenda for tomorrow?" Jen asked.

"Maybe Val and Angel can finish their shopping trip?" Carly offered, pushing chips in.

"Sounds like a plan, I didn't get a chance to get much," Angel sighed, as she folded.

"Maybe we could check in with Sam, see if any work needs to be done. Though I can't think of anything. I guess we could go gather some gasoline," Matt suggested, as he also folded.

Jen called and it was just the two of them. Pushing more chips in, Jen called Carly's bet.

"Three Kings," Jen smiled.

Carly folded and Jen took the pot.

"Thanksgiving is Thursday. We have plenty of food, but we should plan our meal. What should the main course be?" Val smiled, pushing chips in.

"Marlin," they all replied, causing Angel to look up.

"You guys caught a marlin?" Angel asked, folding.

"Yep, over 400 pounds. It was Matt's dream fish," Jen laughed, pushing chips in.

Matt raised the bet and they all called, Angel was the only one out.

They took their cards; Matt didn't take any and that earned a look from Jen. He pushed all of his chips in and Val immediately folded.

"Your sister folded; she knows you. You don't bluff, I'm betting," Jen smiled, as she called.

Carly had the least amount of chips between the three of them, as Matt teased her.

"If you want in Carly, you are going to have to put something else on the table," Matt grinned.

Carly shook her head and pushed her chips in, then reached underneath her shirt and put her bikini top on the table.

"Wow," Val beamed.

"Let's see it Matt," Jen laughed.

"Straight flush, seven high," Matt smiled.

Carly buried her head in her hands and tossed her cards away as Jen could only laugh, also folding. Matt took the pot, and the bikini top.

Val offered Carly more chips but she declined, taking her loss.

"I can tell you guys are overly friendly, but I can also see that Matt is the only guy available. I guess I will have to make due on my own," Angel sighed, as Matt dealt the cards.

"Maybe we will get more guys," Val offered.

"But Val is fine with not getting more guys, don't let her fool you," Jen laughed, pushing chips in.

"Angel decided she hated me within the first couple of minutes, so I guess all you can do is hope," Matt grinned, folding.

"Hard to believe she sided with Yuktrap," Val laughed, pushing chips in.

Yuktrap raised his hands in the air three times again, but no one was paying attention. Val took the pot again, as Matt passed her the cards.

"Carly? Can you start prepping dinner, since you busted out?" Val beamed.

"Sure," Carly smiled, standing up and moving into the kitchen.

"So, Jen? What do you do for a living?" Angel asked, pushing chips in.

"I am a treasure hunter, from a wealthy family in England," Jen smiled, pushing her own chips in.

"So, a successful treasure hunter then?" Angel smiled.

"Extremely," Matt whispered, folding.

"You could say that, yes," Jen laughed.

"And Carly? What about you?" Angel shouted into the kitchen.

"Retired superhero," Carly laughed.

"Okay then, and Sam?" Angel asked.

"Superhero. Don't mess with him Angel, your superhuman strength won't help you," Val grinned. "I am 100% in your corner, but that's not a winnable fight for you."

"I don't fight people, I told you. Witches, vampires and demons only," Angel shrugged, pushing chips in. Jen raised, forcing both Val and Angel to go all in or fold. Val folded, she was fading, but she wasn't going to lose with a bad hand. Angel called and promptly regretted it.

"Four Queens," Jen laughed.

Angel threw her cards away and stood up to help Carly. Yuktrap followed behind her, reaching his hand out. She interpreted it as him trying to grab her ass, and threw him out the door, into the rain. He was pounding on it, but no one moved.

"Do you think we are bullying him too much?" Val whispered, as she went all in. This was her last hand.

"Yeah, but I don't care," Matt shrugged, calling her bet. Jen called as well, and they took their cards.

"He got another chance today and it lasted less than a minute," Jen laughed, raising the bet. Matt called and they tied with the same two pairs. Laughing, they split the pot as Val got up to move into the kitchen. She opened the front door, and let the soaking wet robot inside.

"If you track water anywhere, you are back outside," Val laughed at him. "You have to stand there, a doormat."

"Ouch," Matt smiled, as he dealt the cards to Jen. "How long do you want to play?"

"Until someone wins all the chips," Jen beamed. "I have to get you back for that thrashing you gave me at dominos."

"I am good at dominos," Matt admitted.

"You aren't as good at poker, I can tell," Jen teased. "You haven't bluffed a single time."

"Maybe I will against you, you never know," Matt grinned. "I have been waiting for the head-to-head."

"A legitimate strategy, we will see," Jen smiled, as she pushed chips in. Matt called and they continued to play. Dinner was almost ready, and Val told them to wrap it up. Their chip count had barely moved, as they had traded wins. Jen was reading him very intently as she waved Val off. They wanted a legitimate finish.

Relenting, Val wasn't going to interfere in their continued courtship, even Angel took notice of their buzzing chemistry as they gossiped. Matt got a hand and pushed more chips in, Jen immediately folded. Jen pushed chips in and Matt folded. It was just a matter of waiting until they both got a strong hand.

Twenty minutes later, the rest of the group were back in their seats, watching and eating. The two players didn't even notice, as even Yuktrap was focused on their game. Matt had taken the lead on a flush, but they both still had a lot of chips. Finally, what would be their final hand arrived.

"One card," Matt requested, as Jen took none. He had pushed a lot of chips in, and she had already called once. He checked to her, and she pushed all of her chips in, then added her own bikini top.

"This is for the game," Jen teased. "Push your chips in."

Matt smiled and agreed, pushing his chips in. The group stopped eating and watched, as Jen slowly laid her cards down.

"Four kings," she grinned. She had a bad feeling, even the group of onlookers didn't think it was enough.

"Straight flush," Matt smiled, laying his cards down.

"Ugh!" Jen threw her hands in the air, as Matt took the chips and the bikini top. "You are good at this! I knew I should have folded; you don't bluff at all. But you got in my head about it."

"Matt is hyper competitive at everything he does. I don't care at all about winning or losing, Matt only thinks about winning," Val laughed, as she served them some food.

"Can you imagine playing Sam at poker? I would just fold, every time," Matt laughed.

"Oh, for sure. That guy is a stone, unreadable," Jen smiled, as she took her plate. Matt pushed the poker chips to the side, but he kept the bikinis close as he also took his plate.

"That was fun, thanks everyone," Matt smiled.

CHAPTER 36

THANKSGIVING

Waking up, Matt rolled out of bed and went to get them some juice. He didn't have to go far, Yuktrap was there waiting by their door with two glasses. Thanking the stupid robot, Matt walked back into his room and set Jen's glass on the nightstand.

"Happy Thanksgiving Jen," Matt grinned.

"Happy Thanksgiving Matt. This is an American holiday, but we always celebrated it back home. It's good to appreciate what you have. We have a lot to be thankful for this year," Jen smiled.

"What are you thankful for, Jen?" Matt asked.

"Meeting you. Just an ordinary country bumpkin that has treated me better than anyone I have ever met before," Jen smiled.

"Country bumpkin? I lived in a big city," Matt scoffed.

"I think I nailed my description," Jen beamed. "What are you grateful for Matt?"

"I have told you repeatedly, being blessed with your continued affections," Matt grinned.

"I never tire of hearing it," Jen laughed, as she sipped her juice.

They heard a noise outside in the living room, and just laughed. They knew it was Angel kicking Yuktrap out of her way. Jen got out of bed and put some clothes on, as Matt stepped out again. Yuktrap was picking himself up, and sulked to the back porch, letting the dogs inside. Rolling to the kitchen, he fed them. His mood had been constant depression since Angel rebuffed him, but it was his own fault. She gave him a chance and he had utterly humiliated her.

"Morning Angel, how are you?" Matt whispered.

"Morning Matt. Happy Thanksgiving," Angel grinned.

"Happy Thanksgiving. Did you get all your shopping done?" Matt smiled.

"Yes, complete with dresses and bikinis. I probably ran a 5k tab up, but uh, they can just send me the bill?" Angel laughed.

"I'm glad you are adjusting to this whole thing. How are things going with you and Yuktrap?" Matt teased.

She looked down at the robot, who was holding his hand out. "I kicked him across the living room this morning, but he keeps coming back for more. I hate him with every fiber of my being," she growled, emphasizing the last sentence. He continued to hold his hand out, undaunted.

"We are going full formal tonight for the feast. If Yuktrap misbehaves, we throw him out with the dogs. Otherwise, he can mope around and serve drinks," Matt shrugged.

"I look forward to it Matt. I hear Jen sets a high bar, but I will be ready," Angel grinned.

"She does, yes. You got your color picked out?" Matt smiled.

"Black, of course," Angel smiled, as she poured herself some old-fashioned coffee. "Do we need to start any meat right now?"

"Nah, we aren't doing a turkey, it's all marlin. Grill it. We have plenty of time," Matt grinned. "It's going to be a big feast—I don't know if there will be dancing after. I don't know if you want to dance."

"I wouldn't say no, but we will see how much energy we have," Angel grinned. "Is Sam coming?"

"Yeah, Val wouldn't let him say no. He isn't dressing up, but it's okay. He can do whatever he wants after he saved us from Jack," Matt shrugged.

"What is that guy's story, for real?" Angel whispered.

"Oh, I guess you haven't spent any time with him, but he heals his wounds instantly, and has metal claws that come out of his fingers. He has killed Yuktrap a few times, so you can bond with him over that...I guess.." Matt shrugged.

"Killing Yuktrap makes him okay in my book," Angel laughed, as Yuktrap threw his hands in the air. "Stupid robot."

"Hey, I have been meaning to tell you something," Matt offered.

"What is it?" Angel asked.

"You looked really good in that lingerie," Matt teased.

"It would be a shame for you to die on Thanksgiving Matt. I think your room is that way," Angel pointed.

Matt could only smile as he took some breakfast back to Jen. She was sorting through her makeup, in preparation for the evening. He offered her a pop tart and she accepted. There was a knock on their door, and surprised, Matt opened it. He was surprised to see Angel again.

"I have decided to forgive you for your joke, because the fact is, I would strip down again for you all if it meant Yuktrap was going to remain silent. That's all," Angel offered, turning away.

Matt shrugged and closed the door, while Jen eyed him slyly. "You made a joke about her underwear, didn't you?"

"How could I resist, she folded so fast to his voice box, I didn't even ask her to strip and she was half naked," Matt laughed. "Come on, let's get started with the day. We have a lot of food to cook."

Jen rolled her eyes and exited with him, as they moved into the kitchen. They had decided to slow cook some frozen veggies, it wasn't ideal, but it was the best they could do. Angel was drinking her coffee, while Yuktrap hovered beside her. Moving towards Jen, she waved him off and he returned to Angel.

"Let's slow cook the frozen potatoes, carrots, and broccoli. I know they won't taste as good, but the fact is, we don't have fresh vegetables anymore. The garden is only doing okay, I think it needs more time. As a backup, we also have 15 bean soup, we can slow cook that as well," Matt offered.

"How many slow cookers do we have?" Angel asked, confused.

"A lot. We have looted all kinds of stuff—supply isn't ever going to be an issue. We also have cornbread mix, frozen Hawaiian rolls that I have been saving, canned cranberry, stovetop stuffing, canned green beans, hmm…the milk is running low, it's the first thing we are going to run out of, we have been freezing it, I don't think we need it today," Matt reflected.

"We will help as long as we can, but I need two hours to get myself ready. Val probably needs the same. Angel? How long would you say you need?" Jen smiled.

"Oh…not two hours. Probably just one," Angel stammered.

"I don't need that much time either," Carly shrugged, she had come to get Val some coffee. "I will help for as long as you need, Matt."

"Honestly, the biggest challenge is going to be the marlin, I have never cooked it before. I have no idea what is happening there, I will start out with small pieces. Fortunately, there is a lot of it," Matt grinned.

"Perhaps you should research it? Google is still up and running, a lot of other websites are down, but I think you could find some recipes," Jen grinned.

"Val has been monitoring the internet, most of the bigger websites are still up. It's the smaller ones that probably paid monthly service fees that are programmed to be deactivated when the check doesn't clear, they are the ones that are dropping off. Where is Val, anyway?" Matt asked.

"She doesn't like to get up before the sun," Carly smiled, as she took two cups of coffee back to their room.

"That's fair," Jen shrugged.

Matt was pouring the 15 bean soup into the slow cooker, added some water, put the lid on and turned it on. Pushing it to the back of the counter, it could be largely forgotten about. He put the frozen veggies in another slow cooker, added water, and turned it on as well.

"I don't feel as optimistic about the veggies, but we will see how it goes," Matt sighed.

"What should we do now?" Angel asked.

"Whatever you want. We are a long way from needing to cook any-thing else, the marlin is defrosting, so—" Matt shrugged.

"We could go to the pool Val told me about?" Angel intercepted.

"Sadly, when Jen and I went to the pool, we discovered that the chlorine was off, and the water was turning green. No one is maintaining it, cleaning it, that sort of thing. Unless we can go find some chlorine, our days of swimming in the pool are over," Matt sighed.

"We still have the beach, so…that's all we really need in my book," Jen smiled.

"I completely agree, I prefer the beach anyway," Matt grinned.

"Let's come back in a few hours, Val has a point, the sun isn't even up yet," Jen laughed.

"Okay, see you later Angel," Matt relented.

They left Angel there with Yuktrap, who was standing close to her. She looked at him and sighed. "Well, this sucks."

Matt and Jen got back in bed and snuggled. "Think Angel is feeling left out?" Matt asked.

"Not much we can do about it. She needs to sleep in later, that's all. She has Yuktrap, she can spend time with him, since she loves him so much," Jen laughed.

"I don't think you are reading that relationship correctly," Matt grinned.

"We are doing everything we can to make her feel like part of the group, but she needs another person to keep her company. Five is a bad number. Maybe she will get someone next week. Someone short," Jen stifled a laugh.

"Ouch," Matt rolled his eyes. "I think we should stop making fun of her height. Even though she is adding some inches to it, it angers her. And her strength is real, she could hurt us. It's also not earning any good points."

"That's fair. Thanks for taking care of most of the food today," Jen whispered. "Is there something specific you need help with?"

"Yeah, Val will have to make the cornbread, I have no idea how. Other than that, finding out how to cook marlin is my biggest need," Matt reflected.

"We can start out cooking one piece at a time, to make sure you are doing it correctly. I think we should rejoin Angel, keep her company. As you said, earn some good points," Jen grinned.

They stood up and reentered the living room, Angel was lying on the couch, holding Yuktrap's hand. She quickly let go of it when they entered, sitting up.

"You alright?" Matt asked her.

"I'm fine. I'm just…very bored. I feel like I have nothing to do," Angel lamented.

"We realized that and came out to keep you company," Jen smiled.

"I appreciate that. I was settling for Yuktrap, who I hate," Angel glared at him.

"Ordinarily, we map out our days ahead of time. Because as you said, we can feel bored easily. It was harder at the start, when it was just Val and I, but now we each have a partner. And we realize it's not your fault you don't have that, so I would suggest sleeping in later. Val really likes you, but she also really likes the sun," Matt grinned.

"It makes sense," Angel relented.

"Do you play sports?" Jen asked.

"No, I have to hide my strength. Most of my free time I spent stopping witches from being stupid and being with my friends and family," Angel reflected.

"Well, okay. We are probably going to start leaning on the fishing, the golf courses are turning into dirt, the pools are turning green, and five people can't play tennis together. We could also try horseback riding, if we could track down some horses. They are pretty much wild at this point," Matt sighed.

"I can't imagine what happened to so many animals out there," Angel whispered.

"That's another thing, Sam is taking care of a female Beagle, if you wanted it, I'm sure he would let you take over. But you would have to move next door. She can't be here with Buddy, we are in no condition to deal with puppies," Matt offered.

"Honestly? I would like that. It beats Yuktrap. Can I leave him here?" Angel asked.

Yuktrap threw his arms in the air and simulated crying. She kicked him across the room again.

"He doesn't have his voice box, so you can leave him here, yes. Yuktrap! Get back over here," Matt grinned.

The robot picked himself up and rolled over to them, looking depressed.

"We are giving you a new friend, a female Beagle. When we are out, you will have to take care of her as well. Just go house to house, don't give me any grief about closed doors, I know you were made to open them," Matt laughed.

"I would prefer to not have him in my house, if it really is going to be mine," Angel growled.

"It will just be to feed and walk Gracie on days that we aren't here. You can keep the doors locked while you are home. You can move in right now, take an inventory, tell us the things you would like to have. We will see if they are being stored elsewhere, if not, go loot them," Matt offered.

"Honestly, yes. I will do that. Thanks Matt," Angel relented. Standing up, she headed to the door, Yuktrap following close behind. She stopped to kick him across the room again, and left.

"He is just a glutton for punishment, it seems," Jen smiled. "That was nice of you, by the way."

"I know that she is lonely. Beagles are the face of therapy dogs, it makes sense. I hope Sam goes along with it," Matt shrugged.

Val and Carly walked out of their room, looking rested and refreshed. "Good morning," Val smiled. "Happy Thanksgiving. Where is Angel?"

"Happy Thanksgiving to you too," Matt smiled. "Angel is scouting out the neighboring houses in preparation to move into one of them. She is lonely, and I offered her Gracie to keep her company. The caveat is, she can't live here. The upside is, she doesn't have to take Yuktrap."

Yuktrap threw his hands in the air and flipped Matt off, while Val just rolled her eyes and laughed.

"That makes sense. How is the food going? What do you need help with?" Val asked.

"I will definitely need you to make the cornbread, and whatever other dessert dishes you want to make. I also need you to Google the best ways to cook marlin," Matt offered.

"Why can't you Google it?" Val chided him.

"Honestly, I don't even know where my phone is anymore. I haven't been carrying it," Matt shrugged.

"Don't offer to help then ask him why he can't do it Val," Jen grinned.

"Okay, both of those check out," Val beamed. "I will start working on that recipe now."

"Anything you need from me?" Carly smiled.

"Did you go find those missing items I talked about in the bedroom?" Matt teased.

"Oh my God," Carly rolled her eyes. "I have one of them."

"Well, work on the other then," Matt grinned.

"Not on Thanksgiving Day," Carly smiled. "Oh, did I tell you guys I found something the other day in a house we are taking care of?"

"What did you find?" Jen asked.

"A pool table, in good condition," Carly smiled.

"Oh, that is fun. We can put it in one of the bedrooms. We can even ask Angel to help us move it, her strength is real," Matt grinned.

"Finally, something I am confident I can beat Matt in," Jen beamed.

"Oh? You're good at billiards? Matt teased.

"Absolutely," Jen laughed.

"How far is it Carly?" Val asked, while searching on her phone.

"Three blocks down," Carly laughed.

"Let's not interfere with Angel's work, but if she comes back, we can ask her to help us today," Matt nodded.

"I have a recipe here for striped marlin, lots of ways to cook it," Val reported.

"It's not a striped marlin Val," Jen replied. "It's a blue marlin, the meat is different."

"Oh...how many kinds of marlin are there?" Val stammered.

"Swordfish, white marlin, striped, sailfish, blue, that's all I can think of," Matt offered.

"Okay, one minute," Val grumbled. "Here, look at this. It looks easy."

Matt took her phone and read a recipe, just marinate the marlin and grill it. Simple enough. "Okay, yeah, this is what I thought. I'll use the charcoal grill—I like it better. Long way away though, it's only 9am. We should radio Sam, tell him our plans."

"Let's wait to see if Angel comes back soon, if so, we can go get that pool table. I want my bikini top back," Jen beamed.

"I'm not putting that on the table until I follow through with my plans for you two," Matt laughed.

"Well…I guess I have to take other things off the table if that's the case," Jen glared.

"Fair enough. I'm not backing down," Matt grinned.

"I will play along Matt. I think you have something devious in mind, and I want to have fun with it," Carly smiled.

"Thanks for being fun Carly," Matt laughed.

Some time passed while Jen pouted, and Angel came back in. "Hey guys, the house next door is fine, I just need to move my clothing over there. Hi Val," Angel smiled.

"Hey Angel," Val beamed, standing up to hug her. "We need your help with something."

"Oh, what is it?" Angel asked.

"I found a pool table a few blocks down. Can you help us carry it back? It's too big for the trucks," Carly offered.

"Oh, sure. Lifting things seems to be in my immediate future for the time being, I can live with that I guess," Angel shrugged.

Hours later, they were finishing up their last game so Matt and Val could go start dinner. As expected, Jen was a monster, having not lost a single game, barely missing any shots at all. Carly was second, Matt and Angel were about the same in level of talent, and Val didn't care about her lack of experience. After establishing the pecking order, they started playing team games. The current team was Matt and Carly against Jen and Angel. Jen and Carly weren't allowed to be on the same team, and Jen had to call her shots.

The handicap was barely affecting her, but fortunately, the last shot was coming down to Angel.

"Corner pocket," Angel called.

She struck the eight ball and it went straight into the corner pocket, but she had hit the cue ball way too hard and scratched out, ending the game.

"All right, free win!" Carly laughed, high fiving Matt. Yuktrap asked for a high five, and Matt ignored him. Carly obliged him though, for some reason.

"Angel, I told you to take it easy," Val chided her. "Surely you are better at hiding your strength than this."

"It's okay, I can take my one loss for the day. Matt you are on the couch until I get my bikini back," Jen chided him.

"Okay," Matt shrugged. "That was fun everyone. I am going to go start the grill, then prepare the green bean casserole. Jen? You can teach Val how to play, since you are a professional."

"I was expecting a more frustrated response to you being on the couch," Jen glared.

"Well, sorry to disappoint you, but as I said, I'm not backing down," Matt grinned, setting his cue stick down and heading outside to the grill.

"What do you think he is planning?" Jen growled as Matt walked out.

"To have fun, obviously," Carly laughed. "If it bothers you so much, why did you put the bikini on the table?"

Matt couldn't hear the rest of the conversation, as he stepped outside with Buddy and Fred. Yuktrap followed him, raising his hands.

"You want to help? Go get the zip locks off the counter and bring them out here," Matt pointed.

Yuktrap offered a salute and headed back to the kitchen. Matt added charcoal and lighter fluid, then fired up the grill. He had already brought the baster out, along with a fork to flip the fillets. He had lemon juice and seasoning to add, he just needed the meat. Yuktrap brought the zip locks and handed them over. Matt actually said thanks and began to prepare the meat.

Jen came out on her own, hugging him from behind. "You don't have to sleep on the couch, I was just trying to get you to fold. I'm not mad at you at all. I'm actually really happy I found something I can kick your ass in," she whispered into his ear.

"Ha, there are a lot of things you are infinitely superior to me at Jen. I can't even do half the stuff you do," Matt grinned.

"Yes, but it's not as fun that way," Jen smiled. "Even if the list is enormous."

"Oh you. It is an enormous list," Matt laughed as he let the fire heat up. "You can probably cook this meat better than me."

"Oh, I know I can. But maintaining a positive mindset involves you all doing stuff on your own," Jen grinned.

"No argument there. How is Angel doing?" Matt asked.

"Oh, she is good. She is in there with Val helping her prepare the food. Carly is too," Jen smiled. "What were you talking about with Carly earlier, about finding those missing things?"

"Ha, I noticed a few things were missing from her outfit when you had her chained up against the wall. She said she would work on them," Matt grinned.

"You were enjoying yourself then? Think I will let you do that to me?" Jen teased.

"No, I don't," Matt smiled. "Which is why I am taking advantage of having your bikini."

"Well, you never know, we could have some fun in that department. Maybe over Christmas," Jen whispered into his ear.

"I know you liked having that power over Carly. You don't seem to be the type that would trade places with her," Matt teased as he threw the meat on the grill.

"I've never put myself in that position, I have been put there against my will a few times. But I will...hmm...I will leave you out of it for now. You haven't been behaving," Jen whispered into his ear.

"Is that so? Did you answer Carly's question in there as I was walking out?" Matt teased.

"I did, yes. But I'm not telling you what I said," Jen whispered, finally breaking away with a smile and sitting down in the chair. "Yuktrap—drinks."

Yuktrap dutifully went inside to get them some drinks, as Matt flipped the meat and eyed her. "You want to take a break after these fillets?"

"Maybe I do," Jen grinned. "I'm in a good mood," as she took her drink from Yuktrap and sipped it, keeping her eyes on Matt.

CHAPTER 37

THE CRASHING

"Maybe I should let you win more often," Matt grinned, as he was back on the grill after their quick break.

"You think you could fool me like that?" Jen teased, sitting in her chair with her drink. Carly had joined them as well, drinking from her glass.

"No," Matt admitted.

"So, Carly, Matt tells me he was trying to adjust your outfit from the other night. What adjustments exactly was he making?" Jen grinned.

"I think he wanted a wardrobe piece, specifically," Carly whispered, not sure whether or not it was okay to tattle on him.

"Are you nervous about ratting him out?" Jen teased.

"Yep, you caught me. He still has my bikini," Carly laughed.

"I see. Well then, perhaps we should have this conversation later," Jen smiled. "Yuktrap, refills all around."

Yuktrap took their glasses and rolled inside, taking care to avoid Angel while he was carrying the drinks. He refilled their drinks and rolled back out, serving them.

"You are so much better without your voice, Yuktrap," Jen observed.

Yuktrap went back to sulking, as he helped Matt with the fillets. Angel and Val were inside prepping their dishes, Angel had added yams to the menu.

"In all honesty Matt, how far away do you think we are?" Jen asked.

"I am done with about half of the fillets, so we are probably approaching the two-hour mark. You should go start getting ready," Matt offered.

"I will, thank you. It's been a fun day so far, I hope we can have a great evening," Jen smiled, as she stood up and headed inside. Val was heading to her room as well, while Angel came and did a final check.

"The oven is pre-heating; do you need anything out here?" Angel asked.

"Nah, I've got Yuktrap to help me. Thanks though," Matt grinned.

Yuktrap held his free hand up to Angel, causing her to scowl. "The only reason I don't punt you over the fence is because you have those fillets in your hand," she stormed off.

"She is still really mad at you dude. You humiliated her," Matt grinned at Yuktrap.

"You warned her, I was standing there when you did," Carly laughed.

"Yeah, I know. You were missing the fishnets and gag, but you still looked great in that blue lace," Matt teased.

"Oh you. I liked it, but my wrists were sore after. I think I will push for my hands to be free overnight next time," Carly reflected.

"Oh, so there will be a next time?" Matt teased.

"You didn't catch me there or anything. Yes, there will be a next time," Carly laughed.

"I know everyone has offered, but before I go, do you need anything?" Carly stood up.

"How about a hug?" Matt smiled.

"Absolutely," Carly laughed, hugging him. "It's still nice of you to give me the attention you do."

"Come on, we are friends, right? I doubt I will ever have this kind of friendship with Angel, but Val has her handled," Matt grinned.

"Angel will come around; she is straight as an arrow. She will start to appreciate your company more, just stop teasing her about her height. Or lack thereof," Carly beamed.

"We have agreed to stop doing that, we think it earns bad points," Matt chided her.

"Fair enough. I will see you soon Matt. I have a new dress, I hope you like it," Carly smiled.

"You know I'm not dumb enough to not like it," Matt teased.

"Again, fair," Carly laughed as she headed inside.

It was just Matt, the dogs, and Yuktrap now. He finished grilling the fillets and put them on the plate, carrying them inside. The group followed, as he made his way into the kitchen. The kitchen itself was quite large, and had an oven warmer, so he put all of the meat inside of it and started preparing the green beans. The cornbread was made, the Hawaiian rolls were thawed and just needed to be broiled, and the Jell-O that Val had added to the dessert menu was in the freezer.

"Yuktrap, put yourself in the oven, make sure it's hot enough," Matt ordered.

Yuktrap hesitated, looking at the oven, then back at Matt, then back at the oven, raising his hands.

"Just kidding, learn how to take a joke Yuktrap, sheesh," Matt teased.

Yuktrap waved his arms in the air and flipped Matt off. Matt just laughed as he put Angel's yams in, along with his own green bean casserole. He checked the slow cookers, the 15-bean soup was coming along just fine, and so were the veggies. He probably wouldn't serve the soup tonight—it had been a backup if something went wrong. But since the veggies were coming along nicely, he figured he was safe.

"Okay, I think I got everything taken care of for now. The stuffing only takes a few minutes, the cranberry comes right out of the can, the cornbread is done thanks to Val. Let's go slack off on the couch Yuktrap," Matt grinned.

Matt led the robot into the living room, once again the dogs followed, along with Yuktrap. Matt picked Buddy up and lay down on the couch, placing Buddy on his chest. Yuktrap waved his hands in the air, and Matt pointed to the nearby chair. The robot relented and rolled over to it, as Matt petted Buddy.

"Nothing bothers you huh Buddy? All the people gone, you still have your people, so you are fine," Matt whispered, poking his nose and playing with his ears.

About half an hour went by, and Angel came out of her room, dressed to the nines. Wearing a long black dress, hair tied up, makeup, and heels. Matt was surprised, he had dozed off. Buddy jumped down as Yuktrap rolled over to Angel, admiring her. Standing up, Matt tried to recover.

"Oh uh, Angel. I'm sorry, I wasn't expecting you. I haven't even changed clothes yet," Matt stammered.

"Was I not supposed to come out of my room?" Angel asked.

"Well, uh, as I said, you are very early. Normally, you each come out at a preset time, and I'm dressed and waiting to seat you. But we still have at least an hour," Matt managed.

"Oh…well I guess you should have gotten ready then, instead of lying in here slacking off," Angel chided him.

Yuktrap looked at Matt and mocked him, as Angel looked on disapprovingly. "Yuktrap, go get her some wine," Matt growled.

Yuktrap continued to mock him as Angel looked on. "Yuktrap, come sit with me at the table. I guess we are operating on our server's schedule," she observed, taking his hand and leading him to the table.

Matt shrugged and headed into the kitchen. He was reasonably confident that if he was doing all the work in the kitchen and she wasn't offering to help, things wouldn't go well for her. Opening the oven, he checked on the yams. He had no idea how to cook them, or when they were done, or anything. He also wasn't going to eat them regardless.

"Angel? Do you know how long it takes to cook the yams?" Matt called out.

"No, but I know it doesn't take *this* long to bring me wine," Angel replied.

"Okay," Matt shrugged. "Yuktrap! Whenever you want to bring Angel some wine, it's okay with me! I won't be doing it."

He had no intention of breaking the wine open before Jen arrived. And if Jen walked out and saw Angel there not helping, Matt just smiled at the thought. The door opened again, and Carly came out. Walking by the table, she was surprised to see Angel.

"What are you doing? It's not time to eat yet," Carly stammered.

"I am sitting here waiting for my wine," Angel calmly replied.

"If Jen walks out here and sees you have just been sitting there while Matt is doing all the work, you are going to be eating outside," Carly pointed out.

"Look at this dress, I am not staining it," Angel scoffed.

"Yuktrap, I hope you are ready to clean your girlfriend's brains off the ground," Carly waved at him, as she joined Matt in the kitchen. "Hey, do you need any help? What the hell is going on in there?"

"I have no idea, she just walked out, said some mean things, and sat down. She expects me to bring her some wine," Matt scoffed. "Can you check the yams? I don't know how to cook them. I find their entire existence disgusting."

"How about a hug first," Carly pressed, as she hugged him. He was surprised, but he appreciated it. Carly had her makeup on, but not her dress yet. "Okay, Val asked me to check on you. I will give her a full report. Don't forget to broil the Hawaiian rolls, she said. She also said for me to get all the serving utensils on the table, so I will do that now, then go finish getting ready."

"Sure, thanks Carly," Matt grinned.

She walked out and stopped at the table. "If you aren't going to help get dinner on the table, you should just go back into your bedroom and wait until dinnertime. Because you aren't getting any wine."

Angel scoffed and stood up, coming into the kitchen. "Will you open the oven door for me? I have these gloves on and don't want to stain them."

"Sure," Matt grinned, opening the door.

She looked at the yams. "They aren't ready yet, the marshmallows will be a lot more melted, and the yams themselves will be incredibly soft."

She walked back towards her room, while he shouted a "You're welcome" at her. Yuktrap came into the kitchen, waving his hands disapprovingly.

"Hey, she is the one acting like a you know what. We are a team, I'm nobody's slave. If there is a slave here, it's you, Yuktrap. But at least she looked good in that dress," Matt shrugged.

Yuktrap gave him a nod, as Matt handed him the plates to take to the table, followed by the silverware. He heard a door open, then close, and thought nothing of it. Taking the green beans out, he gave them to

Yuktrap, who carried them to the table. Opening the cans of cranberry, he served them in small dishes and off Yuktrap went. He started cooking the stuffing, this had been his favorite course as a kid. He wanted nothing to do with homemade stuffing, just the box was fine.

"A door opened again, and Val came in. "How's it going?" she asked.

"Fine. Everything is almost ready. I am about to go change clothes. How are you?" Matt asked.

"I'm good. I checked on Angel—she was crying in her room. I guess she got pretty embarrassed when Carly brought the woodchipper down on her," Val sighed.

"She came out like an hour early dressed to the nines, and told me off. Didn't even offer to help with the food. She owes me an apology, at the very least," Matt shrugged.

"I still think she is trying to work this whole situation out. She agreed to clean up all the dishes after, so there is that," Val laughed.

"I'm over it. She has Yuktrap, she is fine. I am going to cook this stuffing, then go change clothes. All that is left is getting the veggies out of the slow cooker, and serving everything. Oh, and the Hawaiian rolls," Matt whispered.

"I can do everything but the stuffing, so finish that, then go get dressed. Yuktrap can carry everything to the table," Val offered.

"Okay, thanks. The stuffing should only take a few minutes," Matt relented, pouring the box into a skillet and adding water, then butter. "Think Angel will even join us? Maybe we should skip her when asking what we are thankful for."

"I do think she will eat with us…and maybe that's a good idea. She probably isn't thankful for a lot right now," Val admitted.

"Maybe you should check on her again while I finish this stuffing," Matt offered.

"Okay," Val nodded. "Yuktrap, keep helping Matt."

Yuktrap nodded and stood by, waiting for Matt to tell him to do something. Matt finished cooking the stuffing and served it onto a platter, handing it to Yuktrap. He followed the robot into the dining room and continued walking into the empty bedroom. He had his clothes set out there, along with his cologne. He didn't want to spoil Jen's surprise, so he was once again changing in a different room.

He got his suit on, wearing a blue dress shirt this time, and added his cologne. The time was getting close, as he walked back towards the kitchen. Yuktrap was making trips back and forth, while Val and Carly were finishing up the food. All that was left was the Hawaiian rolls.

"Oh Matt. You look very handsome, thank you," Carly smiled.

"Yes Matt, thank you," Val beamed. "Can you finish the rolls? We already have three done. We followed your method, only doing three at a time, so if we burn a few, we don't burn them all."

"Yeah, I've got it. You both look amazing as well," Matt grinned. "Do you have the timing set up with Jen?"

"Yes, she will be appearing at 5pm on the dot, we will come out right before her. Angel knows as well; she is feeling better. Yuktrap even got to hug her," Val smiled.

"Wow, she must have been really down," Matt whispered, as he put some rolls in the broiler.

"Apparently. Okay, see you soon Matt," Val laughed, as they walked out.

There was a knock on the door, and Sam walked in. "Hey kid, I brought some smoked venison for the feast."

"Oh! Sam! I uh, yes, thank you. We love venison, can you just hand it to Yuktrap? Can I get you a drink? We don't have any beer, sorry. Plenty of alcohol though," Matt offered. He had completely forgotten about Sam. Yuktrap had the common sense to add a plate to the table, then silverware, while Sam dug in the cabinet and poured himself some tequila. Matt gave him a thumbs up. Getting the rolls out, this batch had come out a little crunchy, but he liked them that way.

Putting the last batch in, he checked the time. Ten minutes to go until Jen came out, he had plenty of time. Everything else was on the table, as Sam sipped his tequila, standing to the side. He was woefully underdressed, wearing his seemingly standard plaid shirt with blue jeans and boots. Yuktrap had put him next to Angel's seat—because there was nowhere else. He hoped Angel would be okay with it, this would never be Sam's thing.

"Hey Sam, you are going to be next to our newest member, she is still a bit...chippy. Try not to antagonize her too much," Matt prodded.

"No problem kid. I like chippy," Sam growled.

"Yes, of course," Matt sighed.

Angel came out first, and Matt was ready to receive her. She was wearing a long, sparkling black dress, with white gloves, and her hair was tied up. She had reapplied her makeup as well. She was taken aback by his appearance, and openly recoiled when she saw Sam. "Oh, Matt. You look very handsome; I have to admit. I am very sorry for my behavior earlier. I can see now, I messed this up."

"You look lovely as well Angel. Let me escort you to your seat," Matt smiled. He took her arm and led her to her seat, pouring her some wine.

"Thank you," Angel stammered, still looking at Sam. Yuktrap came over and extended his hand towards her, and she took it for a bit.

Carly and Val came in next, Val in a new red dress, with her hair down. Carly was wearing a sparkling white and gold dress, also with her hair down.

"Hello Val, Carly. You both look lovely as well. May I escort you to your seats?" Matt smiled.

"Thank you, Matt, you look handsome as well. And hello Sam, thank you for joining us. Your company is always welcome, despite appearances," Val grinned.

Matt escorted the couple to their seats and poured some wine, Angel was still looking away, trying not to blush.

"Angel, you look beautiful. Is everything okay?" Carly asked.

"Everything is great! Happy Thanksgiving!" Angel shouted.

Jen came in last, even Sam looked her way. Angel couldn't bear it, as she emptied her wine glass. Jen was wearing a new purple, sleeveless gown, that was see through in the middle. Sparkling on her chest and legs, her hair was down and looked perfect.

"Jen...you look as lovely as always. Thank you for joining us, may I escort you to your seat?" Matt managed.

"Thank you Matt, I love how handsome you look in that blue. Sam? Thank you for joining us, you may be seated," Jen smiled.

"The pleasure is all mine, Jen," Sam growled, as he sat down next to Angel, who was asking for more wine.

Matt poured Jen some wine, as he seated her at the head of the table. He poured Angel some more wine, and then himself, as he sat down on the other end. Yuktrap was holding Angel's hand, as she was squeezing it.

CHAPTER 38

THE DINNER

"Shall we begin the evening with a toast?" Jen smiled, raising her glass. The others followed suit, as Jen toasted them. "To our continued growth and happiness as a family," she beamed.

"To family," they toasted.

Angel fought back tears as she drank her wine and squeezed Yuktrap's hand.

"Angel? Are you alright?" Jen asked.

"Oh! Yes, I'm fine. Thank you. I'm fine. How are we serving the food?" Angel managed.

"Serve whatever is closest to you, and pass your plate around the table. We will serve each other a little bit of everything. Obviously, this is a tremendous amount of food," Jen offered.

The group passed the plates around, Matt declined the yams, but took everything else. He wasn't sure how he was going to eat it all, but he focused on the meat. They took some time and dug in, before Jen started the conversation again.

"Sam? What have you been working on lately? Is there anything we can do to help?" Jen asked.

"I've been collecting and storing fresh tires, car batteries, alternators, even car engines, from various auto repair stores. No big deal, I don't need help. We will likely be able to sustain ourselves on that front for years to come," Sam growled. "This marlin is good."

"We appreciate all of that Sam. We did have a request regarding Gracie," Matt offered.

"Does Angel want to take care of her from now on?" Sam growled.

"If you don't mind," Angel whispered. "May I have some more wine?"

"I don't mind, you need a companion," Sam shrugged, as Matt poured her another glass of wine. Her fourth. Val was eyeing him, thinking he should cut her off, no doubt. The woman was 5'2 with heels, it was going to go right through her.

"Thank you both," Angel managed, putting her glass down and continuing to eat.

"Are you kids going fishing again soon?" Sam asked.

"Who are you calling a kid," Angel growled.

"Yes Sam, we are probably going to go on Saturday, weather permitting. Head to the sea cottage tomorrow night, wake up in the morning, shove off," Matt replied.

"There are a lot of deep freezes on the other side of the neighborhood, I can start bringing those over. How much marlin is left?" Sam asked.

"Oh, a lot. I only cooked four zip locks' worth, out of 20. And we still have the cobia. We can help with the deep freezes, Angel is a power lifter," Matt grinned.

"Yep!" Angel declared.

"How is the rest of the food guys?" Matt asked.

"Oh, it's wonderful Matt. I love the marlin as well, plus the vegetables came out great. I know you were worried about them, but they taste just fine," Jen beamed.

"The meat is really good, both the venison and the marlin. Thanks for bringing the venison, Sam," Val smiled.

"You are welcome. I'm not a freeloader, I know the work you kids are putting in," Sam growled.

"There is that kid again," Angel offered. "You aint exactly that much older than us."

"How old are you, Angel?" Jen asked.

"27," Angel declared.

"Sam?" Val laughed.

"Older," Sam shrugged.

"See? That aint old," Angel pointed out. "Is there more wine?"

"No, we are out, actually," Jen replied.

"Does anyone want seconds?" Matt asked.

All of their plates were relatively cleaned out, even Angel's. No one was even thinking about seconds.

"I think we have some desserts, but let's get the table cleaned off first," Matt offered.

"Matt? You can sit that out, thank you very much for cooking most of the food for us," Jen smiled. "Yuktrap? You are up."

"I will help get the table cleaned off, then go get Gracie. Which house is Angel moving into?" Sam asked.

"That one," Angel pointed straight up.

"The one on the right, Sam," Matt rolled his eyes.

"Matt? Can you carry her to her bed? She can move out tomorrow?" Val whispered.

"Sure," Matt grinned. He walked over and tried to pick up Angel, but she fought back.

"Get your hands off me you lummox," Angel growled, and shoved Matt backwards.

Her strength surprised him, as he lost his balance and went down. Carly was closest and checked on him first, as they were all concerned.

"Oops," Angel lamented. Standing up, she shuffled to her room, or actually Val's room. Val redirected her and pushed her inside her own room, closing the door. Matt stood up, and Jen called the night done.

"Okay, we are leaving everything for Angel tomorrow. Let's just retire to our rooms for a bit, change clothes, then come back and eat dessert. Yuktrap? Clean off the table as best you can while we are gone," Jen growled.

"Are you okay Matt?" Carly whispered as she helped him up.

"Yeah, I'm good. I guess her being drunk made me forget about her strength. Thanks," Matt managed.

"Have a great night guys. Thanks for cooking Matt," Sam growled, as he headed out.

"Thanks for coming, Sam," Matt waved.

"This is not how I envisioned the night ending," Val whispered.

"It doesn't have to end this way, we can still dance," Matt offered.

"I think the moment for that has passed, Matt," Jen whispered.

"I agree. Let's go change clothes, take a break, then regroup for dessert," Val pressed.

"Okay," Matt shrugged, as Jen led him into their room. They shared a hug, and then a kiss, as he held her in his arms.

"Your marlin was delicious Matt," Jen beamed.

"Not as good as this dress," Matt grinned.

"Do you want to see what I have underneath it?" Jen teased.

"I have no objections to that," Matt laughed, as Jen slid her dress off. She helped him get undressed and they fell into bed, kissing.

———

An hour later, they were all sitting in the living room, minus Angel, as Val was serving them Jell-O. Sitting down herself, they ate.

"This is the best colored Jell-O," Matt smiled.

"Are they not all the same? It's just food coloring?" Jen asked.

"They are completely the same Jen. He is just being a kid again," Val laughed.

"I mean, green Jell-O does taste pretty good," Carly beamed.

"What did we just say?" Jen exclaimed.

"What are we going to do about Angel?" Val sighed.

"If she isn't insanely apologetic tomorrow, we are going to the beach without her," Jen shrugged.

"Someone should go make sure she got those heels off, or else she will wake up with sores," Carly offered.

"I will do it. I seem to be the only one she likes," Val stood up and slowly entered her room. A few minutes later she came back to rejoin them.

"I got them off, she had passed out with them on. That dress is going to be wrinkled, but I'm not stripping her."

"I'll go strip—" Matt started but Jen clasped her hand over his mouth.

"Silence. You didn't deserve that treatment tonight, but there will be none of that," Jen laughed.

"Fair enough," Matt shrugged. "Will you let her keep her clothes tomorrow, I wonder?"

"We will have to see," Jen grinned. "Thanks for the Jell-O, tomorrow we head to the beach. Matt is finally going to go through with his plan, I have accepted it. Happy Thanksgiving everyone. Despite the literal hiccups, it was a wonderful evening. Good night."

Jen led Matt back into their room, while Val and Carly retreated to theirs. Val was definitely a little disappointed with Angel's behavior, but they all hoped she would come back to them in the morning.

CHAPTER 39

PENANCE

Waking up the next morning, Matt rose from the bed to fetch their drinks. Opening the door, he expected to find Yuktrap, but was surprised when the robot wasn't there. Shrugging, he walked to the back door and let the dogs out, then went into the kitchen to pour two glasses of juice. He headed back for his room, and he heard Angel sobbing in hers.

Letting out a sigh, he walked into his room and gave Jen her juice. "Good morning," she whispered.

"Good morning, Angel is next door sobbing, probably hugging Yuktrap. What do you think I should do?" Matt asked.

"Go try to comfort her. She will likely beg for forgiveness, grant it. It's better if she just apologizes to you," Jen whispered.

Matt nodded and exited the room, knocking softly on Angel's door. He could still hear her crying, and he felt bad. He decided to give her more time, and went to make her some coffee. He wasn't particularly good at making a great cup of coffee, but he did his best and came back to her door, cup in hand, knocking again. Slowly opening it, she was on the ground, crying in Yuktrap's arms.

"Oh...Matt," Angel managed.

"Hey Angel. I brought you some coffee. Are you alright?" Matt whispered.

"That's so...so nice of you Matt. I don't deserve it," Angel cried.

"Well, I brought it anyway," Matt smiled, offering her the cup. She dried her eyes and took it, sipping it.

"You aren't very good at making coffee, are you," Angel whispered.

"No, admittingly not," Matt grinned.

"It's the thought that counts. Yuktrap? Go take care of the dogs," Angel pointed.

Yuktrap wheeled himself out of there, and Angel looked up at Matt. She was still in her dress; she had worn fishnet stockings as well.

"I'm very sorry for treating you so badly yesterday, Matt. I was horrible to you. I hope you can forgive me. I understand if you want to banish me, I'll go," Angel cried, wiping tears away.

"You were pretty cold to me yesterday, and the shove really hurt, but we haven't considered banishing you Angel. At least I haven't," Matt whispered.

"Um, the shove?" Angel managed. She didn't remember.

"You shoved me to the ground, yes," Matt whispered.

"Ohh," Angel sobbed again. "I'm sorry! I can't even remember that!"

She was crying again, as Matt tried to comfort her. She waved him away.

"No, I don't deserve it. Here, let me stand up," Angel cried. "This is what you like to do, right?"

Angel slid her dress off and put her hands against the wall, looking back at him. He looked away—this conversation had taken a weird turn.

"Come on Matt. This is what I really deserve," Angel whispered.

"Alright, if you insist," Matt managed and walked over to her. Offering her a harsh spank, she winced in pain. He grabbed her chin and clasped his hand over her mouth, telling her to look at him. She complied and he spanked her some more. She winced but kept her eyes on him. "It ends if you give me your top."

She shook her head no, and he kept spanking her. She took it for a while, before finally giving up. Unstrapping her bra, she handed it to him. Accepting it, he let go of her and retreated.

"Matt?" Angel called after him.

"Yes?" Matt whispered.

"I promise, I will be part of the family from now on. You won't get any trouble out of me. And I'm very sorry for shoving you, I hope I didn't hurt you," Angel offered.

"You didn't hurt me. We are going to the beach today—you are welcome to join us, Angel. I think you should apologize to everyone else as well," Matt suggested.

"I will," Angel nodded. "May I get dressed?"

"Hmm, stand there for five more minutes, then get dressed," Matt grinned, closing the door behind him.

Matt walked back into his own room and tossed Angel's bra at Jen. She took it and laughed.

"Really? I guess things went well then?" Jen giggled.

"It didn't go the way I expected, she apologized, then offered me some spankings. I guess she thinks that is what we are into, thanks to Carly. She promised me she would be part of the group from now on," Matt laughed.

"That's good," Jen smiled, as she got up and put some clothes on. "So, the beach? I am to wear the outfit you have chosen for me? Then I get my bikini top back once we get to the sea cottage?"

"That's right. Maybe Angel will help you out on that front. I wonder if I should allow it," Matt teased.

"Oh you. I admit this is a fun idea, I can see why you didn't let go of it easily. I don't mind, it's not like there will be any people there with cameras," Jen laughed.

"We can't leave until Angel cleans up though, that was the deal. She doesn't even know about it yet," Matt grinned.

"Oh, that's fair. I had almost forgotten," Jen nodded, as they headed out. Angel was coming out as well, having put some clothes on.

"Oh, good morning Jen. I am very sorry if I ruined your evening. There is no excuse," Angel bowed.

"You certainly brought the mood down, Angel. You can make it up to me by cleaning the kitchen now. The faster you finish, the faster we can all go to the beach," Jen pointed.

"Yes, that's fair. I'm sorry again," Angel whispered, as she moved into the kitchen.

"Yuktrap, help her," Jen waved at him.

Yuktrap was already rolling that way, following Angel into the kitchen. There were a ton of dishes, they had piled them up.

"Um? Is it okay if I use the dishwasher?" Angel asked. "You can say no and I will accept it as part of my punishment."

"In that case, no. Handwash them, and put them in the dishwasher to dry," Jen replied, as she sat down on the couch. Matt sat next to her, and they waited for Val and Carly, who were always the last to come out. They had at least waited to get moving until the sun came up.

"I feel bad making her do that all by herself," Matt whispered.

"She needs to serve her penance Matt. You can go help her if you want, in say half an hour. I can tell just by looking at her she feels awful," Jen whispered back, as she lay down in his lap.

Carly came out of their room first, walking into the kitchen and turning the Keurig on. Ignoring Angel, she started to walk to the living room.

"Carly? Carly!" Angel stopped her. "I'm sorry for ruining your evening."

"How sorry?" Carly asked.

"Well, I gave Matt my bra, and now I'm handwashing these dishes for Jen. How can I make it up to you?" Angel offered.

"Well, we are going to the beach today, and you can loan me your bikini top," Carly smiled.

"Fair enough," Angel relented.

Carly turned and joined the group in the living room, offering Matt a hug. He couldn't get up because Jen was on his lap, but he accepted the hug as best he could. Val came in last, heading into the kitchen. She gave Angel a long hug, holding her tightly. Angel didn't even offer any words—she just held the hug.

"Angel? I hope you have gotten it all out of your system. You have likely earned a lot of bad points since you arrived, more than anyone else. So please, if you could join our family, we would all appreciate it," Val whispered.

"I will Val. I promise," Angel whispered back.

Val nodded and broke the hug, joining the group in the living room.

"Good morning. How is everyone?" Val smiled.

"Good. We are going to let Angel finish the dishes, then get ready to go to the beach," Matt grinned.

Angel came into the living room, and fell to her knees in front of them all. Matt tried to stop her but she waved him off.

"I'm sorry, I still don't fully understand what is happening here. You said…you think it's a Puppetmaster testing humanity? And we are in… some kind of different world? Where Matt and Val, Jen, Carly, Sam, the vampires, and myself are all from different places, merged into one? And we are being judged by our behavior? Literally every second, of every day? How long do you think we have to do this?" Angel whispered.

"Our theory holds weight Angel, and I believe in it. We decided to go with it, instead of exploring other possibilities. The Puppetmaster is on some kind of vampire kick the last month, excluding Yuktrap. But I can't answer your question. I honestly have no idea how long this experiment is designed to last. It could be six months, it could be a year, it could be the rest of our lives. We could be living the rest of our lives like this, a new person every week, to prove that humanity is capable of rebuilding itself. We aren't even sure how death works, Sam killed Jack, but the vampires killed each other and kept coming back. I emptied a shotgun into Yuktrap, he kept coming back. It's borderline nonsensical, I think at times they are making it up as they go along. I'm sorry to say that you are stuck here with us, until they decide it's over," Matt sighed.

Angel sighed. She closed her eyes and thought about it for some time. Finally, she stood up. "Okay, I will go finish the dishes now." Walking back into the kitchen, she left them in silence.

"If I have to live here the rest of my life, I can happily say at least it's with you guys," Carly offered.

"I haven't wanted to think about it. But, I'm very happy with Matt. So, whatever happens, I hope we can stay together," Jen whispered.

"I think maybe we should refocus our efforts on work. We have been completely focused on recreation, we should probably do some productive things, check on the houses, see what we need. Sam works every day, it's not fair to him," Matt offered.

"At the same time, fishing puts food on our table," Val countered.

"Yes, but we have plenty of fish for a while. That said, we have one more mouth to feed every week. Theoretically, at least. We have added one mouth in four weeks, so we have lucked out there, I guess. But the more people we add, the more food we will consume. Even rationing, two meals a day, we will eat a lot. I'm not saying I regret yesterday, far from it. But we have to make sure we eat all those leftovers. We can't throw anything out," Matt pressed.

"I agree. Do you want to change our plans for today?" Jen asked.

"No, let's head to the beach still. If nothing else, Angel deserves it. Plus, I'm looking forward to your outfit. And Carly's," Matt grinned.

"I traded outfits with Angel, remember?" Carly beamed.

"Oh, that's right," Matt laughed.

"You won fair and square but I am going to get you back for this and it's going to be hard," Jen laughed.

"What about the fishing trip tomorrow?" Val asked.

"I think we should push that back, get some work done here. Move those deep freezes, like Sam said. Angel said she would help, even though she probably doesn't remember. What do you guys think caused her to hit the wine so hard?" Matt asked.

"Lots of things, but if I had to pin it on one instance, when Jen walked into the room. She had just put two hours into her wardrobe, and Angel put in less than 30 minutes, and it was obvious. You were as nice as you could be Matt, but us ladies notice stuff like that," Val smiled.

"I was shocked when Angel came out here after 30 minutes, treating me like crap, no less," Matt whispered.

"I was surprised to see her sitting at the table, I did a double take," Carly grinned.

"We can't say we didn't tell her the plan in advance, she just did whatever she wanted. But that doesn't excuse the way she was treating Matt," Val sighed. "I think for our next dinner date someone else needs to host. It feels like he is doing all the work."

"I agree, maybe Angel will volunteer," Jen nodded.

"That's fair. We will get ready to go now," Val smiled, standing up. Carly followed her, as Angel came back into the living room.

"The dishes are mostly finished. Am I okay to get ready for the beach?" Angel asked.

"Yes, of course. Thanks for doing the dishes," Matt waved.

"You don't have to thank me for serving my punishment Matt," Angel smiled.

"Wear your bikini and sarong, with a see-through beach top," Jen pressed.

"I um, I promised Carly my bikini top. If I wear a see-through top.." Angel started. "Oh...I see. This is the game that Matt is playing with you two. And I am taking Carly's spot."

"Are you okay with that? You can say no," Matt offered.

"I'm good with it," Angel nodded. "I'm probably just going to sunbathe, I doubt we can get in the water. "It's winter, is it not? I'm sure the water is freezing. Where are we, anyway?"

"You don't know where we are?" Carly asked, bewildered.

"It's not like there is a sign on the front door," Angel countered.

"Well, there have been a lot of water towers, a lot of flags...anyway, we are in South Texas. This is Harlingen, we are going to South Padre," Matt grinned.

"Never heard of it. I'll go get dressed now," Angel headed towards her room.

"Are you sure she is a witch hunter?" Matt looked at Val.

"You felt her strength last night. But she has been a bit off," Val relented.

"I've been meaning to ask—do you think she qualifies as medium?" Matt asked.

"Yeah, I heard her story, mainly because I had forgotten it. She slept with demons, felt bad about it, but didn't stop for the longest time. Then she gave her weapon away, and it punished her for it," Val nodded. "That's all she was willing to talk about."

"There are worse things to get graded down for. Killing people, for starters," Carly whispered.

"Let's all get ready to go," Matt grinned.

———

An hour later, they were driving to the beach, crossing over the bridge and coming to a stop. They were all wearing their favorite colors, and Jen and Angel just had their see-through tops on. Angel was looking around nervously for some reason.

"There are literally no people Angel. You are fine," Val assured her.

"Did you guys have to push all those cars out of the way?" Angel asked.

"We had to push a lot of cars, yes. Sam and Jack did the ones on the bridge, that's why there are such big pile-ups. It was a big hassle in Austin for Matt and I," Val reflected.

"I'm not taking this seriously enough, I know. It feels like I am coming into a much better situation than some of you. I've honestly never thought about what I would do if every single person on the planet just vanished," Angel whispered. "Drink a lot, probably."

"Oh, the first night, we ate a lot of ice cream," Val laughed. "I didn't really drink heavily until the hurricane hit. Come on, let's catch up to the others."

Matt, Jen and Carly had left them behind, walking to the beach and starting to set up their camp. Jen had taken her top off and Matt was applying suntan lotion to her back and chest. Carly was watching with amusement; she had stolen Angel's black top. Val and Angel got there and lay the towels down, setting up the umbrellas.

Matt finished caressing Jen and walked to the water with her, she was just rolling her eyes as she put her cover back on. Putting his feet in, it was as cold as they expected. Jen looked at him, but he never went to the beach without getting in the water. He had never cared about people watching, and now there were no people.

"You coming?" Matt grinned.

"The water is cold, but I'm not backing down," Jen smiled.

"Let's just stand here in it, let our bodies get used to it," Matt offered.

Slowly, they waded out, gasping as the water rose around their bodies. Carly surprised them by stepping in as well.

"Wait for me!" Carly smiled.

"Okay. I didn't think you were coming," Matt teased.

"You seem to keep forgetting how tough I am," Carly laughed.

"Sorry," Matt offered.

"I'm just teasing. You got dropped by a drunk last night, so I will give you a pass," Carly beamed.

"Oh, come off it. She does have superhuman strength, it's abnormal," Jen chided her.

"I've seen it before," Carly shrugged. "It doesn't even bother Sam. Nothing seems to bother Sam. I guess when you have seen everything, this is just another adventure."

They were pretty far in now, the water was up to their shoulders as they hovered, bouncing in the waves. There was barely any wind, so the waves weren't too serious. Looking back, they could see Val and Angel lying on their stomachs sunbathing.

"How's it going with Val?" Matt asked.

"Oh, it's good. We have figured each other out. I was never upset or anything, Val was going through a lot when I got here. Angel was right, she has missed a ton of the drama. But that is going to be true of every new member," Carly offered.

"Yeah, it definitely is. We have definitely reached a good comfort zone, I mean, Jen is walking around topless," Matt teased.

Jen splashed him and laughed. "I could never do this in my world, the paparazzi were ruthless."

"I have lived that as well," Carly smiled. "We got lucky with that storm, as I think about it. It was just the one."

"I don't think it was luck, more like a fluke. We aren't in a hurricane zone, it's very rare for them to hit this far south. One a year is too much, it's closer to one every five years. I think the last time the neighborhood flooded was 20 years ago," Matt reflected.

Carly came closer to Matt, "Will you hold me, it's getting pretty cold. You don't mind, right Jen?"

"He can hold us both. Matt? I'm fine, but don't keep us out here too long, okay?" Jen grinned.

"Okay, we can go in at any time," Matt offered, as he put his arms around their shoulders, snaking his hand down Jen's chest. She slapped him and they just laughed.

"I want another shot at you in poker, just so you know. We know you can't beat me in pool, but I think I have you figured out in cards," Jen teased.

"Anytime," Matt shrugged.

"We are going to have to enforce stricter rules on her in pool," Carly grinned. "Call every shot, every ball that gets hit in the process."

"It won't matter," Jen shrugged.

"Make it so she has to sink two balls per shot, or her turn is over," Matt grinned.

"That's a better rule, I admit," Jen laughed.

"Matt?" Carly looked at him. It was time to get out. He nodded and they headed for the beach and the sunbathers. Drying off quickly, they wrapped their towels around their bodies and sat down, getting some waters out of the ice chest.

"How was the water?" Val asked.

"It was a bit chilly," Matt observed.

"I think it's time to fully forgive Angel and bring her into the family," Jen grinned.

Angel looked her way—Matt knew she was scheming something. "Take your cover off and run out there into the water, diving in headfirst," Jen pointed.

Angel sighed and pushed herself up. She wasn't going to back down, as she took her cover off and walked down to the water. Putting a foot in, she recoiled at the temperature. Letting out a sigh, she waded in and dove into a wave. Matt stood up and walked a towel out there, as she was coming back in, shivering.

"Oh, thank you," Angel managed, as he wrapped the towel around her. Walking back, she sat down as they helped her warm up. "Part of the family."

"Part of the family," Matt grinned.

"Crummy family," Angel beamed.

They shared a laugh, Matt understood the reference, he wondered if anyone else did. Packing up, they began their journey back to Harlingen.

CHAPTER 40

THE FIST

V al drove them over the causeway, Matt was in the passenger seat and the girls were in the backseat, gossiping.

"Praying for a hot man for me!" Angel exclaimed.

"Just remember, they will need a few days, or you can throw your boobs at them," Carly grinned.

"It seems like some of you can't keep your clothes on," Val beamed.

"I admit it was a little fun to be bad, as I have said, the paparazzi would have never allowed it back in my world. But if it is another guy, I will be much more conservative. So, behave yourself Matt," Jen smiled.

"You are the ones that have been taking your clothes off, I never asked for them," Matt waved his hands in the air.

"But you accepted them," Angel pointed out.

"Who wouldn't?" Matt countered.

Val shook her head and parked the truck. Sam hopped out of the tailgate, while the others piled out. Jen took the shotgun in hand, and they walked down the pier. Peering out, Matt could tell it was a woman.

"Damnit," Angel hissed. "Val is winning."

Val was smiling as they approached her. Long black hair, wearing red and blue, she looked up at them. Matt didn't recognize her, she was older than them, in her late 30s. He asked Val if she knew anything.

"No, I have no idea who she is," Val shook her head.

"I recognize her," Sam growled, extending his claws slowly.

"Who are you guys?" the woman asked.

"We are the only humans left on the planet. Who are you?" Matt asked.

"The fire told me I was the Fist of the Chosen Ones," the woman growled.

"Hmm. The Fist? Isn't that the elite martial artist with the glowing fist? I thought it was a man, but I guess it could be a woman," Matt wondered out loud.

"Yep. She is a threat, I think we should put her down," Sam growled.

"I recognize you, old man. You have killed me so many times, yet I keep coming back," The Fist stared Sam down.

"Yeah, you are kinda stupid like that, I guess," Sam growled, as he stepped forward.

The Fist drew a pair of daggers out of her coat, standing up.

"Yeah…this is a problem. Her title is a bit off, I guess that's intentional. I mean, she is called the Fist but uses daggers. Okay," Matt sighed. "She can't come back with us. Let's get out of here. Sam? I will leave it to you."

They backed up, Jen kept the shotgun pointed at them, as Sam surged forward and they started fighting. Climbing back into the truck, they drove away.

"I said a hot man, not a hot woman. Are you listening??" Angel shouted at the sky.

"They seem to be listening to Val. I guess Jen can continue to take her clothes off," Matt laughed.

"Someone is on the couch tonight," Jen proclaimed.

"Let's try to review Matt. Start at the beginning, if you would?" Val prompted.

"Okay, first we got Sam, the Protector. Bang up job, by the way. He is a medium comic book character, we think. Probably multiple characters fused into one. Right down the middle. Then we got Jack, very, very low medium. As in, if the Medium Place had to make cuts, they would go down to the bottom of the list, and Jack would be the first cut. Also seemingly fused into one person. Then we got the opposite end, Jen. Totally amazing, great at everything, the highest medium. If the Good Side was taking new people, she would be first on the list. Maybe she has been fused? I have no idea," Matt sighed.

"If you could skip the flattery," Jen rolled her eyes.

"That's not flattery, that's fact. Continue Matt," Val beamed.

"Then we got Carly, again, medium. Right down the middle. Possibly fused, no way to know. Killed people, uh, did good things as a superhero. Then it got weird. We got the Sunwalker, is he medium? Sure. But what? Then it got even weirder, we got the Nightwalker. Is she medium? I guess. Both of them seem to be definite fusions. Then…Yuktrap. He isn't medium, he is the worst. Bottom of the Bad Side bad. I think he was a prank, or a butt dial. I'm guessing a butt dial. Then we got Angel, a witch hunter. Probably a fusion. Team medium," Matt offered.

"Um, I am firmly Team Good Guys, thank you," Angel cut in.

"Girl you slept with hot demons, the very people you were supposed to be hunting," Val laughed.

"Team Medium," Angel conceded.

"And now this woman, a regular femme fatale," Matt sighed. "So, despite Val's gloating, we have gotten three men, five women, and a male robot. It just so happens that one of the men died, and the other is hibernating, along with one of the women. Maybe the Fist signals the Puppetmaster is off their vampire binge. I wonder what they were watching."

"Still, is the Fist medium? How much do you know about her?" Val asked.

"Nothing? I don't know who she is. Like I said, a Fist that uses daggers, pretty weird. Most likely several fused characters. But again, she and Sam recognized each other. I honestly don't understand how it works. But I hope she likes dying, because those daggers aren't going to do anything against Sam," Matt grinned.

"Probably should keep that tidbit to yourselves if you see her again," Jen offered.

"I expect Sam to bring her back home to the table at some point," Matt sighed.

"Let's move on for now. Since I am out a hot date, what are our plans?" Angel asked.

"Wait a minute Angel, we aren't off of this yet. How did the Puppetmaster land on the Fist? Think they are just choosing hot women to throw at you, Matt?" Val teased.

"I mean, she could have done a lot better if that was the case. But I really don't know. I think she could be another saboteur, similar to Jack. That is certainly what Sam believes, I can guarantee that," Matt sighed.

"What do you think we should do?" Jen asked.

"Just…keep soldiering on. Try to earn good points. That has to remain the focus, earn good points, live good lives. Take care of each other. Angel is probably deep in the hole, sorry Angel," Matt whispered.

"It's my fault," Angel sighed. "I was pretty bad. I want to make it up to you guys. What can we do now?"

"I have another theory, it's wild, but…it might be possible. Sorry, I know you want to get off this Angel," Matt sighed.

"What is it?" Val asked.

"That woman, I mean, it could be a girl for Sam," Matt shrugged.

"Do they have any kind of a connection?" Val asked, bewildered.

"I don't know, I honestly don't, but they knew each other. Everyone knows everyone in the comic book world, apparently. Even if they are fused," Matt waved his hand. "Besides, knowing one another doesn't seem to be the criteria. Look at us."

"So, he gets a lover, and I don't?" Angel demanded.

"We aren't saying that Angel. Look, I know you are upset, I'm sorry for that. It's not our fault, we have no control over the situation, literally none. Sam however, has been with us the longest, he was the first person to arrive. The rest of us have had partners drop in over time. You have been here the shortest amount of time, well the second shortest now. You just need to be patient," Matt sighed.

"We are also assuming that Jen and Carly were dropped in with the purpose of helping us as partners. Well, I am assuming that, I don't think Matt ever looked at Jen as a potential partner until she informed him that's what was happening," Val beamed.

"Matt was very honorable, and remains so," Jen smiled.

"It took Val and I less than 24 hours to hook up," Carly laughed.

"I wish I was going at that speed," Angel sighed.

"We know the situation sucks, it always has. We will just pray you get someone next week," Carly assured her.

"Can we get off of this now? What are we doing this week?" Angel sighed.

"We will let you decide Angel. What do *you* want to do?" Matt offered.

"I still want to host a dinner date, but I want to actually have a date. So, can we finally go deep sea fishing?" Angel asked.

"Sure. We can head back tonight, wake up in the morning, go. Val? Do you mind sitting out? There isn't enough room in the boat," Matt sighed.

"Oh, I don't mind, I can just sleep in. Honestly, if you guys start heading back at say 11, I can be waiting for you at the cottage with food and cool drinks. Buddy and Fred will keep me company," Val smiled. "As much fun as it was, I was wiped out for days."

"We don't have to go out as far this time, so we can leave a bit later, say 6:30. Go out until the sun is coming up, start fishing wherever we are. A wahoo was just a luxury fish, it's no big deal," Jen shrugged.

"We still have those frozen benito to use as cut bait, and we can even fish for another marlin," Matt grinned.

"Sounds like a plan," Carly smiled. "What about Sam?"

"I guess we just have to wait for him to come give us a report on what happened with the Fist," Matt sighed.

"Let's give him a few hours to get back to us, pack up all your stuff, your swimsuits, and leave around 8," Val offered.

They drove the rest of the way in silence, Angel was frustrated, as Carly and Jen took her hands. Finally arriving, they got out of the truck, and everyone offered Angel a hug.

"Oh, thank you," Angel stammered. "I'm sorry, I'm just frustrated."

"We get it. Val was frustrated for a while, then Carly. We have all been there. Matt helped them both in different ways. He can help you too. We can talk about it in your house, come on," Jen offered, taking Angel's hand and leading her to her house next door.

Matt, Carly and Val walked into their own house, where Yuktrap came to greet them.

"Hey Yuktrap, did you take care of the dogs in both houses?" Matt asked.

Yuktrap nodded an affirmative, and motioned with his hands to the truck. He wanted to know where the new person was.

"We left the new woman on the beach with Sam, they are probably killing each other," Matt shrugged. "You have no shot, don't even try with this one."

Yuktrap threw his hands up in the air and rolled away to sulk. Carly and Val went into their room to pack, and Matt sat on the couch with Buddy to wait for Jen. He understood that Angel was sexually frustrated, he had helped Carly with it. Maybe a little too much, but no one seemed to mind. There were two couples in very happy places at the moment, and Angel was completely left out.

Jen came back in, beckoning him. "Angel is just asking for your company for a bit, we all know what's going on. I'm fine with it. Give me a kiss first and head over there. No, not you Yuktrap."

Yuktrap threw his hands in the air again and went back to his corner to sulk. Matt just shook his head and stood up, giving Jen a kiss on his way out the door. Walking over, he knocked on the door. Angel came to open it, inviting him in. He had never been in this house before, so he looked around. Gracie came to say hello, she could smell Buddy on him.

"Hey girl. This is a nice house Angel, I have actually never been in here," Matt offered.

"Oh? I thought you guys were taking care of all the houses in this area?" Angel asked.

"We are, but I go left each morning, and Jen goes right," Matt shrugged.

"Well, you can sit down anywhere in the living room, can I get you a drink?" Angel smiled.

"Sure, anything except for coffee will be fine," Matt grinned, as he sat down, Gracie in tow.

Angel rolled her eyes and got him some ice water, coming into the living room. "May I sit next to you?" she whispered.

"Yeah, of course," Matt replied, taking the water and thanking her. "You doing okay?"

"Not really, I am really frustrated with everything. Literally every-thing," Angel sighed.

"I feel like some of that is my fault, you and I got off on the wrong foot, and I regret that. I couldn't resist taking shots at your stature, I'm sorry for that," Matt sighed.

"It's nice of you to apologize. And I'm really sorry for how I treated you on Thanksgiving, believe me, I was suffering for it very soon after. It was humiliating to see Jen come out of that door. But really, I was embar-rassed way before that," Angel sighed.

"I don't think it does any of us any good to relive our first week to-gether, Angel," Matt whispered.

"I agree. I am discovering how tough this whole situation is on one's mental health. I can't imagine how bad it was for you and Val, coming down here and seeing your parents gone. Jen and Carly must have been a godsend. But I hear Carly was struggling a bit as well, what happened? You don't have to tell me, if you don't want to," Angel waved.

"Carly was an immediate help to Val, she came in during a hurricane, a literal storm, that's how we ended up in this house, instead of our parents. But soon after that, Carly was feeling a little bit...ignored I guess. I don't know what word to use that isn't too hard on Val. Carly needed some help of her own, and Val wasn't seeing it. So, I helped her a bit. I took her out in the *Invictus II*, we caught a few fish, just the two of us. Then we came home, got in the shower, she kept her bikini on, me my own swimsuit, she asked if I would kiss her, I obliged. It stopped there, she went back to Val, who I nudged in the right direction. She picked up on it right away. Now everything is good," Matt reflected.

"That's really nice of you Matt. And now here you are, with me. Offering me the same attention. I appreciate it. We don't have to do any-thing, just hearing how you helped Carly helped me. I know you guys are all good people. If it's possible...can we just lie on the couch? Hold me in your arms? I would appreciate it," Angel whispered.

"Yeah, sure Angel. Let me lie down here," Matt nodded, as he moved to the couch. Angel lay on her back on top of him, and he wrapped his arms around her. She closed her eyes and held his hands on her stomach.

They just lay there in silence for a good long while. Finally, she sat up and let him up. He headed for the door but she grabbed his hand, silently looking down.

"Please…just a little more," Angel whispered very softly.

Matt turned and hugged her tightly. "More?" he whispered into her ear.

She closed her eyes, "Yes please," she whispered.

He leaned down and gave her a kiss, she had to stand on her tiptoes to reach him. They held on for a while before he broke away and hugged her again. She couldn't say anything as he turned and headed out. Walking back to his house, he went into his room where Jen was waiting.

"Hey, how did it go? You kiss her?" Jen teased.

"Yeah Jen, she asked me for a kiss, just like Carly. And I gave her one. That's it," Matt rolled his eyes.

"You are earning good points for that Matt. Don't worry, it's not cheating. Now come make out with me," Jen smiled.

Matt fell into the bed and started kissing Jen, she wrapped her legs around him and they made passionate love. She laughed as he tickled her ribcage and kept trying to hold on to the kiss. Finally, they broke away and she caught her breath.

"That was fun. I love you Matt," Jen beamed.

"I love you too, Jen. Every second of every day," Matt smiled.

"Let's rest up for tomorrow, then head out later as Val said," Jen laughed.

———

Hours later, they were getting ready to head out when Sam and the Fist walked up and into the house.

"Oh, Sam. We were about to head to the island, everything uh, everything okay?" Matt stammered, as he looked at the Fist.

"Yeah kid, everything is fine. This is Tali. We have made peace with each other—she is going to stay with me. We have a pretty long history, not sure if you knew that," Sam growled.

"Nope, I'm not familiar with her at all," Matt shrugged. "If you have cleared her, she is okay with me."

"What are your names?" Tali asked.

"My name is Matt. That's Val over there, Jen, Carly. Angel is next door," Matt pointed. "All of our memories are kind of hazy, that's just how it's been. We can't explain it. Such as, you can't remember your name, can you?" Matt asked.

"I cannot," Tali relented. "Sam has largely apprised me of the situation. We are going hunting in the morning, I am told you are going fishing?"

"Yes, we have caught many prize fish out there, we will bring some more tomorrow. Can you two meet us at the dock like last time?" Matt asked.

"We will meet you there. Tali will see that you all are capable of pulling your weight. I will further drive that fact home by touring the neighborhood with her. Have fun tomorrow," Sam growled, as he and Tali exited.

"Wow, okay then. I think you were right," Val smiled, coming out of her room.

"Yeah, that was kind of crazy, but okay. As long as he doesn't lose focus protecting us, I don't care," Matt shrugged.

"He isn't the kind of man to lose focus, ask Jack," Jen grinned.

"Right. Still, Jen? Can you start carrying a gun around? I will too. I just...don't want to take any chances," Matt sighed.

"Matt? Can I use your katanas?" Carly asked.

"Yeah, go ahead. They are fake anyway. Jen really burst my bubble on those," Matt grinned.

"I'm sorry, but it's not my fault they are fake," Jen put her hands up.

"You are right, I should have had them appraised I guess," Matt shrugged. "Let's head out when we are all ready."

CHAPTER 41

BACK TO THE SEA

Angel gave the boat a firm push off, and Matt steered into the channel. Accelerating, he drove them out towards the jetties. It was Matt, Jen, Angel, and Carly, each wearing their respective colors. The girls were helping each other with the suntan lotion as Matt broke into the Gulf. Jen walked to the front and was trying to apply Matt's lotion, but the waves were running high, and she sat down instead.

Matt pushed the boat on, the waves were being a little mean, but they would make it. The girls were getting splashed a lot so he slowed down a bit. Finally, they got about five miles out and he stopped.

"Okay, the waters are a bit rough, did you two take the medicine?" Matt called out.

"Yes, thank you," Angel nodded.

Jen applied Matt's suntan lotion while he dropped the artificial line into the water. The benito still needed to be cut up, so they just went with the one line for now. He got the boat going again, while Jen sliced the fish up. Setting up the cut bait line, she dropped it into the water as well. About five minutes later, the artificial line started singing.

"Okay, Angel you are first up. Carly, why don't you come sit up here, I know the waves are worse back there," Matt offered, as Jen set Angel's rod in front of her.

"Be careful not to break the rod with your strength," Jen whispered, as Angel started pulling.

"It's heavier than I expected," Angel admitted. "But it's nothing I can't handle."

As Angel reeled Carly came to sit next to Matt, smiling. "The waters are a little worse today, but I'm looking forward to the chair. I heard you helped Angel a bit yesterday, that's really good of you. You know how much I appreciated, and continue to appreciate, your company Matt."

"Is it okay to tell you I love you as a sister? I have from the very beginning, when you were stitching up my arm," Matt grinned.

"Yes, it's okay. Still, being the only man on the planet that is…you know…available for affection, you have been a true gentleman about it," Carly teased. "Except when you squeezed my ass."

"I regret nothing," Matt laughed, as Angel got the 10-yard ribbon in. Jen pulled the line in and gaffed the catch, a big yellowfin tuna.

"Nice job Angel, how was it?" Matt asked, as he stood up to get the live bait out again.

"I think I made it a bit harder on myself, but it was fun," Angel smiled.

Jen got the lure out and dumped the fish into the storage bin, pulling out one of the dead benito. Matt moved over to drop the artificial lure back into the water, as Jen readied the marlin line. He got the boat going again, as Jen dropped her line into the water. They trawled for another five minutes, when the live bait line started singing. Carly was excited, as Matt asked Angel to reel in the benito.

They got all the lines in and Carly was in the chair, moving with the fish. She was learning a lot, not even reeling when the fish was swimming away from them. Matt encouraged her and soon enough she got the 10-yard ribbon in as well. Matt got the benito ready again, as Jen gaffed the fish and let out a cry.

"Wahooooo!" Jen shouted.

"Hey hey, we are eating good tonight! Great job Carly!" Matt laughed.

Jen dumped the wahoo into the boat, it was a big three-foot fish, sharp teeth and green scales. She got the hook out as Matt dropped the benito into the water. Moving over to the artificial lure, he threw it in as well and got them going while Jen cut up more of the other benito. Carly came to join him again.

"I love this," Carly beamed.

"You are doing a lot better. I can see you are trying to move with the fish. It's fun to watch you," Matt smiled.

Before Jen could even finish the artificial line was singing again, as Matt was going to grab the marlin line they looked in shock as another big blue marlin jumped out of the water and hit the benito. The line started screaming as the marlin jumped again. This one was enormous—they could already tell it was much bigger than the last one.

"It's a monster! Jen just cut the artificial lure and strap Angel into the chair!" Matt shouted.

"Right!" Jen nodded, as she took out a knife and cut the artificial line free. Moving to put the fighting vest on Angel, they weren't sure how needed it was given her strength, but they weren't going to take any chances. The rod was still tied to the boat, as the marlin jumped again. It was already way out there, as Matt saw the 100-yard ribbon race out.

"Ready Matt!" Jen pressed, as he took the rod out of its holder. Jen came over to unhook it from the boat, and they moved it to Angel's chair together. Hooking the rod to the chair, and Angel to the rod, they bid her to let the fish run. A useless gesture, as the 200-yard ribbon raced out next. They saw the marlin jump again, way out there, as Carly pointed.

"It's going to dive at some point, don't start fighting yet Angel, it is still at maximum energy," Matt pressed.

"I've never done this, are you sure it should be me in this chair," Angel stammered.

"You are the one with super strength, it's okay, I will be right here to help you," Jen assured her. "Just breathe."

Angel took some breaths and collected herself, nodding to Jen. She was ready, as she started to pull back on the rod with both hands. Even with her enhanced strength, Jen needed to help her.

"Pull back, and then as you lower the rod, reel in. If you can't reel, that's okay. Don't break the rod," Jen whispered.

Matt drove the boat on, pulling the marlin, trying to tire it out. Carly lightly sprayed Angel in the back with some water, as they settled in for what would be a long fight. The 300-yard ribbon slowly went out, and Matt assured her it was okay, it was a special 500-yard line on that rod. Angel actually got the 300-yard ribbon back, as she was reeling efficiently. The marlin had indeed gone deep, but they were slowly but surely pulling it back up.

Almost two hours passed, as Angel was still in the chair. The 100-yard ribbon had just passed by, and Angel assured them she was okay. Matt nodded and asked Jen if she thought the fish was close to the surface, and she nodded an affirmative. Sure enough, they saw the marlin jump again, still a good distance out, but Angel was encouraged. Carly was in awe of its size.

"How are we going to fit that in the bin?" Carly whispered.

"We aren't, plain and simple. We will throw it in the lower storage compartment where we put our stuff. Can you get our gear out of there, put it in the left bin, and put a towel down?" Matt asked.

Carly nodded and set to work, as Matt looked out at the line. Angel had settled into the rhythm, and she was efficiently winning the battle.

"Gloves Matt," Jen whispered, as he got three pairs of gloves out. Carly finished her task and came out, asking for instruction.

"We are going to untie Angel, and you are going to trade places with her. We just need you to hold the rod and reel, the fish is losing energy. The three of us will get her in," Matt assured her. He handed a pair of gloves to Jen, as the 10-yard ribbon passed. The marlin was in sight, tired. They saw it first in the waves, then it came up to the surface, rolling onto its side. The fish was enormous, as Jen unhooked Angel and she got out of the chair.

"Are you good to help us get it in the boat?" Matt asked.

"Yes, what do I need to do?" Angel asked.

"Put these gloves on, try not to touch it's body, the slime is acidic. Jen will grab the sword, I will gaff it, and you and I will pull it over the side and into the boat. Make sure to step back quickly, it has a sharp dorsal fin," Matt pressed.

Jen nodded as Carly was in the chair now. Matt handed her the gloves, and they leaned over the side. Jen grabbed the sword, and pulled it forward. The fish was just too enormous to believe, as Matt gaffed it, and pulled it up. Angel grabbed the underbelly and helped pull it into the boat. Her strength was a huge help, as Matt and Jen were both surprised at how quickly it came out of the water. Dropping it into the boat, they stepped back.

"Wow…" Matt whispered.

"Great job Angel, thank you so much. Are you okay?" Jen beamed.

"Oh yeah, I'm good," Angel smiled.

Jen tied the weight line onto the tail, and asked Angel to hoist it up. She made it look effortless as she got the fish into the air.

"880 pounds," Matt whispered. "It's over seven…close to eight feet."

"We will get a picture when we get home. For now, let's get it below, then regroup. Angel? Can you help us?" Jen asked.

"No problem," Angel smiled, as she lowered the fish and shoved it down below deck. She didn't even need any help, as Jen just shook her head and got a new artificial lure for the other rod. Matt cut up some benito while Carly hosed Angel down. They got both lines back into the water and resumed their trawling.

"How are you Angel?" Matt shouted.

"Will you stop asking? I am fine," Angel waved him off. She didn't appear to be tired at all, her super strength had definitely paid off.

The live bait line started singing, as Carly was excited to be up again. Matt got the artificial line in as Jen set Carly up. She started pulling, reporting it was a heavy fish.

"Not as heavy as mine," Angel beamed.

"Oh stop," Carly rolled her eyes, as she once again moved with the fish. It went left so she pulled right. It turned right and she reeled aggressively as it was swimming towards her, then she pulled left again. Repeating the process, the fish was trying to turn a lot, which just hurt its cause. The 10-yard ribbon passed, as Jen readied the gaffe.

"Hey Matt?" Angel asked.

"Yes?" Matt grinned.

"Are you going to throw the marlin line out again, we still have a benito, right?" Angel smiled.

"I can, yes. But...we don't have anywhere to put a big one like yours. But if you want to, we can put it out," Matt grinned.

"Yes please," Angel beamed.

"Alright then," Matt shrugged, as Jen landed another big yellowfin. "Great job Carly!"

They got the lines out again, as Matt prepared their last benito. He dropped it into the water and they pressed on. Carly landed another big dorado, and then the marlin line started to sing.

"Hey hey, Angel you are up again," Matt smiled.

"I don't see it jumping," Angel looked out.

"I don't either, it feels much lighter, but that's not saying a lot," Matt grinned, as he got the marlin rod down while Jen got the last line in. Hooking the rod up to the chair, he signaled Angel to go for it.

"Oh yeah, way smaller. That's okay though," Angel grinned.

The 100-yard ribbon came back, as Angel was making steady progress. Only about 30 minutes passed and the 10-yard ribbon passed. Matt got the gloves and the gaff ready, handing a pair of gloves to Jen. They finally saw the fish, it was big, but it was still in the waves.

"Sailfish, maybe?" Matt whispered to Jen.

"It looked like it, yes," Jen replied.

The fish came up to the boat, and it was indeed a sailfish. Angel offered to help, but Matt assured her they were okay, as Jen grabbed the sword again and Matt pulled it into the boat. It had a big sail on its back, but it was much smaller than the marlin. About four to five feet long, Angel got up and tied the weight line to it. Hoisting it up, Matt checked the scale.

"66 pounds. Jen? You think we should throw it back? I have no idea how to cook it, the US has a strict rule about sailfish, they are catch and release only. So, no one really eats them," Matt offered.

"I do think we should throw it back, yes. We can catch a much bigger fish that is worth keeping. Let's get it back in the water," Jen nodded.

"Angel, did you want a picture first?" Matt asked.

"Nah, this one is too small. How do we throw it back? Just chuck it?" Angel grinned.

"No," Matt rolled his eyes. "We should help it recover. Let's lower it back into the water, hold onto its sword, and drag it along, get the water going through its gills."

Lowering the fish from the weight line, Angel untied it and picked it up on her own, no gloves. Matt tried to warn her, but she was already lowering it into the water. She held its sword as Matt sighed and slowly got the boat going.

"Carly, get the water hose ready please," Matt motioned.

Carly nodded and stood up. Jen was securing a wrist cuff with a rope attached to it to the boat. She knew what was going on, as Angel was holding onto the fish as they dragged it. Letting go of the sword, it paused for a moment, then swam away.

"Success!" Angel beamed, as she turned around.

"Yeah, come here," Jen shook her head, securing the wrist band around Angel's arm. "You have to listen to us Angel. You are super strong, but Matt and I are the experts here."

"What do you mean.?" Angel started. "Ahhh!! It burns! Oh God, my skin is burning!"

"Ready Matt?" Jen sighed.

Matt stopped the boat, and pushed the anchor release, causing it to fall off the bow. Angel was screaming, as he signaled them to go for it. Jen walked Angel to the edge of the boat, she was crying at this point, and pushed her into the water.

"Oh my God!" Carly gasped.

"No amount of hosing was going to help, she needed to go for a swim," Matt shook his head. "That sailfish was rubbing all up against her body."

Angel came up, still yelling in pain. She tried to swim to the boat but it was already drifting away. Jen assured her she was okay—she was tied to the boat. They were all holding onto the rope, as a super extra precaution. The anchor finally caught and they stopped moving. Angel was treading water instead, soaking her skin.

"Ohh....okay...that actually feels good. Okay," Angel managed.

She swam towards the boat, coming to the side, Matt reached over and pulled her up and into the boat.

"Thank you," Angel managed. "Okay, I'm sorry about that. I might have gotten a little too full of myself."

"It's okay. How are you feeling? You okay to continue? You don't have to fish, Carly can do it until she gets tired," Matt offered, as he raised the anchor.

"My hands…my hands are a little burned. I think…I might be done for the day. I'm sorry," Angel sighed.

"You don't have to be sorry. We will just fish until Carly is spent, or the appointed hour for our return comes," Matt shrugged.

"Let's soak your hands in some ice, and get going again," Jen offered.

"Yes, thank you," Angel nodded.

They fished for another two hours. Carly was having a great time. She landed ten dorado, four benito, two yellowfins, and one kingfish. The dorado were much smaller, Matt called them chicken dolphin, but they would still taste amazing.

"Okay guys, it's almost eleven. We are about 15 miles out, it will probably take an hour to get home. Shall we say one more fish again, and hope it's not a shark?" Matt grinned.

"How about just putting the artificial lures out?" Carly smiled.

"Good idea. One more fish, then we can head in. Angel? Are you okay?" Jen asked.

"I'm hanging in there. My hands are sore, but I'm starting to feel a little nauseous. I can do one more fish," Angel nodded, as she held her hands in the ice bucket.

They nodded and got the lures out, while Carly hosed Angel down. Not fishing was actually tiring her out. She needed to stay active, but she couldn't because of her burns. It didn't take long for one of the lines to start singing. Jen got the other one in as Carly sat back in the chair.

Again, she leaned to the left and right, fighting the fish. Matt enjoyed watching her, as Jen was helping her pull. This was definitely a good size fish, as the 10-yard ribbon passed. Getting the gaffe ready, they saw the big yellowfin in the waves. Smiling, Jen gaffed it and got it in the boat.

"Woo, big yellow!" Jen laughed. "Let's throw it in the bin and start for home. Carly? Can you tie the last rod to the boat please?"

"Sure thing," Carly beamed.

Angel moved to the front seat, where Matt was pointing. Jen stored the tuna and came back to sit next to Carly.

"Good to go!" Jen shouted with a smile.

"Hey Angel? You are going to like this part," Matt grinned, as he opened up the throttle. The engine roared to life, as they raced back home. It took no time at all for their escorts to arrive. Angel looked in shock and joy as the porpoises broke the water, calling out in midair. Riding the bow waves, Angel was laughing as they followed them all the way in.

An hour later, they broke through the jetties and turned towards their channel. Spotting Val, Sam, and Tali on the dock, with Buddy and Fred baying at them. Offering a wave, Jen tossed Sam a line and they pulled in.

CHAPTER 42

TREATMENT

"Hey guys! Welcome back! How was it?" Val beamed.

"It was awesome, Angel really helped us out with her strength!" Matt laughed. "But she accidentally got some acidic slime on her from the marlin, I am going to need to take her inside and give her some first aid. But first, Angel? Can you help us lift said marlin out of the boat? They can get the rest of the fish. I will bandage you up, then we can come get our picture."

"Oh…yes Matt. Thank you," Angel said sheepishly.

"How big is the marlin?" Sam growled.

"Twice the size of the last one," Jen beamed.

"Um…really?" Sam managed.

"Wow you surprised Sam! No one has ever done that before Angel! Way to go!" Matt laughed.

Angel smiled and went to put some gloves on, then dragged the marlin out of there. Tali was shocked at the size of it, even Sam was impressed.

"880 pounds," Carly smiled.

"You were right, these kids are pulling their weight," Tali whispered.

"Yep," Sam growled.

Angel got in the middle and Matt and Jen got on opposite ends, and they lifted the big fish up and onto the dock. Matt threw the measuring tape to Tali, and she didn't hesitate to measure it. Val took one end of the tape and Tali walked the other down to the tail.

"101 inches," Tali reported.

"Let's hang it up and get a picture, then I will take Angel inside for some first aid. Can you guys take care of the boat and the fish?" Matt offered.

"Absolutely. Take care of Angel Matt," Jen winked.

Angel and the group lifted the fish up again, taking it onto the porch and hanging it up on their fish board. Val got the camera out and Matt got out of the shot, leaving just Angel, who was trying her best to smile.

"Got it!" Val beamed. "Head on inside, that rash looks bad."

Angel had skin rash on her chest and hands, and walked up the steps and into the cottage. Matt directed her to the bathroom, where the first aid kit waited. She sat down and started crying.

"It hurts so much, please Matt help me," Angel pleaded.

"Okay, okay, get in the shower," Matt urged, as he helped her into the shower and turned the water on.

"Oh—it's cold!" Angel cried, trying to get away from the water. It warmed up and she held her hands up to it, letting it come down on her chest as well. Matt closed the shower curtain and dug some skin cream out, as well as some bandage wrap for her hands. Letting her take her time in the shower, he leaned against the sink and waited.

"You okay?" Matt whispered.

"Yes, the water feels amazing on my skin. Thank you for not telling them the truth out there, I know I was stupid," Angel sighed.

"There was no reason to humiliate you like that Angel. You were a huge help out there, you don't even realize it," Matt shrugged.

"Oh please, I embarrassed myself and you know it," Angel shook her head.

"While the sailfish wasn't smart, you landed that huge marlin in under two hours. If you hadn't been there, it could have taken Jen and I over four hours. We would have quit for the day after that. But you made it look so easy, we were able to stay out and catch even more fish. So, rest assured, you were the MVP out there," Matt pressed.

"Thank you for saying those things, Matt," Angel whispered. "Will you come…help me?"

"Sure," Matt stood up and walked over, pulling the curtain back. She was still standing there in her bikini and sarong, holding her hands up to the water. Turning to face him, he looked at the rash on her body.

"How does it look?" Angel whispered.

"It looks pretty bad Angel. It starts at your neck and goes all the way down to your belly button, I can't imagine how much it hurts, I'm sorry," Matt sighed.

"Ordinarily I would tease you for saying my body looked bad, but I will pass this time. I am in a lot of pain—can you help me?" Angel asked.

"Yeah, lay down in the tub, plug the drain. We will do a soak in salt water. Listen, it's very important you don't rub it, scratch it, anything like that. You have done a good job so far of not touching your chest, keep that up,' Matt pressed.

Angel nodded and plugged the drain while Matt dug some Epsom salts out of the medicine cabinet. That was a standard ingredient for all fishermen, Angel wasn't the first person to touch a fish she shouldn't have. She lay down in the tub as Matt added about two cups of the salts to the water.

"Okay, I am going to leave you here for about 20 minutes, come back and get you out, then apply some skin cream to the rash. Again, don't touch it," Matt whispered.

"Thank you, Matt, I mean it, thank you," Angel whispered.

"You're welcome, Angel. I'll be outside if you need anything, but people will be in the house, if they aren't already," Matt assured her.

Angel nodded and he left her, going outside to survey the scene. Val and Carly were washing the boat, while Jen was on one fillet table and Sam the other. Tali was standing by to take the platters inside. She spotted Matt and headed his way.

"Matt? Can I ask you something?" Tali asked.

"Yeah, go ahead. Tali, isn't it?" Matt whispered.

"Yes. What is with that girl you took inside? She lifted up that fish like it was nothing, and she is smaller than even me. I can't even move it," Tali asked.

"Oh, right. She is a witch hunter, she has superhuman strength. I guess you could say she is the equivalent of Cap—" Matt started.

"Bucky Barnes!" Val cut him off from the boat.

"Right," Matt grinned. "Winter Soldier. You familiar with him?"

"Yes. I see. A witch hunter, you say? I would not have guessed that, but I am used to not being taken seriously because of my height and gender. So, I will accept your explanation," Tali finished, turning away and back towards Sam.

"Hey kid!" Sam called out to him.

"Yeah Sam?" Matt walked over, spotting some fish carcasses in the water, along with some dead seagulls. They were all over the place, as loud as ever.

"Tali and I would like to start taking the bay boat out, go fishing in the mornings. It's something we used to do together," Sam growled.

"Uh...well that's no problem, Sam. You guys can go out whenever you want. The bay fishing gear is all stored upstairs. Poles, nets, artificial lures, everything. I can show you some good spots, if you like," Matt offered.

"We are competent, thank you Matt," Tali waved him off.

"Okay, sure. I will leave you to it then," Matt shrugged, turning towards Jen. He walked up and goosed her, she leaned back into him and laughed.

"Hey. How is Angel? It was really nice of you to shield her from further embarrassment," Jen beamed.

"That was a layup, come on," Matt grinned. "She is in there getting a saline soak. I cheered her up a bit."

"With a kiss?" Jen teased.

"No actually, but I have a feeling she wants one. She was pretty embarrassed, but I assured her she did a great job. She landed that marlin in less than half the time it would have taken you and I," Matt grinned, wrapping his arms around her.

"Oh, definitely. It would have taken all morning, and into the afternoon. Look at it, we can barely move it," Jen pointed.

She finished up her fish, tossing the carcass into the water, where the seagulls swarmed it. "Val said she made some ice, and more is freezing.

We are tired, we should nap, then head home. Sam and Tali are here in their truck, so they can finish the work and go whenever."

"I agree. Before I sleep though, I need to take care of Angel. I could leave her with Val, but I think we both know she wants me to. Her rash is actually really bad, going from neck to belly. I need to get some skin cream on her. Then she will likely want to nap," Matt offered.

"She can sleep with us," Jen smiled. "She is going to pass out from that medicine, if she hasn't already. Go check on her."

"Yeah, okay. Not enough time has passed, but you are right, we don't need her drowning in the tub," Matt grinned.

He turned and walked back to the cottage, carrying the fillets Jen had carved up. Setting them on the counter, Val and Carly followed him in.

"You okay Carly?" Matt asked.

"I'm good Matt, thanks. I'm wiped out, the medicine is kicking in. Val is going to handle the rest, I'm crashing," Carly laughed.

"Okay, get some rest. Thanks for taking care of this Val, I am going to go check on Angel," Matt waved.

"You're welcome, Matt," Val laughed.

Matt knocked on the bathroom door, calling out before peeking in. Angel had her eyes closed, she was probably asleep. Running his hand along her cheek, she stirred.

"Oh...I think I passed out. Could you help me?" Angel whispered.

"I've got you, I'm going to pick you up, dry off your backside, then carry you to bed. I will put the skin cream on there," Matt whispered.

She nodded and lifted her arms as he picked her up out of the tub. Standing her up, she leaned forward against the sink as he dried her off as best he could. He took her sarong off, she didn't stop him, understanding it was soaking wet. Picking her up again, he carried her to the bedroom and lay her down on her back. Retreating to get the skin cream, he sat down on the bed next to her.

Slowly, he dabbed it all around her body. "Don't rub it, okay?" Matt whispered.

It was useless, she was already passing out again. He took her palms and dabbed some on those as well, then laid her hands down facing up. Standing up, he went to check on Val and Jen.

They were in the kitchen, bagging the fillets. Looking up, they asked how Angel was.

"Did you give her a kiss?" Jen teased.

"She was passing out, no. She is already down—you want to go nap? Val? You got this?" Matt asked.

"Oh, of course. They haven't even started the marlin yet, it will be a while. Carly is already gone. Go rest up guys," Val laughed.

"Okay, thanks," Matt whispered.

Matt and Jen walked into the downstairs bedroom, where Angel was sound asleep. She hadn't moved a muscle, as the skin cream was soaking in. Matt applied some more, while Jen teased him. He shook his head and they lay down next to her.

"That was fun today. Thanks for being so amazing Jen," Matt whispered.

"More flattery?" Jen teased.

"I just enjoy every moment with you, that's all," Matt grinned.

"That's sweet Matt. I also enjoy every second with you. Let's rest," Jen smiled, as she took his hand and they fell asleep quickly.

A few hours later, Matt felt Angel stirring. He sat up and looked her way, she was slowly waking up. Getting out of bed, he got some more skin cream, as Jen scooted over. Matt sat down next to Angel, and started applying the cream.

"How are you feeling?" Matt whispered.

"It itches a lot. The cream feels amazing. But it's so hard to resist scratching it," Angel closed her eyes.

"It will probably take about two days to pass, in the meantime not only should you not touch it, you should keep your hand use to a minimum. Don't grab things, pick things up, close your palms at all. Let Yuktrap be your slave," Matt grinned.

"I hate that robot and his unrelenting affection and determination to grope me," Angel rolled her eyes.

"This is the one instance where you should use Yuktrap, we all know how annoying he is, but he actually is helpful," Jen smiled.

"I would rather have Matt, if you two will allow it," Angel sighed.

Matt just smiled and continued dabbing the skin cream onto her chest. Jen got out of bed and went to check on the progress outside. Offering Matt a wink, he rolled his eyes and continued.

"Matt," Angel whispered.

"Yeah?" Matt asked.

"I appreciate your continued support, it must be so hard for you to take care of all these women in bikinis," Angel rolled her eyes.

"It's uh, no big deal," Matt grinned.

"I'm going to keep it together here, and ask you to trade places with Jen, if you would," Angel whispered.

"Oh? Okay, if that's what you want," Matt shrugged and stood up.

"Matt? Look at the rash on my chest. Follow it down by body. You have made everything you can see feel a lot better with the skin cream, and I definitely appreciate it, but my boobs are on fire. And I'm not *that* desperate...yet. So please just go get Jen," Angel whispered.

"Sure Angel, she will be right here in a moment," Matt whispered.

Matt walked out and waved at Jen. "She needs you, you will understand," Matt pointed.

"Okay," Jen shrugged and walked into the bedroom, but not before giving Matt a nudge with her shoulder. Matt just grinned and sat down with Val and a refreshed Carly.

"How's it going out here? You feel better Carly?" Matt asked.

"I do yes, I was never sick or anything, maybe just when Angel was on that marlin, but I feel good. Thanks Matt," Carly smiled.

"You did really well out there today, it was fun watching you in the chair," Matt grinned.

"It's really fun out there, I enjoy it a lot," Carly beamed. "I was telling Val the waves were rough today, she is glad she stayed behind."

"I have some lunch for you," Val smiled, handing him a plate of fish and chips.

"Thank you. What's going on with the fish?" Matt asked.

"Sam and Tali loaded up all they could fit in their truck and headed home. I am still making ice, we can head home whenever Angel is ready, how is she doing?" Val asked.

"Well, she has a skin rash all over the front of her body and hands. I gave her a saline soak, and then skin lotion. But uh…I think I will refrain from telling you guys what she just told me," Matt grinned.

"Must have been pretty devious," Val teased.

"When you see her rash, you will be able to figure it out," Matt shrugged.

Jen came back out and joined them. "I think she needs another saline soak. The rash is pretty severe. She asked for your help again Matt, she was very polite about it, making sure it was okay with me. And it is, just go help her get into the bath again," Jen pointed.

"Okay, sure," Matt shrugged. Walking back into the bedroom, Angel was there, fighting back tears. "You alright?"

"It just hurts so much, can you get me in the bath again?" Angel pleaded.

"Yeah, I will get the water on, then carry you in there," Matt nodded. Walking into the bathroom, he turned the shower on and plugged the drain. He went back to pick up Angel, and carried her into the bathroom. Setting her down into the bathtub, she gasped as the water hit her. Pouring some more Epsom salts into the tub, he sat on the side and held her wrist while the water filled.

"Thank you, Matt," Angel whispered.

"You're welcome," Matt whispered back. "You want a drink or anything?"

"No, I have the water," Angel opened her mouth to drink the water coming out of the shower head. "This is going to be a rough couple of days. It seems like that's all I have had down here."

"Don't say that," Matt sighed. "We all know what you need, Angel. We are all sympathetic, and we are all on your side. I can offer you some more affection, but it stops at making out. I'm not going to cheat on Jen. But if there is something else that you want to do, just say it. We will try our best to make it happen."

"I....I appreciate that Matt. I would never ask you to cheat on Jen like that. I can't do anything until this darn rash stops crushing my skin. You guys knew right away, I was so stupid," Angel closed her eyes as Matt turned the water off.

"I can't disagree with that, sadly. We did know right away you were in trouble," Matt sighed. "Is there anything else you need?"

"Please don't go, just sit here with me," Angel whispered.

"Okay, sure," Matt relented.

———

A couple of hours later, Matt carried Angel into their house. Yuktrap was there to greet them, and she allowed him to come into her old room with her. Setting her on the bed, Matt went to get some skin lotion.

"Yuktrap, get your ass over here," Matt waved.

Yuktrap obediently rolled over to him, looking on with curiosity.

"Angel is injured, she has a skin rash, your job is to apply skin lotion onto her chest every 20 minutes or so. Just dab it on there, don't rub it. If you screw this up, hanging from a tree. If you grab her boobs, hanging from a tree. You got it? I will check in on her every so often, or if she asks for me, you come get me. Screw anything at all up Yuktrap, hanging from a tree. Is that clear?" Matt growled.

Yuktrap nodded an affirmative and took the lotion and cloth from Matt. Rolling back to Angel, she thanked Matt as he left. Looking at Yuktrap, she asked him to proceed. Matt figured the robot must secretly be in heaven, while still being concerned about Angel. He hoped she recovered soon; he knew she was suffering.

CHAPTER 43

TOUCHING THE SKIES

Three days later, Angel was feeling a lot better. Yuktrap had obediently stayed by her side for almost the entire time, and she didn't mind. She was ready to go back to her house for a bit, as she entered the living room, where the group was sitting.

"Hey, feeling better?" Val asked with a smile.

"I am, thank you. I would like to go back to my house for a bit, spend time with Gracie and reward Yuktrap for staying by my side so obediently. I appreciate everything you guys did for me, especially you Matt. I thought of something I would like to do tomorrow, I will share it with you later," Angel offered.

"Okay, sure. See you later Angel," Matt waved.

She walked out with Yuktrap in tow, they all had a pretty good idea what she was plotting for him. As long as he stayed out of their house, it was fine. Still, they didn't think it would last long.

"What do you think she wants to do with us?" Val smiled.

"No idea. I assume it's something new, I look forward to it. Tomorrow we go get our next member, I really hope it's someone for her," Matt sighed.

"What do you want to do in the meantime?" Jen smiled.

"Well, I have some ideas, but I will let you take the lead as always," Matt grinned.

"Oh you. Why don't we play some pool? Just casually. Val is getting better. She can partner with me, we will use the rules you established," Jen offered.

"Sure, let's go," Matt smiled, as Carly took his arm and smiled.

Hours later, they had played a few games, rotating partners, and Jen's team still won them all. Angel came back with Yuktrap, who was of course silent again. He looked to be in better spirits, but no one cared too much.

"Hey guys, do you think it's possible for us to go parasailing? It's something I have always wanted to do," Angel beamed.

"Oh uh…sure. Sure Angel, that would be fun. We just have to loot everything from wherever the parasailing charters were on the island. Which, I have no idea where those were. We can split into a few teams, drive cars, and the boat, up and down until we find them. We need the parachute and the winch, specifically," Matt offered.

"We will have to figure out how to secure the winch to our boat, it could be difficult," Jen pointed out.

"Yeah, let's just take it one step at a time. Everyone go and change into boating outfits," Matt smiled. "Yuktrap, take care of the dogs while we are gone."

Yuktrap gave a salute, and the group began preparing to leave. An hour later, they were pulling into the driveway of the sea cottage in two cars. Matt got out with Angel, shotgun in hand, and they walked over to the bay boat, while Jen and Val backed their cars up and headed to the island. Angel was carrying a radio with them, so they could keep in contact with each other.

"Who do you think has it easier, us or the cars?" Angel smiled.

"Oh us, definitely. We only cleared the roads that led to the pier where the light is closest. The rest of the island is still packed with vehicles. Even if it was late at night, the island had a busy night life, there are cars everywhere. We can just cruise in the water, looking through binoculars," Matt grinned.

He hopped into the boat, and Angel handed him the radio before jumping in herself. Starting the engine, Angel untied the mooring lines and pushed off. She came to stand next to him and held his arm as he accelerated into the channel and towards the island. It had been a while since he had taken the bay boat out, but he never tired of it. Pointing at some porpoises, she smiled as they spotted the trucks driving over the bridge.

Honking their horns, the two boaters waved at them as they turned towards the southern part of the island. Angel started looking through the binoculars, searching for any sign or parasailing logo. There was a big marina in front of them, with lots of boats, none of which would likely start.

"You see anything that looks like it could be a parasailing hub?" Matt asked.

"I'm not sure, it feels like a place this big would offer it. Do you think we should get out and look around?" Angel asked.

"Yeah, this was a big deep sea charter marina, I would think they would offer parasailing as well. These boats look like they are in bad shape, it makes me think about ours a little bit. We should probably get them out and clean the underbellies," Matt reflected. "They have been in the water for over a month now."

"We can do that today, if you want," Angel nodded.

"Yeah, I think that's a good idea. We might as well spend the night, since we have the light to deal with tomorrow," Matt nodded, as he pulled up to the dock.

He had spotted some steps, and Angel grabbed the pylon and tied the mooring line off. Climbing out, Matt took the shotgun and they headed for the front door of the marina hub. The door was locked, but Angel just ripped it right off the hinges. There was no power, and they had forgotten a flashlight. Walking in, they explored a bit. Matt was on the lookout for critters, Angel didn't seem concerned at all.

Approaching the front desk, she walked around it and looked through the logs. Opening a book, she reported success. "Look, here are reservations for parasailing. This place should have the chutes and stuff. One of the boats out there must have a winch attached to it. Go get on the radio and report in while I look for the parachutes," Angel smiled.

"Right, check the employee-only sections, they wouldn't have them lying around out here. I'll go radio Jen and Val, then look for the right boat. It should be easy to find," Matt nodded, as he turned towards the exit. Hopping back into the boat, he picked up the radio.

"*Jen, Val, you guys read?*" Matt transmitted.

"*Go ahead Matt,*" Jen replied.

"*We found a parasailing charter down here in the Sea Ranch, on the south bay side. We are looking for the chutes and winch now. You two want to head down here?*" Matt offered.

"*Copy that, on our way. Fisherman's Wharf is still a dump,*" Val laughed.

"*As I expected. See you soon,*" Matt signed off.

Matt got out of the boat and walked around the pier, it was a big marina, he figured the parasailing boat would have an obvious name. Sure enough, he came to a purple boat that was aptly named *Touch the Skies,* and spotted the winch bolted into the back. Hopping in, he examined the mechanism. It was pretty securely bolted into the stern, where a fishing chair would normally be. Their boat had a plate like that, but he needed tools, and probably Angel's strength.

While he waited, he could move their boat closer to this one, as he hopped out and walked back over to it. Starting the engine, he untied the mooring line and pushed off, getting back on the wheel and slowly motoring over next to the parasailing charter. He cut the engine and let the boat drift forward, grabbing the pylon and tying the line off. Disembarking, he walked back into the building and looked for Angel.

"Angel! Any luck?" Matt shouted. "Where are you?"

He was about to fire the shotgun off when she poked her head out of the employees' locker room. "Over here Matt, I found some chutes, but I don't know if they are good to go or not," she offered.

"Well, I don't really know either. Fortunately, we have Jen. I'm sure she has done this before, or at the very least, parachuted before," Matt grinned.

"Should we just take all three?" Angel asked.

"Yeah. Did you happen to see a place where they stored keys to the boats?" Matt asked.

"No, nowhere," Angel shook her head.

"I wonder if the boat captains just took them home, in which case we will never find them," Matt shrugged. "Let's head outside and meet up with the others."

Angel carried two of the parachute bags, while Matt carried the other. Heading outside, they walked down the pier and deposited them into their own boat. Waiting for the others, they saw them drive up and waved them down. Jen, Val, and Carly walked down to meet them, asking for an update.

"We found three chutes and the winch. We need the drill with some bolt heads to get the winch out. Not sure what size, just bring a bunch," Matt shrugged.

"Roger that," Jen smiled as she went back for the tools.

"Is this going to work?" Val smiled.

"If we can get the winch secured to the plate in our stern, yes. It will work," Matt grinned.

Jen came back with the drill, and started unscrewing the winch from the other boat. Angel lifted it up effortlessly and set it on the dock, hopped out, boarded their boat and picked up the winch, setting it on the stern plate. Jen screwed it in again, and declared them good to go.

"Do you have sunglasses, Angel?" Matt asked.

"Oh…I forgot them. There were a bunch in the store, be right back!" Angel shouted, as she ran back into the store. Coming back with some, they had untied the lines and gotten the boat going, as she hopped in.

Matt steered them out into the open water, while Jen put the parachute on Angel. She was securing the winch cord to the chute harness, and asked if she was good.

"I am! I am nervous, but excited," Angel beamed. "Just two thumbs down if I want to come down?"

"Yep. And should you uh, you know, break the line or anything, just parachute down, we will pick you up. Are you good to go?" Matt laughed.

"Yes!' Angel beamed.

Jen pulled the ripcord and Carly started unreeling the winch line, as Angel ascended into the air.

"Wooo!" Angel screamed, as she went higher.

"Wow, what a great idea," Val beamed. "And no, I am not going up."

"There are two other chutes if one of you wants to," Matt offered Jen and Carly.

"I might take a turn," Carly smiled. "She finally looks happy."

"It feels like it's been such a slog for her. I am glad we found her something to enjoy," Matt relented.

They could see Angel laughing, as Matt coasted them around the bay. Staying well clear of the causeway, there was no pressure to come down. She stayed up for almost an hour, before she gave the two thumbs down sign. Jen started reeling her in, and Carly helped her, it was a tough go. Finally, she was close to the boat, as they reached out and grabbed her. Falling down into Matt's waiting arms, she took a breath.

"Oh, that was so much fun! But coming down was kind of scary," Angel managed.

"It's okay, we got you," Jen assured her, as she unhooked her from the winch line and got the parachute harness off of her. The chute had come down in the water, that was probably not the proper way to retrieve it, but they didn't care.

"Oh, I loved that, thank you guys for helping me make it happen," Angel smiled.

"You are welcome. We still have plenty of daylight left, Carly did you want to take a turn?" Matt offered.

"Yes, if you guys don't mind," Carly smiled.

"It's worth it, believe me," Angel laughed.

Soon enough, Carly was up in the air, shouting in joy, as Jen and Val were trying to repack Angel's used chute. It was too wet, and they gave up.

"We need to let it dry," Jen shrugged.

"No big deal," Matt offered. "We can always find more chutes if we can't repack that one."

Carly stayed up for almost the same amount of time, and they started to recover her. Angel was on the winch, all by herself this time. Jen and Matt were standing by to catch Carly, as she came in. Falling into Matt's arms the same way, Jen saved the chute from falling into the water this time. Then she unhooked Carly.

"That was amazing," Carly panted. "But yeah, coming down was a little scary."

"Are we done? Anyone else?" Matt offered.

"Matt? Why don't you go up?" Jen smiled.

"I'm...pretty scared of heights Jen," Matt relented.

"You came up in the plane with me a few times," Jen chided him.

"Let's go easy on him," Angel offered. "If he doesn't want to, he doesn't have to. It's a lot of fun Matt, but we aren't going to pressure you."

Jen was just smiling, as Matt gave in. "Okay, I'll take a trip. It probably won't be as long though."

Jen nodded and got the third chute on him, hooking him up to the winch. He put his aviators on as she gave him a kiss and a hug. "I won't let anything happen to you, Matt," she whispered into his ear.

"That is very reassuring," Matt relented.

Jen pulled the ripcord and Matt started to ascend. It was pretty scary at first, he had no control at all. Finally reaching maximum height, he tried not to look down at the boat, but instead at the island and the rest of the bay. It was an amazing sight, he could see porpoises swimming around the bridge, and the lighthouse in Port Isabel. He could even see the convention center way down the island, with the orcas painted on the side.

He lasted about 20 minutes, as Jen was driving him around. Giving the thumbs down signal, they reeled him in. It was actually really scary, as he was descending towards the water with no way to stop. Jen was there though, as she grabbed him. She didn't even stumble as Carly grabbed the chute, saving it from the water. Jen unhooked him and he jumped down into the boat.

"How was it?" Jen beamed.

"It was amazing, and scary. Coming down—it's scary," Matt managed, as Jen hugged him tightly.

"I'm proud of you Matt. I love you," Jen whispered into his ear.

"I love you too Jen," Matt whispered.

"Carly? You got the chute under control?" Jen checked.

"Yes, I got it," Carly nodded, as she had gotten it in the boat.

"Let's head in then. I'll drive," Jen smiled.

CHAPTER 44

THE SPACE TROOPER

Waking up in the sea cottage the next morning, Matt got them going. Angel had slept with the two of them, still seeking company. No one had any objections, as he walked into the kitchen and made Val's Keurig go. He usually stayed away from the coffee maker. One failed try was enough. Angel came in and shot him a smile, seemingly reading his mind.

"You have done a lot of things for me Matt, which I deeply appreciate. But making a good cup of coffee has not been one of them," Angel smiled.

"I confess with the invention of these Keurig's, coffee makers have become virtually obsolete to our age group," Matt relented.

"I still prefer my way," Angel grinned.

Carly and Val walked in, with Jen behind, as Val thanked Matt and collected her cup. Sam and Tali also walked in, surprising them.

"Hey," Sam growled.

"Hey Sam, Tali," Matt replied.

"What have you guys been up to?" Tali asked.

"We went parasailing yesterday, it was a lot of fun," Jen smiled.

"An invite would have been nice," Tali growled.

"We still don't know if you even want to talk to us Tali, much less be around us. Every word you utter is dripping with scorn," Matt countered.

"Kid has a point. You marvel at how much they accomplished on their own, but have shown them nothing but hostility," Sam shrugged.

"That's just the way I am. They don't complain about your never changing disposition," Tali countered.

"Sam has also saved our lives quite a few times. Whereas we still aren't sure you don't want to kill us! We have already one saboteur, and you fit that profile more than you check the friend box," Matt offered.

"Again, the kid has a point," Sam shrugged.

"You are a big help," Tali growled.

"Have you guys gone fishing at all?" Val tried.

"Yeah, a few times. We have caught some fish, but your analysis has proven correct. Live shrimp is the best bait, and we don't have any. Still, it's been calming for Tali. She understands that right now, you kids are the ones putting food on our table," Sam growled.

"It's true, your exploits in the Gulf have been remarkable. I cannot contest that," Tali conceded. "Given the traitor that has already appeared once in your group, I don't know how I can convince you I can be trusted. I promise not to appear without Sam, that's all I can offer."

"That's fair," Jen nodded.

"If she does appear without me, just shoot her," Sam shrugged.

"Yes," Tali conceded again. "Shall we go to the light?"

"Yes, let's head out. Two trucks, or one?" Matt offered.

"We will take our own, Tali doesn't like sitting in the tailgate," Sam shrugged.

Less than an hour later, they were parking their trucks and walking down the pier, Jen had the shotgun in hand, while Carly was wearing her new Korean katana knockoff on her back. Matt scowled at the sight of it, he was still sour about that. Jen just shook her head and they approached the fire.

"What is that?" Val asked. "It looks like...a toy?"

"I just want a hot, straight, human male. Is that so much to ask??" Angel demanded.

"I cannot believe this," Matt sighed.

"Oh! Hello there! My, your planet has much larger beings than I am accustomed to!" the toy shouted at them. He was about a foot and half tall, black and blue, dressed like a spaceman. He had red wings folded up on his back.

"It's the toy, I feel like I recognize him…but I just can't place it…I cannot believe it either," Val shook her head.

"I'm Bozo Star Reacher, Space Trooper! Who is in command here?" Bozo asked.

"Did you just say your name was Bozo Star Reacher?" Matt laughed.

"Yes! That is correct! I am glad we have been able to successfully establish communication! Now, if you could point me to the person in charge, I can begin peace negotiations!" Bozo proclaimed.

"I've got your peace negotiations, right here!" Angel shouted. "Jen! With me!"

"Odd that the leader of your group happens to be the shortest of you! But I hold no judgment! Ahh!" Bozo offered a shout of surprise.

Angel had picked him up and was walking towards the water. The tide was out, and the third sandbar was visible.

"Jen? Ready?" Angel hissed.

"I am Bozo Star Reacher, Space Trooper! And I demand that you set me down!" Bozo shouted.

"You got it!" Angel shouted back, as she hurled him into the air as far as she could.

The group looked on as Bozo actually deployed his wings, but he was spinning violently, as Jen lined up the shot. Pulling the trigger, she clipped Bozo's right wing, and bits of him flew off as he was redirected and came crashing down into the sea, well beyond the third sandbar.

Angel stormed away, heading back towards the truck. Holding up one finger, no one uttered a word.

"I have nothing to say," Tali managed.

Jen came walking back, shaking her head. "Shall we go?"

"No reason to stay," Sam shrugged.

The group turned towards the pier, leaving Bozo Star Reacher to his fate, whatever that may be. Piling into the truck, they drove back to Harlingen in silence. Angel was pouting, as Matt offered his sympathies.

"Sorry Angel. I think that was another mean prank," Matt sighed.

"I don't want to talk about it. Jen? Can I take Matt into the shower with me? I will do anything in return," Angel sighed.

"Sure Angel, we had already discussed that contingency should this happen. I admit though, I did not expect a talking toy," Jen stifled a laugh.

"I'm cursed," Angel whispered, as she got out of the truck and led Matt towards her house.

An hour later, they were reconvening at the dinner table. Matt had made out with Angel in the shower, and she had appreciated it. Now they needed to decide what the rest of their week looked like. Everyone was looking at Angel.

"If we could…if I could host you all to dinner tonight…I would deeply appreciate it. My behavior on Thanksgiving Day still haunts me. I have been trying to wait until I had a date, but I just can't go on anymore. I want to do everything. I want to cook all the food, I want to take my time to look my best, and I want to host you all. I don't want you guys to even come out of your rooms. If I need help, I will have Yuktrap. If I need more help, I will knock on one of your doors. Please?" Angel pleaded.

"That's fine Angel. Do you want to invite Sam and Tali?" Matt asked.

"I…I don't know. Sam's attire on Thanksgiving was revolting—and I doubt that would change tonight. And I don't know if Tali even has anything to wear to such a formal event. Does anyone know what her color is?" Angel whispered.

"I am almost positive it's red," Matt replied. "She was wearing red when we found her, at least."

"I have lots of different colors, I can wear something else if you want to invite them. I think we should give Tali a chance. Provided she has something to wear," Val offered.

"I'll get on the radio, see if they are interested. In the meantime, I guess we should retire to our rooms, per Angel's request," Matt shrugged.

"Thank you," Angel bowed her head.

"You are very welcome," Jen smiled, as she stood up.

Matt picked up the radio and started transmitting.

"Sam, Tali? Are you guys receiving?" Matt called.

Some time passed, and Tali responded.

"Yes Matt. What is it?" Tali called back.

"We have decided to have a feast tonight, and we would like to invite you and Sam. It's a black tie affair. We understand Sam will come dressed like Sam, but you are welcome to dress as formally as you wish. Am I correct in believing your preferred color is red?" Matt offered.

"Yes, you are correct Matt. Thank you for inviting us. What time is the feast?" Tali asked.

"What time? What time is it now?" Matt asked Angel.

"It's noon. Let's aim for six," Angel replied.

"Six o'clock Tali. Is that acceptable?" Matt called.

"Yes Matt. We will be there. Again, thank you for the invite," Tali signed off.

"Okay, they are coming. I know you want to take this on, but if you need any help, you know where to find me," Matt pressed.

"Yes, thank you Matt. For everything today," Angel smiled. "Please, go and rest with Jen."

Matt nodded and left her with Yuktrap. Stepping into the bedroom, Jen was lying in the bed on her side, just wearing her lingerie.

"Hello," Matt grinned.

"Hey there. Let's have some fun, then maybe some *more* fun, then we can start getting ready," Jen beamed.

"What's the occasion?" Matt smiled.

"Do we need one? But really, I'm proud of you for once again facing your fears and going up in that parasail," Jen laughed.

"You are just so encouraging, you always make me feel comfortable," Matt shrugged, getting undressed.

"I know this whole new reality is taxing on one's mental health, and I know it's crushing Angel. I feel bad for her, she asked me if she could stay with us for a little while, I guess she liked the feeling of waking up next to someone. I agreed, of course," Jen smiled.

"Yeah, I guess that explains why we are having fun now," Matt grinned.

"It's one of the reasons, yes," Jen laughed. "Come over here already."

An hour later, Jen was picking out a dress while Matt lay in bed. She had looted quite a few over time, lots of colors, but mostly purple and green. She decided to stay with purple, since she didn't know what color Val was switching to.

"So, a toy Space Trooper," Jen smiled.

"I feel like I know him but I just can't place it. It has to be the powers that be messing with our memories again. But he really was a talking toy, that's crazy. How is he medium? I don't know. How does he contribute? Beats me. I think he was another prank, like Yuktrap. Angel was so mad, I couldn't help but laugh. But you, that was a nice shot, she really heaved the poor guy, but you still hit him," Matt grinned.

"I only winged him. I was expecting it to be a strong throw, her strength is real. A talking toy, wow. How many bad points do you think we accumulated with that stunt?" Jen shook her head.

"Quite a few," Matt grinned. "Leaving him out there in the water was probably mean. If she had just thrown him along the beach, we could have gone to pick him up, put him in a cage or something. Maybe make him Yuktrap's slave."

"I think Angel wanted him out of her sight, forever. Especially after that joke about her height," Jen giggled.

"It was all I could do to not burst out laughing at that comment," Matt laughed. "And his name. Bozo Star Reacher, I mean, I can guess what his slogan was, he didn't even have time to utter it. Just up and away, then crashing and burning. I think he was literally smoking after you clipped him."

"I take it that was not his name in the movies?" Jen smiled.

"No, I can't remember his actual name, as usual. But it wasn't that, I'm sure. They would never name a character Bozo, he seems like another fused character," Matt rolled his eyes.

"Do you want to join me in the shower? We can have some fun, then I have to wash and condition my hair, and start getting ready. I don't want to overdo it like on Thanksgiving, I know I humiliated Angel," Jen sighed.

"Angel made the decision to put 20 minutes into herself when she had two hours. It was her own fault, and she knows it. I know she is determined to look her absolute best tonight, which will still not come close to you," Matt grinned.

"Oh you. Come on, into the shower already," Jen laughed.

CHAPTER 45

REDEMPTION

Another hour later, Matt was back in bed being lazy while Jen was sitting in front of the vanity mirror next to the bathroom. She was working on her face, and Matt didn't offer any questions. Suddenly, they heard a *whoosh* outside and Angel screamed. Jen looked in curiosity as Matt stood up and headed for the door.

"Any guesses?" Matt grinned.

"Yuktrap used too much lighter fluid," Jen offered.

"Not bad," Matt laughed.

He stepped out, and looked towards the back porch. Seeing the charcoal grill was indeed burning way too high, he asked Angel if everything was okay.

"Yes, sorry. Yuktrap poured way too much lighter fluid on there, stupid robot!" Angel hissed, kicking him across the yard.

"Wow okay. Just let it burn down. Um, some of your hair is singed, you might want to take care of that," Matt sighed.

"Thanks. I will do that now," Angel growled, as she stepped inside and slammed the door in Yuktrap's face. Heading towards her room, Matt walked back to his and flopped down on the bed.

"You were right, too much lighter fluid. The robot took a trip across the yard for that one," Matt grinned.

"He is hopeless. Angel tries to throw him a bone, and it always blows up in her face. Literally!" Jen laughed.

"Wow, and here I thought I was the one with the better sense of humor," Matt laughed.

"That was an easy one," Jen beamed.

More time passed, as they began to smell the food. Jen was taking a particularly long time on her eye shadow, but Matt continued to remain silent. They heard Yuktrap setting the table, it was still just 4pm. Matt didn't need to start moving yet, so he dozed. Opening his eyes, he saw Jen had moved to steaming her dress with a hand steamer, and she told him it was probably time for him to start moving.

Looking at the time, it was a little after 5. He stood up and started getting dressed himself, asking if she knew when they were supposed to make their entrance.

"Last. Yuktrap will knock on the door, providing his arms haven't been severed," Jen grinned.

"Well, as possible as that is, Angel has surely been leaning on him for help. She probably took a lot of his decision-making ability away though. Not sure why she gave it to him in the first place. I never do," Matt shrugged.

"She said she allowed him to speak the other day, and he actually behaved. Apparently, even he can see that she is struggling with this," Jen whispered.

"I'm sure she misses her family. Val told me she had a strong social support group. Whereas everyone else that has arrived is accustomed to either being completely alone, or in Carly's case, conscripted to a team that she really had no investment in. Angel feels our compassion I'm sure, but she definitely needs more. Liking her isn't enough, she needs love. The Space Trooper was just mean," Matt sighed as he finished getting dressed.

Jen came out of the walk-in closet, ready to go. Wearing her standard purple, she looked amazing once again.

"You are so beautiful, Jen," Matt whispered.

"You look handsome as well Matt," Jen smiled. "I never liked dressing up like this, but it's been fun, if only to see your reactions!"

"Oh stop, the entire room stops to look at you when you walk through that door. I bet Tali looks nice though, you might finally have some competition," Matt grinned.

"Remember the focus is Angel," Jen pressed. "She needs to see you look at her, feel your eyes exploring her body, hear you say how beautiful she is. Hearing that from other women means nothing to her, and Sam is useless. You have to check that box for her."

"Yes, I will do my job," Matt grinned.

"You are the only one that can, don't mess it up Matt," Jen growled. "Or the couch awaits."

"I hear you, loud and clear," Matt waved her off.

There was a knock on the door, they knew it was Yuktrap. Matt went to open it, and the robot motioned them to come out. Matt collected Jen, and they walked out together. The rest of them were standing behind their seats to receive them, as Angel herself was waiting in front of the table. Matt noticed Tali's look of surprise, but quickly turned his focus to their hostess.

"Good evening, Jen, Matt. Thank you for coming," Angel beamed.

She was wearing a black evening gown with gold trim, with a low-cut slit. Her hair was down this time, and she looked very happy as she smiled.

"Good evening, Angel," Matt smiled. "You look beautiful tonight."

"Thank you, Matt. Please allow me to escort you to your seats," Angel smiled.

She seated them next to her, as they all took their seats. Angel sat at the head of the table, as she poured Matt and Jen some wine. The seating arrangement saw Matt, Jen, and Sam on one side, with Val sitting on the other side of Angel, with Carly and Tali finishing out the line. Yuktrap was trying to squeeze next to Angel but she ignored him.

"Shall we make a toast?" Angel smiled.

They raised their glasses, as Angel offered her toast. "To Bozo the Space Trooper!" Angel proclaimed.

Val stifled a laugh, as Carly couldn't and burst into a giggle. Even Jen was shaking her head.

"We only knew him for a short time, and it was long enough. I hope he is enjoying his resting spot on the bottom of the sea," Angel beamed.

"To Bozo!" the group laughed, clinking their glasses.

"I have to admit that was one of the strangest things I have seen, and it's been a wild week," Tali offered. "A talking toy."

"I'm kinda sad we didn't get to hear his slogan, but oh well," Matt shrugged with a smile.

"Before Angel begins the dinner conversation, I should apologize to you all. Sam was right, and I was wrong. I'm glad I listened to him," Tali offered.

"Oh? Were you not taking this formal event seriously? I have been there myself," Angel teased.

"That's exactly it. 3:30 rolled around, and Sam asked me if I was going to start getting ready. I waved him off, saying I had set a dress out, I didn't need long to get ready for you…kids. Sam asked me if I heard Matt specifically say 'black tie affair' and again, I waved him off. Claiming you…kids…didn't even know what that was. And Sam assured me I was wrong, and he also assured me he would get me home, because I would start drinking heavily the second Jen walked out that door. I thought about it, and I decided it was most assuredly not worth the risk. I am *very* glad I listened to Sam," Tali finished. "You all look very elegant, and Matt, you look handsome as well."

"Thank you, Tali, both you and Sam look lovely tonight. Thank you, Sam, for dressing up a little more. Your Thanksgiving attire was almost as bad as my behavior," Angel teased.

"Oh, I made him wear a nicer outfit, I did hear about how he had been going as is, and if I was going to spend two hours getting ready, he was at least going to spend ten minutes. Which he did, barely," Tali smiled.

"So where are you from Tali? What did you do for a living?" Angel asked.

"Well…my memory is really not too clear, but I believe I worked for the Yakuza in Japan. As an enforcer. I seem to remember dying a few times, and coming back," Tali offered.

"So, you got paid to do work for a secretive Yakuza like group? That's interesting," Angel smiled.

"What about you Angel? What did you do with your super strength?" Tali tried.

"I was in the supernatural business. That was my primary...duty. Just stave off invasions and takeovers from the supernatural. I died and came back, that whole thing," Angel waved.

"I've also died and come back," Carly piped up with a smile.

"As...have I," Tali relented. "What did you do for a living, Carly?"

"Superhero business. I remember getting marooned on an island, dying there, coming back, then it was the superhero stuff," Carly shrugged. "This marlin is delicious Angel—you did a great job."

"I agree, it does taste excellent," Matt smiled.

"Thank you," Angel beamed.

"I guess I should stop tap-dancing around my occupation. I am also an ex-assassin, died and came back quite a few times, killed plenty of people. Which seems pretty normal for you guys," Tali waved her hand. "And I also agree, this marlin is cooked very well."

"Thank you," Angel beamed.

"What about you Val? What did you do for a living?" Tali asked.

"Oh, Matt and I are very ordinary when compared to all of you. We went to school, graduated, worked regular jobs while taking night classes for our Masters. Honestly, just, super normal, happy people," Val waved her hand.

"Well, that might have been your life before, but you aren't ordinary anymore. You are sitting at the table of the social elite—the best humanity has to offer. Because by all accounts, we are the *only* humans left. So, be proud of that," Tali pressed.

"We often said we were the best golfers on the planet, we teed off from the professional tees," Val beamed.

"Best fishermen as well," Sam growled. "This marlin is just as tasty as the first one."

"Thank you," Angel beamed, as she refilled everyone's wine glass.

"And you Jen?" Tali asked.

"I was a famous treasure hunter. A globetrotter, I guess you could say. I had to live this glamour life every now and then to pay the bills, it was always my least favorite part of the job. But I got by," Jen smiled.

"You miss it, don't you?" Angel whispered.

"I do miss it. I never thought about settling down, I just wanted to be outside. But I am very happy with Matt. And we spend a lot of time outside," Jen smiled.

"If I get the opportunity to get you back to your world Jen, I will take it," Matt assured her.

"Would you go with her?" Angel asked, seemingly taking the words right out of Tali's mouth.

"Oh, you don't have to answer Matt," Jen started.

"I would. I would go with you, Jen. If it was possible, I would definitely go," Matt nodded.

"Oh," Jen looked away.

"I take it that question has come up before," Tali observed.

"On the second day of our relationship, yes," Matt nodded.

"That's a bit too early for that kind of commitment. But I can tell by the tone of your voice, you answered honestly. You don't have to be embarrassed Jen, he loves you," Tali offered.

"Yes," Jen whispered.

Angel sensed her embarrassment and moved things along. "Sam? Again, thank you for wearing a nicer suit. What did you do for a living?"

"A lot," Sam growled. "But let's just stick with the superhero business. And now I am here, protecting you."

There was a hushed silence, as Tali tried to get them going again. "Honestly, there are very few people that I would trust more to protect me than Sam here. My old flame, that is probably the list."

"What did your old flame do for a living?" Val offered.

"I struggle to remember, but he was a warrior, a talented one. But... if it really came down to it...it would be hard to say that he would do a better job than Sam. The one difference between my old lover, and really everyone else is he refused to kill people. For Sam, that's a Tuesday."

"Are you sure it constitutes a full day?" Val beamed.

"No," Tali smiled. "Maybe just breakfast."

"I hope you don't have to kill anyone else. I know everyone here has killed someone, except for Val and I. But we have tried to avoid that. Perhaps I was naive about Jack, but he was only the second person to arrive. He plotted against us, thought himself the better killer, delusional. Just delusional. His death saddened me at the time, but I look back now and it was very amusing," Matt grinned.

"Again, very, very few people that I would say are better at their jobs than Sam. Especially if the job involves killing," Tali smiled. "I think everyone is done eating? Thank you again for the invite. Next time, we will bring a dish to share. We didn't have anything worthy of this event at our house."

The group stood with Tali and Sam, as Angel escorted them to the door. Bidding them goodnight, they parted ways. Angel turned around and rejoined the group.

"I think that went well with Tali. It seemed like she came into the conversation looking at us as kids, and went out having a much different opinion. Carly, your story just continues to boggle my mind. And Sam's… well…moving on. Would you all like to dance?" Angel beamed.

"We would love to dance with you, Angel. Why don't you take the first dance with Matt? You deserve it," Jen smiled.

"Thank you so much, Jen," Angel bowed her head.

"Do you have a favorite song? We have a good playlist," Val smiled.

"I um, you probably don't have it. I had to sing a song once, while I was working. It was pretty weird, but I liked it. Just…whatever you have is fine Val," Angel whispered.

"Matt?" Val asked, probably already knowing.

"Sinatra, of course," Matt shrugged.

"Play 'The Best is Yet to Come', Sinatra's other song is my song with Matt," Jen smiled.

"Okay!" Val beamed.

She hit the music and joined Carly, as Angel and Matt came together. Matt looked into Angel's eyes, she looked so happy as she stared back.

They danced around, lost in Sinatra's voice. Jen watched from the couch with Yuktrap sulking close by.

"It's okay, Angel, you have my permission," Jen teased.

"Really?" Angel whispered.

"Yes, you have been a great hostess, go ahead. I have never minded," Jen laughed.

"Okay," Angel relented. "Matt, please come down here."

Matt smiled and leaned down to kiss her. He felt her relief, her loneliness as she held the kiss. Breaking away, Angel looked away and gave Jen a hug. Thanking her, she sat down while the next Sinatra song played. Matt and Jen danced together as Val and Carly stayed together.

"When did this become our song?" Matt whispered.

"The first time I danced with you to it," Jen smiled. She leaned closer, "You did your job Matt. I'm proud of you."

"It wasn't too hard," Matt whispered.

"Still, you did everything right," Jen assured him.

The couples danced together, switching out with every song. They hoped Angel would have a date next time, for all their sakes. They knew her mental health was barely hanging on at this point. Breaking up after the last song, Angel addressed them one last time.

"Thank you all for the wonderful evening. I feel like...I have redeemed myself. Why don't we retire on this note? Um, Jen? Are we still okay?" Angel whispered.

"Yes Angel. Change clothes first, then come knock on the door," Jen smiled.

"Thank you," Angel bowed again.

CHAPTER 46

CHORES

Waking up the next morning, Matt tried to sit up but both Angel and Jen were lying on his shoulders. Instead, he just lay there and gently nudged them. Jen stirred and offered a smile, hugging him tighter. Not moving. Angel copied her, so he just lay there and held them both.

"Thank you for letting me be here, it feels so much better," Angel whispered.

"You are welcome," Jen whispered back. "We know how hard it has been for you."

"I swear I will make it up to you both someday," Angel assured them. "But for now, I need coffee. I will bring you both your juice back, hopefully Yuktrap is there waiting."

"He better be— he has one job," Matt grinned.

Angel rose from the bed and it was only then that Matt noticed she was wearing fishnets.

"You slept in fishnets?" Matt smiled. "Are those just for me?"

"Maybe they are," Angel grinned, as she took them off and tossed them his way. Putting her sarong on, she walked out to a waiting Yuktrap. Taking the juice glasses, she handed them to Jen and Matt, and continued on to the kitchen. A few minutes later she came back and lay down in her spot.

"What are we going to do today?" Angel asked.

"Matt thinks we need to get some work done. Head to the island, clean the undercarriage of both boats. They have been in the water a while—we need to do a thorough scrubbing. Clean out both engines, run them, the works. Maybe leave Val and Carly here to check the houses thoroughly. We usually just run through them, make sure everything is working and scoot. But we should make sure the food is holding up," Jen offered.

"So, the three of us head to the island, when do we leave?" Angel smiled.

"As soon as we are all ready," Matt grinned.

"I've been working on a surprise for the two of you, maybe it will be ready tonight and we can have some fun," Angel laughed.

"Do I even want to know?" Matt smiled.

"I will offer no hints, to make the surprise better," Angel teased.

"Come on, after you drink your coffee, let's all shower together, to save time. And as she said, have fun," Jen laughed.

"Um, okay. I didn't expect that, but I have no objections," Angel stammered, as she hurried to retrieve her coffee.

———

A few hours later, Jen was backing the trailer down the boat launch, as Matt drove the *Invictus II* up it. Angel hopped in the water and pushed it up, as Jen tied the bow onto the front of the trailer. She then got back into the truck and drove it out of the water, as Matt helped Angel into the boat. Heading back to their sea cottage, they parked the truck and got ready for the deep clean.

"Having someone with super strength really helps get that boat out of the water," Matt laughed.

"It was nothing," Angel waved him off with a smile.

They crawled underneath the boat to inspect the hull. It needed a good cleaning, there were barnacles and grime stuck to the bottom. Letting out a sigh, it was a dirty job, but Angel didn't mind helping.

"Okay, Matt and I will scrub the bottom. Jen? Can you clean out the engine?" Angel beamed.

"Sure thing," Jen rolled her eyes, as she tossed them some sponges and a bucket of water. They set to work, scrubbing off the barnacles as the water dripped on them. Matt could sense Angel was in much better spirits.

"You seem pretty happy today, Angel," Matt grinned. "I hope you had fun last night."

"I did. I needed to get that monkey off my back, and I feel like I accomplished that. I was pretty happy when I got Tali to back down on her arrogance. Sam really saved her, if she had shown up underdressed it would have been such a hit to her pride. She couldn't hide her surprise when I opened the door for them, and it was pretty much a surrender when you and Jen came out," Angel beamed.

"She has been pretty harsh to us, but I think listing out your occupations gave her a reality check, she isn't unique. I had been pretty sure she was some kind of assassin, I figured Carly would be the first to expose her. Carly isn't what she seems, she is a really good fighter. She has been going to the gym on her own, she needs a sparring partner, maybe Tali or Sam will oblige her. I'm not...entirely sure what your fighting skills are—but your super human strength can hurt any of us," Matt tried.

"It's okay, I know you were just trying to save it there, and you didn't have to. I can't spar with Carly, as you said, my strength would flatten her," Angel assured him, as they continued to scrub.

Jen was hooking up the water hose to the engine, and signaled them she was about to start the motor. They acknowledged and she fired it up. Resuming their work, they were about a quarter of the way done.

"I really like spending time with you guys, Matt. And now you are letting me sleep with you, I feel as if I am finally settling in. I definitely could use a lover, no reason to even deny that, but I am making due. I wish you would use your hands more. I have heard about that particular fetish you have. I liked when you had me pinned against the wall like that," Angel teased.

"I didn't expect that to happen at all. One minute you are crying and I am trying to comfort you, and the next you are stripping and I am spanking you," Matt laughed.

"Well, I didn't expect to walk into your room and find Carly standing against the wall in chains and lingerie, so I guess that makes us even," Angel laughed. "That reminds me of that joke you made, when I stripped for you. Remember?"

"Yeah, you threatened to kill me. How much worse off would you have been?" Matt teased.

"Oh, if I had survived Sam, which I have my doubts, we all would be suffering," Angel whispered. "Moving on, stripping for you seems like nothing now."

"It's not something I ask for, it just seems to happen," Matt shrugged, as they moved up the hull. They were almost done, as Jen was finishing up cleaning out the engine. Reaching the bow, they quickly finished up and rolled out from under the boat.

"Now what?" Angel asked.

"Get it back in the water. Get the bay boat out. I will drive the bay boat over there to the launch, while Jen drives the truck back. I would ask, but I know you are coming with me," Matt grinned.

"See you guys there," Jen beamed, as she got back in the truck.

Matt and Angel hopped down into the bay boat and got it going. Matt cruised towards the launch, taking his time.

"What's wrong, you usually zoom on over there?" Angel asked.

"Maybe I am just increasing our time together, or maybe I am waiting for Jen to actually drive there," Matt grinned.

"Solid romantic line, Matt. I will continue to say this, thank you for spending time with me instead of your incredibly hot, amazing girlfriend. And just so you know, you did flatten her last night when you answered that question," Angel beamed.

"I could spend the rest of my life with Jen," Matt whispered.

"But you still don't know if she could settle down with you?" Angel offered.

"I am trying to convince her that having a love in your life doesn't mean settling down. I would never try to stop her from going on her treasure hunts. I mean, I would probably want to go with her," Matt whispered.

"She has to know that Matt. She is way too smart to not see that," Angel assured him.

"I'm trying to frame this as nicely as possible, because I am not implying anything related to you...but I think she and I will talk about it soon," Matt whispered, as he pulled up to the boat launch. Jen was getting into position to back the boat in, but she needed a spotter. Matt waved Angel towards the dock as she helped him tie the bay boat off, out of the way.

Jen backed the trailer into the water, with Angel guiding her, as Matt climbed into the *Invictus II.* Starting the engine, he put it in reverse as Angel untied the straps. Backing the boat into the water, he steered it towards the closest dock as Angel ran over to help him tie it off as well. Finally getting it secured, they climbed out and ran back over to the bay boat, untying it and pushing off.

Matt turned the boat around so he could come at the trailer in a straight line, as Angel got ready to jump out and push it up. Revving the engine, Matt drove it onto the trailer as she pushed it up. Jen pulled it forward again and tied it down.

"Okay, drive the *Invictus II* back to the sea cottage, and I will meet you guys there," Jen beamed.

"Right!" Matt shouted as he jumped out of the bay boat. The pair walked over to the *Invictus II* and jumped down into it. Untying the line and pushing off, Matt got them going again.

"If you need me to spend the night with Val and Carly tonight, I am sure they won't mind. Maybe I can find out what kind of games they play," Angel offered.

"Maybe you will get yourself captured, you mean," Matt grinned.

"I will accept it," Angel grinned.

"I think Jen does want to have that conversation, thank you for understanding," Matt relented.

"I mean, I saw you two buzzing at that poker table, I have promised myself not to interfere, only do what Jen allows," Angel observed.

"We are all on the same page, kissing is completely allowed, Angel. You are a good kisser, if you were wondering," Matt grinned.

"Oh..." Angel looked away.

Matt just smiled and remained silent, driving the boat. Pulling up to the dock, Angel tied the bow line off, as Matt tied the stern line. Getting out, they walked across the deck to their driveway and waited for Jen. She pulled up soon after, and they repeated their positions. The bottom of the bay boat was in much better shape, but Jen reported the engine really needed a good scrubbing. They set about their tasks, quiet for a while.

"Did I say something wrong?" Matt whispered.

"Of course not," Angel assured him. "You just made me blush, which isn't a gentlemanly thing to do. But as I said, I have to limit myself. I could use your help in that regard, by avoiding overly flirting. You are in fact, being very courteous to me. Above and beyond, really. But please, don't surprise me like that. You have a solid arsenal of romantic lines Matt, and I don't object to hearing them. Just make sure you time them appropriately."

"Copy that," Matt grinned.

Angel smiled and they scrubbed away. Jen was working on the motor, having hooked the water hose up and scrubbing away herself. Finally, they were done.

"We have to get this boat back in the water, drive it back here, then we can head home. That was a good day's work, but it was a great idea Matt. We have to keep these boats operating," Jen smiled.

"Yeah, I don't think they have ever been in the water this long, but I think it's okay. Some of these boats always stay in the water," Matt shrugged.

"It doesn't hurt a boat to be in the water, I understand your concern though. Let's head back to the launch together," Jen laughed.

They piled in the truck, Matt and Angel sat in the back, with Jen's permission. She laughed and drove them to the boat launch.

"So, you two scheming anything for us?" Jen teased.

"No, I am actually going to spend the night with Val and Carly, with their permission that is. I know you want to talk to Matt about that dinner conversation last night," Angel smiled.

"Perceptive," Jen grinned. "I appreciate that, Angel."

"It's the least I can do for how much you have shared Matt with me," Angel assured her.

Jen nodded and they arrived at the boat launch. Matt and Angel hopped out, with Matt climbing into the boat while Angel spotted Jen. Backing up, Angel untied the straps and pushed the boat into the water. Matt started the engine, and she hopped into the boat with him, as he turned it back towards the sea cottage. Jen drove the truck back that way as well.

Matt and Angel drove in silence, with Angel just grinning, as they arrived first. Tying the boat off, they jumped out and waited for Jen. She stopped in the street and they unhooked the trailer, Angel pushing it back into the adjacent driveway with ease. Hopping back in the backseat, Jen pointed them back home.

As they were driving over the swing bridge, they were completely shocked when Bozo the Space Trooper jumped onto their windshield.

"I am Bozo Star Reacher, Space Trooper, and I order you to pull this vehicle over AT ONCE!" Bozo shouted.

CHAPTER 47

ARRESTED

Jen slammed on the brakes, causing Bozo to fly off the front hood and onto the ground. Picking himself up, he walked around to the driver's side.

"Out of the vehicle, now!" Bozo shouted.

"What in the world?" Jen asked, bewildered.

Matt was just covering his face with one hand, laughing. "Okay, come on guys, let's hear him out. Angel? Restrain yourself."

"Are you sure? We could easily just drive on, leaving him here," Jen offered.

"Yes, but it wouldn't earn any good points. We should at least listen to what he has to say," Matt grinned. They exited the vehicle and looked down at the talking toy, completely surprised to be seeing him again. He had some damage to his right side, and his right wing looked to have a couple of holes in it. Jen had indeed clipped him.

"You have willfully attacked a member of the Star Force—I am placing you all under arrest! Will you come quietly, or do I have to subdue you?" Bozo demanded.

"I will show—" Angel started to step forward but Matt stopped her.

"Wait," Matt held his arm out. "We are willing to discuss the terms of our...surrender to you, Space Trooper, but first, allow us to confer with each other for just a moment."

"Very well!" Bozo declared.

Matt pulled them in close, Angel was demanding an explanation. "Listen, our theory is we are being tested by a Puppetmaster. And we have to acquire good points to pass. And Angel…you have acquired quite a few bad points, I'm sorry to say. Throwing him in the air and having Jen blast him was definitely bad points for both of you. Sure, we could throw him into the bay again, but that is guaranteed bad points. I think we should at least try to get back into good territory. So, let's just play along. And it's literally playing. He is a toy. We are people. Jen? What do you think?"

"I agree Matt. Let's just play along Angel. See what he really intends to do," Jen whispered. "But I think there is going to be a lot of eye rolling."

"Fine," Angel waved her hand in the air. "This is so ridiculous."

They broke up and Matt did the talking. "Okay Bozo, we are willing to surrender to you. What are your terms?"

"You are making a wise decision. I intend to arrest the three of you, take you back to a holding cell, and put you on trial for attacking a Space Trooper with no provocation," Bozo declared. "Get down on your knees and put your hands behind your head."

Angel started to object but Matt waved her off. "Bozo, we aren't kneeling on this hot, asphalt road. Is there something else we can do to placate you? Where is this holding cell of yours anyway?" Matt sighed.

"It's a long way from here, I admit. Perhaps you could turn around and put your hands on the vehicle's hood. Are any of you carrying weapons? I will make sure that you are not," Bozo declared.

"No, we are not actually. But we will still comply with your request," Matt rolled his eyes.

They turned around and put their hands on the hood of the truck. Bozo came forward to search Angel, who was just wearing her bikini and sarong, as was Jen.

"If you touch me in any way I deem inappropriate, I will—" Angel started.

"Report you to your superiors," Matt cut her off.

"Have no fear! I know how to handle female prisoners," Bozo declared.

Angel rolled her eyes while Jen just smiled. Matt tried to get Angel to take it easy, but she was clearly annoyed. Bozo jumped up on the hood and searched Matt's pockets, and declared himself done.

"Now, I will march you all to the holding cell. Line up, and put your hands behind your heads," Bozo ordered.

"How about we drive to a house that could pass as a holding cell, instead. You can keep us there as your prisoners for as long as...needed," Matt offered.

"Hmm yes, marching under this hot sun could be considered inhumane. Very well, let us get in your vehicle! I will sit in the front seat, so don't try anything!" Bozo declared.

They rolled their eyes as a group and got in the truck, Jen let Bozo hop in her door and jump over to the passenger seat, while Matt and Angel sat in the back.

"Everyone, restraining harnesses!" Bozo ordered. "You there, can you assist me with mine?"

Jen just shook her head and reached across to fasten the front seatbelt. Bozo slid underneath the waist strap. It wasn't a terrible idea, as a toy he would fly around in that seat if Jen wanted him too.

"Jen? Just take us back to Harlingen," Matt grinned.

"Roger that. Bozo? Permission to drive?" Jen asked.

"Permission granted," Bozo declared.

Jen smiled and drove them home. Matt took Angel's hand and winked at her, she finally allowed herself to smile and roll her eyes. The whole affair was utter nonsense.

"Unbelievable," Angel whispered.

They arrived home without incident, Jen parked in Angel's driveway. Unfastening Bozo's seatbelt, she got out and waved goodbye.

"Have fun guys, I'm going home," Jen laughed.

"That prisoner is escaping!" Bozo started.

"Just let her go Bozo, you have your main culprit, and I will take that one's place. Let's head inside to the holding area," Matt smiled.

"Very well! You two, inside. No funny business!" Bozo ordered.

Letting out a sigh, they walked inside, where Gracie came forward to greet them. Reaching down to pet her, she quickly moved to inspect Bozo, who also petted her.

"Ahh, a friendly face finally!" Bozo declared. "We will play later, friend! For now, I have to process these two prisoners."

"Sometimes the friendliness of a Beagle works against you," Matt laughed.

Suddenly Carly walked in carrying a bag, surprising them all.

"Ah! Another perpetrator! You there! Stop!" Bozo ordered.

"Hello Bozo Star Reacher, I come in peace. I brought you some gifts for your two prisoners," Carly beamed, as she dropped the bag. "Jen says to play along and earn those good points back, both of you." She laughed and exited.

Bozo was looking in the bag, and let out a cry of excitement. "Ah! Restraining devices, excellent! Okay you two, on your knees, hands behind your backs!" Bozo ordered.

"Are you serious? She brought the cuffs?" Angel demanded.

Matt was just shaking his head. "This is a fine mess you've gotten us into Angel. Start playing along, you aren't earning any good points by hating it."

Angel bit her tongue and they got on their knees, placing their hands behind their backs. Bozo came around and cuffed Angel.

"Too tight?" Bozo asked.

Angel shook her head no, and Bozo nodded. He repeated the process with Matt, who really could not believe what was happening.

"Okay you two, stand up," Bozo ordered. "Walk over to that couch."

They stood up and headed over to the couch, sitting down. Bozo dragged the bag over and dug the leg shackles out.

"Oh, come on!" Angel whined.

"Just play along, with your strength you can shut this down if he goes too far," Matt grinned.

Bozo applied the leg shackles to both of them and resumed digging in the bag.

"What else could he have in there?" Angel whined, as he pulled out a ball gag. "If you put that in my mouth I will rip you limb from limb," she hissed.

"This is a cruel and unusual device, not appropriate for prisoners!" Bozo declared, dropping it back in the bag.

"I think you would have looked really good in that, Angel," Matt teased.

"Shut it. I am cooperating, but I have my limits," Angel growled.

"All right! The two prisoners have been secured! Now, what are your names?" Bozo demanded.

"Matt," Matt shrugged.

"Angel," Angel stared up at the ceiling.

"Matt and Angel. Very well, your names have been entered into the log. Now, you there! Angel, you threw me in the air for no reason, and I was later badly damaged as a result. I suffered even more damage in the water. Explain yourself!" Bozo barked.

"I was frustrated by you calling me short," Angel offered.

"That is not true. Lying will do you no good here!" Bozo declared. "You had started walking forward with the intention of picking me up and throwing me into the sea before I called you short! Now, try again!"

"He is right," Matt shrugged.

"Whose side are you on?" Angel hissed at him.

"There are no sides here! Only justice!" Bozo declared. "Now, explain yourself Angel! Why did you decide to throw me in the air after I offered peace?"

"I was frustrated by your presence," Angel growled. "I still am!"

"I was no threat to you! I extended a peace offering, and you not only rejected it, you attacked me! This is an open declaration of war against the Star Force!" Bozo declared.

"Again, accurate," Matt pointed out.

"I am going to break out of these cuffs and rip your limbs off," Angel snapped at Bozo.

"Another threat! I have no choice but to escalate this interrogation!" Bozo declared.

"Bozo Star Reacher, wait!" Matt sighed. "May I request a private recess with my fellow prisoner here?"

"Very well! I suggest you use this time to get her back in line!" Bozo declared, and walked away out of earshot.

"What are we doing?" Angel hissed in a low voice.

"Angel please," Matt urged. "I am literally asking you to please stop earning bad points. Please. You are just racking them up with every syllable."

"How am I supposed to earn good points in this situation?" Angel hissed.

"By doing the right thing!" Matt pressed. "Everything he said is true, you threw him up in the air for no reason. He wasn't a threat to us—he is a toy. You were frustrated because you wanted a hot, straight, human male, and you got a toy. I get it, I am on your side in your desires. But now we are where we are. Prisoners to a Space Trooper!"

"A toy. We are being dominated by a toy Matt," Angel corrected him.

"Yes, we are. I admit, we are being dominated by a toy. And we have to find a way to earn good points. And maybe our freedom," Matt whispered.

"How?" Angel relented.

"Plead guilty. Ask for mercy. See what he says," Matt shrugged.

"Fine," Angel sighed. "Fine. Bozo Star Seeker?"

"Star Reacher," Bozo corrected her. "Have you come to your senses?"

"Yes, I have," Angel replied. "Please come over here."

Bozo came walking over. "Well, let's hear it."

"I would like to plead guilty to the charges you are bringing against me. There is no excuse for my behavior. Will you show leniency?" Angel asked, falling off the couch and getting on her knees, looking down.

"Hmm," Bozo studied her. "I will accept your guilty plea. As for leniency, you attacked a member of the Star Force, severely damaging him, possibly beyond repair. I'm afraid the penalty must be severe."

"Please Bozo, show mercy. I am so sorry!" Angel fake cried.

"Begging will get you nowhere," Bozo declared, waving his hand.

"Fine," Angel shrugged, climbing back onto the couch and looking at him.

"You there, Matt. You were an accessory to her crimes, how do you plead?" Bozo demanded.

"Not guilty," Matt shrugged.

Angel shot him a glare as Bozo studied him. "Explain your plea."

"Simple. Our leader, Angel, made a decision to throw you into the air before I even had a chance to object. However, my objections would have been irrelevant, seeing as how she is the leader and I am not. Everyone was just following her orders. How can following orders from your leader be a crime?" Matt shrugged.

"Very well! I accept your plea, and find you not guilty!" Bozo declared.

"Thank you, will you release me now?" Matt asked.

"I will!" Bozo declared, as he took the keys and unchained Matt's feet, then his hands. Angel was furious but bit her tongue as Matt smiled and rubbed his wrists.

"Thank you for being fair, Bozo Star Reacher. Will you hand down Angel's sentence now?" Matt grinned.

"I will!" Bozo declared. "Her legs shall remain shackled, and she will be locked in the smaller room adjacent to this one for a period of ten days!"

Angel started to object, but dialed it down just in time. "Bozo Star Reacher, I would like to appeal for mercy, and request five days."

"I would also like to appeal for your mercy Bozo Star Reacher. Angel is our day-to-day leader, to have her removed for ten days will have a significantly negative impact on our society. Almost assuredly crippling it. If necessary, we are willing to share the sentence with the other members that were at the beach," Matt offered.

"Starting with Matt," Angel offered.

"Negative! The leader shall start the sentence! How many of you are there, Matt?" Bozo demanded.

"There are six of us," Matt replied. "Including Angel."

"Six?" Angel looked at him.

"Uh, yes. I am absolutely offering Yuktrap," Matt grinned.

"Oh yes, there are six of us," Angel beamed.

"Very well! Angel will serve three days, the person that shot me will serve two days, one other person of your choice will serve two days, and the remaining three will serve one day each!" Bozo declared. "This will be the only leniency I show, I suggest you take it!"

"We accept," Angel relented. "Will you please take these handcuffs off of me, and I will head to my room, peacefully?"

"I will!" Bozo declared, as he took the cuffs off of Angel's wrists.

"Please allow me to leave final instructions with Matt, seeing as I am his leader," Angel offered.

"I accept!" Bozo declared, again walking out of earshot.

"This is so ridiculous, and I'm a little mad at you for pleading not guilty there, but I will accept the fact that this is my fault. Thank you for speaking on my behalf. After this is all over, we will have a good laugh about it, I'm sure. Will you give me a kiss goodbye?" Angel whispered.

"Sure," Matt grinned, as he leaned down and kissed her, grabbing her ass.

"Matt!" Angel hissed as he let go.

"What? You said use my hands more," Matt teased.

"I did say that yes, but he is right there," Angel whispered.

"He is following protocol to the letter, it's pretty funny, you have to admit. He isn't going to look back this way," Matt grinned.

"It's actually pretty absurd how much he believes he is a real Space Trooper," Angel smiled. "Okay, my final instructions as your leader are to go back and chain Jen up, apply that ball gag, and spank her."

"How many spanks?" Matt grinned.

"One hundred," Angel grinned.

"As you command," Matt beamed.

Angel smiled and turned towards Bozo. "Bozo Star Screamer?"

"It's Star Reacher. Are you ready to begin your sentence?" Bozo demanded.

"Yes, I am. Please, take me to my cell," Angel offered.

"Very well! This way," Bozo declared, waving her forward. Angel followed him, along with Gracie, as Matt picked up the shackles, put them in the bag, and walked out, laughing.

CHAPTER 48

THE SENTENCES

Matt walked into the house, still laughing. The others were sitting on the couch, very curious about what was going on.

"Hey, where is Angel?" Jen beamed.

"She got convicted of war crimes and is serving her sentence," Matt waved with a laugh. "That was the best."

"Oh my God, what was her sentence?" Val laughed.

"Ten days of home confinement in leg shackles," Matt grinned. "She appealed for leniency, and shared punishment, and Bozo granted it. So, she will serve three, the person that shot her, Jen, will serve two, someone else, Yuktrap, will serve two, and the rest of us will serve one."

"I'm not wearing leg shackles for an entire day, we will just make Yuktrap serve mine," Val waved with a laugh.

"That's completely fine. But Angel and Bozo were clear, Jen has to serve hers. She is the one that blasted him, after all. She also had some more punishment for Jen lined up, and we can address that later. Is there food?" Matt laughed.

"Yes, your plate is on the counter," Val pointed, shaking her head.

"How did Angel look in that ball gag?" Carly teased.

"Oh, she vehemently refused to wear it, and Bozo declared it cruel and unusual—it wasn't used," Matt smiled, as he sat down at the bar and ate his fish.

"Lame!" Carly declared.

"So honestly, what do we do about Bozo?" Jen asked.

"I don't know. We didn't even talk about that," Matt shrugged. "Maybe I can take Angel's plate and discuss that with him. He really thinks he is a Space Trooper, I swear that was a movie. I mean, if Angel wasn't so desperate for a lover, it would be pretty hilarious."

"How did he get off the beach?" Val asked.

"I'm assuming he walked back in," Matt shrugged. "Poor guy."

"How bad did Jen hit him?" Val grinned.

"Oh, there is a small chunk of him missing, you can see where the pellets hit. Like I said, it was a good shot," Matt grinned. "Thanks for cooking Val. Jen? Can we retire to our room for a bit? Then I will take Angel her plate."

"Sure," Jen smiled, standing up. Matt picked up the bag of chains and walked into the bedroom behind her. "Did you enjoy the gifts I sent?" she teased.

"I did, yes. I think Angel hated them though," Matt grinned.

"Did he really put them all on?" Jen smiled.

"Oh yeah, everything except for the gags. He couldn't interrogate us if we couldn't talk," Matt laughed.

"I imagine Angel wants some revenge? She wants you to put those on me?" Jen smiled, as she laid in the bed on her side.

"She does, yes to all of those," Matt smiled.

"Very well, I will allow it. I was an accessory after all. I feel a little bad about shooting him, he didn't do anything to us," Jen grinned.

"That was his whole point, yes. He was no threat, and we blasted him out of the sky," Matt laughed.

"You have to tell me what she wanted first," Jen offered.

"Chained, gagged, and spanked," Matt grinned.

"Hmm alright," Jen whispered. "Let me change into something sexier."

"Okay, take your time," Matt smiled. He noted she didn't ask for more specifics, deciding not to offer them just yet.

She slid into the closet and came out wearing black lingerie and fishnets. Posing for him, he admired her long legs, as she laughed.

"Hands in front," Jen whispered, holding her hands out. He obliged her, then shackled her feet. Lying down in the bed, she allowed him to gag her, without even asking how many spankings. He pulled her feet off the bed, so they were touching the ground, and started spanking her. She reacted immediately, groaning.

"I notice you didn't even ask how many spankings, she gave me a number you know," Matt teased, as he spanked her.

Jen looked back at him with curiosity, moaning into the gag as he spanked her. She started to drool, closing her eyes and taking the spanks. Lifting one foot off the ground, she raised her arms as well, as he kept going. He was counting in his head, but was still not telling her the numbers. She tried to squirm away but he held her in place, continuing.

"MMPPHH!" She screamed into the gag, as he stopped for a moment.

"You good?" Matt whispered.

She shook her head no, and he ungagged her. Catching her breath, she demanded to know how many spankings he intended on giving.

"Angel demanded 100," Matt grinned.

"And what number are you on?? You better not be lying!" Jen hissed.

"57," Matt smiled.

"Okay, that's fair," Jen relented. "I should have asked how many at the top. You can re-gag me, but please, change positions. Lay me on my back."

"Okay," Matt nodded, as he gagged her again and she crawled onto the bed. Rolling over onto her back, she raised her legs part way and Matt lifted them up, admiring them. She giggled through the gag as he resumed the spankings. She groaned in protest, but didn't tap out. Finally, he finished and let go of her legs. Ungagging her, she caught her breath.

"Oh, my ass hurts," Jen groaned. "I'm afraid of sex while being gagged."

"You don't have to do anything you don't want to," Matt assured her.

"You making me feel comfortable is working," Jen grinned. "Re-gag me and let's do it. Don't unshackle me just yet."

An hour later Jen was resting while Matt took Angel some food. Knocking on the door, he walked in, figuring Bozo couldn't actually answer it.

"Bozo? I have brought the prisoner some food, will you allow it?" Matt offered.

"I will! I will stand guard out here!" Bozo declared, emerging from the living room.

"Very well, I will feed her and then come back out to discuss your future here," Matt grinned.

"Very well!" Bozo declared.

Matt shook his head and walked into the bedroom, where he found Angel laying on her stomach petting Gracie. She greeted him with a smile as he tried to look away.

"Hey you, how was the sex?" Angel laughed.

"It was good, thanks for asking, and setting it up," Matt rolled his eyes. "I brought you some lunch."

"Thanks, I appreciate it," Angel smiled as she took her plate and pushed Gracie away.

"How is the Space Trooper treating his prisoner?" Matt teased.

"This is so absurd Matt. I told him not to come in without knocking, and he agreed. I'm not even sure he can open the door, and certainly not if I locked it. I hear him out there talking to himself, reporting his discoveries. I'm not sure if I can do this for three days, honestly. If you could plead our case with him, I would appreciate it. I don't want to be alone for that long," Angel sighed.

"I planned on talking to him after you ate. I am very curious about his intentions going forward. What does he intend to do?" Matt smiled.

"Well, we have to earn good points, I am trying to remember that. Because I have a few ideas," Angel grinned.

"Keep focusing on the good points, I will go talk to Bozo," Matt laughed.

"Thanks for the food, again I appreciate it. I will continue to sit here, earning good points. Perhaps I should change into something sexier?" Angel teased.

"How are you going to do that with your legs being chained?" Matt grinned.

"You think these can hold me?" Angel smiled.

"Alright, well, I will hopefully talk to you soon," Matt rolled his eyes, standing up and taking her plate.

"Bozo Star Reacher? Will you talk to me over there on the couch?" Matt asked as he exited the bedroom, closing the door behind him.

"Very well!" Bozo declared. He had been standing on the windowsill above the sink, looking outside. Jumping down, he ran into the living room and hopped onto the coffee table again.

"Looks like you are missing some chunks of yourself there, Bozo. How are your wings?" Matt asked.

"Inoperable. I will never fly again, unfortunately. Which means I am stranded on this planet until the Star Force sends a ship here to rescue me," Bozo declared.

"How unfortunate," Matt shrugged. "What do you plan to do while stranded here?"

"I am currently trying to figure that out myself. This house can serve as a base of operations for me, until I find a mission objective," Bozo pondered.

"This house belongs to our leader, are you just going to kick her out?" Matt asked.

"Negative. No matter how much of a criminal she is, I will not sink to her level. She can live in the guest room," Bozo declared.

"Oh, how generous," Matt laughed.

"Indeed! She is a horrible criminal, the likes of which few in the Galaxy have seen! She should count herself lucky I am allowing her to even live!" Bozo declared, pointing a finger in the air.

"Uh huh," Matt offered. "I'm sure she is saying the exact same thing right now."

"As she should! She narrowly escaped execution!" Bozo declared.

"Yeah, okay. Let's just move on," Matt waved his hand. "Our society is collapsing because you have taken our leader away. No one is doing any work, I myself just slept with my girlfriend. Three more days like this and we will all be dead—you would have committed a genocide. How does the Star Force look at genocide?"

"It is the most horrible crime in the galaxy!" Bozo declared. "Were I to be found guilty, I would be executed on the spot by being shot into the sun!"

"Well, we don't want that, do we?" Matt teased.

"Definitely not! How can we rectify this situation?" Bozo asked.

"Let our leader serve the rest of today, then release her tomorrow. We will send someone else to take her place for one day, then we will send another 'person' to serve the remaining eight days," Matt offered.

"I accept! I want the person that shot me and rendered me flightless to serve tomorrow!" Bozo declared.

"I am positive our leader does as well, we will send her tomorrow, you have my word," Matt waved his hand.

"Very well! You may inform your leader of the situation, while I resume my patrol!" Bozo declared.

"Right," Matt grinned as he stood up. Bozo hopped off the coffee table and headed back into the kitchen. Matt knocked on the door and Angel said to come in.

Opening the door, he offered a smile. "Well, what's the verdict?" Angel smiled.

"He will release you tomorrow, and we will send one more person, Jen, over here to serve for a day. Then Yuktrap will serve the remaining eight," Matt grinned.

"I completely accept that. Thank you. I will personally bring Jen over here," Angel beamed.

"I thought you would like that," Matt grinned. "I'm going to head back—I'll bring you dinner tonight. Maybe you will put on something nice."

"Maybe I will," Angel smiled, as Matt left.

———

The next morning, Bozo had let Angel go, and she was waiting on Jen to change clothes, along with Matt. Carly had loaned her another bag of toys, and insisted on being present for Jen's send-off, so she was sitting on the bed as well. Jen finally came out, wearing purple lingerie and matching fishnets, in high heels.

"Is this sufficient?" Jen rolled her eyes.

"Absolutely," Carly beamed.

"I understand why I have to serve a day, but this is too much," Jen whined.

"You sent Carly with a bag of toys over, and we were humiliated. Now it's your turn," Angel smiled. "Hands behind your back."

Jen complied, she knew she was outnumbered, and Angel was physically stronger, regardless. Angel cuffed her hands, then her leg shackles, closing the distance between them which meant Jen would have to take much shorter strides.

"Ow, that's not fair," Jen whined. "Really? A blindfold?"

Angel put the blindfold on her, then the ball gag. Jen protested the entire time, moaning into the gag. Angel finished her off with a neck collar and a lead, pulling her out, as Jen shuffled her feet. Walking outside, Matt and Carly followed. That hadn't been part of the agreement, but there was nothing Jen could do. Entering Bozo's new house, he was ready to receive them.

"Hello there! This prisoner has been subdued quite heavily, was she giving you a hard time?" Bozo demanded.

"Yes Bozo, I apologize for her behavior. We had to gag and blindfold her, leave them both on for the entire length of sentence," Angel beamed.

"MMMPPPHHH???" Jen screamed into the gag, shaking her head.

"I see she is already resisting. I have ways to get her in line! Take her into the bedroom!" Bozo pointed.

Angel pulled the lead and Jen shuffled into the bedroom. She was shoved into the bed, and Angel rolled her onto her stomach and secured the lead to her ankle shackles, completing the hogtie.

"There, she isn't going anywhere. Bozo? If she is making too much noise, feel free to spank her. She hates it, but you have to be firm. Here is a paddle to make it easier. Are we good?" Angel beamed.

"MMMPPPHHH!!!" Jen screamed again, as Bozo brought the paddle down on her ass.

"Yes! I will get this prisoner in line! You have my word!" Bozo declared.

"Glad to hear it, Bozo," Angel laughed. "Enjoy yourself. Bye Jen. Remember, good points."

"MMMMMMPHHHHHHH!!!!!!!" Jen howled, as Bozo spanked her again.

"Quiet prisoner! You will behave!" Bozo declared.

CHAPTER 49

THE DEMON

Val drove them over the causeway, with Sam and Tali following behind. It had been a very long few days for some of them, Matt and Angel, specifically. Jen had broken free and gone on the warpath, throwing Bozo into the washer machine and chaining up Matt, Angel, and Carly. Angel could have stopped it, but she wisely chose to earn good points. They were having a good laugh about it now, but it had taken a while to get there.

"Hoping for a straight, human, hot male," Angel beamed.

"You better be, or else you are back in my bed," Jen teased.

"As much fun as it's been, your nights always end with something that I desperately want," Angel laughed.

"It certainly was an interesting week," Val beamed.

"I had fun," Matt shrugged.

"I did too," Carly laughed.

Coming to a stop at the pier, they hopped out. Jen once again had the shotgun, as Sam and Tali led them on.

"I still wonder how Jen broke out of those chains," Matt pondered.

"I told you, I have been in that position before," Jen grinned.

"How long did it take you?" Carly smiled.

"Oh, an hour, Bozo wouldn't leave until I was completely submissive. He untied me and everything. It was fun, but annoying at the same time," Jen laughed.

"Wait, he unchained you? That's not nearly as dramatic as you escaping," Matt offered.

"Yes, he spanked me a few times and asked if I was going to behave, I nodded yes. He let some time go by then took the gag out, I further pleaded my case, and he agreed to my conditions. Leg shackles, solitary confinement. As soon as he left, I got free and went out the back door," Jen laughed.

"So, he didn't go in the washer machine?" Val asked.

"Nah, I was just being dramatic. He never knew the difference, I went back in the very early AM, reapplied the shackles, and he came to release me. Stupid toy," Jen beamed.

"Looks like you got your man, Angel," Sam growled. "Not sure if he is human though."

"Finally!" Angel exclaimed, looking at the fire.

"Oh—." Matt whispered.

"You recognize him?" Val asked. "It's a video game character, right?"

"Once again, his identity is on the tip of my tongue. He isn't human, check out that sword, and the weird hair. I can't place him, probably because he is a fusion, but I don't think Angel cares too much," Matt grinned.

"Not one bit!" Angel beamed, racing forward.

"Who are you kids?" the man asked.

"Before you leave with your booty call, what did the fire tell you?" Matt tried, as Angel was already waving him off.

"Never mind them, I am here to pick you and take you back to my place. The name is Angel, I know you don't remember your name, and it doesn't matter to me one bit. Come on, are you ready?" Angel beamed.

"No thanks, I'm not into short human girls. Too fragile," the man waved her off with a laugh. "The fire said I was the Demon of the Chosen Ones, whatever that means. I don't care! Think I will go find something else to do."

"Um, fragile?" Angel stammered.

The Demon stood up and started to jump away, literally vaulting in the air, but Angel was not having it.

"Oh no! You are not leaving!" Angel shouted, grabbing his foot out of the air and pulling him back down.

The Demon was surprised, looking back at her, and even more surprised when she slung him across the sand, some 20 feet.

"Whoa!" he shouted as he flew through the air.

"Oh!" Val exclaimed, surprised at the aggressiveness.

"I am getting what I came for, one way or another!" Angel shouted.

The Demon stood up, dusting off his blue trench coat. He was wearing a huge two-handed sword on his back, the handle extended over his head and the tip of the blade was a few inches off the ground. Crazy red hair, boots, he fit the cyberpunk theme well. But Angel didn't seem to care.

"Maybe I was wrong about your fragility," The Demon laughed. "But you are still just a human, you can't reach my level."

Angel was stomping towards him, as he jumped in the air again, about 30 feet high, drawing his sword with one hand.

"He's got hops!" Val exclaimed. "And style, he isn't bad!"

"Yeah, watch out Angel! He isn't kidding around!" Matt laughed.

Angel stood undaunted as the Demon hurled his sword at her, she took one step to the side as it landed in the sand.

"Was that supposed to hit me? Because it didn't," Angel crossed her arms.

The Demon just smiled as he hit the ground, and dashed forward, in breathtaking speed, right up to Angel's face. Smiling, he extended his hand a little bit and sent her flying. She landed in the sand, about ten feet from where she had started, slowly picking herself up.

"Like I said, fragile. I'm outta here," The Demon laughed, as he jumped again, well over them and onto a nearby gas station.

Angel followed after him, unfazed. The rest of the group followed, maintaining a safe distance.

"This guy is right up her alley, the problem she has is convincing him to bed her," Matt grinned.

"So, he is clearly not human. Is he a threat to us?" Jen asked.

"Nah, he isn't giving off that vibe. I think he is another fusion, of several really fun, unserious anti-heroes. But he is very strong, she is no match for him, I'm sorry to say," Matt smiled.

They walked out into the street, Angel had followed him to the gas station, which he was standing on top of, looking around at everything else.

"Hey! I'm right here!" Angel shouted.

The Demon scoffed and drew one of his guns, it looked like an enormous .50 caliber-long pistol. Pointing it towards her with a smile, it was dark black, and he fired off a round. It missed Angel, who stood there, still undaunted. He fired off some more rounds, and she didn't flinch. He finally finished his drawing, and jumped off the gas station and onto a larger building, and then an even larger hotel.

They walked up to Angel, who was looking at the ground. He had shot a heart shape into the pavement around her.

"If this is your idea of courtship the answer is yes!" Angel screamed up at him. He jumped a few more times, landing on top of one of the skyscraper hotels, 50 stories up. She walked over to the bottom of it, looking up at him. The rest of the group maintained a safe distance, as they could really only make out the blue coat up there.

"We are going to leave, he doesn't seem to be a threat, good luck Angel," Tali waved her hand, as she led Sam off.

More shots rang out, and hit the ground next to Angel, who again didn't move. He was using a second gun now, carving out a message in the pavement. From 50 stories up. Jen was marveling at both his precision and her courage.

"She really wants to sleep with him," Val beamed.

He finally stopped shooting, as they crept forward to read the message. "Is it Love?" was carved out into the pavement.

"GET DOWN HERE!!" Angel screamed.

They looked up at him, he seemed to be burning orange flames, as he jumped off the roof.

"Is he burning?" Carly asked.

"He said he was a demon," Matt shrugged.

He landed the typical superhero landing, standing up, his horns were visible, eyes burning blue, red claws. Angel again didn't flinch.

"Take me to bed already!" Angel demanded.

Reverting to his human form, The Demon scoffed, "You that desperate huh?"

"Yep," Angel nodded, as the rest of the group nodded along.

"I don't take it easy, might be into some real kinky stuff, won't be there when you wake up in the morning, won't bring you food, and might just be gone for good one day," The Demon laughed.

"I'm still standing here," Angel growled.

"I notice this place is completely deserted, save you lot. We will meet you by where the fire was," The Demon laughed.

Before they could say anything, he picked up Angel in his arms and jumped away. They could only shake their heads as they headed back for the beach.

"Well, I am thrilled for Angel, but I hope they find a place that's not 50 stories up. There is no power, no AC, they are going to suffocate," Val beamed.

"I don't think that's on her mind at all," Matt shook his head. "I'm happy for her as well, he isn't going to help us too much, but there are plenty of freeloaders right now."

"Let's just wait on the beach here for them to come back. I know this has been a wild week, but I am happy for Angel as well," Jen smiled.

———

"Hey Carly?" Matt offered.

"Yes Matt?" Carly smiled.

They were sitting on the beach, waiting for Angel to come back. They had no idea what building the Demon had chosen, but it was no big deal.

"I think Jen had some requests regarding your toys," Matt laughed.

"I'm going to kill you for that, Matt," Jen rolled her eyes.

"I would be happy to listen to them, Jen," Carly beamed.

"Fine. The ball gag is too big and too painful. Can you find something a little more comfortable? Bozo made me wear it for 30 minutes, I was practically in tears. I'm not taking it off the table, but if I'm going to spend extended amounts of time being captured, I want something more comfortable," Jen whispered.

"Sure, no problem. Why are you whispering? Is this an embarrassing topic for you?" Carly teased.

"It is, yes," Jen admitted. "Can we please talk about anything else?"

"Let's talk about Christmas then. The best time of the year," Val beamed.

"It's what? Two weeks away? Today is the 13th I think?" Matt smiled.

"Yes, I think we can start decorating today, I know we wanted to wait to see if we got another roommate, but I think the answer is going to be no. He doesn't seem the type to even care about Christmas," Val laughed.

"Not at all," Matt waved his hand.

"I know we need to conserve electricity, so I will forgo the lights, but I want everything else up in our house," Val beamed.

"Absolutely, we can transport all of our stuff from our old house to the new one, and hang everything. Then we can loot other people's stuff, and hang that as well. Angel will want to decorate her own house I'm sure," Matt smiled.

"I want to talk about gifts," Jen teased. "I don't want to hear any excuses—we have plenty of time to find some great ones."

"I think a road trip might be in order, the shopping locations in this city don't seem to be up to snuff. Where could we go that wouldn't be a huge inconvenience?" Carly asked.

"Back to Austin. We know the city well, we can break up into groups, two people with Val, one with me. We could even wait until next week, to see if we do indeed get a new roommate. At this point, it could be anyone or anything," Matt grinned.

"I think we should wait until next week to go shopping as well. This week can be all about decorating. What do we want to eat for Christmas? How much marlin do we have left?" Jen asked.

"Not a lot, we still have plenty of the smaller fish, mahi-mahi, tuna, stuff like that. But the shark and cobia are long gone, and we probably won't have that much marlin left by Christmas. We consume a lot each week. Do you think we should go fishing again?" Val asked.

"I wouldn't say it's a need, we just need to spread our meals out a little better. How many bags of marlin do we have left?" Matt asked.

"Twenty zip locks," Val replied.

"See? That's a lot. We just need to eat the smaller fish, some other meat, even pasta. We don't have to eat fish every day guys. Val made chicken fettuccine over a month ago? That was the last time we had pasta," Matt laughed.

"I feel bad about this, you and Val have done almost all of the cooking. I can't cook at all, it's just not something I have ever done. Jen? What about you?" Carly sighed.

"I'm okay at it, but yes, it has pretty much fallen to just the two of you. But we at least clean up after you, so I guess it balances out. Whatever you want to feed us is fine," Jen relented.

"It's not like we are complaining. You two have done so much for us. And as long as you wash the dishes, I'm fine with it," Val shrugged.

"I think as long as we eat at the table every night, nothing needs to change. Dinner is a big deal for Val and I, and we really enjoy having you all with us," Matt offered. "But that has never been an issue, so let's just move on. Here comes Angel."

Angel was indeed walking up, beaming. "Hey guys! Ready to head home?"

"Yeah, how was your booty call?" Matt asked.

"It was amazing. He didn't want to talk or anything, he just banged away and left shortly after. I am completely okay with it," Angel laughed.

"Okay, let's go then," Val rolled her eyes.

They stood up and headed back for the truck, Angel was just glowing, and everyone was happy for her. Piling in, Val pointed them towards home.

"Where is your demon?" Carly teased.

"Who knows? Who cares? He will come find me when he gets bored," Angel laughed.

"Wow," Matt whispered.

As they were driving over the bridge, they spotted the demon standing on the railing. He backflipped into the tailgate, and shook the whole truck when he landed. Sitting down, he didn't even look their way as Val rolled her eyes and continued to drive.

"We don't have his favorite food, maybe we can make some. I doubt it will be very good though," Angel whispered.

"What is it?" Val asked.

"Pizza," Angel grinned.

"That is the one dish that I have no confidence in either of our abilities to make," Val laughed.

"I miss pizza," Matt offered with a smile.

"How many supernatural creatures are we going to get, sheesh," Carly sighed.

"It does seem like a lot, even though the Sunwalker and the Nightwalker have gone to hibernate and haven't been seen since. But if we ever need something to be killed that Sam and Tali can't handle, I mean, we have plenty of options. That guy in the tailgate seems to be a real beast," Matt smiled.

"Can confirm!" Angel beamed.

"Let's just keep him away from Bozo and Yuktrap, we don't need either of them getting blown to bits. Remember, Yuktrap respawns with his voice box," Jen smiled.

They felt the demon hop out of the truck as they pulled into their neighborhood. Apparently, he wasn't a suburbanite either, as Val parked them in front of their house.

"Angel? Go make peace with Bozo once and for all. Everyone else is off the table," Matt smiled.

"You got it!" Angel beamed.

"Come inside with me Matt," Jen whispered, taking his hand. "We have some things to discuss."

CHAPTER 50

TIS THE SEASON

Jen closed their bedroom door, and Matt sat down in their recliner next to the bed. She came over and sat in his lap, facing sideways.

"You good?" Matt asked.

"Yes, I am. You know what I want to talk about?" Jen whispered.

"Our long-term future?" Matt guessed.

"Yes. Where do you see yourself in a year Matt?" Jen whispered.

"With you. Either here in Harlingen, continuing the experiment, or in your world," Matt replied.

"You didn't even hesitate. You didn't hesitate at the dinner table either. Would you really come to my world with me? Even if it meant never seeing your family again?" Jen whispered.

"Yes, I would. I could spend the rest of my life with you Jen. I'm a simple guy, my mental health hasn't taken that big of a hit in this crazy situation, because I was never into people. My sister is here with me, and now you, Carly, and Angel. And even Sam. You are all my family now," Matt whispered.

"I was never into people either. I never thought about being with anyone for very long. This is the longest relationship I have ever been in. And it's only been a few months. But I don't want it to end. If you came into my world, what would you do?" Jen asked.

"Well, the first thing I would do would be to make out with you passionately," Matt grinned.

"Score," Jen laughed. "You nailed that one. But I'm serious, what would you do on an everyday basis?"

"Whatever you wanted to do. I would, in all likelihood, try to follow you on all of your adventures. The things I would need to learn, you would teach me. That is what I would hope to do," Matt whispered.

Jen hugged him tighter. "I have always thought about a relationship as settling down. But we haven't come close to settling down here. We are active every day. I have to be active, and this situation demands it. If we were back in my world, I would want to be active. And…hearing you say you would want to go with me…it checks that box for me Matt. I love you."

"I love you too, Jen. I hope I am making you as happy as possible," Matt offered.

"Every day Matt," Jen smiled. "Come on, let's start preparing those Christmas decorations."

Jen stood up and Matt followed her out, and to their surprise, Carly was sitting there at the dinner table, seemingly waiting for them.

"Oh, hi Carly. Everything good?" Mat stammered.

"Yes. Jen? Can I borrow Matt for a bit? No foreplay," Carly assured her.

"Sure, I don't care what you do," Jen smiled.

Carly pulled Matt into his room and sat down on the bed. He closed the door and asked what was going on.

"What do you think of Val and I eloping?" Carly asked.

"Val always said she would never do a formal wedding, sign some papers and that's it. What are you asking me for? I'm her brother—not her Dad," Matt asked, bewildered.

"Okay, let me rephrase. Do you think I am good enough for Val? I have killed dozens of people, it still bothers me," Carly pressed.

"Yep. Next question?" Matt deadpanned.

"You aren't really helping me here, Matt," Carly growled.

"Then take off your clothes," Matt shrugged.

"What? No, I said no foreplay. This is serious," Carly hissed.

"It's not serious, it's silly. Do you love Val? Do you want to stay with her forever? If yes, elope. If no, then don't elope. I mean, marriage is a lifetime commitment. I just got done telling Jen if I could go to her world and stay with her, I would. Would you bring Val into your world if you could?" Matt asked.

"I would prefer to stay here, honestly. My world is a screwed-up place," Carly whispered.

"Fine, would you stay here with Val, if given the chance?" Matt asked.

"Yes," Carly nodded.

"Then elope. That's all I got. I don't even know how you would make it official," Matt shrugged.

"You're not being a big help here, but it's not entirely your fault, you probably weren't expecting this topic from me. Why don't you come sit down?" Carly patted the bed next to her.

Matt relented and sat down next to her, as she took his hand. "You have actually done a really good job of supporting Val and I, among other things. Being the only guy here, you accepted the responsibility that came with pretty well. I know Angel was a complete handful, but you even spent time with me that I appreciated. I'm happy here with you guys, I didn't choose the superhero life, it just happened.

Kind of like how this just happened. Val misses the people, sometimes she misses them a lot, but if one person a week drops in for the next year, I don't know..." Carly shrugged. "I mean...I kind of ran out of things to say there."

"I can tell," Matt laughed.

"Oh stop," Carly pushed him. "You say something."

"If one person a week continues to drop in for the next year, that's a lot of mouths to feed. We can't assume it's going to be a living person each time, given how we have what? Six non-humans? Maybe five, I'm not even sure anymore. You and Val checked the houses last week, how did they look?" Matt asked.

"All of them had power, freezers were full, cabinets had non-perishables, found four dead mice, Val ejected from the house each time. I reset the traps. Despite our concerns about food, we still have so much. You guys did a great job looting two entire grocery stores. I don't think meat will ever be a problem for us, we have the fishing, and herds of cows out there. Get back on topic," Carly smiled.

"Alright. I just talked to Jen about this, but we didn't even talk about marriage. We aren't that far along in our relationship. We love each other, but marriage is still...just a little too far away. You and Val are there, obviously, and that's great. I have always worried about her mental health during all this, but you have taken care of her really well. And she likes Jen, and Angel. I think she helped Angel more in the beginning, then I stepped in and helped her from there.

But it's going to continue. Angel is good now, but there will be another person that drops in and struggles with it. And we will have to start over. I still worry about threats like Jack. I will probably never fully trust Tali, and she would say that's a good thing. The powers that be seem to be good at dropping in comic relief, Bozo being the biggest one. I mean, Yuktrap was absurd, but Bozo thinking he is a real space trooper, then arresting us, that was just so far out there!" Matt laughed.

"What is going on with him now?" Carly smiled.

"Angel is over there trying to make peace, I guess. No idea what that situation looks like going forward. He is a toy. The good thing is he doesn't eat. Maybe we can send him to take care of the houses, take care of the dead mice," Matt shrugged. "Or maybe he will continue to try to imprison us."

"The aftermath of that craziness was fun, I liked being chained up next to you, and I really liked how Jen blindfolded you and refused to let you see me. I was wearing something special for you and you never got to see it," Carly beamed.

"I liked that too, it was really mean," Matt grinned. "Think you can find some more toys for us? We need something that Jen can't escape from."

"I know exactly what to get," Carly laughed. "But wow did she look great in those chains when we first took her to Bozo."

"Smokin," Matt grinned.

"Now come on, get back on topic. Me and Val," Carly chided him.

"Like I said, I'm her brother, not her father. I think you are a great couple. If you want to elope, you don't need to clear it with me. Go for it," Matt shrugged. "It would be kinda weird to be tied up next to my sister-in-law though."

"You will get over it," Carly laughed. "Like I said, I liked it. Which means it will happen again."

"Okay," Matt smiled.

"Thanks for talking to me Matt. You want to go get started on this Christmas adventure?" Carly beamed.

"Yeah, let's go," Matt grinned.

They stood up and walked back into the living room, only to find Angel there waiting for them. "I'm next," Angel declared.

"Come on, this is getting a bit silly," Matt tried.

"I promise I will keep it short and have already cleared it with Jen," Angel insisted, pushing him back into the bedroom and closing the door. She reached up and pulled him down to her, giving him a nice kiss. "Thank you for supporting me even when I didn't deserve it Matt," she whispered.

Turning around, she exited, he followed her out. Carly had barely made it to the couch as she looked up. "That was short," Carly laughed. "Kiss and go?"

"Yep," Angel beamed.

"Jen and Val drove the truck to your old house, we should walk down and join them," Carly laughed.

"Sure, let's go. I would ask about Yuktrap's whereabouts, but I don't really care," Matt shrugged.

"He is still fighting it out with Bozo," Carly laughed. "They destroyed a couple of things, but they aren't mine, so whatever."

"Okay then," Matt laughed. "Let's go."

Walking out, they joined arms and headed by the dead golf course. Almost all of the grass was dormant, and the greens were yellow. The fountain was still going, but that was the only attraction. They also passed by the pool, which looked like it had a green to it. The tennis courts were in perfect condition, they had taken a couple of nets down to preserve them, but the front two were still ready to be used. They had only played once, before Jen and Carly were there, so no one knew how good Jen was.

"We should play tennis soon, I am curious about how good Jen is," Matt reflected.

"Well, if she is half as good at tennis as she is at pool you are in trouble," Carly teased.

"Nah, I am much better at tennis than pool," Matt laughed. "Do either of you play?"

"No, never," Carly waved. "I told you, I have never played any sports."

"Same. My strength was difficult enough to hide, sports were a total no go for me," Angel shrugged.

"I guess I should have known that," Matt grinned.

"It's okay," Angel smiled. "Oh, is this your old house? The one where Val parked?"

"Yeah, this area got flooded out, you can still see the damage. But our Christmas stuff is hopefully okay, it was in the attic," Matt whispered, thinking about its location.

"What happened Matt?" Angel asked as they stepped inside the house.

"Our avocado tree came down on the house during the storm, it hit the back, caved the roof in. It was an add-on....the attic didn't extend that far. So, hopefully our decorations are okay," Matt sighed.

Jen and Val were in the living room, organizing boxes. They looked up and offered hugs all around.

"Hey guys, our Christmas stuff is all okay," Val beamed. "It didn't take any water damage."

"That's good, I was a little worried about that. Did we get the tree down?" Matt asked.

"Not yet, I think we will put it in your truck," Val smiled.

"Oh uh, we walked," Matt shrugged.

"Oh, that's okay. We will just come back to get the tree then," Val laughed. "Let's start loading our truck. Three of us will drive it back, while you and Jen can get the tree down."

"Sure, that sounds like a plan," Matt nodded.

They loaded the truck up with what seemed like hundreds of boxes, and the three of them drove home. Matt and Jen walked to the stepladder leading up to the attic, looking up.

"How many trees do you have?" Jen asked.

"I know this might seem unusual to you, but we just have one big tree," Matt grinned.

"Oh, sorry," Jen smiled. "Don't ask me how many were in my old place."

"Now I have to ask," Matt teased.

Jen was trying to look away, blushing. "That was a silly moment. We had at least seven. I didn't decorate any of them. Honestly, I tried to be home for Christmas, but I failed a few times."

"Well, we can...borrow...another tree and put it in our room. One thing we have an overabundance of is ornaments, there will be plenty to spare," Matt smiled.

"I can tell you are hesitant to loot other people's homes," Jen whispered.

"I think it would earn bad points, and it's just bad karma in general to steal Christmas decorations. I think...it would be much more appropriate to search homes, and put people's Christmas decorations up for them. In their own homes, I mean," Matt offered.

"Oh, I completely support that Matt," Jen agreed. "And I know Val will too."

"Okay, I will go up and hand the parts of the tree down to you," Matt nodded, as he climbed up the ladder.

Crawling over to the tree, it was easy to just take one piece at a time and hand it down to Jen. Half an hour later, Val was pulling up again and they loaded the tree up. Piling into the truck, they headed home. As they were unpacking the tree, Bozo came running out of Angel's house—apparently he had figured out how to open the door.

"Stop right there!" Bozo ordered. "You all are in direct violation of the agreement I made with your leader! No crimes of any kind! You are stealing a Christmas tree!"

"Seriously?" Carly asked.

"Well, since our leader made the agreement, she can answer for it. Angel? Deal with it," Matt waved at her.

"Listen here Space Trooper, you are on thin ice!" Angel started.

"Don't get an attitude with me, you are the one in violation of our agreement!" Bozo countered.

"Maybe he will put her in chains again," Carly whispered.

"I don't think that's going to happen," Matt grinned.

Angel followed Bozo back into her house, and Yuktrap came flying out the front door, landing in the street. Picking himself up, he flipped the bird in the direction of the house, probably directed at Bozo, even though Angel had tossed him. Rolling over to the group, he started waving his hands frantically, flipping the bird and pounding his open hand with his fist. No one was really moved, as Matt handed him the tree stand.

"Take this inside Yuktrap. Don't drop it," Matt pointed.

They went inside and started setting up the tree, Val had carved out a corner for it in the living room. Angel came back inside and they asked what was going on with Bozo.

"Nothing. I explained it was our Christmas tree that we had gotten out of storage. He is resuming his watch," Angel shrugged.

"Does he just stand in the window all day?" Matt asked.

"He walks from room to room, talking to himself, taking logs, as he calls it. He plays with Gracie, feeds her, lets her out, so he is a slightly less annoying version of Yuktrap," Angel smiled.

Yuktrap raised his hands in the air three times, everyone knew what that meant by this point. He went to his corner to sulk as they finished getting the tree up.

"Let's take a break to eat lunch, then continue on. It should be a fun week," Val beamed.

"I agree. I love Christmas. I'm looking forward to it this year," Matt smiled.

CHAPTER 51
TACTICAL RETREAT

"Ahh! Damn slice!" Jen exclaimed as she lunged fruitlessly at a backhand that sailed past her. Matt took the game and they started to switch sides of the tennis court. He picked up his water and drank while she came up to join him. Picking up her own water, she smiled.

"That backhand is sneaky, you are way better at tennis than you are at pool," Jen laughed.

"You aren't going to get anywhere attacking my backhand, I can control that slice really well," Matt teased.

"I know, and I keep going back there like some kind of idiot," Jen exclaimed.

"Your serve is really good, you put a lot of topspin on it, and it has good velocity. I can tell you have had lessons," Matt smiled.

"And I can tell you have played competitively. You treat it like a marathon, conceding points you can't win," Jen offered. "You play at university?"

"No, just high school. Pros here are a different level, I was never that serious. I enjoyed the sport a lot, but I was never going to hit the circuit," Matt shrugged.

"You are being a good sport about not teasing me that you are about to serve me off the court," Jen grinned. "It's 5-2 in your favor, you ready?"

"Yep. Maybe you will stage a comeback," Matt grinned.

"Again, good sport," Jen laughed as they took their positions.

It was 40-0 in no time, and Matt paused for a second, seeing how it was match point. Jen smiled, as she readied herself. She had had lessons, but probably not played against too many live opponents. She had stood on the baseline for the entire match when he was serving. He decided it was finally time for a wake-up call.

He sent a power serve right at her body, as she shrieked and barely got her racquet on it. The velocity knocked the racquet out of her hands, as it clanged on the ground.

"Oh! You tosser! That's how you end the match??' Jen hissed at him.

"I love how your British comes out when you're angry," Matt laughed. "But no, the match is not over, the serve was a foot long, you didn't even see it."

"Whatever," Jen growled, picking up her racquet.

Matt laughed, she still didn't realize her mistake, as she stayed on the baseline. His second serve lost velocity, so that was probably okay. But he knew it was just luck, not her actually learning. He sent the second serve to her forehand, and she was so angry she sent her return back at him. He laughed and sent the backhand slice away from her, as she just tossed her racquet at it.

"Now now, don't be angry," Matt chided her from afar.

"Oh come on, that was completely unnecessary, you hurt my wrist," Jen growled.

Walking over to her side, he looked at her wrist, it was a little swollen. "How often have you played against a real opponent?" he whispered to her.

"Only a couple of matches, I know it was obvious to you," Jen shook her head.

"It was. Look, I will show you why," Matt pointed. "Where were you standing when I was serving?"

"On the baseline, where I am supposed to," Jen waved her hands.

"That's the result of lessons, not experience, or even common sense. Nothing is forcing you to stand there Jen. You should have learned right away to back up. Your stance should be at least two feet off the baseline for my first serve. I was taking it easy, but I could have aced you every time with you standing on the baseline," Matt grinned.

"Oh…I hate you right now. But I know you are right. Good match Matt. I'm sorry for my behavior," Jen lamented.

"And I'm sorry about your wrist. But I did love that British," Matt grinned.

"Stop," Jen rolled her eyes. "Let's pack up and head home. This was fun. I really did enjoy it, next time I will try harder."

"Me too," Matt smiled.

"You really are going to die at some point," Jen laughed, as they packed up their gear and began their walk home.

Entering the house, Val and Carly were setting up their Christmas village on an empty table in the dining room, and they looked up to greet them.

"Hey! How was the match?" Val smiled.

"She has had some lessons," Matt waved with a smile.

"So, she beat you?" Carly asked.

"Saying she has had lessons is Matt's nice way of saying she was over-matched," Val rolled her eyes.

"I am pretty sure he let me win the two games that I did," Jen sighed.

"I don't know the rules at all, what was the score?" Carly asked.

"6-2. Tennis lessons are different from golf lessons," Matt grinned.

"We are going to go jump in the shower, then come back and help with dinner," Jen offered.

"Jump in the shower, then head to Angel's. She has some house guests," Val waved.

"They tried to come here but Val said they were disturbing the Christmas Spirit," Carly laughed.

"Okay, sure," Matt shrugged.

Half an hour later, Matt and Jen knocked and entered Angel's house. To their surprise, Angel was sitting at the table, with the Demon to her left, feet resting on the table as well, Bozo across from him, Sam, Tali, and the Sunwalker. Matt was really surprised to see the Sunwalker.

"So, this looks ridiculous," Jen whispered.

"Turning into a real clown show I see," the Sunwalker growled.

"Yeah, we just need someone representing the New York Mets, and the clown show will be complete. What are you doing here?" Matt asked the Sunwalker.

"This freak woke me up, started kicking me around, Sam got there in time to stop him, else he probably would have killed me given the state I was in," the Sunwalker growled.

"There is still time," The Demon grinned.

"You good now?" Matt asked.

"Yeah, the girl gave me some blood, thanks kid," the Sunwalker growled.

"Sooo....now what?" Angel asked.

"Send the Sunwalker back to bed, tell the demon to stay away from him, story end?" Matt offered.

"Why are you keeping a couple of vampires around? They eat humans, you know that right?" The Demon grinned.

"What are you doing in this city?" Matt asked.

"No idea, I wish I could leave. Not a single pizza place to be had. And this human girl is already losing steam in bed," The Demon sighed.

"That is not true, and I hate you for saying that," Angel hissed as she kicked his chair out from under him, sending him crashing to the ground.

"Inappropriate talk about the bedroom will not be tolerated! This will be your only warning!" Bozo declared.

"What is this?" the Sunwalker pointed at Bozo.

"It's a toy," Sam growled.

"I am Bozo Star Reacher, Space Trooper! I am certainly not a toy," Bozo glared. "I am marooned here on this planet until the Star Force comes to rescue me."

"Whatever," the Sunwalker growled.

The Demon had picked his chair up and sat down again, putting his feet back on the table. Bozo started to object again, but he was cut off by the Demon drawing one of his guns and pointing it at him. Bozo remained silent, but that didn't save him. The Demon shot a hole right through his helmet.

Bozo was knocked down by the force, and immediately started gasping for air, as the others looked on, quickly recovering from the gunshot to watch the toy's performance.

"So familiar..." Matt whispered.

Bozo continued to gasp for air, until realizing nothing was happening. Recovering, he stood up, unhappy.

"How dare you shoot a Space Trooper's helmet on a contaminated planet! My eyeballs could have been ripped out of their eye sockets, my lungs frozen, my brain exploded, any number of terrible things! I have no choice but to declare you a hostile enemy of the Space Force!" Bozo shouted.

"Please don't shoot our ears again...!" Angel pleaded, but the Demon ignored her and blew Bozo's arm clean off.

"Bozo! Retreat already!" Matt waved at him as he tried to cover his ears.

"I think you are right Matt. This is Bozo Star Reacher, sounding the retreat!" Bozo declared, jumping off the table and running away into the other room. He stopped to pick up his severed arm on his way.

"Okay, no more guns in the house, please," Angel pleaded.

The Demon shrugged and holstered his gun. "That guy was annoying. So, we are stuck here, no other humans, demons, anything, and one of us drops in every week. What's the point?"

"We have been trying to figure it out, it just keeps getting stranger and stranger. We don't know who is doing it or what the point is. Our theories are barely hanging on. You got a name yet?" Matt shrugged.

"Nope," The Demon shrugged. "I guess you can call me Damien."

"Not very creative there, buddy," Sam growled.

"Oh well," Damien threw his hands in the air.

"Damien is fine. So...what are we all doing here? Sunwalker? You want to go back to bed? We have added a couple of humans, but it's still not enough to sustain you. Certainly not you and the Nightwalker," Matt sighed.

"What would I do if I was awake? Try to kill this clown? Nah, I'll head back. Just see that he doesn't bother me again," the Sunwalker growled, standing to leave.

"This is a weird bunch," Damien grinned.

"Yep," Sam growled.

"I guess I will head out too, hope you enjoyed your booty call human, might be a while before I come back this way," Damien laughed, as he stood up and headed out himself.

"Wow," Jen whispered.

"Well then, I don't even know where to begin," Tali threw her hands in the air.

"I guess I can begin by asking the obvious. Angel. Did you in fact, enjoy your booty call?" Matt grinned.

Angel had collapsed her head onto the table, but looked up to glare at him. "Read...my...mind."

"I'm glad you have the weird ones in your house," Jen laughed.

"Sam? Tali? Are you two alright? What brought you over?" Matt sighed.

"Sam detected the Sunwalker and the Demon approaching, and he wanted to make sure you guys were safe. If there is nothing else, we will be going," Tali rolled her eyes.

"Have a good night," Sam growled, as they also stood to leave.

"Okay, Jen? Let's get out of here as well, this is too much craziness," Matt waved.

"Wait!" Angel called out, standing up. It was only then that Matt noticed she was just wearing a robe. "Bozo? It's safe to come out now."

Bozo peeked his head out, noticed the house had emptied out, and approached them, carrying his arm. "What a relentless assault, I fear we could not hold them off should they attack again," Bozo declared.

He hopped onto the table and flopped down, dropping his arm. "I need medical attention. Are any of you a trained field medic?" Bozo asked.

"Jen," Matt pointed.

"Seriously?" Jen exclaimed.

"Is that not correct?" Matt shrugged.

"He is a toy, find some tape," Jen waved her hands.

"While you fix him Jen, I am going to borrow Matt," Angel offered, pulling him into the bedroom, leaving Bozo there asking Jen for help.

"What is it Angel?" Matt asked.

"I just want to make sure I'm not in trouble, or causing problems, or earning bad points," Angel pressed. "It's not my fault my boyfriend is a gun toting whack job."

"I mean, unless sleeping with him is earning bad points, I don't know how you would be in the wrong. He isn't a slave—he can do what he wants. I wish he wouldn't have shot his guns in the house, but the results were amusing. Probably earned some bad points for that," Matt shrugged. "You want me to leave so you can put some clothes on?"

"Why would I want you to leave?" Angel grinned. "I promised you the other day I would put something nice on for you."

Angel dropped her robe and Matt tried to look away, but she pulled his face back to her. "I can make you look at me, Matt."

She was wearing a black corset, and turned around to find some clothes. Matt checked her out long enough for her to feel his eyes then looked away again.

"Want to have some fun tonight?" Angel offered.

"I have no idea what you mean, so I am going to decline," Matt whispered.

"I can capture you and Jen, if she will allow it. I like the idea of dominating you two together. I know you love it, but it's up to her, of course," Angel smiled.

"I will try to find the right opportunity to bring it up," Matt shrugged.

"Any requests?" Angel smiled as she pulled some clothes on.

"I notice your confidence has quickly returned since you got a boyfriend," Matt smiled.

"I feel like I owe you a lot for your support, and I know you like this. Don't bother denying it," Angel teased as she walked towards him and the door.

"If it happens, I at least want to see you for a bit," Matt whispered.

"I'll keep that in mind," Angel whispered back, opening the door.

They came into the living room to see Jen had taped Bozo's arm back on, as well as the damage to his other side from the shotgun blast. She had also taped both sides of his helmet.

"Looks like you are barely keeping it together, Space Trooper," Matt laughed.

"The situation is not ideal," Bozo admitted.

"I haven't forgotten how you spanked me without permission," Jen hissed, as she shoved him down and walked to join Matt and Angel. Matt immediately waved Angel off, she got the message. Not today.

"I did not do anything untoward—" Bozo started.

"Listen Bozo," Matt cut him off. "How well are you functioning right now? Give me a percentage."

"I would say at best 35%, losing my ability to fly, then an arm, it has definitely crippled me," Bozo relented.

"Perhaps it's time to consider resigning your position as a Space Trooper," Matt offered.

"Never! A soldier serves until the end!" Bozo declared.

"You are coming up on the end here buddy," Angel nodded. "Look in the mirror."

"Are you fit for combat? If we are attacked again, can you hold them off?" Matt grinned.

"No, I could only advise a tactical retreat," Bozo relented.

"Let me put this in a less diplomatic way, because I am tired of talking to you. Our peace agreement is at an end, Bozo. If I see you again as a Space Trooper, you really will go into the washer machine," Jen finished, as she headed out.

Matt and Angel watched her go, a little concerned. "Bozo," Angel started. "What did you do to her?"

"Nothing!" Bozo declared. "I simply got her back in line the way any guardsman would a misbehaving prisoner."

"What, specifically, did you do?" Angel growled.

"I...pulled her hair until she was completely silent and still," Bozo admitted.

"I see," Angel observed. "She is correct, our peace agreement is over. Unless you resign, we will have no choice but to treat you as hostile. What is your decision?"

"I will...step down from active duty, effective immediately!" Bozo declared.

"Good. Know that you no longer have any authority over anyone, but you will be allowed to stay here to take care of Gracie. Step out of line with your attitude and there will be consequences. Goodbye for now, Bozo," Angel finished, as she and Matt turned to leave.

Walking back into their own house, Val was finishing up the meal prep, and Carly was setting the table. Matt asked where Jen was and she pointed towards his room. Nodding, he left Angel and went to see her.

She was sitting on the recliner, flexing her wrist. "Hey, are you okay?" Matt whispered.

"I'm fine Matt. I just don't like that toy, that's all," Jen shrugged.

"You should have told me about the hair pulling," Matt whispered.

"It's just a little embarrassing. I'm not comfortable with the unknown. A lot of things happened there that weren't agreed to, and I was humiliated by a toy. I mean, I get it, I did send Carly over there to humiliate you two, and it did happen, so I had a little bit coming back my way. But it went a little too far," Jen sighed.

"We don't have to do that stuff anymore, Jen. I don't care," Matt assured her.

"It's fine Matt. I will come back around in time. Thanks for being nice about it though," Jen smiled, as he leaned down to kiss her.

"Come on, let's go eat," Matt smiled.

CHAPTER 52

THE LAST

Waking up, Jen nudged Matt out of bed with a smile. He stood up and opened the bedroom door, taking the drinks from Yuktrap and handing her a cup.

"It's always nice waking up next to you. I think that's one of my favorite things about our relationship," Matt grinned.

"I know you like it," Jen whispered. "Could you handle an empty bed from time to time, I wonder?"

"I think I could, as long as I knew where you were," Matt smiled.

"An acceptable answer," Jen grinned. "Come on, let's get ready to go get our new member, then make plans for our road trip."

"I know I have been saying this a lot, but it's anyone's guess at this point in regards to what we will get," Matt shrugged.

An hour later, the two vehicles were once again crossing the causeway, heading towards the light. Angel was in high spirits, knowing she had a fallback option in case it was another bust. Damien wasn't with them—he hadn't been seen since that day in Angel's house. Parking their trucks, the group hopped out and headed down the pier.

"Looks like another man," Sam growled.

"Hooray!" Angel exclaimed.

"How many boyfriends do you want?" Tali teased her.

"Just a normal, straight, human will suffice. That Demon has stamina, I'll give him that, but come on!" Angel laughed.

They approached the man sitting by the fire, looking exactly like what Angel was asking for. "Oh..." Val whispered. "Well, he definitely checks all those boxes!"

"Hey, I'm supposed to tell you guys I am the Last," the man smiled.

"The Last? Hmm, okay. That's interesting. You want to get out of here?" Matt tried, but Angel rushed forward.

"Hello there," Angel beamed, taking his arm. "I'm Angel. Do you remember your name?"

"No....but I can remember my son's name, it's Jake. So, you can call me that. Hi Angel," Jake smiled.

"Oh...that's new. Well, that's a lovely name. Come on then, let's get out of here Jake," Angel stammered, but managed to hold her gaze on him.

"I...can't believe he is here. And able to remember stuff..." Val whispered, looking at Matt.

"Maybe the Puppetmaster is making a statement," Matt reflected.

"Well...let's just go," Val relented.

"Those are some big buildings," Jake observed.

"Right, so Jake here, was born in Space, after a nuclear apocalypse wiped out mankind. So....he should fit right in here...as soon as we introduce him to all the luxuries humanity had to offer before his time," Matt managed.

"Yeah, thanks for that. What's your name buddy?" Jake asked.

"It's Matt. This is Jen, my sister Val, and Carly. The two walking away already are Sam and Tali," Matt managed.

"Matt huh? Have we met before?" Jake asked.

"I don't think so, no," Matt shrugged.

"You seem familiar. Well, I'm sure it's impossible. Let's get going, as you said," Jake offered.

"Carly? Can you catch up with those two and ride with them? Otherwise, one of us has to be in the tailgate. And Jake is sure to have questions," Matt offered.

"Sure thing," Carly nodded, as she ran forward.

"So, Jake. Tell me about yourself," Angel beamed, as they climbed into the truck. Jen got in the front seat while Angel sat in between Matt and their new member.

"As Matt said, born in space, lived there for 20 years. Got sent down with a bunch of other conscripts to see if the Earth was survivable. It was a rough situation, but we had a couple of real leaders in that group. I can't remember their names, but there was another guy, and another girl, they were special. The guy had a sword he had somehow gotten on the Station, we needed it. Later on, the rest of our people came down, he took command, became Chancellor," Jake reflected.

Val was eyeing Matt; as they listened to his story. "So, you have never even been in a car before?" Angel asked, holding his arm.

"I have, we found a running one from...a group of survivors. But uh, this is all very new," Jake looked out at the window at all the buildings.

"There are going to be a lot of things that are very new to you, take your time to acclimate. Angel will surely help you with everything. Uh, good luck explaining Bozo though," Matt grinned.

"He can stay with you for a while," Angel shrugged. "Jen? Is that okay?"

"Sure, the washer machine is open," Jen smiled.

"What is the situation here, exactly? I don't see any other people, the city looks abandoned," Jake observed.

Val was driving them over the causeway, as he looked out the window into the bay. "All of the people just vanished one day. We would get one new person a week, on the beach. It started out with just me and Val. Now you say you are the Last, I wonder if that is a literal meaning," Matt whispered.

"Two people surviving on the entire planet? What could have caused that?" Jake asked.

"We have a working theory—we can go over it a bit later. It doesn't seem as weird anymore, given the characters that have been dropped in," Matt grinned.

"Tell us more about your Chancellor, if you would?" Val prompted.

"He is the bravest man I know. We met a Commandant on our way along, and she was amazing. They clicked right away, perfect matches, but they weren't sexually compatible. At least, that's how it appeared on the outside. They pushed up against that boundary quite a bit. I felt like when they were together, along with our other two leaders, they were unstoppable.

That theory got pushed to the ultimate test when a robot left over from the old wars tried to conquer us. Our Chancellor, his right hand, a General, the Commandant, and her lover, our other leader—they led us on. I was right by them, the whole time. We lost thousands of people, but we won. The cost was high though," Jake reflected.

"You lost the Commandant," Matt whispered.

"Yea. Nothing was ever the same after that. We pressed on, but the nuclear reactors melted down, destroying the Earth. At least, that was our theory. Our part of the world was definitely wiped out. We survived because of our Chancellor. We lost him for a while. He went to space to survive the blast, he finally came back down and crashed in a pool of water we built for him. We found happiness again. But they never truly got over the loss of our Commandant," Jake finished. "That's my story."

"That's uh...quite a story," Jen whispered.

"Isn't he just a dream? He has suffered so much, don't worry, you will be safe with me now," Angel smiled.

"Wow, okay Angel," Val rolled her eyes.

Matt was grinning for a few reasons, but he just kept silent as they drove home. Jake was looking out the window the entire time, as Angel just admired him. Pulling into the neighborhood, they hopped out. Jake was still looking around, as Matt pulled Angel towards him.

"What is it?" Angel demanded.

"I know you don't care about me right now, but I'm just going to tell you, slow down a bit. He has literally never seen anything like this?" Matt waved his hand. "I mean no houses, no paved roads, no coffee makers, nothing. This is all completely new to him."

"Yeah, I get it. I will give him a huge tour, after I sleep with him. Loud and clear," Angel hissed, as she took Jake's arm and pulled him inside her house. Bozo came flying out the door, and she slammed it behind him.

"Wow," Matt sighed.

"Hey," Val smiled. "So..it looks like someone has been brought to life from a book series we know."

"Yeah, I wonder who wrote it," Matt grinned. "He looks exactly like the concept art I had drawn."

"I don't want to think about how many bad points I earned not reading your book series, but if this is the Puppetmaster's way of rubbing it in my face...I....I will accept it. Because Jake lives," Val rolled her eyes.

"I think that is the message they are trying to send, yes," Matt smiled.

"Matt? You wrote a book series? Like, a real series?" Jen asked.

"Yeah, six books and a short story. It's over 900,000 words," Matt grinned.

"Wow," Jen whispered. "That's a lot."

"It's absurdly long, I haven't read it, I accept my bad points," Val rolled her eyes. "I have a mental block on it."

"It's a lame excuse," Matt grinned.

"I see. Well then, I guess let's head inside and wait for the two lovers to join us," Jen waved them on. Bozo was heading their way, which was a mistake, as she kicked him as far as she could. He flew backwards, his arm came off as he hit the ground. Matt shook his head and ignored the toy; it was his own fault.

Entering the house, Carly greeted them, having been dropped off by Sam and Tali. "How are the two lovebirds?" she laughed.

"Currently loving," Matt grinned.

"Let's start planning out this road trip. Getting back to Austin will be easy, but getting into the downtown area could suck because of all the cars," Matt offered.

"We have a lot more people this time, so that will help. Angel can push cars easily," Val smiled. "Let me cook us up some food, focusing on things Jake has never eaten."

"Good plan," Matt grinned.

"I am even going to bake some cookies for him. Let's be clear, I loved Jake, he was one of my favorite characters, before I burned out of the series. So, the fact he is here makes me very happy. I know he isn't available, but I plan on getting very close to him," Val beamed.

"That's fine Val, I am happy for you," Matt smiled. "I liked him too. I wrote a book series that I became very attached to. So, yeah."

"You wrote a book series Matt?" Carly asked.

"And Val refuses to read it," Jen laughed.

"Bad points allocated to Jen!" Val shouted.

"Um, wow," Carly stammered.

Bozo was trying to open the front door, but was unable to. Jen had locked it. He was reduced to knocking. "Yuktrap! Where are you? Go open the door for Bozo. And yes, you may resume your fighting. You have a clear advantage now," Matt laughed.

Yuktrap had been in the kitchen and fist pumped, rolling over and opening the door.

"I am requesting...oh.." Bozo stopped and scowled, but it didn't matter, as Yuktrap yanked his loose arm out of his hands, and hit him with it, repeatedly.

"Go Yuktrap!" Jen cheered.

"Stop! I demand! That you! Stop!" Bozo shouted.

"Try surrendering instead, you are in no position to make demands, toy," Jen laughed.

"I give up! Please stop!" Bozo shouted.

"Okay Yuktrap, he surrendered, let him up," Matt waved. Yuktrap threw his arm into the yard and rolled back inside, leaving the door open and doing a twirl.

"This is all earning bad points," Carly offered.

"He deserves it for what he did to me," Jen shrugged. "All he has to do is admit he was at fault and apologize. No one will help him with that, however. Yuktrap, all you need to know is that he hurt me. Keep piling on."

Yuktrap gave a salute and rolled outside, as they heard the commotion. Bozo was shouting at him, demanding to be left alone, but Yuktrap apparently was not hearing it. Finally, Yuktrap rolled back into the house, closing the door. He wheeled to the back and opened the door, letting Buddy and Fred in.

"Where is the toy?" Matt asked.

Yuktrap waved his hands, signaling Bozo had run away. Matt accepted it and they sat down for lunch, hoping Angel and Jake would arrive soon. When they didn't, they decided to take lunch to them. Knocking on the door, Angel came to open it after a bit. Again, just wearing her robe.

"Hey guys. Everything okay?" Angel beamed.

"As long as you aren't Bozo the ex-Space Trooper," Val laughed. "We brought lunch. Is that okay?"

"Oh, of course. We were just lying down in bed, Jake had never seen a ceiling fan before," Angel laughed, letting them in.

"Well, the table is looking a lot more normal this time," Jen observed.

"What happened last time? We thought we heard shots," Val asked.

"You did, hence Bozo's condition. The Demon was here, with the Sunwalker, Sam and Tali. It was then we realized how off the rails this was getting," Matt grinned.

"I hope you aren't including me in that bunch of weirdos," Angel offered.

"Oh sure, exclude the witch hunter, because that makes sense," Carly laughed.

"Fair enough," Angel sighed, as she went to get Jake.

Coming back in, he offered greetings and sat down. "This is certainly quite the welcome wagon," he smiled.

"We have been doing this a while. Although, I think you are the first person to have sex this soon," Matt grinned.

"I will say nothing," Carly smiled.

"What is this food?" Jake asked.

"It's marlin fillets, with lemon juice. A side of Lays potato chips, and some cranberry sauce. Your drink is a cold soda. Even though it's not technically good for you, I know you have never had it before. And it does taste really good," Val beamed.

Jake was struggling with the soda can, and Angel helped him. He thanked her and took a sip. "Oh wow, this does taste good," he offered in surprise.

"We will have a bigger dinner tonight, I promise," Val smiled.

"So, Angel tells me it's almost Christmas? Do you guys think it will snow? I really loved my first Christmas on the ground. Our Chancellor... he nearly died from a certain snowball," Jake laughed.

"It probably will not snow, no. It doesn't really snow in this area. Has Angel shown you where we are?" Matt asked.

"No, I don't have a map handy," Angel shrugged.

"I am familiar with the geography though. What state are we in? I am assuming we are in the United States, I saw the flags. But I don't know state flags," Jake offered.

"Texas, the southern tip, close to Mexico," Val smiled.

"Oh, okay. Sure," Jake nodded. "This is really amazing food, by the way."

"Glad you like it," Val beamed.

"So, what's next for us?" Jake asked.

"We are going to drive north tomorrow, about four hours. The goal is to go Christmas shopping for each other. We are dividing up into teams, so it can be you and Val, Angel and I, and Jen with Carly," Matt grinned.

"I don't recall signing off on that," Angel cut in.

"You signed off on it yesterday," Jen pointed out. "We literally laid the teams out in case we got a new, contributing member."

"Oh, I forgot. I've had a lot of sex since then," Angel tried.

"Anyway Jake, it will be a good opportunity for you to continue to take in the sights. We know this is a lot, and Angel is barely helping, but we will break you in slowly," Matt laughed.

"I wouldn't even say she is barely helping," Val teased.

"Watch it!" Angel hissed.

"Thanks for the food. Um? Maybe Angel and I could go for a walk around the...whatever this place is called.." Jake tried.

"The neighborhood? Sure, go for it," Matt smiled.

"Would anyone else like to come?" Jake offered.

"It's nice of you to offer, there was no way Angel was going to, but no, we will let you two continue to acclimate," Val laughed.

"I...I promise to be on my best behavior tomorrow," Angel managed. "Thank you for the lunch. We will be sure to be on time for dinner."

CHAPTER 53

SHOPPING TRIP

The convoy drove north, Matt and Jen were in their truck, with Val, Carly, Angel, and Jake in the one behind them. They had just pulled out of Robstown, stopping to charge their trucks. They had agreed to shoot a deer, if one came into view. The Go Wild was in the back seat, having not been used for some time. Otherwise, it was straight on to Austin.

"So, your sister really likes him," Jen grinned.

"Yeah, she does. I don't think Carly or Angel need to be worried, but she is definitely happy he is alive, and here," Matt smiled.

"He has a pretty solid smile, as far as those go," Jen laughed.

"Yeah, he was a really likable guy in my story. Everyone liked Jake," Matt reflected.

"I'm curious about this book series. Will you let me read it? I think Carly wants to as well," Jen offered.

"Oh sure, we have it downloaded on the computer at home, I realize I'm barely holding onto it, but I can't publish it, so the computer is all I have," Matt sighed.

"Can you print it out?" Jen asked.

"It's over 4000 pages, it could take...days," Matt grinned.

"So what? I think you should print it out. We can figure out a way to keep it safe," Jen shrugged.

"Alright, maybe we can use multiple houses, multiple printers," Matt reflected. "Here comes our exit. We are going to stop at my old house, trade partners, show you all how boring I was, then split up."

"You paid for that house with your own money Matt. That's more than Carly or I can say," Jen assured him.

Pulling into his old neighborhood, he parked in front of his old place. Jen got out and admired it. The dead plants, the dead yard, it really stuck out. "Can we go inside?" Jen laughed.

"Sure," Matt shrugged.

The rest of the group piled out, smiling. "This is a nice house Matt. Don't let these rich kids tease you," Angel laughed.

"Thanks Angel, I am doing my best," Matt grinned.

Walking inside, the room temperature was probably in the 90s. Matt promptly walked back outside, where it may have been cooler. Val stood out there with him while they explored the interior.

"How is Jake?" Matt asked.

"He is doing alright. This is all very new to him," Val grinned.

"Jen wants to print out my story, any idea how to make that an easier process?" Matt whispered.

"Use multiple computers, just do one book per house," Val offered.

"Yeah, that's what we were thinking. You know what you are going to get Carly?"

"Pretty good idea, it's just a matter of finding it. What about Jen?" Val beamed.

"Couple of small ideas. And yes, getting there will be hard. We might have to just park the truck and walk," Matt shrugged.

"Traffic was probably still consistent enough to be annoying, and the offramps will probably be flooded. We will just go slow, we have plenty of food and water. And Angel's strength," Val smiled.

The group came back out, looking overheated. "I like your house Matt, but it's hot. Can we get going now?" Jen asked.

"Sure, let's go. Angel? Come on," Matt waved her along.

They switched vehicles and Matt led them out again, handing Angel a water.

"Thanks, I did like your house Matt. It looked like you and Buddy were happy there. I am here, by the way. I promised you I would be here today, and I am. Jake is really nice to have, but I know Christmas shopping is important to the group," Angel smiled. "Val was telling me he has memories of your book series?"

"Yeah, it's pretty weird. His memory seems to be completely intact, except for his name. Which, I mean that's better, clearly, but still..weird," Matt admitted

"As weird as a demon, a toy, a robot, and some vampires?" Angel laughed.

"Point," Matt grinned. "Don't forget to include yourself in that group. We are going to need that strength today."

"I'm here, as I said. What do you want to get Jen?" Angel beamed.

"She doesn't want anything glamorous I know that. I do want to get her a ring however. But I think she would appreciate a gift closer to her field. I just don't know what, I think we should head to a museum I know. Maybe a Native American theme, I'm not sure how much experience she has exploring US dig sites," Matt whispered.

"Okay, head that way, and if we have to get out and push...we will," Angel smiled.

They drove on, weaving around traffic, Matt just drove in the shoulder, deciding it was easier. Finally, they came to their exit ramp, and it looked rough. Stopping the truck, there were about 20 cars blocking the road.

"This is just as daunting as you said. Let's get out and shove them off the road," Angel offered.

"Where though? The pile-up goes all the way down the road," Matt lamented.

Angel got out and walked to the first car. She looked over the side of the road, and shrugged. Lifting the car up, she flipped it over the side, sending it crashing down below. Matt was thoroughly shocked, as she laughed at him.

"One down," Angel beamed. "Come on, it will be easier if you help me."

"R-Right," Matt stammered. They walked to the next car and lifted it over the side again, pushing it off the edge. It hit the ground and the alarm started going off, which was annoying. Continuing on, they pushed ten cars off the ledge until they were down to the grass part of the off-framp. They knew they could drive around those, so they headed back for the truck.

Driving around the traffic in the grass, Matt turned onto the road leading towards the downtown area. There were still a lot of cars on the road, and Matt parked the truck under a tree. There was a sign for their museum, pointing them in the right direction.

"You don't mind walking, right?" Matt asked, as he got out.

"Not at all, I have good company," Angel teased.

"Let me see if I can get the other team on the radio, just to check in," Matt offered.

"Val? Jen? Do you guys read me?" Matt transmitted.

"Yes Matt, just moving cars. How are you and Angel?" Val replied.

"We finished moving our cars and are going to walk the rest of the way, it's only a few blocks. Remember whenever you get to where you are going, take the guns. Jake knows how to use them as well," Matt pressed.

"Roger that, Matt. Good luck," Val signed off.

Matt took the shotgun out of the back seat and they started off. Angel took the flashlight in one hand, and his arm in the other, and they enjoyed the scenery. Austin always had a nice downtown area, and with no people, it was even better. Within ten minutes, they heard a dog barking behind them. Turning around, it was a wild dog, for sure. Just barking, not approaching.

Keeping an eye on it, they kept walking, as it followed. Matt didn't want to take any chances, as he raised the shotgun and shot over the dog's head. The noise didn't even bother the animal, as he kept approaching.

"Matt? Shoot it," Angel pressed.

"Yeah," Matt sighed.

He let the dog get a little closer and then pulled the trigger again. Turning around, they resumed their walk, she was holding his arm a little tighter, trying to comfort him. One of the few things he had not enjoyed about this ordeal was the dog killing.

Arriving at their museum, Matt asked Angel to do the honors. Again, she ripped the door right off the hinges, and they walked in. The emergency power was on, as Angel shined the flashlight. Looking at the directory, the Native American section was to the right, up the stairs.

Walking up the steps, it was a nice exhibit. "You thinking a spear maybe?" Angel offered.

"Yeah, I think a bow and arrow is lame. A spear would be nice. It's hard, I don't know what she doesn't have in her collection," Matt lamented.

"You are out here trying Matt, she will appreciate it. Look, here is one," Angel pointed.

Angel found a long spear complete with feathers and a tip. She picked it up and Matt nodded. Content, they headed back into the street.

"What's next?" Angel smiled.

"I want to get her a ring, but that can wait, I know where an open jewelry store is," Matt grinned. "Let's head to the shopping mall near here, there is a music store we can find, maybe it has some memorabilia. Queen is a little dated, but they might have something."

"Oh, is she a Queen fan? Yeah, that fits. England," Angel rolled her eyes.

"Is there anywhere in the downtown area you want to stop at?" Matt offered.

"No, I think the shopping mall will be fine for both of us. Let's get back to the truck," Angel smiled.

Arriving without incident, they stored their gear and Matt got the truck going again while Angel called Val.

"Hey Val? You out there?" Angel transmitted.

"Yes Angel. How's it going?" Val asked.

"One stop complete, heading for our second location now. How are you guys?" Angel asked.

"We have just arrived at our first stop. Any trouble to report?" Val asked. "Jen wants to know."

"Yeah, Matt had to shoot a wild dog, he didn't like it. Other than that, all clear," Angel replied.

"I'm sorry that happened. Good luck on your next stop. We will try to check in soon," Val signed off.

Matt navigated back onto the highway, going up the offramp they had cleared. The shopping mall was a few exits down, as he drove on the shoulder again. Arriving at their exit, it was a little less crowded, but they still needed to clear the road. Angel was happy to throw cars over the side again, as he helped her push them off. The alarms started blaring, but they pressed on. Finally clearing the road, Matt weaved them into the grass and down the road. The mall parking lot was empty, it had been closed when the people vanished.

Parking in front of the doors, Angel checked in with Val again, but there was no answer. She got the flashlight as Matt got the shotgun, and they entered the mall, the same way as always. Matt immediately recognized that there would be a problem. All of the stores were barricaded shut.

"Oh…well…this could get complicated.." Matt sighed.

"Why?" Angel teased. "Did you forget I was here?"

"Maybe," Matt shrugged, before smiling.

"Come on, let's go shopping Matt," Angel beamed, taking his arm.

Heading in, they made several stops. Angel lifted the barricade up for each store they wanted to stop in. Matt found a ring for Jen, a Queen poster, and some new clothing. Angel found predominantly clothing, but she also insisted on modeling some lingerie for him. He found it pretty awkward which just added to her fun.

"Why don't you like looking at me Matt?" Angel teased.

"Probably because you like me looking at you," Matt waved her off.

"I got basically all the colors, so if Jen or Carly wanted to match one night, it's definitely possible," Angel laughed.

"Jen has been pretty distant from the roleplay thing since her encounter with Bozo, she didn't like it, plain and simple," Matt sighed.

"I know, she told me about it. We are going to play soon though," Angel assured him.

"Is there anywhere else you want to go? If not, we will head south, back towards my place and the jewelry store. I think I can find a better ring there," Matt grinned.

"I'm ready. We got what, ten bags of clothing? Probably a huge bill, oh well!" Angel laughed.

"Yeah, thanks for your company. Thanks for being so willing to spend time away from Jake," Matt smiled.

"You are very welcome, Matt. I still enjoy your company very much. Having a boyfriend isn't going to change that," Angel beamed.

"That's kind of you to say," Matt looked away.

"Oh! Did I finally make you blush?" Angel laughed.

"Stooooopppp," Matt laughed.

Arriving at the truck, they threw the rest of their bags in and stored the shotgun. Matt tried calling Val again but there was still no answer.

"Hmm, I know you don't want to move out of range without checking in. Why don't we get our prepared food, and go back inside to eat?" Angel offered.

"Yeah, we can take the radio," Matt nodded.

———

An hour later, Val finally checked in.

"Hey Matt, Angel? You guys receiving?" Val transmitted.

"Yeah, go ahead Val," Matt replied.

"We just finished our first stop, moving on to our second now. How are you guys?" Val asked.

"We have finished our second stop, preparing to head south again. I'm not sure what the plan is just yet, one moment, let me talk to Angel," Matt replied.

"Any ideas? They have four people, so they are going slower I guess. Do you want to go anywhere else?" Matt asked.

"Why don't we go back to your old house?" Angel offered. "Turn the A/C on, use the kitchen to cook some of our food. Just relax."

"Okay, sure," Matt nodded.

"Val? We are going to head back to my house, we can use that as a rendezvous point. Whenever you finish up, meet us there. Let's say no later than seven?" Matt offered.

"Copy that Matt. See you soon," Val signed off.

They packed up the radio, left their trash on the tables again, and headed out. Matt figured that might have been bad points, but there were no people. The mice would appreciate it.

———

Couple of hours later, they were lying in Matt's bed, just relaxing. The A/C was on full blast, and they had both lost some clothes due to the heat. Angel hadn't teased him this time, it was legitimately hot.

"Want to get in the shower?" Matt grinned.

"Yes, but I don't have a bikini," Angel smiled.

"We don't have to shower together, you know," Matt teased.

"Where is the fun in that?" Angel laughed. "How about this? I will go get in, then call you when I am ready."

"Okay," Matt shrugged.

She stood up first, and walked into the bathroom. He heard the water turn on and got up to change into one of his old bathing suits. He looked around his room, he had liked living here with Buddy, but he didn't have any special memories. Certainly nothing like the last few months.

"Matt? Come on," Angel called.

Thinking this might have been a bad idea, he walked into the bathroom and opened the shower curtain. Angel had kept her bottoms on, but nothing else as she covered her breasts with her hands. Smiling, she couldn't resist teasing him again.

"I have a confession, Matt. I am addicted to feeling your eyes on my body. I think I will be able to kick it once I am with Jake, but for now, it's still you," Angel laughed.

"When did this addiction first start, I wonder?" Matt grinned as he stepped into the shower. The water felt good, as she approached him.

"The dinner I hosted. I needed that so much, and you did your job. We don't have to kiss, but I won't stop you if you want to," Angel grinned.

"Come up here if you want a kiss," Matt smiled.

"Oh you," Angel rolled her eyes and reached up on her tiptoes to kiss him. He got a good laugh out of it until she slapped him. "Get down here," she growled.

"Alright alright," Matt relented.

Almost three hours later, Angel was napping in the bed while Matt was cooking some food, when the second truck pulled up. It was good timing, as he was just finishing up the meal. The group walked in, asking for the food right away.

"Let's eat up and hit the road, I still need to make a stop at the jewelry store, but we can make it back to Harlingen before dark," Matt pressed.

"You, Angel, and Jake can go. The rest of us need a short break," Val waved.

Angel came in, giving Jake a kiss. "How was the city?"

'I've...never seen anything like it," Jake managed.

"You good to go Jake?" Matt asked.

"Oh yeah, I'm always ready," Jake grinned.

"Let's go then," Matt smiled, giving Val and Carly hugs, and Jen a kiss. He playfully grabbed her ass as she slapped him lightly.

"Be safe guys, we will radio when we are moving. See you in Robstown," Jen laughed.

CHAPTER 54

THE REFUGE

Matt was sitting at the picnic table at the Robstown rest area, as Jake and Angel were getting it on behind the visitor center. They had had some questions about what happened to the jewelry store entrance, but Matt just played dumb. Now they were charging the truck, waiting for the rest of the group. Jen had radioed they were about 30 minutes away. He was currently trying to figure out if he was looking at a deer under a tree several hundred yards away.

Deciding to check it out further, he got the Go Wild out of the truck and took it out of its case. Peering through the scope, it was in fact a small buck, about 400 yards out. They didn't have a ton of room in the tailgate, he would have to hit it in the head to reduce the bleeding. Loading the gun, he looked again, and the deer was still there. Taking a breath, he exhaled and pulled the trigger.

The gun fired, and the deer bolted. Letting out a sigh, he figured he had shot too high. Unloading the gun, he put it back in its case and closed the door.

"What are you shooting at?" Angel yelled at him.

"A deer," Matt yelled back.

"Did you hit it?" Angel demanded.

"No, I was high," Matt waved her off.

"Then be quiet, you are disturbing my sex life," Angel hissed.

"Sorry, won't happen again," Matt laughed. It was so amusing to him because Jake was accustomed to being with a sex addict, so this was nothing new for him. Literally everything else was very new, but this particular aspect of life was right up his alley.

Half an hour later, the second truck pulled up. Matt stood up to greet them again, offering hugs all around. Jen asked about Angel and Jake, seemingly the only one that didn't know exactly where they were.

"Behind the visitor center, of course," Matt laughed. "How are you guys? How was your shopping?"

"The cars were frustrating, but once we got inside our destinations, it was a success. You?" Val beamed.

"Angel threw the cars off the highway, so it was fun all the way around," Matt laughed.

"Of course, she did," Val rolled her eyes. "How high is your charge?"

"It was at 78% a few minutes ago. Does anyone want to come with us? We have one spot, I missed the deer so I didn't have to empty out the tailgate," Matt offered.

"Oh? You took a shot at a deer? How far?" Jen asked.

"400 or so yards. He was under that tree over there," Matt pointed.

"Your depth perception sucks Matt. That tree is over 700 yards away," Jen laughed.

"Oh, well that explains why I missed," Matt shrugged.

"I'll come with you Matt. That way you aren't by yourself when you get home. See you girls later, it was wonderful today," Jen waved.

They parted ways; the truck was at 85% now, enough to get them home. Matt honked the horn, and Angel and Jake came around the corner carrying their blanket. Exchanging hugs and eyerolls, they piled into the backseat.

Setting off, Jake continued to look out the window. "What are those?" he asked.

"They are cows, the primary meat dish for humans during this time. We have some at home, we can cook it for you. It's delicious," Matt grinned.

"There are so many of them," Jake whispered. "Are those horses?"

"That's right, those are horses," Angel smiled.

"Sorry, it's just...I've never seen anything like this," Jake grinned.

"You never have to apologize, Jake," Angel beamed.

"Let's do something fun tomorrow for him. I wish we could take him to a zoo, but we have plenty of wildlife refuges around here. The best one is Santa Ana, it's a birding refuge. Honestly, it will have species none of you guys have seen. Like the green jay," Matt offered.

"Is that like a blue jay, but green?" Angel smiled.

"Yes, that was a blonde moment, in case you were wondering," Matt laughed.

"How far is it, Matt?" Jen asked.

"It's west of us, towards McAllen. We drove to McAllen for the fourth electric truck, the road was pretty clear. It should be easy enough to get to. Maybe an hour, tops. Honestly, it's as close as the island, just the other way," Matt assured them.

"That sounds like fun, you up for it, Jake?" Jen smiled.

"I'm always up for something fun," Jake grinned.

"Okay then. Do you have any tricks to attract birds, Matt?" Jen asked.

"Just one. It always works," Matt smiled, as he drove them on.

———

The next day, as promised, Matt led the convoy into the parking lot of Santa Ana Wildlife Refuge. To their surprise, Sam and Tali had agreed to come along. Jake still didn't know anything about Sam, so they figured they would get it out of the way in the parking lot.

"Jake? This is Sam. He is our Protector. He does a good job. Doesn't talk too much, but he is being a little more social now that Tali is here. He is uh...you know, not human," Matt offered.

"I was about to say it was nice to meet you, but maybe you could run that last part by me again?" Jake smiled.

"Sam?" Val beamed.

Sam extended his claws, and Jake took a full step back. He watched as Sam cut his arm, and the wound healed instantly. Jake looked on, not believing it.

"So uh, can you explain that?" Jake managed.

"He is from another world, just like you. We have kept you away from our supernatural clown show, but Sam isn't the only aberration we have," Val laughed.

"For example," Jen growled, as she went to the tailgate and opened up a locked toolbox. Inside, laid poor Bozo. Picking him up, Bozo was too dejected to offer much.

"Is that a…. living toy?" Jake examined him.

"I am alive, yes. But I am not a toy. I am an ex-Space Trooper, beaten, half dead, wanting it to end," Bozo sighed.

"Bozo here crossed the line with me, and refuses to apologize. Therefore, he continues to suffer," Jen shrugged, as she put him back into the toolbox.

"Wait!" Bozo pleaded. "I am sorry for degrading you, Jen."

"Apology accepted. You are free Bozo, goodbye," Jen waved at him as she rejoined the others.

"Bozo, I actually have an idea that could fix you to 100%, we will try it soon. Of course, if it doesn't work, it really will be the end for you. In the meantime, stay here in the truck," Matt laughed.

They left Bozo and walked towards the park entrance, Jake still absorbing things. The green jays that were flocking around them cheered him up.

"Oh, they are beautiful," Angel smiled.

The jays had green bodies, blue heads, and yellow tails. They were much prettier than the more common blue jays.

"These are why I wanted to come, even I have never seen them," Tali smiled.

Matt heard the ever-obnoxious chachalacas singing from within the park, and knew this had been a good idea, despite Bozo's torture. "Come on, let's head inside. This is an expansive park, and we can take our time."

"Yes, let's go," Jen beamed.

Walking around, the groups had split up, and Matt was sitting with Jen on a bench looking out over the river. "I didn't know about Bozo, that seems pretty mean Jen. That's not good point territory," Matt whispered.

"He refused to acknowledge he did something wrong. Even Angel apologized for going too far. He claimed he knew how to handle female prisoners when he arrested us, yet he participated in humiliating me? No. I am completely okay with leaving him here with the birds," Jen shrugged.

"Okay, we won't do that, but I won't press it anymore," Matt grinned. "Are you having fun?"

"Oh yes, this was a great idea. The birds are beautiful. I'm glad this area has been able to endure the lack of humans," Jen smiled.

"I am too," Matt nodded.

A couple of peacocks were headed their way, apparently trying to establish their territory. Matt was pretty surprised to see them this deep in the park, but he had promised not to shoot any birds. It would have to be an extreme situation to do that anyway, but this was one of the scenarios he envisioned.

"Come on, let's get away from these two aggressors," Matt smiled.

Jen nodded and they resumed their walk. They spotted a couple of kingfishers sitting in a bush over the water. Matt couldn't remember their names, but he knew they were the ultra-rare ones, so he stopped them.

"Look, these are famously rare. I can't remember what they are called though," Matt smiled.

"It's okay. You can tell me when we get Val's bird book back," Jen smiled. "Thank you for pointing them out to me."

They continued to walk, spotting various birds, all fairly normal. The chachalacas were still as loud as ever, and even Jen had to laugh at them. It was a nice break for them, the shopping trip was a bit more challenging than everyone had expected. Coming back around to the visitor center, Sam and Tali were already there.

"How was your walk?" Tali asked.

"Wonderful. And yours?" Jen smiled.

"It was very nice, Sam won't admit it, but he has always preferred to be outdoors. Anything that allows him to be outside is okay with him," Tali grinned.

"That Jake kid, you said he was from a post-apocalyptic world? It seems like he has seen a lot," Sam growled.

"He has, we are trying to give him some peace," Matt whispered.

"Peace is what we all long for, Matt. If this…ordeal has given us anything, it's peace," Tali assured him.

"Not entirely. We still got that Demon out there, doing whatever. He doesn't hurt humans, but he is a weirdo, for sure," Matt sighed.

Carly and Val came walking up, followed by Angel and Jake. Offering greetings, Jake looked extremely happy.

"Hey Jake. Did you have fun?" Jen smiled.

"I did, yes. I have never seen anything like this. Animals were few and far between in my world, and at a certain point, they disappeared entirely," Jake smiled.

"Well, let's get out of here. You can take any mementos you want from the gift shop," Val laughed.

"I think I will do that," Jake nodded, heading that way with Angel.

"So, does anyone else think they found a nice place to have sex?" Carly teased.

"Angel promised she wouldn't, but he didn't," Matt grinned.

"I think they held off. We are cooking beef for him tonight, she will want him for dessert," Jen rolled her eyes.

"Let's get going. They will catch up," Matt grinned, as they slowly made their way back towards the parking lot. Sure enough, Angel and Jake caught up to them in no time. Jake had a stuffed animal in hand.

"Whatcha got there?" Val beamed.

"It's a hippopotamus. Inside joke, you wouldn't get it," Jake grinned.

"You would be surprised," Matt laughed.

"I have no idea what is going on, and I accept that," Val rolled her eyes.

"So, what's next?" Jake asked.

"Head home, regroup. Decide what to do. Christmas is almost on us, but I know you want to do things. I think you would really like the fishing, but we can't all fit in the boat," Matt offered.

"Oh, we didn't tell you, but Sam and I got another Gulf boat up and running. We found it in a dealership. It's in perfect condition, in the water, docked by the sea cottage," Tali offered.

"Oh, no, you did not tell us that. Thank you, guys," Matt managed.

"If that is the case, why don't we go fishing tomorrow morning? Matt, Angel, Jake, and Carly in one boat, Jen, Sam, Tali, and me in the other?" Val offered.

"I can trade places with you Val, I know you like Jake," Carly laughed.

"And I know you like fishing with Matt," Val countered with a smile.

"Why don't I take Tali, Sam, and Carly?" Matt laughed.

"Thank you, Matt," Tali offered. "Sam and I are capable fishermen, but we don't have a lot of experience piloting a boat in the deep seas. Clearly, you and Jen are the experts."

"Make sure you dress warmer, the water will be colder," Matt smiled.

"I have no idea what's going on, but I will be there," Jake laughed.

CHAPTER 55

THE NEW FLEET

Sam and Carly pushed the *Invictus II* off, while Angel waited for them to clear and pushed off their new boat, *The Hat Trick,* and they headed out to sea. Breaking into the Gulf, Jen pulled up beside them.

"*Last one to the second buoy cleans the fish,*" Jen laughed over the radio.

"*You're on. On three,*" Matt grinned.

They counted down and opened up their engines. The seas were rough, but Matt knew how to handle the boat and raced on. Jen drove her boat right into a wave and lost a lot of speed, as Tali just laughed. As long as that didn't happen to Matt, they would be fine. Jen relented and pulled her boat into Matt's wake, which was no way to win a race. Speeding past the second buoy, Matt eased off the throttle and Jen pulled up beside him.

"*You took that wave right to the face,*" Matt laughed over the radio.

"*I know I did. What is the plan?*" Jen asked.

"*We will leave the marlin to you, you have the superhuman. We will just fish normally. Give each other a wide berth, but stay within sight. Make sure your passengers take their medicine, the seas are rough,*" Matt offered.

Matt gave Carly the motion sickness pills, and she offered to share them with Tali. She declined, and Carly shrugged and put them away. Matt got the first artificial lure ready while Jen steered her boat away from them. Dropping it into the water, he offered Tali a smile.

"I notice you didn't take my advice, wearing a bikini and sarong," Matt teased.

"I wasn't going to be shown up by everyone else. We both have pants in there if we need them," Tali grinned. "I noticed that was the first time you looked at me however. I wouldn't think a young man like you would be able to resist."

"I have had a lot of practice learning to be a gentleman," Matt offered, as he dropped the second line into the water.

"An unnecessary gesture with me, I enjoy the empowerment," Tali laughed.

"The day is young. Who is up first?" Matt smiled.

"We will let Carly go first, she loves it, after all," Tali offered.

The first line started singing, and Sam got the other one in while Carly sat in the chair. She started pulling and immediately noticed how heavy it was. Tali helped her pull and confirmed it. Switching places with Sam, he helped her pull. Carly turned with the fish, but they knew it was a big one, as it pulled harder. Matt accelerated a bit, curious as to what they had.

Finally, the 10-yard ribbon passed and Matt got the gaff ready. Sam took it from him and nodded. It wasn't his first rodeo. He gaffed it and got it in the boat, it was a huge dorado, over 30 inches.

"Wow, that's a big one, nice job Carly," Matt smiled, as Sam got it in the bin. Matt dropped the other line in and Sam got the second one back out.

"Matt, we just hooked a big marlin. He is running your way—can you turn away from us?" Jen transmitted.

"Copy that, good luck. Who you got in the chair?" Matt asked.

"Jake, of course. Angel is standing by though," Jen laughed.

"Good for him," Matt signed off.

"Already a marlin?" Tali observed.

"The fish are abundant, no one is fishing for them. Look," Matt pointed. The line was singing again, as Sam got the other one in. Matt sat Tali down in the chair and signaled her to go for it. She was aggressive early, but eased off after a bit, turning with the fish, the way Carly had been.

"Too aggressive Tali," Matt encouraged her. "Don't reel against the fish when he turns away. Let him finish his turn then pull in the opposite direction."

"Thank you, Matt," Tali relented, taking his advice. She made steady progress until the 10-yard ribbon passed, and Sam got the fish in.

"Kingfish, a nice one," Matt nodded. "Carly? Can you see them? How far out is the line?"

"It looks like a long way still," Carly reported, as she looked through the binoculars. "Jake is still in the chair."

"Good for him," Matt smiled, as they prepared the lines again.

Before long they all had taken their turns in the chair, and Tali was back at it. Carly was looking through the binoculars, the other boat was close to landing their marlin, it had been over an hour. Sam got Tali's fish in, it was a nice wahoo.

"Oh, nice job Tali. It's a wahoo, a delicacy fish. Jen's favorite," Matt laughed.

"This is honestly more fun than I expected Matt," Tali smiled.

"I'm glad you are enjoying yourself," Matt grinned, as he got the other line ready. Tali put her legs up on the stern, wanting him to check her out. He obliged her, she was very beautiful, and she knew it.

"521 pounds, Matt. Jake is exhausted, but he did it all on his own," Jen laughed.

"We are all proud of him, Jen," Carly laughed. *"We have landed two big dorado, a king, and a wahoo."*

"Wahoooo!" Jen laughed.

Matt was cutting up the benito Sam had landed, and tossing some chunks of it in the water. He wanted a shark, but he wasn't sharing that detail just yet. Tali was watching him and he winked at her. Two fish later, and a lot of pieces in the water, the live bait line started screaming. The rod was bending heavily, and they all looked at it.

"It's a big one, who wants it?" Matt grinned.

"Oh I do. I'm not afraid," Carly beamed.

"Good girl," Matt laughed, as he hooked the rod to the chair and she started in.

"It feels like a whale," Carly laughed, as Sam helped her pull. Even he noted how big it was.

"I think we have a shark on the line, Jen. How are you guys over there?" Matt laughed.

"Good, we have landed about five fish. Good luck with your shark," Jen shouted.

The 100-yard ribbon went out, as the fish was diving. They weren't in deep water though, as it had to stop when it reached the bottom. Sam and Carly worked the rod, pulling and reeling him back up. An hour went by, and she could feel the fish still pulling hard. Sam traded places with her, and she caught her breath. Matt hosed her down, as Tali helped Sam pull.

Sam made a lot of progress, getting the 100-yard ribbon in, and continuing to pull hard. They could feel the fish tiring, as Sam continued to reel. Another 30 minutes went by, the 10-yard ribbon passed, and Carly took the chair again. Tali was slightly confused but Matt assured her everything was okay. Getting the gaff ready, Matt looked to Sam.

"If it's a shark Sam, right in the head with the claws, okay?" Matt pressed.

"Got it Captain," Sam growled.

Matt grinned at that compliment and they waited for the fish to come in. "Look, there it is. It's a big tiger," Matt pointed.

He gaffed it, and tried to pull it up, but it was too heavy. It didn't matter, as Sam leaned over and extended his claws right through the shark's head, killing it. Matt called to Tali for help and the three of them pulled it in together. Flipping it down, Carly couldn't believe it.

"Matt? What's your progress, we saw you landing it, what is it?" Jen transmitted.

"It's a 10-foot tiger, not sure about the weight yet," Matt grinned.

"Oh! Good catch! We have landed about 10 fish since you hooked it, what do you want to do?" Jen asked.

"We have a tiger and a marlin, we can go in now, or stay out a bit longer. How is Jake?" Matt asked.

"He will deny this, but despite taking the medicine, he is green Matt. Want to race in?" Jen laughed.

"We need a bit to secure this shark, but I'm sure you won't give it to us," Matt laughed.

Turning, Sam and Tali were pulling the shark towards the storage bin, and he helped them get it in there. "Okay guys, do you want to do a 30-minute count, or just head in now? Jen is probably already racing in. It's up to you," Matt shrugged.

"They are still cleaning the fish, regardless, right?" Tali laughed. "Why don't we catch one more. I would like to, at least."

"Sure, I'll get the line out," Matt smiled. "You good Carly?"

"Yes, of course. I'm tired, but I am used to this by now," Carly beamed.

Matt got the line out, as he looked to see what *The Hat Trick* was up to. They were actually heading towards them, as he got them going one last time. The line started singing quickly, as Matt slowed the boat down and Sam got the rod into the chair.

Jen pulled up beside them, seeing Tali was fighting.

"Hey! You guys decide on one more?" Angel shouted.

"Yeah, Tali wanted another!" Carly yelled back.

"How many fish you got?" Jen shouted.

"Five or six, plus the shark!" Carly yelled.

"Want to wager again on who cleans them?" Jen offered.

"Nope!" Sam shouted.

That caused Matt to laugh, he had never seen Sam that vocal. It even surprised Jen.

"Well, okay, have it your way!" Jen shouted.

"We will!" Sam shouted.

Matt laughed again, he could tell Sam was actually enjoying himself, as even Tali was laughing. The 10-yard ribbon passed, and Matt got their last fish in, a big yellowfin.

"You're still here!" Tali shouted at Jen.

"They are stalling! They want to follow my wake in, they have a sick passenger!" Matt laughed.

"You got us!" Val laughed.

Matt and Sam secured the boat, as Tali put her legs up on the stern again for them. Carly joined Matt in the front, and he gave Jen a signal.

She nodded back and Matt opened the throttle, racing home. Jen fell in behind them, and their escorts came. Tali was laughing as the porpoises jumped with them, riding the waves all the way home.

Breaking through the jetties, Matt slowed down and waved Jen on, knowing Jake needed dry land. She passed him and they all waved, as he moved their boat into the wake. Jen docked at the first pier, they had rearranged the boats a while back, putting the bay boat two docks down. Matt docked at the second pier, as Sam and Carly grabbed the pylons and tied the boat off. Jen and Angel were helping Jake out, he looked pretty weak.

Angel helped him to a patio chair, and sat him down. That wasn't going to last too long, they needed her help. Matt signaled Val to switch places with her, and she nodded and headed that way. Sam and Tali were pulling the shark out of the storage bin, as Jen handed the smaller fish to Carly and Matt. Finally, Angel came back to help with the marlin and shark.

She got gloves on this time, and they handed the marlin up to her, tail-first. She grabbed the tail and pulled it up with ease. It was another big blue marlin, as they smiled.

"We will get a picture when Jake is back on his feet. Come on, help us with the shark, we haven't even weighed it," Matt grinned.

Angel was surprised at the size of the shark—it was even bigger than the marlin. Sam and Tali handed her the tail, and she pulled it up onto the dock with ease. They were still surprised at her physical strength, but said nothing.

"How did you catch this? Were you fishing for shark?" Jen asked.

"I cut up a couple of fish, but I think it was a fluke, honestly. I was hoping for a blacktip or mako, but hooked this big guy instead. I think the lack of fishermen is really affecting marine life, they are more abundant, closer to shore. Come on, let's get it over to the scales, then Angel can go back to Jake. How is he?" Matt grinned.

"He started feeling the waves after the marlin, he said he had been in a boat before, but it was larger, and he didn't feel the waves nearly as much. He was also very afraid of getting into the water," Jen offered.

"Yeah, I know his background, I wrote it," Matt smiled.

"Yes...I keep forgetting that strange tidbit," Jen admitted.

Angel dragged the shark over to the scale, and tied the rope around its tail. Hoisting it up on her own, Jen read the news.

"*880 pounds,* wow. This will certainly feed us all for weeks, combined with the marlin, we won't have to go fishing again for a while. Just drive the boats on a weekly basis," Jen smiled.

"How are we going to handle the cleanup?" Tali asked.

"Val and Carly can wash the boats, then head to bed. Jen has to clean the small fish, after taking that breaker to the face," Matt grinned.

"Watch it," Jen growled. "You blocked me from seeing it until it was too late."

"I mean...if the wave had been coming from the other direction, the same thing would have happened to me. I can't control the waves," Matt laughed. "Sam, Tali, and I can work on harvesting the big fish. Angel can take care of her booty call."

The group broke up, Angel at least helped them get the shark over onto the filleting table, then headed back to Jake, who looked to be passed out on the lawn chair. No one minded, her strength had helped them enough. Matt got them some fillet knives, but Sam had already extended some of his claws and was cutting into the shark.

"Oh, you really can just extend just a few claws," Matt observed, setting a knife down.

"Should we cut the shark in half to make it easier?" Tali offered.

"No—" Matt started.

"Wastes meat," Sam growled.

"Yes," Matt nodded. "Despite the fact there is so much meat, no one likes to waste. We can each work on opposite ends, working towards the middle."

Tali nodded and Matt and Sam worked on the shark, as she made runs back and forth to the sea cottage. She also checked in on Jen, who was going through the smaller fish easily. The seagulls came quickly, waking Jake up. Whenever one landed on the perch next to Sam, it died. Matt just shook his head and grinned.

Jake and Angel came walking over, he still looked a little woozy, but he wanted to see what was going on. Matt greeted him, asking if he was okay.

"Yeah, I'm alright. What is this?" Jake pointed.

"It's a shark. A predator of the sea, this is a big one. I know you are afraid of what's in the water, but rest assured, these are very rare. In this world, the water is much safer. None of the creatures have mutated due to radiation. We will head to the beach soon, so you can see for yourself. Angel? Why don't you hoist the marlin up, so we can get a picture?" Matt smiled.

"You got it," Angel smiled.

"Oh, I can help you," Jake tried.

"She has probably been too focused on you to actually tell you she has enhanced strength; she can lift it all by herself. But she will remember the slime this time, and not get any on her," Matt teased.

"Thank you for the reminder, Matt," Angel glared.

She grabbed the marlin's tail and pulled it over to the weight scale, hoisting it up again. She motioned for Jake to come and stand next to her, while Val took a break to get the camera.

"What are we doing?" Jake asked.

"Taking a picture, silly," Angel beamed.

"He has never seen a camera Angel, give him a break," Matt laughed.

Val snapped the photo, and changed places with Angel. She wanted a picture with Jake as well. They finished up and Val said the boat was clean, and she was going to take a nap. Carly came up to Matt and offered a hug.

"This is my favorite thing to do here with you Matt. Thanks for getting me on your boat," Carly beamed.

"I always enjoy your company, Carly. And I noticed you wore your sarong the whole time as well. The other boat team all put their pants on, but not my ladies, for some reason," Matt smiled.

"I'm glad you appreciated it," Carly laughed, as she headed inside to nap as well.

An hour passed and they finally finished harvesting the shark. Angel helped them get the marlin onto the table, and then she and Jake headed inside as well. Jen had finished her fish, and was sunbathing in the patio chairs. Matt took the water hose out and sprayed her, causing her to laugh.

Another hour passed and they finished the marlin, in total they had almost 100 zip locks of fish. Tali was asking how many more zip locks they actually had and Matt assured her they had looted dozens of boxes and there were still dozens more out there.

"What now?" Tali asked.

"Let's load up the ice chests, collect Jen and head home. The other group can join us when they wake up. None of us took the medicine, so we aren't feeling the effects of it. They will sleep for another two to three hours, no sense in waiting around for them," Matt shrugged.

"Agreed," Sam growled.

Matt walked over and pounced on Jen, kissing her. She had been dozing, and just had to laugh.

"Ready to go home?" Matt whispered.

"We will have the house to ourselves," Jen whispered back. "Let's go."

CHAPTER 56

MOVIE NIGHT

"So, it's Christmas Eve, and in the Spirit of Christmas, we are going to try to make amends with Bozo, and fix him. Bozo? Step into the respawning device here," Matt offered.

The group was standing out beside the house, as Bozo the ex-Space Trooper stepped into the respawn device, still sulking, still silent. His left arm was completely gone, he had two large bullet holes in his helmet, bits of his right side were gone, and there were holes in his right wing from the buckshot. Some of that damage was completely undeserved, and they were going to see if they couldn't fix him for good.

"*Scan completed. You may now safely, or unsafely, die without worries. We hope!*" the voice sounded.

"Step out Bozo," Matt waved. "Stand over there."

Bozo stepped out and walked over to an open area. Facing the firing squad, he stood at attention.

"We think this is going to work, but if it doesn't, any last words?" Matt grinned.

"I did my duty to the best of my abilities. And Jen, I am sorry for degrading you. I should have stopped it immediately," Bozo declared.

"Jen, earn good points," Val prompted.

"I accept your apology, Bozo. Should this work, we will establish a fair punishment for you," Jen offered.

"Jen, try again. He has suffered a lot already," Matt laughed.

Jen relented, "I accept your apology Bozo. I hope this works, if not, rest in peace."

Jen raised the shotgun and blew Bozo into bits. Jake was looking on, confused about the whole thing. He was even more confused a couple of seconds later as Bozo respawned in the device.

"Welcome back, we hope you enjoyed your death," the voice sounded.

Bozo stepped out of the respawn device, completely restored. Looking at his hands, he couldn't believe it. "I'm…okay. I'm a Space Trooper again. I am a Space Trooper again! You there! What is the fastest way off this planet?" Bozo demanded.

He had been pointing at Jen, who shrugged and blew him away again.

"Jen!" Val shouted. "Bad points!"

"What? Was my answer not correct?" Jen demanded, only to break into a grin as the device hummed.

"We are sure that was just an accident. If not…you do you!" the voice sounded.

"Alright, let's try that again," Bozo declared. "You there, the one they call Matt, what is the fastest way off this planet?"

"Jen," Matt pointed.

Jen took that as a prompt and blew Bozo into bits again.

"Oh my God! Stop shooting!" Val exclaimed.

Jake came forward and took the shotgun away from Jen aggressively. "Whatever is going on here, we are done killing this toy," he pointed.

The respawn device hummed once again, *"Oh hey, it's you."*

Bozo stepped out and looked at Jake, who was holding the shotgun now.

"Friends?" Bozo offered.

"Yeah, friends. Listen, you can't get off this planet, so stop asking. You are a toy, don't be annoying," Jake pressed.

"I am not a toy, friend. I am Bozo Star Reacher, Space Trooper, sent to stop—" Bozo started.

Jake pointed the gun at him, "What was that?"

"For now...we are friends. But I am unhappy with being blown away after apologizing to Jen," Bozo glared.

"Well, you will just have to get over it," Jake shrugged, as he secured the shotgun. "Let's head inside."

"Scan complete, you may now safely, or unsafely die, without worries. We hope," the voice sounded.

They looked to see Val stepping out of the respawn device. "Better safe than sorry!" Val beamed. Matt rolled his eyes, but they all took the time to get scanned, before heading inside, followed by Bozo.

They found Yuktrap playing with the dogs, and he looked up at the women, then Bozo. Throwing his hands in the air, he charged.

"Look out! Hostile robot inbound! Have no fear, I am at maximum charge on my laser now!" Bozo declared, as he rushed forward to engage Yuktrap once again.

"Take it outside!" Val pointed, not wanting them to mess up the house. Yuktrap ran outside, and Bozo, smartly, slammed the door behind him.

"Threat neutralized!" Bozo declared.

"Wow, nice job Bozo," Matt laughed.

Yuktrap was pounding on the door, as Angel locked him out. Jake handed the shotgun to Matt who took it to their room. Coming back, he asked the group what they wanted to do.

"We could watch a Christmas movie, one that Jake hasn't seen...which is any and all of them!" Val managed.

"Nice save," Matt teased.

"Shut it! It was a nice save!" Val laughed.

"I've never seen a movie before, I would like that," Jake managed.

"How do we decide which one?" Carly asked.

"What is the musical where they are practicing at a ski resort? I have always enjoyed that one," Jen smiled.

"I don't think I have ever sat through the whole thing," Carly admitted.

"Me neither. Does anyone know what it's called?" Angel sighed.

"'White Christmas', I really like that one. We danced to one of the actors' songs already. Bing Crosby," Matt smiled.

"I have been saving something special for this occasion, I will get it ready. Matt? Will you set up the movie in the living room? Oh uh…I guess all of our parents' movies are back at our house," Val realized.

"It's okay, we can go get them. Jen and I will pick out a few. I'll let Yuktrap back in, explain to him the war is over, behave. Bozo? Behave, got it?" Matt pressed.

"I will!" Bozo declared.

An hour later, they were set up in the living room, each couple snuggling, as Val cooked smores over a portable smore maker she had looted from somewhere. Matt thought it was lazy, but a fireplace was too much work. And the smores were delicious. Jake's eyes were glued to the screen, as they enjoyed the experience. He started crying when the cast started to sing the title song.

"It's just as amazing as the first time I heard it," Jake managed.

"You have heard this song? How?" Angel looked at Matt.

"Read the books to find out," Matt shrugged. They had in fact, printed out all 4,000 pages and stored them in a safe place. And they were downloaded offline on multiple computers.

The movie came to an end and Jake asked if they had anything else. Angel took his hand and assured him they had hundreds of movies, then asked if anyone else had any requests.

"We can watch anything, honestly. I am very comfortable here with Matt. So, someone else will need to put the movie in," Jen beamed.

"'It's a Wonderful Life?'" Val offered.

"I worry about the themes of that movie and their impact on our current situation…but sure. It's over there," Matt pointed.

Val was voted unanimously to be the one to start it, as she rolled her eyes and switched the old school DVDs out. Angel made out with Jake while they waited, and Matt offered Jen a kiss as well.

"Whoa!" Bozo shouted, as Matt looked to see him flying through the air. Bewildered, he looked back to see Yuktrap innocently trying to hold a baseball bat behind his back.

"Yuktrap," Matt sighed.

"That does it! I can no longer tolerate this robot's presence. I will sit elsewhere!" Bozo declared, as he stood up and sat on the nightstand next to Matt and Jen.

"Must be feeling pretty good to sit so close to Jen," Carly teased.

"Hello Jen," Bozo offered.

Jen ignored him and kissed Matt again, giggling. Val finally got the movie going, after some booing. Waving them off, she sat back down on top of Carly and they resumed cooking their smores. It was 2pm, and Sam and Tali would join them for dinner at six. Then they would likely watch another movie, then retire.

"We are playing tonight," Jen whispered into Matt's ear.

"Oh? I look forward to it," Matt grinned.

"I thought you might," Jen smiled.

They sunk into their seats and watched the movie, once again Jake was glued to it, giving Angel almost no attention. She didn't mind, she had come around on the idea that he had never experienced their society before, only fragments.

Matt actually dozed off; the recliner was so comfortable. Jen kissed him awake and smiled. "It's ending," she whispered. Matt looked and sure enough the movie was wrapping up, Jake had been crying again. His body was asleep but he didn't want to move at all.

"What's next?" Angel smiled.

"What time is it?" Jen asked.

"It's a little after four. We have time for another shorter one," Val smiled.

"'Home Alone?'" Matt offered.

"I'm not going to be the one to get it this time," Val smiled.

"I couldn't get up if I wanted to," Matt laughed.

"Have no fear! I will complete this mission!" Bozo declared, hopping off the nightstand and running towards the stack of movies. Holding them up one at a time, they finally said he had the right one. Somehow, he knew how to operate the DVD player, and switched movies out. "I watched Val complete this task very closely! It is a delicate process!"

Yuktrap threw some candy at him, but he missed so badly Bozo didn't even notice. Completing the task, Val pushed play and the movie actually started. Bozo took his spot back on the nightstand and they watched. Jake once again was completely enamored with it.

"It's really adorable how much he is into this," Jen whispered.

"Well, I am just as into this particular position as he is, so there is that," Matt grinned.

"Oh you," Jen smiled.

"Having fun?" Matt teased.

"Oh yes, this is wonderful," Jen whispered.

"I don't recognize any of these actors, they are less famous than the ones we saw earlier, and those guys aren't even alive!" Val laughed.

"Joe Pesci is the biggest name in this movie. The kid flamed out," Matt grinned.

"Oh, I love him. We should watch 'Goodfellas' next," Carly smiled.

"I don't know if that fits the Christmas spirit even a tiny bit," Jen laughed.

"Not even remotely," Matt laughed.

"Shh!" Angel waved them off. "We can't watch if you are all laughing."

"What's the world coming to?" Carly shouted, throwing her hands in the air.

"Oh my God!" Matt burst out laughing. "That's great, perfectly timed!"

Even Angel was giggling, as she rolled her eyes. Val was bewildered, she didn't get the reference at all. They finally quietened down and enjoyed the movie once again. Matt assured Jake nothing with the family was relevant, he wasn't missing anything.

"'Goodfellas' is much better than this movie," Jen whispered.

"Don't make me laugh right now I have the giggles," Matt grinned.

"If I have to enforce a silent mandate, I will," Bozo informed them.

"If I have to stand up and shoot you Bozo, I will," Jen smiled.

"Oh...hello Jen," Bozo whispered, turning his attention back to the movie quickly.

"I think he is terrified of you," Matt whispered.

"Good," Jen smiled. "Bozo? Bring me a smore."

The Space Trooper stood up and moved to cook a smore for her, and as he was doing so, he started to burn himself. No one was paying attention until he screamed out as his hand fell off. Val rushed forward to save the smore, handing it to Jen.

"It's okay, it's just Bozo's hand," Val shrugged.

"Just—" Bozo started.

"Shh. We will kill you later," Angel growled.

Hours later, they were setting the table as Tali and Sam arrived with freshly barbecued beef. Thanking them, Matt asked Sam to kill Bozo. Without questioning it, he sliced Bozo vertically all the way through. Disintegrating, he came around and walked through the still open door, offering his own thanks.

"The side dishes are almost ready; everyone can start sitting down. Tali, Sam? What would you like to drink?" Matt asked.

"Oh, we will drink the wine with everyone else, thank you Matt," Tali smiled.

"Alright, here Val comes with the sides, let's be seated everyone," Jen beckoned them to sit.

Val had made macaroni and cheese, garlic bread, and steamed cauliflower. Things Jake had never eaten before would be the ongoing theme. As they sat down, Bozo hopped onto the table and Sam promptly killed him again, enforcing a 'no toys at the table' rule. He had to break the 'no claws at the table' rule but they were gone as quick as Bozo.

———

"So, how were the movies Jake?" Tali teased as she sipped her wine.

"Oh, they were very nice, I had never seen anything like them before," Jake managed, as Angel not so subtly knocked his elbow off the table.

Tali ignored the slip and continued. "What do you think of the way society…appeared to be, before it came to an end in your world?"

"Honestly it's everything we dreamed of. Our lives were hard on the Station, one child policy, any crime committed by someone over 18 was a capital offense and they were immediately sentenced to death—by sucking the oxygen out of an airlock," Jake sighed. "Even things like stealing a food ration, stealing medicine, punching a guard, the smallest crimes meant death.

It makes me really appreciate this meal right here. There was nothing like this on the Station, no meat, no bread, no wine. We did celebrate Christmas though, but nothing like this. We didn't even have trees," Jake whispered.

"It was a hard life, from the sounds of it. But you survived, got down to Earth, had a family. Now you are here, for who knows how long," Jen offered.

"Yeah, I hope I can get back to my people soon," Jake nodded. "Not that I am complaining about the company, but...I fought really hard to carve out a piece of land for my family. I need to get back there."

Angel was looking at him, as Jen gave her a look of concern. "Matt?" Jen offered.

"Yes?" Matt asked.

"Do you think Jake fits your medium theory?" Jen whispered.

"As much as you do. Killed people, that's it," Matt shrugged. "I think the Puppetmaster is sending some messages."

"How long do you think this...experiment...is going to last?" Jake asked.

"No idea. Right now, we are very curious about your title, the Last. Are you the last person that's going to drop in? If so, I mean, that's fine. We can't handle too many more weirdos. Or Yuktrap," Matt sighed.

Yuktrap gave his customary three waves in the air, as Bozo spoke up. "It's true, this robot is a depraved lunatic. Thank the stars he isn't able to speak, can you imagine how much his voice would grate against our ears?"

"Oh, he had a voice. We just ripped his voice box out. You are right Bozo, it's horrible," Val laughed.

"Bozo isn't much better," Jen grumbled.

"Hey, I heard that. Who said that?" Bozo grumbled. "Oh, hello Jen."

"Moving on, how is the food? Thank you for cooking it, Sam, Tali," Val beamed.

"You're welcome," Tali smiled. "All of the food is wonderful. Getting back to Jake, you wouldn't stay here if given the option?"

"No, again, no offense, but I have my people," Jake replied.

"I'm not offended. I'm not sure if Sam and I would stay here either," Tali assured him.

"We have never discussed the concept of staying here. We have always talked about following each other back to our own worlds. I'm not sure if any of us would want to live here for the rest of our lives. Although I think Matt could live anywhere with me," Jen reflected.

"Really Matt? Could you stay here with Jen for the rest of your life?" Tali asked.

"Absolutely," Matt shrugged. "There are still so many things we haven't done. I wouldn't enjoy it as much if it was just the two of us, but…I could make it work."

"It would definitely be harder with just the two of us. But if Val and Carly were here, I think we would be alright," Jen nodded.

"I've never thought about staying here either. I always thought about either going to Carly's world, or bringing her back to mine," Val offered. "I probably wouldn't be happy if we had to stay here permanently."

"I don't think it does us good to dwell on it, I think we should continue to enjoy each other's company and try our best to earn good points," Matt reflected.

"I agree," Val nodded. "No more randomly killing Bozo."

"That wasn't random," Jen tried.

"No more killing Bozo," Val reinforced.

"Very well," Jen relented.

"Thank you for your concern, Valerie! It is much appreciated!" Bozo declared.

"Quiet," Jen glared.

"Oh…hello Jen," Bozo looked away.

"We have dessert as well, if everyone is done eating," Val beamed. "I will get it."

Val had baked a strawberry shortcake while they were watching movies, and went to fetch it from the kitchen. Bringing it in, she put it in front of

Jake and Angel. Angel raised the cake knife and started cutting into it, serving it to everyone.

"This is delicious, another first for me," Jake managed.

"Thank you for the feast, everyone. We will help clean up a bit, then retire. Do we need to bring anything for tomorrow?" Tali asked.

"No, we have everything prepared. Marlin and shark are the main courses, we will do the same sides as Thanksgiving, maybe a few different ones, I don't think many people ate the stuffing," Val beamed.

"Hey—" Matt started.

"It takes more than one person to justify a single dish, Matt," Jen laughed. "The yams are probably being cut too."

"Hold on—" Angel started.

"As Jen says," Val laughed.

They stood up and started to clean off the table, as Angel led Jake back to the living room. She was comforting him; he was feeling pretty down. Of the entire group, he was the only one that had a family and kids. Having his memories intact was likely starting to weigh on him. Carly pulled Matt aside.

"Hey," Carly grinned.

"Hello," Matt smiled.

"I have been granted permission by multiple sources to join you and Jen at 10pm tonight. Got any requests?" Carly teased.

"Well, let's see. Did you pick up those new toys Jen requested?" Matt grinned.

"Yes. But I'm not sure who is going to be on top," Carly beamed.

"Me neither. Just don't wear white, okay? I know that's your color, but—" Matt started.

"I'm not wearing white lingerie, I promise," Carly beamed. "I will see you later Matt."

"That was weird," Matt sighed. Finishing loading the dishwasher, the group said their goodbyes, and Tali and Sam departed. Angel was still on the couch snuggling with Jake, as Val and Carly bid them goodnight and headed to bed. Checking the time, Matt saw it was after 8pm, and asked Jen what she wanted to do.

"Let's head to our room," Jen smiled.

CHAPTER 57

CHRISTMAS MORNING

Waking up the next morning, Carly nudged Matt. "Good morning. Merry Christmas, will you please take this armbinder off of me so I can go elope?" she whispered.

"Um, what?" Matt whispered, as he woke up. "What was that?"

"I asked you to take this armbinder off so I can go elope. You know that was the plan all along, right?" Carly grinned.

"Um, no. I did not know that was the plan," Matt admitted, as he sat up.

"Wait, so what do you think was happening last night, you goofball?" Carly teased.

"Just...fun?" Matt tried.

"It was a bachelorette party, oh my God you are such a guy," Carly giggled. "You really didn't know that?"

"No, I guess I never officially heard that," Matt shrugged.

"Unbelievable. Well yes, it was my bachelorette party," Carly laughed. "Did you have fun?"

"Oh, definitely. I loved it. What about you?" Matt grinned.

"Every. Second," Carly beamed.

"Did uh, Angel and Jen know it was your bachelorette party?" Matt asked.

— 478 —

"Yes, of course. You really didn't know—this isn't an act. You are completely clueless," Carly laughed.

"What about Val? Did she just get left out entirely?" Matt asked.

"No, but she wasn't going to do THIS with her own brother. She watched movies with Jake all night. That was the plan at least. Jake was supportive, he understood the situation. Apparently, you are the only one that didn't know what was going on," Carly laughed. "Now will you please set me free?"

"No, I will not. I think you have earned some spankings," Matt laughed, as he pulled her over his lap. She didn't object at all, instead just laughing as he spanked her. She barely winced as she couldn't stop smiling. Giving up, Matt started to untie her. Finally free, Carly stretched, not even caring that she had almost no clothes on. Leaning over, she gave him one last kiss.

"Thank you for the wonderful evening, Matt. You were amazing. Yes, this was our last time playing with me on the bottom, and I probably will never grind on you again, but I still love you as a friend and a brother," Carly beamed.

"I love you too Carly. You are family now, I guess," Matt grinned. "What if Jen and I elope? Will you do that again for us?"

"Okay Matt, that is the one instance when I would be fully available for anything," Carly rolled her eyes, as she put a robe on.

"Merry Christmas, Carly," Matt smiled.

"Merry Christmas Matt," Carly beamed.

Standing up, they got dressed and stepped into the living room, looking for signs of life. Seeing none, he headed to the kitchen to pour himself some juice. Carly made the Keurig go, and they sat down at the table to wait for Angel and Jen. They came out soon enough and exchanged hugs.

"Merry Christmas guys. If you can believe it, Matt here had no idea last night was my bachelorette party. What a guy, right?" Carly laughed.

"To be fair, I think my opening act threw him off the scent completely. It worked to perfection, he thought I was the theme," Angel laughed.

"It's true that Carly didn't seem to take on the role of the bachelorette at all, that's probably why I didn't suspect it. Not that I mind. How much of that was scripted out beforehand?" Matt asked.

"A lot of it, the plan was to always open with Angel on top of the two of us, then Carly submitting as well. The lap dance had already been discussed, Angel added some flavor to it. The only things that weren't discussed was when we broke up, but Carly was always going to decide what happened. Me ending up getting revenge on Angel was Carly's call," Jen laughed.

"Wow," Matt whispered. He was surprised Jen had been in on the whole thing as well. "How was Angel as a slave?"

"Oh, she was good. Very obedient, took her lashes," Jen laughed.

"How was Jen on top?" Carly smiled.

"She did well. If I was to make a comparison, I don't think she was as good as me, but I would like to think I was on fire," Angel laughed.

"You were on fire, Matt really empowered you," Carly beamed.

"And I love him for it," Angel smiled.

"Did you have fun Jen?" Matt grinned.

"I did. The only thing I didn't like was having to give her a lap dance, I don't know what I'm doing, and it showed. But given more opportunities, I think I will enjoy it more and more. Now, Matt and I are going to go have sex, while you go elope Carly. Angel? Be back in a bit," Jen laughed.

"Um, okay," Angel rolled her eyes. "Actually, can I come to add some more spice?"

"It's Christmas, so I will allow it," Jen grinned.

———

An hour later, they walked over to pick up Val and Carly, newlyweds. Offering hugs, Matt was in high spirits.

"Merry Christmas Val. Congrats on your wedding, you always said you would just sign some papers," Matt laughed.

"Merry Christmas Matt. Thank you," Val beamed. "You guys are radiating—did you have fun last night?"

"Yes, we did. How were the movies with Jake?" Angel smiled.

"Great, he held me in his arms and we watched 'A Christmas Carol', 'Miracle on 34th Street', and the classic Grinch, before I went to bed," Val laughed. "I'm glad you guys had fun. Let's get inside and unwind, some of you look pretty tired. How late did you all stay up?"

"Honestly I have no idea," Matt shrugged.

"I think we were up past midnight, for sure. We heard Carly—" Angel started.

"You heard nothing," Carly beamed.

"Past midnight, for sure," Angel laughed.

They walked inside, the dogs leading the way. Feeding them, they spotted Jake coming over with Yuktrap and Bozo. Offering greetings, Jake sat down at the table.

"Merry Christmas Jake. Can we get you a drink?" Val beamed.

"Uh, whatever you have, I guess," Jake grinned. "Merry Christmas to you guys as well."

"You holding up, okay?" Matt asked.

"Yeah, I'm good. You guys are all good people. I just miss my family, especially now," Jake sighed.

"I wish I could say I had a solution for you. I can only tell you what I have told Jen, if I could get you back to your world, I would," Matt offered.

"Yeah, I get that. Whatever is going on here, it has nothing to do with you Matt," Jake assured him. "Any big plans today?"

"Well, we are planning a feast, we just had a wedding, if you blinked you missed it, I don't even know if they got any witnesses," Matt laughed.

"Technically you need a witness to sign the papers as well," Jen smiled.

"Matt? Will you sign the papers later?" Val beamed.

"Sure," Matt rolled his eyes. "We also have gifts—we don't expect you to be there for that though Jake. We know you haven't had the time nor the inclination to Christmas shop."

"I can take care of the dogs, and the toys, while you guys do that. I'll be honest, Buddy here is just a constant, loving animal. Dogs were extinct in my world," Jake grinned as he petted Buddy.

"Yeah, you can love on him forever," Val smiled, serving him some orange juice.

"We will be right back Jake," Matt grinned, as he collected the girls and ushered them into his room.

"So, about Jake," Matt sighed. "He is really down."

"It sucks, what can we do about it?" Val asked.

"I think…part of the Puppetmaster's test has been to see how we can help people that are down. First Angel, then Jake. We didn't help Bozo at all, but I mean…that's a whole different story," Matt laughed.

"He dominated us, I think we helped him plenty," Angel smiled.

"Still, if the test has been to maintain the mental health of every single individual that drops in, our results have been questionable at best. Yuktrap, Bozo, the Nightwalker, Jack, who got scratched off the list completely…I think after today we should re-evaluate," Jen offered.

"All we would have to do to improve Yuktrap's quote 'mental health' is give him his voice back, but that would simultaneously crater everyone else's. I'm not sure what else we can do for Bozo, he thinks he is a real toy and he isn't. The Nightwalker, and the Sunwalker, are alive. That in itself is a big accomplishment, given their scarce food supply. And Jack is dead," Matt grinned.

"Anyways, Angel was difficult, but I think it's safe to say she is in a good place now," Val smiled.

"If not then it's a lost cause after last night," Carly laughed.

"I love you all," Angel beamed.

"Now we need to get Jake into a good place," Val finished.

"Right," Matt nodded.

"How do we do that?" Jen asked.

"I have no idea. Did you take him up in the plane like you said?" Matt sighed.

"Not yet, I'm planning on it tomorrow," Jen whispered.

"These vanities that we are giving him aren't going to do anything for his long-term mental health," Angel sighed. "Being part of the group is what saved me. We are doing everything we can to include him, but as he said, we are never going to be his people. He isn't going to let go of his family in a week, or a month."

"So, what do we do? Cancel Christmas?" Carly offered.

"Absolutely not. Forgive my newlywed wife, last night probably melted her brain," Val waved her off. "I just think we should scale down the gift exchange. Have it privately, throughout the day. Give him the things we got for him slowly. Watch some more movies, prepare for the feast," Val smiled.

"Cancel Christmas. I think that earned some spankings," Matt rolled his eyes.

"What?" Carly threw her hands in the air. "You literally just canceled the gift exchange. That's a big part of Christmas."

"I will deal with my other half later," Val laughed. "For now, let's get back out there. We don't want to make him feel like he is dragging us down."

"Right," Matt grinned. They stood up and headed back to the living room. Angel stopped Matt and Jen on their way out.

"Hey," Angel whispered.

"Hi," Matt grinned.

"Soo...whenever you guys want to play again, I will be there. I know you want your revenge, Matt," Angel beamed.

"Revenge for what?" Matt shrugged. "You didn't do anything I didn't want."

"Oh...I like that answer," Angel smiled.

"We both had fun Angel, I know Matt especially did. But I think we need to adjust the roles a little bit for next time," Jen grinned. "But...I liked your outfits. I wanted to wear mine, but the opportunity never came."

"This isn't how I expected this conversation to go. But as I said, whenever you want to include me again, I will be there. And I will not invite myself, or act inappropriately if I am not invited. I realize one couple already got married, and you two have sizzling chemistry. I just...really had fun last night. And I hope you both did as well. Even though you both just *said* you did. Okay, I'm bailing on this. Merry Christmas, let's go!" Angel shouted.

Walking back into the living room, Val was giving Jake some Christmas cookies she had baked, then retreated to sit with Carly. Bozo came in the front door with Yuktrap, issuing a report.

"All of the houses have been checked and cleared of rodents, there are no threats to report," Bozo declared. "Oh, hello Jen."

"Bozo," Jen replied, pouring herself some juice.

"Val? I am ready for my next assignment!" Bozo declared.

"We are going to need your help later cooking dinner, along with Yuktrap. Until then, you are free to resume your patrols around the neighborhood. Bye Bozo!" Val waved.

"Very well! Patrol initiated!" Bozo declared, running out the door.

Yuktrap threw his hands in the air, even he thought Bozo's act was way over the top. Retreating to a corner to sulk, the group moved on.

"I still don't understand the talking toy," Jake shook his head.

"Neither do we," Val laughed. "But if you treat him professionally, he will behave."

"What do we want to do now?" Jen asked.

"We need to drive the cars; it's been a few days. With six drivers, it will be quick. Should we knock that out really quick?" Val offered.

"Okay, sure," Matt shrugged.

Walking outside, they each picked a car and started it up, driving around the neighborhood. Coming back, they got out and drove the other five, with Angel packing in with Matt.

"So, how's it going?" Angel smiled.

"You are acting so strange today. What's the matter? Yes, I loved last night. No, I don't regret a single thing," Matt teased.

"I can tell you really mean that, I still worry a little though. You can't blame me, I was literally grinding on you while you sucked on my boobs," Angel waved.

Breaking into a giggle, she couldn't contain herself. "It was great though, wasn't it?"

"Yes, every moment. But I think we need to stop talking about it after this last conversation. I mean that. Until then, what was your favorite part?" Matt grinned.

"It's so hard, because Carly's lap dance was amazing. But it has to be grinding on you. It has to be," Angel conceded. "Yours?"

"Carly's lap dance for me was amazing. But I also enjoyed being under your power. Your strength really adds to the roleplay. Those lashes were really hurting. I think when you gave me my hands and I was groping you while you grinded was my favorite," Matt laughed.

"It's addicting, it is. I think we need to take a healthy break before doing anything like that again," Angel laughed.

"I would just say to continue to follow the one rule: Everything goes through Jen. Don't get me wrong Angel, as much fun as it was, I still love Jen very much. And I will never cheat on her," Matt pressed.

"I realize that. I promise I am not going to do anything stupid, just know that I appreciate everything and let me know if you need anything. Looks like we are home," Angel grinned, hopping out.

Matt shook his head, trying to think of ways to get them off the topic of last night for good. Maybe install some consequences for bringing it up. Consequences that involve Yuktrap and/or Bozo. He got out of the car and walked back towards their house, finding Sam and Tali waiting.

"Oh, hey guys. Merry Christmas," Matt offered.

"Merry Christmas Matt," Tali smiled, handing him a bottle of tequila.

"Merry Christmas Matt," Sam growled.

"We understand there was a wedding this morning?" Tali chided him.

"If you are going to complain about not being invited, no one was there for it, Tali. They signed some papers and that was it," Matt laughed.

"I guess I can accept that," Tali waved. "What is the plan for tonight?"

"We are having another black-tie feast. It's at 5pm. Uh, I think the newlyweds are hosting, and the theme is red, green, and gold. That's all I got," Matt offered.

"I would like to prepare my own dish for the group, but I need a list of ingredients, who do I see about that?" Tali smiled.

"Look," Matt pointed at a clipboard on the wall. "Val has made an inventory of everything we have, and what houses they are in. If you are missing something, we can try to assist. It might mean you have to go out in the world and find it though."

"Oh, I see. Thank you Matt. Where are Val and Carly? I want to congratulate them before we depart," Tali asked.

"I think they are in their bedroom," Matt replied.

Tali headed that way while Sam picked up the clipboard and inspected it. "Hey Matt?" Sam growled.

"Yeah Sam?" Matt asked.

"I think the Demon is back in town, keep an eye out," Sam growled.

"We haven't seen him in a while, I wonder what he has been up to," Matt shrugged.

"No idea. But you might want to hide Bozo," Sam growled.

"Is that a joke, Sam?" Matt grinned.

"Maybe," Sam allowed himself to grin.

Tali came back and they headed out, promising to see them later. Jake came walking up cautiously, asking about them.

"What's their story, exactly?" Jake asked.

"It's a pretty long one. You can ask them over dinner for specifics if you want. Sam doesn't talk much, but Tali will I'm sure," Matt shrugged. "How are you?"

"I'm good. What's the plan now?" Jake asked.

"I have no idea," Matt shrugged. "I am just going with it today."

"Do you mind if I put some music on?" Jake asked.

"Go ahead, Val has the Christmas playlist up, but you can play whatever you want," Matt pointed to the jukebox. "Has she shown you how to use it?"

"Yeah, thanks Matt," Jake grinned.

Jake started some music, then sat down with Buddy and Fred. They seemed to sense his sadness, and were content to try to cheer him up seemingly forever. Matt drifted into his own room, looking for Jen. She was sitting in the recliner, sipping some hot apple cider.

"Hey, how's it going?" Matt whispered.

"Oh, I'm good Matt. Come sit with me," Jen smiled.

Matt sat down on the recliner, as she sat on his lap. He deployed the footrest and they bucked backwards, getting comfortable.

"How are you recovering from those lashes?" Matt whispered.

"Those were the hardest things to endure," Jen whispered. "My boobs have stripes on them. How is your chest?"

"Stripes as well. She was really into it. How are you feeling about it, for real?" Matt whispered.

"Honestly, I was having a great time. If it had just been me and Angel, I probably would have loved it even more. But your presence was throwing me off, and the things she was doing to you...let's just say they won't be happening again anytime soon, if ever," Jen grinned.

"You mean the grinding?" Matt grinned.

"Yes, she was so into it, it was crazy. I know you were having fun, but the way she was moving her body, it was a little too much for me. But when we split up, I was having fun. And then Carly just slammed the door in her face. She couldn't believe it, but she honored her word, she switched places with me. I let her boobs have it, believe me," Jen laughed.

"I do," Matt smiled. "You want to exchange a couple of gifts while we have time?"

"Yes. Let me get yours out of my closet," Jen grinned. Standing up, she walked over to the walk-in closet while Matt dug his gift out of the nightstand. Coming back, she had it wrapped up in a blanket, which was a popular theme this year. They couldn't find wrapping paper anywhere, just not the right time of year when all the people vanished.

"Alright, I will go first, okay?" Jen beamed.

"Sure," Matt smiled.

"How many gifts did you get for me?" Jen laughed.

"Three," Matt nodded.

"Hmm, well this is your first one," Jen teased, unwrapping it and revealing a long nodachi. "This is a genuine Japanese made nodachi, the sign said it was from 1975, but I think they got the century wrong," she stifled a laugh.

"Really? Off by that much? Us Americans," Matt laughed, standing up.

"Hopeless I tell you," Jen smiled. "Here, pull it out, I will hold the sheath."

Matt pulled the sword out, it seemed impossible for one person to draw it traditionally. It was well over six feet long, taller than most people.

Certainly taller than any Japanese warriors from the Sengoku period. "How did they draw these weapons in combat?" he asked.

"They didn't. These swords were not designed for hand-to-hand combat, they were strictly designed for morale and intimidation purposes," Jen smiled.

"I have always wanted one, where did you find it?" Matt whispered, admiring the blade.

"A Japanese antique store. They listed it at $1,000 dollars, Val said it was too expensive for the average person. It's not high quality, but I know you will understand," Jen nodded.

"Oh, yes. Thank you Jen—I love it," Matt grinned.

"You're welcome," Jen smiled.

"Here, I have your first gift," Matt picked up the ring and handed it to her. Opening it, it was a big sapphire.

"Oh, my birthstone. It's beautiful. I love both of our birthstones. I have...um...I have dug for them both," Jen looked away.

"What's so embarrassing about that? I have never seen uncut jewels of any kind. Much less rubies and sapphires. I hope it fits you, if not, I grabbed multiple sizes," Matt grinned. "Resizing is currently out."

"Yes," Jen nodded, as she allowed him to slip the ring on her finger. It was a little snug, but there was nothing they could do about it.

"Do you think a size up would be too big?" Matt whispered.

"Oh, definitely. It would fall right off. I will take care of it, Matt, I promise," Jen assured him.

"Well, if not, there are plenty of jewelry stores out there," Matt grinned.

"Very true," Jen rolled her eyes. "Come on, let's go mingle some more."

They headed for the living room, and found Carly approaching their door as they came out.

"Oh, hey Officer Carly," Matt beamed.

"Quiet!" Carly hissed and pushed him back into his room, before breaking into a laugh. "You are the worst."

"I accept that," Matt shrugged. "Whatcha got there?"

"Just a gift bag, a memento, of sorts, for you two. There is no message other than Merry Christmas, don't stop having fun," Carly beamed.

"That seems like a message to me, but okay," Jen teased.

"You both are the worst," Carly rolled her eyes. "Here, take it Matt."

"Thanks Carly. I do have something for you, but I will dig it out later, if that's okay," Matt offered.

"Of course," Carly smiled.

Matt pulled the armbinder out of the bag and laughed. Jen just rolled her eyes and took it, tossing it into her closet. "Thank you, Carly. My review of that thing is a glowing success. It worked perfectly, there was no escaping it," Jen shook her head.

"I know, I slept in it," Carly beamed.

"Good," Jen laughed.

"I have to figure out a way to bury this topic, maybe make the punishment for bringing it up a lap dance for Yuktrap," Matt reflected.

"Seems like it would be effective," Carly laughed, leading them out into the living room. Jake was sitting on the couch with Angel, listening to Christmas carols, petting the dogs. Val was in the kitchen, and they went to touch base with her.

"Hey, do you need any help?' Matt asked.

"I'm just doing the pie right now, but if you want to start cooking the meat, you can grill it outside. We gathered a bunch of lawn chairs, so we will all join you at some point. Jake might want to leave the door open so he can hear the Christmas music though. I do think he is enjoying the entertainment aspect of our society," Val smiled.

"I think it's really early to start grilling the meat. I only expect it to take an hour, maybe a little more. But...I mean I guess I can," Matt shrugged. "Make sure to put Yuktrap to work, he actually is good at helping."

"I thought about giving him his voice back for Christmas," Val teased.

"Yeah? How long did you think about that?" Matt laughed.

"One second," Val laughed.

Yuktrap threw his hands in the air and went to a corner to sulk. Again, he garnered no sympathy at all.

"Do we have any idea what Tali is bringing?" Val asked.

"None whatsoever. But she knows what we are eating, so she will make sure her dish complements the food," Matt shrugged.

"Head outside, fire up the grills, I will have Yuktrap bring you zip locks and platters. Oh, Carly? Can you make some margaritas for us all?" Val smiled.

"Coming right up," Carly beamed.

CHAPTER 58

CHRISTMAS DAY

Matt was grilling the shark meat, as the others were outside drinking their margaritas, another first for Jake. Val had given him a small glass, and he quickly understood why.

"This is so good, but I am already feeling it," Jake grinned, as he set his half empty glass down.

"Hence the small glass," Val beamed.

"Right," Jake relented, as he continued to pet Buddy, who was teaching him the game of fetch. Yuktrap was also trying to convince Jake to throw the ball, using hand gyrations. "Go away Yuktrap," he waved.

"Just throw the ball for Buddy, that's the game," Angel laughed.

"Oh, yeah," Jake relented, tossing the ball. Buddy and Fred were fighting for it, but Buddy was much faster. "It's way warmer here than I am used to this time of year."

"Where was your home, Jake?" Angel asked.

"Old South Carolina. Oh...well I guess it's not that old to you guys," Jake sighed.

"It's pretty much the same concept," Val nodded.

"We were spread out, I would say a 100-mile radius between all of our locations, but we didn't venture out of that area. Mainly because it was a wasteland," Jake reflected.

Matt put some pieces of the shark on the top rack and took some more from Yuktrap, who had brought him some fresh ones. Jen was eyeing the time—it was slowly approaching the point where she had to go get ready. She had a nice green dress picked out; it didn't match her new ring but that was okay.

"You two gonna go on a honeymoon?" Jen asked.

"We are thinking about places we could go. Any ideas?" Val smiled.

"You could go south, to Mexico. Maybe see some Aztec ruins. We haven't done that yet. I could pull up a map, see where the closest ones are," Jen offered.

"That's a great idea, we hadn't even thought about Mexico, despite it being right there. I guess the old cartel situation down there has caused my brain to delete Mexico," Val beamed.

"I know it's getting close to my time to go—I am going to borrow Matt for a bit. Can someone take over the grill?" Jen smiled.

"Sure, go ahead," Val waved them off.

Matt rolled his eyes and followed her into their room. She turned around and kissed him lightly. "You know what I want to do?" she teased.

"I have some guesses," Matt smiled.

"I want to...you know....reenact some of last night," Jen whispered.

"Ah, you want the grinding," Matt realized.

"Yes," Jen laughed. "Angel looked like she was loving it, and I know Carly did it later, at your encouragement. I want that feeling."

"Angel was absolutely loving it, she told me several times," Matt grinned, as he got his shirt off and lay down.

Jen took her shirt off as well, then her pants, pouncing on him. "I'm a little jealous, you sucked on their tits before mine, but we are going to fix that," she laughed. Leaning down, he sucked on her breasts while she started to grind on him. "Okay, yes, this feels amazing."

"Mm," Matt smiled, as he continued to grab her ass as she moved her hips, grinding away.

"Okay, I didn't need long to know. It's time for the real thing," Jen laughed, as she pulled his shorts down.

———

An hour later, Matt was back on the grill, as the girls had all retreated to get partially ready. It was just him and Jake with the dogs and Yuktrap.

"Can I ask you something?" Jake offered.

"You want to know how I know so much about you," Matt observed.

"Yeah," Jake nodded.

"It's a complicated story. Val made a video, but it might not help you as much. Everyone except for Val and I is from a different world than us, worlds we believed to be fictional. That includes you. We are vaguely familiar with all those worlds, including yours. Someone is messing with our memories. There is a certain point in your life where I picked up your story, and it went for about four or five years. That's it," Matt shrugged.

"So, you saw me hit the ground, you saw the battle against the Natives, the robot, the meltdown, and that kid that massacred the village," Jake reflected.

"Yeah, and I know how bad you feel about that," Matt nodded. "I am also aware of the kid that blew up those peace talks, putting your entire people on a path of war."

"I feel bad about that too," Jake sighed.

"Why? That was all him, you told him to stay at the base, he ignored you, started shooting. Just like the kid that opened up in the village. No one told them to start shooting, they just did. Because a bunch of kids have no business carrying guns around. And yes, I know how much your Chancellor hated being called a kid, but I wasn't referring to him. I am talking about the two kids that blew up your chances at peace," Matt pressed.

"He was on me for the second kid," Jake sighed.

"Yeah, he was. But he forgave you. Completely. You were by his side for the fight against the robot. He wouldn't have let you be there if he didn't trust you," Matt offered.

"You seem to know exactly what to say to make me feel better," Jake observed.

"Yeah well, I have had practice," Matt grinned. "Can I ask you something now?"

"Sure," Jake replied, tossing the ball for the dogs.

"Would you sacrifice us to get back to your people?" Matt asked.

"What do you mean, sacrifice you? Like, kill you?" Jake asked.

"I mean if you were given the chance to get home, but you had to delete us, or yes, kill us, would you do it? There are only what? Twelve of us?" Matt asked.

"It wouldn't matter if there was just one of you. The answer is no, I would not," Jake pressed.

"No hesitation," Matt observed.

"Those days of choosing who lives and who dies are over for me. And my people. Every life matters. I couldn't look at my wife, or my friends, if I had to choose death for one people to get back to mine. I don't know what's going to happen here, or if I will ever get home, but I am not falling back into the darkness," Jake finished.

"Seems like I wrote a good character," Matt whispered to himself.

"What's that?" Jake asked.

"Nothing," Matt grinned, handing some fillets to Yuktrap, who carried them inside. Val came out and waved him into the kitchen.

"Hey Jake? Can you watch these fillets? Val is calling," Matt asked.

"Yeah, I've got it Matt," Jake nodded, standing up.

Matt walked into the kitchen and asked what she needed. "I am making the cornbread, but I need you to start baking the macaroni dish. We uh, we are kind of winging it, but I am confident," Val smiled.

"No problem. How are the other preparations coming?" Matt asked.

"Oh, Carly is getting fully ready, except for the dress. So is Angel. I'm sure Jen is you know...on step 12 of 300. Is there a particular step she really focuses on?" Val laughed.

"Eye shadow, for sure," Matt grinned.

"How is Jake doing?" Val asked.

"He uh...he is a well written character," Matt smiled.

"He won't burn us to get home," Val observed.

"Not in a million years. He fell into the darkness with his people, and they cut their way out of it. And he will never go back," Matt finished.

"Well, that's good to know. Too bad we can't say the same for that Demon, or the Sunwalker, or the Nightwalker. But, at least Jake won't burn us," Val beamed.

"The Nightwalker is the one I worry about. The Demon..he is the kind of guy that does the exact opposite of what people of authority want. The Sunwalker, I don't think he would burn us to go back to a world with vampires. But the Nightwalker..I mean who knows," Matt sighed. "How do you think this macaroni is cooked? Bake it in the oven from scratch?"

"I honestly don't know. I don't think the noodles will cook that way. If it doesn't work, we can just scrap it, there will be plenty to eat," Val assured him. "But I would boil them normally, then bake them in the oven with all the cheese."

"Okay," Matt shrugged, throwing a pot of water on the stove.

"The cornbread is going, the timer is on, keep an eye on it. It's very easy to burn, so if you aren't sure, take it out and inspect it. I am going to continue getting ready. We are just barely crossing the two-hour mark, so you don't need to make your green beans yet," Val offered.

"Okay, see you soon," Matt smiled.

Walking back outside, Jake had flipped the shark a few times, admitting he wasn't entirely sure what he was doing. Matt cut into the shark and told him they were good to go, and he gave the plate to Yuktrap.

"When you get back home you will have quite a story to tell...if you keep your memories," Matt grinned.

"What do you think the chances are of that?" Jake smiled.

"No idea, you were the only person that remembered their name. So, it's anyone's guess at this point," Matt sighed.

"You are worried about the final results, aren't you?" Jake whispered.

"Yeah, I am," Matt sighed. "I have no idea what's in store for us, there is nothing I can do about it, and I'm scared."

"I had a friend that told me if you were scared, it meant you were alive," Jake reflected.

"Did your friend ever get scared?" Matt grinned.

"I think a few times, yes. But really, the guy didn't show it. He just walked straight into the jaws of death and laughed. Cutting through to the other side, every time," Jake shook his head.

"Seems like a good guy to stick close to," Matt whispered.

"Yeah, everyone wanted to be around him, at all times. I don't know how he did some of the things he did. I hope to see him again someday," Jake reflected.

"I'm sure you will," Matt grinned.

The timer on the oven was beeping, and Matt headed inside to check the cornbread. Unsure if it was done, he took it out for a moment. Depositing the macaroni noodles into the boiling pot, he took a better look at the cornbread, seeing it wasn't quite the golden brown he wanted. Sticking it back in the oven, he reset the timer and walked back outside.

Angel stuck her head out of her bedroom door, she was using it today, instead of going back to her own house. "Matt? Do you need anything?"

"Maybe those red boots?" Matt teased.

Angel closed her door quickly, and Matt just laughed. They were on the marlin now, as Matt put the fillets on the grill. "We should go parasailing again. I think you would really like that," Matt offered.

"What is it?" Jake asked.

"It's when we put a parachute on you, and hook you to a rope on a boat. We let you ascend into the air, and pull you along. It's almost like flying," Matt smiled.

"That does sound really amazing," Jake admitted.

Bozo hopped over the fence and approached them. Matt was surprised he had figured out how to get over the fence.

"Matt, I am reporting a suspicious person lying on a roof about four blocks from here," Bozo declared.

"Yeah? What's he look like?" Matt asked.

"He is the same person that blew my arm off and nearly killed me!" Bozo shouted.

"Why don't you just say that then, instead of a suspicious person?" Matt sighed. "What's Damien up to?"

"He is lying on the roof, staring up at the sky," Bozo declared.

"Okay, thanks for the update, Bozo. Keep an eye on him for us," Matt waved him off.

"I will!" Bozo declared, running off.

"So, the Demon Damien is around? What is he up to I wonder?" Jake asked.

"It's literally anyone's guess. Wouldn't shock me if he was here for food and a booty call," Matt grinned.

The oven beeped at him again and he went to get the cornbread out for good. Stirring the macaroni, it was done, so he got it in the baking pan and added all the butter and cheese Val had set out. Hoping it would work, he stuck it in the oven. It was also time for the green beans, so he prepped those and got them in the oven. Carly came in to check on him, and he assured her everything was under control.

"Okay, why don't you and Jake get ready, and Val and I will take over," Carly pressed.

"Sure Carly. The marlin is almost done, let Jake and Yuktrap finish it then tell him to go get ready. Angel is helping him, right?" Matt asked.

"Yes," Carly nodded.

Matt nodded and headed for his room. Offering a soft knock then walking in, Jen was sitting at the vanity. Her green dress was hanging on the door, and she asked how much time.

"45 minutes, gonna be ready?" Matt grinned.

"Yes, of course," Jen smiled. "How are you?"

"I'm good. Looking forward to dinner. Apparently, Damien is lying on a roof a few blocks down, no idea why. Maybe he is waiting for his booty call," Matt laughed.

"Seems like a solid plan on his part," Jen nodded. "I had a question for you, Matt."

"Oh? What is it?" Matt asked.

"I know no one in this house seems to be good at this. But, would you like to sign some papers with me tonight?" Jen whispered.

"That is a pretty rough proposal, just so you know," Matt teased. "But the answer is still yes. I would like that. I don't have any rings though."

"We can go get some tomorrow," Jen smiled. "And I know it was a rough proposal. But I heard about the proposals in your books, I don't think it was that bad."

"I would agree with that, barely," Matt laughed.

"I do love you Matt. You know that," Jen assured him.

"I love you too, Jen. And we had our bachelorette party, although Carly promised me that she would be available for another one. Maybe we should sign those papers in two days, so we can capture them both," Matt teased.

"Fully onboard with that," Jen laughed. "For now, we are engaged."

"I accept that," Matt smiled.

"Start getting ready," Jen chided him.

"I am," Matt nodded.

CHAPTER 59

CHRISTMAS DINNER

Matt and Jen walked out of their room, Jen in a dark green dress with some gold trim on the top, and Matt in a red dinner jacket. It was his least favorite color, but he could make an exception for Christmas, and Val's wedding day. Val and Carly were waiting to receive them last, as always. Val in a new red dress, and Carly in a matching green. Each partner was wearing a different color, as they stood around the table.

Once again, Tali caught Matt's eye, wearing a dark red dress, but everyone else was looking at Jen. Angel was beaming, as she also looked very beautiful in her red dress, Matt allowed himself to fulfill her addiction. Jake was standing next to her, wearing a dark green dinner jacket.

"Good evening, Jen, Matt. Merry Christmas," Val beamed.

"Merry Christmas everyone," Matt smiled.

"Allow us to escort you to your seats," Carly smiled.

"Thank you," Jen beamed.

Val was sitting at the head of the table, with Carly, Sam, and Tali to her right. Matt would sit next to her on her left, with Jen, Jake, and Angel completing the line. Yuktrap was on errands duty, and the dogs were circling the table, as usual. Bozo was still out on patrol, likely watching the Demon. Val poured the wine, and they began to pass their plates around, serving each other.

Tali had made a Greek-themed vegetable dish, and everyone made sure to try a portion. Matt and Val's macaroni dish had come out well, and the cornbread was perfectly golden. The shark was the main focus, everyone was enjoying it.

"We have an announcement," Jen beamed.

"Oh? Did you two elope as well?" Val teased.

"No, but we are engaged. We decided we wanted to have another party before eloping. That was the only way Carly would agree to participate again," Jen laughed.

"Oh my God," Carly rolled her eyes. "Congratulations, regardless."

"Congratulations, Jen, Matt," Tali smiled.

The others offered their congratulations as well, as they continued to feast on the shark, specifically.

"This shark is delicious," Tali observed. "We haven't had tiger shark before, is it even permissible to keep them?"

"I don't know, I think so. I have seen pictures of them being caught, so I would assume so. But what's done with the meat, I don't know," Matt shrugged.

"It was probably sold to fish markets," Jen offered. "The angler likely kept a portion for themselves, then sold the rest for profit. A shark that size generates so much meat, it wouldn't be practical to not sell it."

"I agree," Val nodded.

"We were taught that humans lived their entire lives trying to make money to survive, currency was completely dead after the bombs fell. There were so few of us left, we just naturally shared everything," Jake reflected.

"Yeah, I don't miss the concept of currency at all," Matt shook his head.

"I don't think any of us do," Val laughed.

"This vegetable dish is really good, Tali, thank you," Carly smiled.

"You all were right that dealing with frozen vegetables is much more difficult. When Spring comes, we should focus more on gardening. We have plenty of seeds, yes?" Tali offered.

"We are storing a good amount in Angel's house, yes," Val nodded.

"The macaroni also came out well. This was your first time cooking it this way?" Angel asked.

"Yes, we weren't really sure if it would work. But I'm glad that it did. We had backups on standby, just in case. No, they did not include yams," Matt grinned.

"Oh you,' Angel rolled her eyes.

"Val? Have you and Carly decided on a honeymoon?" Tali asked.

"We were just talking about it earlier, Jen suggested south to Mexico, maybe some Aztec ruins, or just the beach," Val beamed.

"I think that's a great idea, but we should probably scout it out first, see how survivable it is. You would need to take all the food you would be eating, because there won't be any down there," Tali offered.

"I can fly the plane south, see how the terrain looks. But yes, with no people, no one has maintained the land for months. We don't even know the power situation," Jen whispered.

"I just assume there is no power at this point," Carly shrugged. "I don't even know how our power is still on, honestly."

"Well, we are maintaining it, that's how. Conserving electricity was a good idea, and we have backup generators. Losing power would dramatically change our lives, the Spring and Summer months will bring blistering heat," Tali observed.

"How hot does it get here?" Jake asked.

"Well over 100 degrees Fahrenheit. Tali is right, it's going to be rough. It's why we haven't been drinking any of the bottled water, just in case something bad happens," Matt replied.

"Sam has talked about a contingency of moving north, but the logistics are a problem. We would essentially be starting over," Tali reflected.

"I have a lot of experience starting over from literal scratch. As long as you have a food and water source, it can work," Jake offered.

"Were we to move north to establish a new base of operations, we would certainly have more than you ever did to start with," Matt nodded.

"Where would we go, specifically?" Val asked.

"No idea. Sam?" Matt looked his way.

"I had this conversation a while ago," Sam growled. "The fact is, I underestimated your ability to put food on our table. Not only is this shark good eating, but the fish are abundant, and you are a capable fisherman.

We have barely hunted at all, and the deer are also abundant out there. There are still herds of cows that are free grazing. I see no reason to move north at this time."

"The only thing I would suggest is look for even higher ground down here. This side of the neighborhood seems to be safer, but you can never be too safe," Jen offered.

"I wasn't here for the storm, but I hear it was a bad one?" Jake asked.

"Yeah, our houses flooded out. It's a very rare occurrence. Let's get off this topic, it's not very Christmassy. Jake? What has been your favorite movie so far?" Matt grinned.

"Oh..." Jake stammered.

"I think you completely caught him there," Angel laughed.

"I think 'Miracle on 34th Street' was really good, but my favorite was 'White Christmas', for sure," Jake smiled.

"Bing Crosby in the flesh did it for you, huh," Matt offered.

"We had...very few pictures growing up. We just learned about people through history passed down. We did find a lot of pictures when we... moved into a nuclear fallout shelter, but even then, I personally didn't have much time to sift through it all. Seeing people is definitely an amazing experience," Jake admitted.

"We have an entire collection of movies you can spend all of your time watching," Val beamed.

"Sadly, there are no landmarks or anything we can show him that are even close to us," Jen lamented.

"Isn't there a dinosaur museum around here somewhere?" Matt asked.

They all shrugged, they had no idea, of course. Matt was trying to think of it, but couldn't place the exact location. Val didn't have her phone on her, so they made a note to check on it later.

"Oh, the Kennedy Center is in Houston," Val offered.

"Yeah, that's true. I mean, he is very familiar with space, obviously. But the Kennedy Center is pretty remarkable. We could probably push through to that in the coming days," Matt nodded.

"Can I have some more of Tali's Greek vegetables?" Jake asked, holding his plate up.

Jen served him a scoop and he thanked her, no one chastised him too much for his lack of proper manners, he had at least learned the hard way to keep his elbows off the table. Out of all of them, Jake was the only one that had completely cleaned his plate off. Val assured him if he wanted more of anything, he just needed to ask.

"Am I holding us—" Jake started.

"Don't ask that. Just eat Jake. I can assure you, none of us mind," Tali cut him off.

Sam managed to finish his plate as well, complimenting them for the food. Tali grabbed his arm when he started to move, he would always be a work in progress. He had at least worn a green jacket.

"Do we have any plans for after dinner?" Tali asked.

"We are probably going to rest for a bit, and then Val made a pecan pie. Also known as the best pie," Carly beamed.

"That is a completely accurate statement, Carly," Matt smiled.

"Thanks for this amazing feast guys. I'm…really not used to eating food like this. We didn't have things like seasoning in my world. It's pretty overwhelming. Thanks Angel, for taking care of applying the right amount, I would have definitely used too much," Jake admitted. "I'll help with the cleanup."

"Thank you, Jake. If you could just put everything on the counter, Yuktrap will handle the dishes. And we will store all the leftovers," Val beamed.

"Also, a completely new concept to me, storing and reheating food," Jake grinned.

"It's definitely a luxury," Carly grinned.

There were too many people in the kitchen, so Matt and Jen moved to the couch and put some music back on. Matt wanted to change into something more comfortable, but Jen didn't allow it. She still wanted to dance, as soon as their food settled.

"So, I've got a question," Matt whispered.

"Oh? What is it?" Jen grinned.

"Are you wearing fishnets under there?" Matt smiled.

"Oh, you noticed," Jen teased. "And here I thought you were a gentleman."

"I'm still in a very playful mood after last night, and I thought I spotted them ever so briefly," Matt tried.

"Mmhmm, I bet," Jen beamed. "Your punishment is the armbinder tonight."

"Can't wait," Matt whispered.

The rest of the group filed in and sat down, letting their food settle. Tali however, had other things in mind.

"Jake? Would you like to dance with me?" Tali offered.

"Oh, of course Tali," Jake stammered, not expecting her invitation at all.

"Come on Matt, dance with me first," Angel swooped in before he could ask Jen.

"Go on Matt," Jen assured him, as he looked at her.

Matt stood up and started dancing with Angel, as she stared up at him. "You look lovely tonight, Angel. But I prefer..." he started.

Angel mashed on his foot, maintaining her smile. "We are all having a problem behaving, it seems," she beamed.

"I accept that," Matt grinned.

"This has been a wonderful Christmas Matt, despite all odds," Angel smiled. "Thank you for the dance."

Angel left him and Jen took her place, while Val and Carly took the floor as well. Jen was very curious as to what had happened there, but Matt knew better. She just rolled her eyes and assured him she would get it out of him later. They danced quietly, rotating partners until everyone had had at least one dance. Sam even danced with Angel one time—it was an odd pairing but no one questioned it.

Finally, it was time for the pie. Val brought it to the table and served each person one plate.

"Thank you, Val, for being such a good hostess," Matt grinned.

"Oh, you're welcome, Matt," Val beamed.

"This is delicious, what did you say it was?" Jake asked.

"Pecan pie," Val laughed. "Pecans are a nut that grows on trees, they taste delicious, especially when frozen. Matt loves them."

"It's true, I can eat frozen pecans all day," Matt admitted.

"This is really good, thanks Val," Jake managed. "I really can't eat any more though, I'm sorry."

"Oh, it's okay. You have eaten a lot," Carly assured him, taking his plate of half-eaten pie. "Why don't you go lie down, rest? You can even go to bed if you want. We have everything under control."

Jake thanked them and headed for his room, no one begrudged him. Fred was following him, and he asked if it was okay. Matt assured him it was and he wished them all good night.

"He is so nice, but so overwhelmed by it all. The concept of a feast must be so foreign to him. He didn't want to stop eating because he doesn't know how to waste food, and he didn't know how to stop and not offend us," Angel whispered.

"He is a great guy, but yes, he has never been around people like us before. I think Tali has done a good job of making him as comfortable as possible, so thank you Tali," Matt offered.

"It's nothing Matt, as Angel said, he is a very good person at heart. He just doesn't know what anything other than his society looks like," Tali waved. "Thank you all for the wonderful evening. Merry Christmas, and good night."

"Good night, Tali, Sam. Merry Christmas," Val beamed.

Sam and Tali left, and the group was winding down. Turning off the music, Yuktrap let Buddy outside one last time. Then he approached Angel, raising his hands. Relenting, (it was Christmas after all), she took both of his hands and held them for a time. Saying nothing to him, he still came forward and hugged her legs. She hugged him back before breaking away.

"Good night, everyone, Merry Christmas," Val and Carly waved, as they headed into their room.

Jen was eyeing Matt, but she invited Angel as well. Surprised, Angel followed them. Matt took his jacket off, finally. It had just gotten uncomfortable, they had turned the A/C down pretty low months ago, so it was never hot.

"Angel?" Jen asked.

"Yes Jen?" Angel offered, standing at the door, unsure of what to do.

"Do you want to sleep with us tonight?" Jen asked.

"Only if it means I'm not intruding," Angel whispered.

"Strip down to your underwear and get in bed," Jen pointed.

"Oh, yes Jen," Angel stammered, as she got out of her dress easily. Stepping out, she got under the covers, while Matt looked away.

"Get the armbinder on Matt when he is undressed and in bed," Jen smiled, tossing her the armbinder.

"As you command," Angel beamed.

Matt got undressed and laid in bed on his back. Angel smiled and extended her legs for him, loving it. She motioned with her finger to roll over, and he obliged. Securing the armbinder, she asked Jen for a kiss and got an affirmative, leaning down and kissing him. Jen got out of her dress, revealing the green lingerie with black fishnets.

"Oh Jen, you naughty girl," Angel beamed. "Did Matt notice those?"

"He did, hence the armbinder," Jen laughed.

"Well, okay," Angel shrugged. "Come join us."

Jen crawled into the bed and started making out with Angel, who was completely shocked. "I know you're straight Angel, tell me no and I'm off you," she whispered.

"Oh...no. Please, go on," Angel managed, unable to resist her as Matt looked on. It was certainly going to be a fun Christmas night.

CHAPTER 60

THE VANISHING

Waking up, Matt was surprised to find his arms had been freed, having never felt the armbinder come off. Jen was beside him, still sleeping. He rubbed her cheek until she stirred.

"Mmm, good morning. Did Angel free you?" Jen whispered.

"If she did, I didn't feel it. Where is she?" Matt asked.

"No idea," Jen whispered. "Go get our juice, please."

Nodding, Matt rolled out of bed and opened the door, expecting to find Yuktrap there waiting with the drinks. Oddly enough, he was missing as well. Figuring Angel was doing something with him, Matt shrugged and headed for the kitchen. He didn't see Buddy and Fred either, so there was no need to let them out. Pouring himself and Jen some juice, he headed back to her.

"The house feels empty, or emptier, at least," Matt whispered, handing her the glass.

"Maybe they went for a walk," Jen shrugged.

"Can I be honest? The way we went to sleep last night, it doesn't make sense for Angel to not be here," Matt whispered.

"You are right," Jen admitted. "Go knock on her door, try to find her."

Matt nodded and walked out, across the living room and to Angel's door. Knocking on it, there was no answer. He called her name and opened it, seeing no one.

"Angel?" Matt called out.

Exiting, he went to the next room, Jake's. Knocking on it, he opened that door as well, finding no one.

"Yuktrap! Bozo! Where are you?" Matt demanded.

Neither of them appeared, which was really strange. Angel and Jake walking the dogs was completely believable, even if it didn't make sense for her to leave them without a word. But taking Yuktrap was a huge stretch. And there was no way they took Bozo and Yuktrap. Going against his better judgment, he went to Val and Carly's door.

Knocking on it, he called out for Carly. She didn't answer, and Matt slowly opened the door, seeing the bed was empty. The sun hadn't come up yet, and there was no way Val would be awake yet. Something was wrong.

Heading back into his room, he waved at Jen. "Something is wrong, the house is completely empty. No robot, no dogs, no Val. Get dressed—okay? I want to go look for them," Matt pressed.

"Okay Matt," Jen whispered, getting out of bed.

Matt went to get on the radio, calling Sam and Tali. They didn't answer, and he called again. Still nothing. Jen came out, handing him his sandals, as he put them on. Leading her outside, all of the vehicles were still there. They pushed out into the neighborhood, looking in every direction. The sun was rising, but visibility was still low. Seeing nothing, Matt was becoming more and more worried, as he ran back into the house.

Picking up the Marlin, he went back outside and fired a shot in the air. He didn't expect a response, but he hoped it would bring anyone that could hear it. Five minutes went by, and he fired another shot. Jen came over to take his arm.

"Matt?" Jen whispered. "We are alone. It's just us."

CPSIA information can be obtained
at www.ICGtesting.com
Printed in the USA
BVHW041508100122
625871BV00015B/782